THIRST

RICHARD COMPSON SATER

RATTLING GOOD YARNS
PRESS

Rattling Good Yarns Press
33490 Date Palm Drive 3065
Cathedral City CA 92235
USA
www.rattlinggoodyarns.com

Cover Design: Rattling Good Yarns Press

Library of Congress Control Number: 2024951529
ISBN: 978-1-955826-85-3

First Edition

I dedicate Thirst *to the memory of my late spouse,
Wayne Robert Comer, in grateful appreciation for his
truest love and never-ending support of my writer's dream.
Wayne, I miss you like deserts miss rain.*

"Sometimes too much to drink is barely enough."

—Mark Twain

I

Since Ranger quit drinking, you won't catch him out joyriding in his vintage cherry-colored 1953 pickup truck at two in the morning, naked except for cowboy boots and hat, singing along with some honkytonk song on the radio, blasting at full.

But I met Ranger before he quit drinking.

I'd finished a late shift at the country club bar and was walking home, my favorite part of the night when the whole town seemed to be asleep but me. At least, that's how I saw it, until this red pickup nearly ran me over. I hollered at the driver to turn the music down, which raised his hackles, I guess. He slammed the brakes, backed up until he was even with me, and stopped.

I immediately wondered how smart I was to engage him. I took a step back.

"Some people are trying to sleep at this hour," I told him over the racket. He leaned from the window of his truck. Under the outline of his Stetson in the streetlamp light, I could make out a mustache that seemed to be the size of Connecticut. He extended the middle finger of his left hand.

"Eat me, pal," he said.

Alice had gotten a similar message in Wonderland. She complied, no questions asked. But I was born and bred to be a cautious man; I could not tell if he was offering insult or invitation. Best, in situations like that, to err on the side of caution. I took another step back; I could turn and run if necessary, but since he was still howling at the moon along with some excruciatingly twangy hillbilly (Hank Williams, I would learn later), I was less frightened than amused. I stayed to watch and listen to his sincere if inaccurate baritone.

He noticed I was still there when the song ended, and he offered a stupid, friendly grin. He could not possibly be as handsome as he seemed to be under that hat, I told myself.

"Well?" he said. "Ya want to?"

"Do I want to *what*?"

"Weren't ya listening?" He repeated the key lyrics of the song. Apparently, he'd decided I was good-lookin,' wondered what was goin' on in my kitchen, and whether or not I would be interested in combining my culinary skills with his. Dancin' and soft drinks were promised, and other unspecified fun to the extent that two dollars could purchase.

"This ain't a hotrod, but it's a Ford. I ain't got two bucks on me, either, but I got this for ya."

He opened the door of his truck and revealed not only his nakedness (except for the aforementioned boots), a furry welcome mat on his chest, and a very impressive erection. In the light, finally, I caught a good look at the rest of him, his angles and bristle, his yearning eyes.

I grew immediately aroused myself, and I wavered. Cock is almighty persuasive, particularly attached to a handsome man, and the possible consequences suddenly seemed unimportant.

"Ya hungry?" His eyes glinted in the dark. "I don't want to take this home with me." Then, the bravado evaporated, "Please?"

Throwing caution windward, I walked around to the passenger side of his truck and climbed in. If I had doubts about his sincerity, he surprised me by taking the lead, unzipping my trousers and reaching in. Clearly, he had an appetite as well, and we both rose to the occasion spectacularly. Stars aligned: anonymity and spontaneity, the lure of danger, the mutual attraction, the undeniability of arousal, the climactic payoff: the last thing I expected after a late shift at work. And possibly the best sex I'd ever had.

When we'd reached our destination, he allowed us perhaps forty seconds of afterglow before he said, "Can I drive ya home?"

I agreed, as it was just a couple of blocks. If operating a vehicle while intoxicated is an acquired skill, he seemed to be well-practiced. We didn't talk so he could concentrate, but what he didn't say told me all I wanted to know. He kept one hand on the steering wheel and the other on the nape of my neck, making me crackle and shiver, excited and anticipating things to come.

He parked in the driveway and turned the engine off, though he declined my offer to come inside and continue the party due to the late hour and the fact that he had to be at work himself by eight o'clock the next morning. He was, he said, a mechanic for the Buick dealership in town. His job sucked, he said (I could have made a bad pun but chose not to), and his wife (wait; what?) was about to divorce him, and good riddance to her, and I should come see his house sometime, which he'd built all by himself, except for pouring the concrete foundation, and it was solid enough to survive an earthquake, and furthermore—

I interrupted him. "What's your name, anyway?"

"Ranger Melusky. Why?"

"I usually try to get at least that much information before getting down to more important matters, but you didn't give me a chance."

"First things first." He offered a handshake.

"You want to know my name too?"

He thought about it. "All right."

"Neil Graham." I wondered at fate, the movement of stars and planets that had put him on my street at exactly the moment I needed to find him. In the dashboard light, I wrote my phone number on his forearm with a ballpoint pen and asked if he would call.

He thought about it. "All right," he said.

Why I'd stayed in this Indiana town, I could not say, but like my parents and grandparents, I was born and raised here. Is that pedigree such an anchor, or is inertia so powerful? Perhaps lack of imagination and ambition factored into my choice.

Maybe I simply liked it here.

I started bartending part-time at a gay club—provocatively named Rumors—during my senior year at the local university, and I did very well. The bar attracted an older crowd, and being young enough and good-looking enough (or so I was led to believe), I did brisk business with tips. The manager happily converted my job to full-time after I graduated, since I had nothing better to do at the time. When the bar closed for the night, I generally had more offers than I could handle, so I rarely lacked companionship when I wanted it. However, none of those encounters led to anything I would call a relationship.

Eventually, Rumors went out of business, and I talked my way into a job in the men's locker-room bar at the local country club, which interested me primarily because it was located within walking distance of my apartment. As drinking establishments go, a country club bar is the polar opposite to almost any other kind, gay or straight. One distinguishing feature is the clientele, members only, presumably the cream of our town's citizenry, or at least those wealthy enough to pay the exorbitant membership fee and required monthly dues.

I was apprenticed to Mike, the crusty old guy who'd run the bar for decades and was thinking about retiring. No women were permitted in the place, which was separated from the men's locker room and showers only by swinging doors. One "perk" of the job was the opportunity to see the mayor, the chief of-police, the high-school superintendent, and countless doctors, dentists, lawyers, bank presidents, and other area business scions fully naked. Had public stature or economy-sized men ever been an aphrodisiac for me, I would have been a happy guy, or at least an occasionally-aroused one.

But, no to the former and no to the latter. Just as well. I learned early on about Mike's rabid homophobia, so I kept quiet about what I liked to do in bed, even if my name, spoken out loud, betrays what I have done any number of times in front of willing men. In the old days, I'd seen eight or ten of our city's A-listers late at night at Rumors, and they recognized me as well, much to their chagrin and my delight. While I would never stoop to blackmail, I found that these gentlemen were significantly more generous with their tips than most of the other members, who were generally the tightest bunch of customers I'd ever had the pleasure of serving.

Mike never guessed my secret, and in fact, we got along famously. We'd been working together for eight months or so when he died unexpectedly of a heart attack. By that time, I was liked well enough that the club manager hired me immediately to take Mike's place. I convinced the club to let me bring in a couple of assistants to work with me three or four days a week as needed, younger guys, reliable and reasonably industrious. They did a little of everything, filling drink orders, serving food, cleaning golf shoes, and keeping the locker room stocked with towels, soap, and toilet paper.

Business picked up in the evenings and on weekends. From spring through early autumn, there was a twice-weekly tournament that started at five o'clock, weather permitting, and that meant late nights, as the teams didn't straggle back into the locker room until well after eight. There were about twenty regulars for the game; when they came in, they wanted to eat, drink to excess, and play cards. The kitchen stayed open late to accommodate them, and I usually didn't get out of there until after eleven.

I worked six days of the week with only Mondays off, when the golf course was closed. The job offered neither challenge nor physical exertion, but there were decided perks. When we had no customers—the bar fully stocked, glasses and mugs washed, tables cleaned and ashtrays emptied—we had nothing to do but sit and wait for our patrons to finish their rounds of golf. We had plenty of down time, during which one of my assistants played video games on his tablet and the other listened to heavy metal and poked endlessly at his cell phone.

I indulged my habit of reading voraciously, acquired as a kid under the enthusiastic tutelage of my grandfather, a retired professor of literature. He was my dad's father, and we'd been best friends ever since we met just before my ninth birthday. Granddad and I shared a love of good books and, as we discovered happily some years later, a similar taste in men.

My college days were far behind, but like a perennial student, I still carried a backpack around, which I referred to as my library, as it mostly contained the current pile of books I was reading. I wasn't particularly choosy; I could lose myself in Mark Twain or Jane Austen as easily as I could in Zane Grey, current biography, ancient history, or the latest lowbrow beach read. The best books made me yearn—and feel guilty for doing nothing more than tending bar while the parchment of my own bachelor-of-arts degree in literature lay at the bottom of a drawer.

The men's locker room itself was accessible all day long, but I opened the bar for business at one p.m., Tuesday through Friday. I usually had a couple of regular customers—retired guys—who required a shot-and-a-beer to make it through the day. On the weekends, I opened at seven to accommodate early-morning tee times, serving innumerable screwdrivers and Bloody Marys to a breakfast crowd unaccustomed to swallowing its juices straight. I took charge of the stereo, too. Nobody complained that I indulged in my fondness for jazz as long as I avoided the squonky third-stream or hard-bop varieties and turned the volume down when the big game (or anything golf-related) was on the big-screen television.

Even on rainy days, I could expect at least a few of the regulars. They came to the bar to commiserate and peer anxiously at the sky, waiting for the weather to break. They watched golf or football or baseball on TV, drank endlessly, smoked cigars, played poker and gin rummy and cribbage and generally made my life hell. I worked much harder on rainy days.

Come the first fall of snow, the golf course closed for the winter and didn't open again until March. I furloughed my two assistants but still opened the bar at one on Tuesday through Friday, as usual. I could count on a few customers, a mournful bunch that missed its golf fix and had nothing else to do. I usually closed by seven; for much of my day, I got paid to read, essentially. Winter weekend hours were curtailed as well. My hours dropped from about sixty a week to fewer than thirty, but I appreciated the extra time off more than I lamented the smaller paycheck.

I'd worked long enough at the country club that I could practically do the job in my sleep. Little happened that surprised or unnerved me. The clientele knew me and I knew it. I could identify anyone who came into the bar, tell you what he liked to drink, how many he'd swallow, what he'd likely order for supper, and what he'd complain about while waiting for his meal.

And the size of his cock....

I considered myself to be openly gay everywhere except at work. I never lost the concern that I'd be fired if my preference for male companionship became generally known at this fiercely straight club, even if fat, balding old guys in striped and plaid golf attire yielded zero temptation. By reflex, I learned to smile at the pale attempts passed off as humor: these two fags go into a bar, see? Particularly since what those two fags usually got was a crude or violent punchline for their trouble.

On occasion, however, I permitted myself to hook up with one or another of them I knew from the old days at Rumors. It was always discreet, no attached strings, and always far away from the hallowed halls of this men's club, wherein we respected each other's privacy. I looked forward to serving them at the bar, perhaps because at least for a moment, when we made eye contact or traded small talk and a smile, we could relax and be ourselves, with no secrets.

Three days after we met, when Ranger still hadn't called, I found myself at the club at the end of a dismal rainy night with only one customer reluctant to leave, a gent named Gary Weston, with whom I'd shared some intimacy rather often. Middle forties, blue-eyed, blond, deeply closeted with a wife and children, Gary owned and operated a large insurance business in town. As busy as he was, he found time to sneak over to my apartment a couple times a month to satisfy his cravings. He was reasonably handsome and fit with an endearing crooked grin, and I usually accommodated him when he asked; had he been agreeable, I might have been interested in something more. But he had his family and his position in the community to consider, not to mention his country club membership.

One simply didn't date the help.

I could tell that Gary was lonely that night, and I imagined he was steeling his nerve to ask if he could follow me home after I closed the bar. But with Ranger on my mind, I wasn't in the mood to say yes. The last time, Gary had told me about a new employee at his firm, a young man who seemed quite promising in ways that had little to do with writing a tight insurance policy. Gary had expressed hope of mentoring the guy by day and undressing him discreetly by night. I commiserated, even if such an arrangement would probably put an end to our own trysts.

After sending my assistants home, I had little to do at the bar beyond washing some glasses, wiping down the tables, and collecting damp towels from the locker room. As I totaled the day's receipts over a cup of coffee and a leftover sandwich, Gary finished his second gin and tonic while he drummed his fingers on the bar, attempting to keep up with the tricky time signatures of Dave Brubeck's quartet.

"How are you doing tonight, Neil?" he asked.

"Can't complain, Mr. Weston."

"Oh, come on. You know me better than that." So he *did* want to follow me home.

"Right. So, Gary, how about yourself?"

He sighed. "Okay, I guess. What are you up to these days? Anything significant to report?"

"Hah! Just what you see. You?"

He shrugged. "Same old same old." In the past, he'd referred to an overweight, nagging wife and a pair of sullen teenagers at home. I imagined nothing had changed, and I didn't envy him. "Buy you a drink?"

I chuckled. "I'm onto you. Get me drunk, and the next thing I know, you'll take advantage of me in the back room."

"Damn. I've got to work on my technique."

"Never change. And thanks for the offer, but coffee's all I want right now. Maybe another night."

"Sure. Any time."

"Making progress with that new guy in your agency?"

He shook his head. "I was a little too optimistic. Damn the luck. As it happens, he already has a husband. I still can't believe those guys can get married now."

Since he was one of "those" guys too, I suspected he would also prefer a husband, but I didn't press the point. "I'm sorry nothing came of it for you."

Gary sighed. "It's hell working beside a man when all you can think about is fucking his brains out. Especially when you know he'd probably let you, under different circumstances."

I couldn't offer much besides sympathy and another gin and tonic on the house. "It's happened to all of us. I met a guy the other night, and I can't get him off my mind either."

That piqued his interest, and he was eager for specifics. If he hadn't been able to seduce his co-worker, at least he could enjoy my experience vicariously.

"That sounds damn hot," he said after I'd narrated my adventure in detail.

"It was."

"Also very risky."

"I couldn't agree more. It wasn't very smart, but I couldn't resist."

He nodded. "You don't have to explain it to me. I'd be all over him, if I got an offer like that. You seeing him again?"

"I hope so. I gave him my number, but it's been three days with no callback."

"If he was drunk, he probably doesn't even remember you."

I conceded that it was possible.

"What do you know about him?"

I shook my head. "His name. He told me he lives outside town, but nothing specific."

"Google him."

"I could do that. Wait a second. I just remembered. He's a mechanic for the Buick dealership here in town."

"Bingo. Maybe it's time for an oil change and a tune-up."

It was the perfect solution. And my old car was actually a Buick, so I had the perfect alibi. It would give me an opportunity to see Ranger again, to find out if he remembered me—and if he wanted to get together. If he didn't, there would be no harm done. At the very least, my car would get some overdue maintenance.

Gary finished his drink and slid the glass across the bar. I passed him the tab for his signature, and he handed it back with a twenty-dollar tip.

"You don't have to do that, Gary." He insisted I pocket the bill, and I thanked him.

"You got room for me tonight?"

Although I'd told myself I wouldn't, I found myself agreeing. Why not? I reasoned as he gave me a lift to my apartment and followed me inside. It's not as if Ranger would be waiting for me on the doorstep.

When we shared a bed, Gary was gentle and urgent, if efficient, but he saw to it that I enjoyed myself, too. He made me feel as hot and sexy as he told me I was. And, as he always reminded me, I never had to worry that he'd wear out his welcome.

Nothing was different this night. Guilt makes one grateful for mercy. But as he walked out my door twenty-five minutes later with a wave and a sad smile, I longed for a man who would stay with me all night and into the day, a man with nowhere to go and nothing to do but please me and let me return the favor.

2

The next morning, I called the Buick service department. After ascertaining that Ranger would indeed be working that day, I made an eleven o'clock appointment for an oil change. My shift at the club didn't start until four o'clock, so I had plenty of time. What better way to spend it than determining if my drunken pick-up from three nights ago wanted to be my Mister Right? Or at least schedule a roll in the hay with me....

You're a fool, I told myself as I swung my twenty-year-old car into the lot at the dealership.

I checked in with the receptionist, and she pointed me toward the door marked "Service Dept." In the small waiting room, I poured a cup of coffee from the complimentary pot, grabbed a doughnut, and took a seat. There were old magazines in a pile and a television tuned to some morning talk show, two bubbly hosts talking with the latest pop princess about her incredibly amazing new album.

The door to the garage swung open and in walked Ranger, looking even better than I'd remembered (and sober, too), effortlessly sexy in dark blue loose-fitting coveralls (unzipped far enough to suggest that he wore nothing underneath), with his name spelled out on the pocket in red script. He'd rolled up the sleeves above his elbows. I could see the phone number written in ink on his forearm, faint but still legible after three days, and my heart lifted.

"You got the Skylark here for an oil change?"

I stood up. "That's me."

"Econo-Lube's just down the street. Cost ya half of what they charge you here."

"Thanks, but I could use a tune-up as well, if you aren't too busy."

He shrugged. "It's your money. Just so's ya know."

"Thanks for the tip. I'll remember it next time."

"Pull 'er into the second bay for me, would ya? And leave the keys in."

"Sure."

Anything you want. Anything.

I hustled out to my car, a bit disappointed that he didn't recognize me instantly and wondering how to proceed. I decided that the smartest option would be to say nothing unless he positively identified me first. Not every man would be thrilled to be confronted at his place of work by the reminder of a beer-fueled blowjob, however satisfactory its conclusion.

"What kind of trouble ya having?" he said as I climbed out of the car.

"Nothing, really. But I haven't had the oil changed in a while."

"How long's that?"

I admitted that I couldn't even remember, probably a couple of years or four. He shook his head, disgusted. "Ya don't change yer oil regularly and yer fucked. Ya change it twice a year, and a good car will last forever. Of course, *this* piece of shit—" and he indicated my old Skylark—"ain't nothin' like a good car. I'm surprised ya got one this old that's still running, especially if ya don't change yer oil regular."

I admitted I'd been careless. "I don't actually drive it very much. I live close enough to my job that I can walk to work."

"Gimme forty-five minutes. Wait inside."

"Could I watch?"

That flattered him, and he grinned. "Makes no nevermind to me."

Now on display, he went about his work with vigor and close attention to detail. If I expected commentary, he offered none. Possibly, he was too engrossed in his task to be aware that I was standing as close to him as I dared. I knew nothing about cars and never lifted the hood of my own if I could help it, so it was foreign land to me.

He checked the fan belts and filters, making adjustments and adding fluids. As he poked around inside the engine, I found myself leaning in closer and closer to observe what he was doing but also just to watch him, so engrossed in his work and so obviously skilled at it. Without even looking up from his task, he reached out unexpectedly with his thumb, black with grease, and swiped it against my cheek. Without looking up, he said, "There, ya nosy bastard. That's for thinking I don't remember who the hell ya are."

He paused to take a look at me, and he grinned from the inside out. I hadn't known what to expect, but he was as good-natured as I could have hoped.

"Neil Graham. See?"

I had to laugh. "Yup."

"I remember. Had lunch?"

I shook my head.

"Let's go get a bite to eat. The oil pan can drain while we're gone."

I needed no persuasion. We washed up at the utility sink in the men's room. To my surprise, Ranger scrubbed his hands and fingernails until not a trace of grease remained. "I hate this place," he said over the din of the electric hand dryers. "I don't take one goddamn thing with me when I walk out the door."

His hands might be clean, but I pointed out the phone number remaining on his forearm.

"Must be something you want to remember."

When he laughed, it rumbled up from deep inside him and spilled over. "You slut," he said.

"Only in the proper company, Melusky."

He liked that, too. "You're my kind of man, Graham."

I was beginning to think the feeling was mutual. It was a strange sensation. I chided myself: You hardly know him.

He stuck his head inside the Buick showroom. "I'm going for lunch," he yelled to no one in particular.

"One hour," a male voice responded, severe. "And no beer. You hear me, Ranger? Ranger!"

"Yeah, yeah." He turned to me. "My boss. The prick."

No one would ever be able to accuse him of playing up to authority.

Ranger took me to his favorite local restaurant, the Blue Plate. I could tell by the way the waitress lit up that she liked him a lot. She offered an enthusiastic hello and black coffee without his even asking. "Great to see you again, Ranger! Meatloaf, mashed potatoes, extra gravy, two rolls, and butter. Right?"

"I eat here too much."

"You're secretly in love with me. What would your wife say?"

"Like I give a good goddamn."

"Ranger! Language!"

"So bring me a side dish of soap."

She laughed a little too much. I tapped her arm.

"Um, I'll have what he's having."

She suddenly noticed me, then looked at Ranger.

"Neil, this here's Marlene. Marlene, Neil."

She offered a nod, but I knew immediately that she didn't like me. Jealous? How quaint.

She scribbled on her pad. "You got a black smudge on your cheek. Restroom's over there." She pointed.

"Thanks."

"Ya gonna wash it off?" Ranger said after she left us.

I shook my head. "Maybe I want to keep it for a souvenir."

He laughed. But he seemed somehow charmed at the same time.

"So tell me about this wife of yours. I meant to ask you the other night. I don't make a habit of hanging out with married men." That was sort of a lie, but he didn't need to know that.

"Nothing to tell. Mistake. She's gonna ask for a divorce any day. And get it."

"Just as well. It's hardly fair to her if you're gay."

That alarmed him. He looked around.

"Keep it down, goddamn it. I ain't gay. Not officially, I mean."

I kept it down, but I begged to differ. "Most straight guys don't drive around at two a.m. looking for blowjobs from other men. Officially, I mean."

"So I have a couple of beers and go out for a little action sometimes. Well, every now and then." He back-pedaled. Cleared his throat. "Hardly ever. But it don't mean nothing."

"It might mean something to me, Ranger. You know, it's actually okay to be gay these days, even in Indiana." My remark was ill-timed, as Marlene chose that moment to bang a cup and saucer in front of me and slosh coffee into it. She glared at me. I smiled, all innocence.

She brought our steaming plates a moment later and lingered, hoping to engage Ranger's attention, but he studiously ignored her.

"Someone likes you a lot," I said after she left.

"Whatever."

Between the meatloaf and the second cup of coffee (into which he splashed some whiskey from a small flask tucked into a side pocket, thus technically adhering to the "no beer" dictum), he started sharing his history, unbidden, our gay-or-not discussion forgotten.

His parents still lived in the Kentucky town where he was born, an only son. Unexpected long after four daughters. Stereotypes leaped into my mind based on what I'd already seen and heard of Ranger, but he cut me off before I could say a word.

"I know what yer thinking, and ya can knock it the hell off. My dad ain't some toothless backwoods hillbilly who married his sister. He's a retired Army sergeant major, 101st Airborne air-assault, and a ranger. How I got the damn name."

"Did I say anything?"

"Didn't have to. I know what people think, soon as they meet me."

"Speaking of hillbillies, who was singing on your radio the other night?"

Ranger seemed genuinely wounded. "Hank Williams Senior ain't no hillbilly either. He's a brilliant singer and songwriter. 'Hey, Good Lookin'' is a classic. Ya don't know fuck-all about music."

He ate in injured silence for a few moments, but another splash of whiskey into his coffee cup made him forget my fuck-allness about music, and the life story continued. At sixteen, he'd started attending classes at the vocational-technical school, spending half the day learning how to fix cars, and he'd proven himself quite talented in that trade. He'd enlisted in the Air Force out of high school.

"Not the Army? Bet your dad was thrilled about that."

"Why d'ya think I went Air Force?"

After basic training, he'd attended technical school for aircraft mechanics. He had two tours of duty overseas and two stateside before transferring to a base here in Indiana. He would have been content to remain in the Air Force. In fact, he could have been retired by now. But, he'd gotten thrown out after several run-ins with the military police and two demotions in rank due to beer-fueled infractions. He earned himself a dishonorable discharge after fourteen years of service.

"My dad was pissed. He helped me get it upgraded to a general discharge instead after a couple years. It was a hell of a lot easier to get a decent job after that. Nobody wants to hire a guy who can't even serve honorably in the military." In his early thirties at that time, he started over, and the Buick dealership had given him a chance, thanks in part to his military veteran status.

"I ain't no drunk, even if I do like to have a beer or two now and then," he said. But only after work. And weekends. And never before eleven o'clock in the morning on any day, and whiskey only on special occasions, he told me solemnly. I would hear him recite this litany on numerous occasions and always exactly the same way, memorized, as if it were a mantra or favorite poem. I suspect he'd repeated it so often that he actually believed it. The service department manager at Buick had learned about Ranger the hard way and thus kept close watch, part of the reason the boss had been branded a prick. On several occasions, Ranger admitted, only his skill under the hood of a car had saved his ass.

It was, actually, a very nice ass and worth saving.

"Buicks are shitty cars, but I can fix 'em in my sleep. So what're ya gonna do? It's a living. Kinda."

He sloshed a bit more whiskey into his coffee.

"I'm pleased that you think our first date is a special occasion."

He recoiled. "This ain't no date," he whispered.

"Sorry," I whispered back. "You invited me out to lunch. It's a damn date. And you're drinking whiskey, and you said you only do that—"

Marlene poured more coffee for Ranger but ignored me when I slid my cup toward her.

"The usual for dessert?"

"What else?"

She scooped up his empty plate but left mine sitting, walking away before I could ask for the same, whatever it was. Ranger didn't notice or didn't care. He told me about his passion for restoring old cars, too. A hobby he'd picked up in his spare time while stationed overseas. "That red truck of mine? Ain't she a beauty? A 1953 Ford F-100 with a 110-horsepower flathead V-8. She was junk when I bought her for a couple hundred bucks in 1990. I rebuilt the engine and did all the bodywork on her. Runs like a top."

I promised to examine the Ford more closely, and he promised some show-and-tell. I had some ideas about what else he might show me after we finished the tour of the truck, and no telling would be necessary....

"How'd you end up in my neck of the woods the other night?"

"Got lost. I reckon. Don't rightly remember."

"I'm glad you have such a lousy sense of direction. How'd you lose your pants?"

He smirked. "How d'ya know I had 'em to begin with?"

"I like you." I don't think I'd ever been more sincere. I couldn't recall the last time a man had shared his life story so guilelessly with me. And I was charmed.

He grinned. A minor side-effect of beer was that he sometimes did things he might not have done had he been sober, he said.

"What kind of things?"

He shrugged, but I could wager a guess.

"Things you enjoy doing? Or don't you remember?" I watched him. And I could tell he remembered, however cagy he tried to be, and likewise enjoyed them. But he didn't incriminate himself.

He swallowed the last of his coffee. Marlene brought him a brownie with ice cream and chocolate sauce. He pushed the plate toward me.

"Have some."

I didn't mind. Marlene seemed to, however. She threw the check on the table and stalked away, fuming, as we shared the dessert and the fork.

"You remember where I live?"

"Over by the country club, ain't it?"

"Yes. Not far from it. That's where I work, actually. I'm a bartender."

His eyes lit up. "You and me'll get along good."

"It's a private club, though. You have to be a member or an invited guest if you want to drink at the bar. You want me to write my address on your other arm?"

He shook his head. "Nah. I'll remember when I see it."

He picked up the check, and on our way outside, I thanked him for the lunch date.

"I told ya this weren't no date."

I wondered what else he could possibly call it. It was unquestionably a date; it had been his idea, and he'd picked up the tab, too, but I didn't press the issue. By that time, I felt as if I had known him for years. The warm fuzzy I felt might have been like his, only mine didn't need whiskey to spread. Why should he have bothered to share his autobiography unless he had great plans for the two of us? I couldn't imagine.

"Well, if it quacks like a duck...."

He gave me a puzzled look. I laughed. "Never mind. Next time, I'll buy lunch."

"Deal." We parked ourselves on a bench outside the restaurant so he could enjoy his after-lunch cigarette at leisure. When he finished, some minutes later, we stood up and stretched and faced each other.

"Ever gone down on a woman?" he asked me, out of nowhere.

I shook my head. "Ever gone down on a man?" I thought for a moment he would say no, but I wouldn't let him get away with it. "How was it? Do you remember?"

He grinned, quickly, like sun breaking through a cloudy day, but it was gone almost as soon as it appeared. I guess he remembered enough.

"Fuck you," he said instead, but it was a reflex, good-natured, not angry.

"I'm game if you are. Come on over. My address is on the invoice at the garage, and there'll be a six-pack of beer in the fridge with your name on it—if you need some additional incentive. Just remember I'm in the apartment around back, and I get off work late. You might want to call first. Fair enough? Just nod your head."

He nodded.

Maybe the red-blooded Bluegrass State boy wouldn't admit to being gay in the afternoon, but he seemed to know what happened after a few beers under cover of the night. If he wasn't inclined to quit drinking, I assumed he also enjoyed the consequences of his behavior.

I reached for the welcome mat of chest hair inside his coveralls, grabbed a handful, and gave it a tug.

"That shit's attached," he said.

So was I. Careful, I warned myself. But it didn't help.

He drove me back to the Buick dealership in comfortable silence. He finished the oil change within a few minutes. I paid my bill, climbed into my freshly-tuned-up car, and drove away. But if I expected him to wave goodbye as I left the lot, I was mistaken.

I checked my phone for messages all afternoon. None. That evening, I hustled my last few customers out of the locker room a little earlier than they liked, and there was some grumbling. I didn't care. I shut out the lights and bolted for home.

But I had no company that night or the next. The morning after that second night, my neighbor from the front apartment—a grouchy old man, single and relentlessly straight—banged on my door to tell me that some naked, drunken fool had practically broken his bedroom window after midnight, looking for me. My neighbor offered to call the police if the fellow didn't leave the premises immediately. He obeyed, grazing the mailbox as he screeched out of the driveway.

"Keep your perversions to yourself," he growled at me. "The next time some freakin' faggot comes banging on my door at one o'clock—"

I was too exhilarated to hear the rest of his rant and tuned him out. Ranger had come looking for me!

That night, when I came home from the country club around ten o'clock, I came across his red truck parked discreetly about a block away from my apartment. He was inside, modestly covered in jeans and a T-shirt, lubricating himself with a forty-ounce malt liquor as he waited for me. We walked back to my apartment together.

Once inside, our clothing wasn't a hindrance for long. Ranger had other things on his mind.

3

I never met Ranger's wife, and he never told me her name, only that she was his fourth one. Four! Why didn't he just come out of the closet already? From his description, I couldn't tell if she was the vindictive type or just guilty of being in love with him and realizing that no matter what she did, she wouldn't be able to hang onto him. At what point did she figure out that all her efforts amounted to little more than groundbreaking for her inevitable replacement?

A couple of weeks after I met Ranger—by which time we had gotten together at least every other night and I was seriously reconsidering my notion that we were meeting only because the sex was good—he informed me that Number Four had moved out. He gave me directions to his house, some miles outside the city limits, and although he didn't explicitly invite me to come over, he must have known to expect me. I wouldn't mind the drive; I'd worried continuously that his drunken luck behind the wheel would run out sooner rather than later, that he'd get himself caught or killed. I'd shared my concerns with him, but he merely laughed.

"I don't get caught," he said. "Or killed, neither."

That same night, after work, I drove out to see him. His directions were careless and inaccurate, and cell service was patchy, so my GPS dropped in and out. I stopped to ask at a convenience store where Ranger apparently bought most of his beer, as the clerk—a young gay man— seemed not only to know Ranger but also how to get to his house. It was certainly remote; as I made my way down the final half-mile of his long gravel driveway, I could not see any other houses or even any lights until I got to his place.

A friendly dog met me first, a solid black and medium-sized mixed breed. He seemed thrilled to find a new friend in me. I heard a transistor radio outside somewhere, blasting a country song at full volume. I climbed the porch steps and knocked at the door. It swung open. Inside, I found nothing. Empty. There was no furniture in any of the rooms, only a pile of soiled clothing strewn across the floor in one bedroom. The kitchen was also bare, with no dishes, pots, or food in the cupboards. Even the fridge was empty except for a few cans of beer and a jar of dill pickles.

Back outside, I hollered his name.

A voice came down from above. "Up here, Neil." In the dim light, I could make out his face peering down at me from the roof. "Took ya fucking long enough. Ya met Spot?"

"Your dog?"

"Yup."

I examined him. "He's all black. No marks on him."

"Yup."

Given Ranger's contrary nature, the dog's name certainly fit.

"Ladder's around back, Neil. Whatcha waitin' for?"

Up there, I found him naked (he certainly seemed to prefer the natural state), with half of a six-pack, his cigarettes, and the radio.

"Aren't you worried what the neighbors might think?" I said.

He laughed. "Ain't no one around for miles. And if there is, they shouldn't be spying on me." He stood up, pounded his furry chest with his fists, gave a Tarzan yell, and then swung his dick in every direction. "Get yer eyes full!" he hollered.

Why argue? I stripped as well, tossing my clothes down below. I put my hands and mouth on Ranger, and he put his on me.

Some twenty minutes later, our initial lust satisfied, Ranger said, "Ya know I ain't queer."

"If you insist. Me, neither." If he felt his announcement freed him from heterosexual responsibilities for a while, I wouldn't contradict. I suspected he wouldn't want to be branded a "fag" any more than he'd want to be labeled an alcoholic. As long as he wanted to spend time with me, I was content. We passed the remainder of the warm evening exploring each other leisurely. When he wasn't otherwise busy, Ranger sang along, smoked, and drank his beer. A thousand stars painted the sky, and I never felt luckier.

When the batteries died in the radio, we climbed down the ladder, and he led me inside.

"Is your house usually this empty?" I said.

"Goddamn bitch," he said. "I get home from work tonight and come inside, and every fucking thing's gone." The divorce had been finalized yesterday, he said. Today, while he was at the Buick dealership, the newest ex-Mrs. Melusky had driven to the house with a big U-Haul and a couple of hired boys. They packed and took it all: the furniture, the TV and stereo, bedsheets, the dishes and kitchenware and groceries, the pictures from the walls, the soap and toilet paper, even the Spot's dish and sack of Ken-L Ration. She left little besides a note, proudly claiming responsibility, tacked to the front door. She and her crew must have worked fast to pack and empty the house in a day.

"I gotta start locking the door one of these days." He laughed. "Guess there ain't much reason to at the moment!"

"What will you do now?"

He shrugged. "Worry about it tomorrow. I got plans for tonight." He steered me into the bedroom (there was no furniture in it, but Ranger is a man of habit) and introduced my mouth to his hard, insistent cock once again. We set off firecrackers, noise, sparks and smoke deep into the night. It was the first time I stayed with him until morning, wrapping myself around him on the floor, inside an old blanket I'd retrieved from the trunk of my car. I didn't kid myself that it was anything more than an accident on his part, but a man can dream. One of these days, I vowed, he'd spend the night with me by choice.

He was equal parts surprised and amused when he untangled himself from me at dawn.

"Jesus fuck," he said. "I was so drunk last night."

On how many mornings had I heard that excuse, from too many other partners who decided I seemed like a good idea the previous evening?

"I know. And you don't remember a thing, right?"

He grinned. "The hell I don't, you cocksucker. I had me a damn good time, and so did you."

What can you do with a man like that? He followed me to my apartment, and I fixed breakfast for him while he showered and dressed in yesterday's coveralls. He raved about my scrambled eggs and perfect bacon, and I made sure he left in time to get to work by eight o'clock.

Ranger seemed a lot less concerned about his empty house than I was. He had little spare cash, so I rounded up what I could beg or borrow, including a card table and four chairs for his kitchen, a couple of lamps, a folding chair, and an area rug for the living room. The local Saint Vincent store provided an inexpensive second-hand bed, dresser, and some framed paintings for the walls. I purchased new towels, bedding, dishes, pots and pans.

An investment, I told myself.

A neighbor of mine conveniently placed a well-worn but serviceable couch on the sidewalk labeled "free," and I notified Ranger, who came by with his pick-up to collect it. He claimed an old, fat television someone had left by the roadside. Over time, he added shelves fashioned from cinder blocks and planks and a large wooden electrical wire spool repurposed as a coffee table.

If he felt comfortable, I had no reason to be concerned myself.

Our relationship (as I began to refer to us) progressed very slowly early on, but I was patient. I had reason to be; I knew what I wanted, and I figured I would wear him down eventually. His first love, however, proved a formidable adversary. Every day, he picked up a six-pack or two of beer on his way home from work. On Saturdays and Sundays, he'd buy himself a case and start drinking at eleven a.m. Maybe only alcoholics started earlier than that, but he had his eye on the clock by nine-forty-five. I'd never seen him drink enough that he actually passed out; he always made a conscious effort to stop for the night, turn out the lights, and climb into bed, but the pattern was too long established.

As for me, I could take the stuff or leave it; beyond an occasional glass of wine with my grandfather, I rarely drank anything stronger than espresso and avoided alcohol entirely when I was with Ranger. Maybe I had more reasons to want to remember our time together than he did, although I tried to convince myself that he needed the physical intimacy as much as I did. It's not that he denied our friendship when he was sober. It's just that alcohol was the necessary catalyst if I wanted the fringe benefits, for him to look me in the eye, raise one eyebrow a fraction, and ask if I wanted to.

I wanted. I surprised myself with how much I wanted—I was even willing to dispense with a long-standing prerequisite of mine because he refused to be bothered with condoms. I assumed I was safe with him, and I decided the risk was worth it. If all he wanted was sex, I was happy to comply, reasoning that he'd realize in time how much more I had to offer him. He certainly knew where and how to apply his mustache to give me the best ride, and he seemed genuinely pleased when I complimented him on his skill. I scoffed at his assertion that he'd (almost) never done such things before. I always let Ranger think it was his idea, but I knew what I was doing and even bought the beer for him sometimes. If I could intercept him between the first six-pack (which made him amorous) and the second (which generally left him belligerent and then sleepy), we had a good night.

My timing improved greatly with practice. Although we never talked about such things, I learned what Ranger liked and how he liked it. However, he wasn't exactly romantic, and he had no interest in foreplay. "Neil," he'd say. "My dick's already hard, so just tell me where ya want it put."

If that was how he approached sex, I told him, it was no wonder he'd been married and divorced four times. "You build up the anticipation. Slowly. There's no need to be in a hurry. Think of it like jacking up car to change a tire. You pump it up one notch at a time."

"Neil," he said gently, interrupting my languid extended metaphor. "In yer mouth or up yer ass?"

By early September, Ranger and I had spent so many nights together that I was busy planning our future. I shared my optimism on the phone with my grandfather, who ordered me to appear at his house the very next morning.

I showed up at nine o'clock, prepared for questions about Ranger, of which there promised to be a carload. Granddad knew I wasn't due at work until four, so there would be plenty of time for a thorough grilling.

He'd made fresh coffee and a pan of buttered scones, the better to bribe me to talk. I'd never seen him happier.

He lit his pipe, pulled his chair up close to mine, and leaned in, confidentially.

"You know how you get 'Dick' from 'Richard'?"

A joke. The latest of hundreds, mostly salacious, he'd shared with me over the years. I started chuckling before he even reached the punch line: "You ask him very nicely!"

He passed me a scone and gave me about thirty seconds to enjoy it before the third degree began. "Now, what about this young man of yours, Neil? It's about time you found a suitable partner."

"First off, he's ten years older than I, so he's hardly my young man."

"*All* desirable men are younger, as far as I'm concerned, Neil. But never mind. Start with the important stuff."

"Such as?"

"Is he handsome, dark and tall? A furry chest? I know how much you appreciate that particular trait."

"Brown hair, all over. You would heartily approve of the generous crop on his chest."

"I always say the best playgrounds are covered with grass."

"And a mustache, almost as fine as yours."

"Good, good. Is he well-hung? Top or bottom? And which do you prefer, anyway? You've never told me. I'm versatile, as you know—I'll go either way."

"Granddad, I suspect there are more than two ways you will go."

"You're possibly right. What's his name?"

"Ranger Melusky."

"Sounds—interesting."

"His dad was a ranger in the Army and liked the sound of it."

"And he's in his forties?"

"Forty-two."

"You've always had a penchant for mature men."

"That's mostly your fault, and you know it, Granddad. You've gone out of your way to make sure I fall deeper in love with you every time we're together." Such banter had been part of our relationship for as long as I could remember, and both of us enjoyed it.

"Don't change the subject. Do you have any naked pictures to show me?"

I laughed. My grandfather was irrepressible. "Not yet." I had no pictures of any kind, and in fact, until Granddad asked, I'd never thought about it. I could grab a few snapshots of Ranger with my cell phone. Maybe, after a couple of beers, he'd even be willing to strip and let me shoot a little video....

"Since you haven't bothered to introduce him to your old granddad, perhaps you'll describe him for me, at least."

"He's not especially tall or dark, but he's kind of sexy in a backwoods-Kentucky way."

"Nothing wrong with the rugged outdoor type. I'm sure you find him handsome. Yes?"

Was he? I tried to explain. Ranger didn't fit the textbook or movie-star definition, but somewhere in the roadmap of his face, his brown eyes full of wonder, his careless haircut and thick haphazard mustache, his sandpaper-and-molasses twang, I got lost. The way he'd stand—like a question mark, curious and cautious, hospital-thin in dirty blue jeans a size too big, the dense crop of fuzz on his chest trapped by a sleeveless undershirt, a Marlboro in his fingers (and the attendant signature cough), how he'd shake his head, muttering "Well, fuck," and then grin. Big. How do you pin down mercury?

I concluded thus: "I love to put my hands on him."

"And I'm sure he enjoys the privilege. You haven't told me if he's well-hung."

"That's correct. I haven't."

"Now, Neil. You can confide in me. I won't breathe a word to anyone. If you had those naked pictures—"

"—I wouldn't share them with you under any circumstances. It doesn't matter if he's well-hung."

"However, It would matter if he weren't, so I'll assume he is at least reasonably well-endowed."

"I have no complaints. That's all I intend to say."

"Have you measured? Give me a ballpark figure."

"No."

"I could loan you a yardstick."

"I don't need one!"

"Bottom or top? You didn't answer before."

"*None of your business.*"

"You're no fun," he grumbled. "You know I'd share all the details with you if I were in your place."

"Of course you would. And it would fall into the category of 'too much information' as always."

Since he retired from teaching at the university, my grandfather had not been shy about regaling me with his sexual exploits, which occurred surprisingly often, given his eighty-one years—aided and abetted, I suspected, by a certain blue pill. With the eagerness of a schoolboy talking smut to his classmates, Granddad notified me of every tight ass penetrated, every hard inch swallowed, and every creamy conclusion (his own and those of his partners as well). He so enjoyed the telling that I couldn't help but take pleasure in listening, and if he exaggerated his prowess—or if it were utter fiction—I cared none.

"What's his profession? Surely you will share *that* information."

"He's an auto mechanic for the Buick dealership in town."

"A working man, and honest work. Splendid. Bad habits?"

"Hmm...he smokes."

"This pipe has never done me any harm."

"Cigarettes."

"Ah. Pity."

"Yes. I doubt if I could convince him to switch to a pipe. I'd rather he quit smoking altogether, but that's up to him, and I won't harass him about it. Oh. He also swears like any three sailors combined."

"Do you find his salty talk to be troublesome?"

"No. It's very colorful. Kind of rude sometimes. Other times, I just want to laugh because it's almost comical. But not troublesome."

"You might want to be cautious about introducing him to your father."

We both laughed. Simply put, my grandfather's son never swore. Dad found it inarticulate and uncivilized, as well as boorish and disrespectful of others' ears. I admired his viewpoint and, for the most part, agreed with his assessment, though I indulged myself on occasion. I think he never discovered the innate satisfaction built into its occasional practical use, however.

"I like your Ranger so far," my grandfather said. "But you haven't told me anything about him that I couldn't discover merely by looking at him. What kind of man is he? What else do I need to know about him before I meet him in person?"

"Hmm. He—drinks."

"All worthy men do, within socially-prescribed limits. And you're a bartender, so that shouldn't be a problem."

"Maybe. I'm afraid I actually *would* have to classify his drinking as problematic at times." That was an understatement, but I couldn't bring myself to admit that Ranger was a card-carrying alcoholic.

My grandfather furrowed his brow. "Hmm...well, that's not good. Does it interfere with his ability to get himself aroused?"

I hedged. "On occasion." It had happened more than once, and the frequency seemed to be ticking upward. I also didn't feel obligated to tell my grandfather that the beer was quite possibly essential as a means of putting Ranger in the mood.

"All the more reason to be moderate. I enjoy a cocktail now and then, but not to the extent that it inhibits other and more satisfying pleasures."

I agreed. And moved on to other subjects. "He's also been married four times."

"Four! To women? Jesus, Neil. Is he married at the moment?"

I knew my grandfather, with good reason, held no truck with married men who sneaked around and met other men on the side. I'd always kept quiet about my country-club hookups for that reason.

"Divorce Number Four is brand new."

"I hope that means you'll be next in line."

"I wish. Somehow, I don't think that's in the cards. He claims he's not really queer."

"A little confused, is he?"

"I think so, but he doesn't. He claims he just hasn't met the right woman, but I doubt if he'll ever find one that meets all of his specifications."

"Of *course* he won't. What does he expect? A woman who's hung like Charlton Heston? Have you met any of the former spouses?"

"No. From what Ranger has told me, the latest ex-Mrs. Melusky is not very nice, but that's just his side of the story. I think she made the mistake of falling in love with him, and I can't blame her for that. I'm dangerously close to falling myself, I'm afraid, and how stupid is that?"

"I suppose it could be very stupid. Unless he feels the same. Does he?"

I admitted I didn't know. Could Ranger ever truly fall in love with a man?

"But first things first. He must admit that he's gay without reservation if you two ever intend to reach some happy ending." He considered for a moment. "Does he let you suck him off?"

Why not tell him? I had no one else to whom I could brag. "He does, in fact."

"Does he return the favor?"

"Yes. And he's extremely talented in that regard, I must say. I know he's been with other men, but he still insists he's straight."

"Do you—excuse my indelicacy—fuck?"

"Yes." Unless he had too much to drink, which I did not volunteer.

As for indelicacy, I almost laughed; as articulate as my grandfather was, he certainly loved the hard consonants and satisfaction that could be derived from the proud and situationally aware usage of such words. They never were mere place-markers in his conversation, or used as adverbs—you would never hear him say, for example, "that's fucking incredible"—or toss out "you cocksucker" as an insult, in part because he genuinely revered the lusty carnality of sexual communion and was proud to call himself a dedicated practitioner of mouth-to-cock stimulation.

"Does he enjoy himself?"

"Thoroughly. And he sees to it that I do, too."

"Let me break the news to him. He's certainly queer. Rest assured. So you're free to move into the next stage of this courtship.""

"I'm ready. But he's the one who maintains he's not one of the family."

"Hmm." My grandfather pondered this conundrum for a moment. "I'd think he wouldn't be able to say a word with his mouth full."

Granddad certainly knew how to turn a phrase.

He put an arm around my shoulder. "I wouldn't worry too much about what he says. His actions speak louder. And wouldn't you much rather be on the receiving end of his actions than his words?"

Yes. I'd merely feel much more secure if Ranger were willing to acknowledge the intimate bond we'd forged, particularly in the daytime, before he got into the first six-pack. If he would let me, I would be his alcohol, let him drink all he wanted of me and never let sobriety intrude.

"Perhaps I could have a talk with him."

"I can manage Ranger. Don't trouble yourself, Granddad."

"It's no trouble, believe me. It's the least I can do for my favorite and only grandson. When will I meet him? Maybe he'll answer more of my questions in person."

Ranger probably would, at that.

Granddad arched an eyebrow. "If I can persuade him to pose for a few revealing snapshots, I'll share them with you."

"You do that." If anyone could convince Ranger to do such a thing, my grandfather would be the man.

"Is he worth waiting for?"

Even Granddad was surprised with the vehemence of my resounding "yes." "Last of the romantics, aren't you, Neil?"

"No. I'm second to the last after you."

As I prepared to depart, my grandfather said, "By the way, Neil. I meant to ask you—"

I sighed. "What now?"

"What do soybeans have in common with a dildo?"

Ah. I started laughing even before he delivered the punch line: "They're both substitutes for meat! "By the way," he added. "I figured out a way to make my dick ten inches long."

I waited expectantly.

"I fold it in half!"

What can you do with a man like that?

I was surprised to learn from Ranger that Granddad visited the garage not long after we had our talk. Ranger even admitted that he'd accepted Granddad's invitation to stop by his home after work one evening for supper.

"So what's your impression?" I asked Ranger.

He grinned. "Horny old bastard, ain't he?"

I sighed. "He didn't try to seduce you, by any chance, did he?"

Ranger's grin widened. "I'm just sayin'. He offered me a bottle of Johnnie Walker Red if I'd drop my britches so he could take a couple of pictures of my dick."

I would have a word with my grandfather.

"Did you accept?"

He snickered. "Never you mind. Johnnie Walker's good shit, though. Hey, Neil, I got a good one for ya. What's the difference between light and hard?"

I gave up.

"Ya can go to sleep with a light on!"

I didn't have to ask where he'd gotten *that* joke.

4

Among the most fascinating attributes of my father is his magnificent name. Unfortunately, he chooses to hide most of it, as if it is something to arouse shame rather than glory. Clem Graham shares a moniker with his own father's favorite author. I wonder what sort of bargain Granddad made with my grandmother to persuade her that their son should be christened Samuel Langhorne Clemens Graham. It's a mouthful, certainly, but one to be savored, shouted, celebrated. Instead, my dad grew up hating the name. Before the divorce, he was known as Samuel; afterward, Grandma called him Sammy, and when my dad left home for college, he adopted Clem—I suspect, in part, because he knew Granddad would be livid, though he agreed that a man should choose the moniker he preferred.

Dad became a pharmacist, all he ever wanted to be. He attended college out of state, but after completing the degree program, he came back home and hired on at a local drug store. He's worked there, satisfied, for as long as I've been alive. I envy him for his certainty and, thus, his contentment with his station, but he's set in his ways, old in ways that my grandfather never would be.

Unlike Granddad and me, Dad is also a fitness fanatic. He exercises every day, calisthenics and weight-lifting, and he and my mom take a speedwalk around their corner of town every evening if the weather permits. Apart from an earthquake or tornado, the weather permits, as far as Dad is concerned. I don't think he ever missed a day, actually. My mom refuses to go out with him in hurricane rain or temperatures below twenty degrees, but nothing stops my dad. He's in enviable shape for his or any age, with enough energy and stamina for two. I think sometimes he should have been a teacher of physical education, but I suspect he decided as a boy that he never wanted to be a teacher of any kind because it would give him something in common with his father.

I would not consider my dad vindictive by nature, but he carried one grudge—a very large one—against his father for breaking apart their family unit over half a century ago. The fact that the divorce resulted from my grandfather's unwillingness to pretend to be straight any longer caused a family scandal, and Dad was never able to get past it. He was nine when his parents split up, and fifteen years passed before he saw his father again. Granddad made an attempt to keep in contact, but Grandma could never forgive. She permitted letters, cards, and the occasional phone call, but no visits. Granddad also sent a generous child-support check every month without fail.

When my dad, fresh out of pharmacy school and married with a child on the way, moved back to his hometown, my grandfather transferred his prescriptions to Dad's pharmacy, just so they would be forced to interact in person at least occasionally. Yet even as an adult, my father resisted Granddad's attempts to re-establish a friendly relationship. Dad disapproved of him across the board and would not—could not—absolve him of his perceived sins.

If I have learned anything from my father, it is the knowledge that such implacability does not come without cost.

I didn't discover this family history until I was grown. I did not even meet Granddad for the first time until I was just nine years old myself, when he showed up at our house uninvited one evening. I don't know why he stopped by on that particular night; when I asked him later, he merely said it was high time he and I introduced ourselves. He'd lost his own son at nine, and perhaps by gaining a grandson at the same age, he hoped to make some reparation for his past iniquities.

I remember the night. The doorbell rang, and my father answered. I was watching something or other on television, and I looked up, because Dad offered no greeting or invitation to the visitor to come in. He merely scowled and then sighed, long and deep. From the other side of the screen door, the man who had rung the doorbell said, "Do you think you might invite me in, Clemens?"

My father sighed again and held open the door. The man stepped inside, an older fellow in a sharp suit who captivated me immediately. I left the couch and the TV program and walked over to the door to get a closer look.

"What do you want, Pop?" was my father's opening remark to this man.

"It's a pleasure to see you, too, son," the man said to my father.

So that's who he was! I had never seen him before. There were no pictures of him in our house. I knew he existed, even lived across town, and I knew he was a college professor—but, never having met him, he didn't concern me until that night. I was charmed immediately. My grandfather was impossibly handsome, impossibly tall, impossibly narrow, built like the Roman numeral I, with a magnificent mustache as dense and irresponsible as his wicked grin, a mustache like a welcome mat, so wide and scratchy you could wipe the mud from your boots in it.

My mother joined our trio.

"Clem, you be civil," she said to my father. "Welcome, Dad. We haven't seen you in so long." She greeted him with a warm hug, took his hat and coat, and then introduced him to me. He shook my hand courteously and gave me his name: Sixtus James Graham. Then he insisted on a hug, which I willingly returned. I liked the feeling of his arms wrapped around me, warm and tight and protective, and I could feel his whole heart. My dad was more reserved and less generous with physical contact.

Mom served lemonade and cookies, and my grandfather spent an hour or so with us, pretending there was nothing unusual about my father's disapproving glare and limited contributions to the conversation, but otherwise, it never flagged. I felt a kinship with this man (who seemed so old to me then, though he was just about sixty) that I'd never felt with my own father.

My grandfather wanted me to call him Sixtus, as if we were fast friends or perhaps co-conspirators, but my dad refused point-blank, so we reviewed the options—Grandpa (too common), Grandfather (too formal), Grandpapa (too sissified), Grandpop (too carbonated, even though my dad used "Pop" himself), Gramps (not on your life)—and settled, by default, on Granddad. "Like the whiskey," he said, wagging his eyebrows. My dad, who never touched alcohol, coughed and said, "Pop, that's enough."

When Granddad left that night, he said he would see me again and wrapped me in another vigorous bear hug. He embraced my mother as well and then faced my father.

"Well, Clemens," he said.

"Pop," he said.

"Thanks for your hospitality. It's good to see you and my lovely daughter-in-law and meet my only grandchild at last. I've been waiting patiently for an invitation, but I wasn't sure it would ever come, so I took matters into my own hands."

My dad didn't say, "You're welcome," or "See you soon," or even "Stop by again when you're in the neighborhood." My grandfather put on his hat, and before he turned to leave, he gave my father a hug, too, and a kiss on the forehead. Dad pushed him away. When they separated, my grandfather said, "Good night, son. I love you dearly." He lowered his voice to a stage whisper: "In spite of the fact that you can be a real prick sometimes."

My father sighed deeply and held the door open. With a wave and a grin, Granddad made his exit. I'm sure I received a lecture after he left, but I didn't pay any attention to it. I only wanted to know why I had not met him before, and my father had no good answer.

"When can I see him again?" I asked. My father was vague about that, too.

After breaking the ice, however, Granddad managed to fit himself regularly into our lives, which wasn't actually difficult. He lived barely a mile away by surface streets (though perhaps a million miles away in terms of temperament and ideology) in the same well-kept two-story brick home where my dad spent the first nine years of his life. Granddad sent a card and a generous check for my tenth birthday and every one after that. Every Christmas, I received a couple of books, inscribed with love. I still have them all: *Tom Sawyer, Huckleberry Finn, A Connecticut Yankee in King Arthur's Court, The Prince and the Pauper.* Always the classics, including everything by Mark Twain that he thought appropriate for a young boy, but others as well: *Black Beauty, Treasure Island, Kidnapped,* the *Just So Stories,* and *Kim.*

When he felt I was old enough, he offered me *A High Wind in Jamaica, The Catcher in the Rye, Sounder, To Kill a Mockingbird, Lord of the Flies, Animal Farm, The Great Gatsby, The Old Man and the Sea, Billy Budd* and dozens more. I knew no other teenager with a similar reading list. To my parents' credit, they censored nothing; my mother in particular encouraged me.

Every time my grandfather gave me a book, he urged me to choose another by the same author, and I was happy to comply. Under his tutelage, I researched each author and even the background of the story so that I'd have an informed reading experience. He expected a written report, which I dutifully provided; such study fascinated me. By the time I was sixteen or seventeen, I'd devoured several hundred of the classics and was the most well-read kid in my high school, the pet of the English teachers, and a target for more than one bully. Realizing that I was also gay alienated me further from the boys my age and only made the library more attractive. My dad, the fitness buff, had a hard time convincing me to put down a book and get some exercise, though occasionally, I would let him persuade me to toss a football or softball around the backyard.

I remember the laceration tattoo my grandfather had on his left forearm: the name Sam in plain letters, two inches high. The letters had been carved deep into his arm with the intent of leaving a permanent scar. When I was a kid, my grandfather declined to tell me about Sam—would only shake his head ruefully when I asked. My father claimed he'd never noticed it. My grandmother gave me the impression that she would rather spit into the dirt (had she been less ladylike) than mention Granddad's name, let alone share any insight into the nine years they spent together. So I learned nothing about the mystery Sam.

I also remember discovering, parked on one side of his garage, a rusty heap that used to be a car, hidden under a dirty grey blanket. I had no idea about the make or model, but it was years old, the kind of vehicle you might see in a 1940s gangster movie driven by Edward G. Robinson or James Cagney. When pressed for details, Granddad identified it as a 1941 Sport Coupe, manufactured by Buick the same year as his birth. He had no particular devotion to the make or the model, but he liked its classic lines and the fact that he and the car were the same age. He'd purchased the wreck for two hundred dollars when my dad was a boy, intending to restore it as a shared project.

Most of his friends had scoffed, he told me. "What do you know about restoring an old car?" they'd asked him. And my grandfather responded, "I can learn. How hard can it be?" After Grandma and Dad departed, Granddad never found an answer to the question. He covered the Buick with the tarp and there it sat.

I had more questions, but that's all Granddad would tell me.

Gradually, with Mom's encouragement, my dad established something resembling a truce with his dad, as long as he remained willing to hold his tongue and respect the boundaries my father set. At any rate, Granddad and I were able to spend time together—not as often as I wanted, but perhaps the infrequency of our intercourse caused me to lionize him so much when I was young. If he had always been around, I might have regarded him the same way most little boys regard their grandfathers, as old and clueless men. Instead, we became the best of friends.

In addition to good books, he introduced me to jazz, which I came to appreciate as much as he did. His extensive record collection ranged from Jelly Roll Morton's classic sides of the 1920s to Miles Davis's more avant-garde experiments of the 1980s. As I grew older, for every book Granddad gave me, I traded him a jazz LP in return, collected from a thrift store or yard sale.

I learned almost by accident that he preferred male companionship. I gathered that his divorce had something to do with another man rather than another woman, but I wasn't able to glean many details as a kid. My mother was reluctant to share what she knew out of deference to my dad and grandmother. I would find out when I was older, Mom said; in the meantime, she believed there was no harm in my cultivating a traditional grandson-grandfather relationship with him. In retrospect, I presume that Granddad hadn't shown a predilection for young boys, or my parents would never have allowed me to see him. Still, I recognized and appreciated my mother's open-mindedness, as well as her willingness to persuade my father to relent a bit. Her own parents had died before I was born, and she argued that a boy deserved a grandfather.

I remember skinny-dipping with him one hot August night at the lake on the edge of town. I'd been dropped at his house one evening when my parents had a rare evening out together. After a leisurely supper at a fancy restaurant, we visited the Dairy Queen for chocolate-dipped cones, which he said used to be a favorite of my dad's. As the sun went down, Granddad drove us to the water. I pointed out the "no swimming" signs posted on the bank, but he merely said, "How can you read the sign in the dark? I can't see a thing. Must be getting old." So we shucked off our clothes (him first, me following suit, somewhat gingerly) and folded them into a neat pile on the shore. The fact that our swim was illicit made it all the more thrilling for me.

The surface of the water glinted like slivers of neon glass, a thoroughly enchanted evening. I can still see my grandfather's lithe figure navigating the water like a seal or fish or some such aquatic creature, as if he'd been born to it. I remember his sheer joy at being naked at the water's edge in the late summer. He splashed and cavorted like Neptune himself, deriving the full measure of satisfaction from his domain.

I vividly recall being fascinated by the luxurious furry pelt on his chest, much to his amusement. In the twilight, it seemed like a field of lush, tangled grass. My father is similarly enhanced, but I seldom saw him shirtless. My father is too proper, too bashful to allow such an indiscretion. (Even in summer, he wears pajamas to bed.) I appreciated my grandfather's lack of decorum. He was justifiably proud of himself, being nearly as trim in his sixties as he was at twenty, and no doubt willing to show himself off to any appreciative audience.

Here was my first close-up look at a naked adult male. My grandfather seemed prodigiously well-endowed, and I inspected his bushy crotch with some amazement. I would have been content to stare much longer than he would permit, however.

"None of that," he growled, stern, impatient. "All men have dicks, and you will have plenty of time to examine them in detail when you're older, if you so desire." Self-consciously, my father would have said "penis" if he ever needed to refer to that particular organ, as he did during our excruciating, painful talk about sex and reproduction when I was about twelve. But my grandfather, unrepentantly exuberant about such things, liked "dick."

He liked it in more ways than one.

After our swim, we dried off—there were convenient towels in the back seat of his car, which led me to believe our excursion was no spur-of-the-moment idea—and dressed, and then he drove me back to his house to await my parents. When they picked me up a short time later, unseen by them, he grinned and put his finger to his lips. I nodded. The night swimming would remain our secret.

On the afternoon of my thirteenth birthday, he got me excused from school on some manufactured pretext and took me to see a matinee of *The Adventures of Priscilla, Queen of the Desert*, the story of a couple of drag queens and a transgendered woman driving across Australia en route to a gig, lip-synching to songs by Abba and the Village People all the way. It was grand entertainment, exhilarating, and highly instructive in its own way. It was certainly more educational for me than an afternoon in class. Even better, Granddad and I managed to pull off the great movie caper without my parents discovering the ruse.

I believed my grandfather was all-powerful, although I doubt that my father shared the same opinion. My mother, bless her, kept her mind open.

From time to time, as I grew older, I wangled permission to spend a night at Granddad's house, and I vividly recall one such occasion when I was fifteen. We shared a pleasant evening, supper and lively conversation, and a game of Scrabble, at which he defeated me by several hundred points. (I vowed to spend more time browsing the dictionary.) The hours passed too quickly, until, finally, he ordered me to bed. I borrowed a book from his library and went reluctantly, leaving him to grade some papers and enjoy a late-night whiskey and soda. He kissed me on the forehead, and off I went to my room to read for a while.

An hour later, I headed to my grandfather's bedroom, intending to ask a question about the book I'd chosen, perhaps, or discuss some matter of importance that had kept me awake, though I can't recall what it was. His door was ajar; I didn't knock, but I peeked in first, and much to my surprise, he was naked, fully aroused, servicing himself with obvious pleasure. In its erect state, his cock was more than impressive; it seemed gigantic.

Of course, I had been actively exploring the pleasures and perils of jerking off myself for a while. I had made the discovery of orgasm with a mixture of fear and astonishment. Given the dire warnings I'd received from the priest and the nuns at my parochial school about the dangers of "touching" myself, I was afraid to do it too often, sure I'd injure myself in some way, or at least damn myself to hell.

He didn't notice me as I watched from the door ajar, mesmerized. I felt a distinct stirring inside my pajamas as I watched him strop himself with expert precision. He was obviously well-practiced and in no hurry at all, but moments later, he persuaded himself to climax, heading over the top with a lusty, animal growl. Seeing my grandfather's erection and the satisfaction he allowed himself from it was an education all by itself and a turning point for me. Watching him come, as the joy of release flooded into his fingers, went down on my permanent record.

Quietly, I padded down the hall, back to my own room. I never did get to sleep that night.

As the sun came up, I kept an eye on the clock, and by half-past seven, I knew Granddad would be up. His door was wide open and the lights were on. I found him in the bathroom shaving.

"Good morning, Neil." He grinned at me. "How did you sleep, young man?"

I confessed: "Not so well."

"Why?"

How could I explain? His glorious (if inadvertent) example the previous night provided me a certain answer to a question that had been nagging at me.

"Granddad, I think I'm gay, too."

He considered. Nodded. He finished shaving and wiped his face. He led me back into his bedroom and sat me down next to him. He put an arm around my shoulder.

"You're old enough to be thinking about such things," he said, all seriousness, "but don't be in a hurry to jump to conclusions. You're still young. Give yourself some time. Don't worry about it. One of these days, you'll figure out it's the right time for you to start exploring. You don't need to be in a hurry for that, either. But then you'll know for sure."

He was thoughtful. "When I was sixteen, my dad engaged a prostitute to educate me about sex, and if you don't think that was a traumatic experience, well—I didn't need any more proof that I preferred the company of men, in bed and otherwise."

He inquired, tactfully, if I had discovered the gentle art of self-service. I nodded.

"Good. It can be endlessly pleasurable if indulged properly and in moderation. As habits go, why not choose one that feels good and causes no lasting harm?" He advised me to ignore the priests and old women who claimed that it was sinful or against nature. "Look at the language they use! Self-abuse! It even *sounds* wicked! Ridiculous. It's perfectly natural, not to mention useful in a tight spot. Trust me. I've got almost fifty years of experience. Okay?"

"Okay, Granddad. Thanks." He'd unwittingly illustrated its merits to me the night before, beyond a shadow of doubt. And, clearly, it had done him no damage in the past half-century.

We exchanged a hug. "If you have any questions, ask. And I mean *any* questions, about any topic. You know I will never betray a confidence." I promised. "Now you get dressed, and I'll see to breakfast."

I appreciated that he didn't, this time, caution me to keep our conversation a secret. He knew I would.

By the time I hit my junior year of high school, I could confidently report to my grandfather that I was indeed gay. He told me how pleased he was to learn that I'd followed his queer footsteps, and my father and grandmother be damned, along with their righteous indignation. It would be a lifelong adventure, he told me, and he envied the fact that mine was just beginning as his had inevitably begun winding down.

I hesitated long and thought hard before coming out to my parents, but I did it just after graduating from high school. I couldn't keep the secret any longer. My mother remained philosophical and supportive; my father ranted and wept, but at least he didn't eject me from the house. I believe he felt outnumbered, with a gay father and a gay son, and it seemed too much to bear. But Granddad proved to be a great role model and resource, answering my many questions honestly and thoroughly, offering advice when asked, and deferring when he believed I had to learn something for myself.

5

Granddad was named after a round of popes, five of whom headed the Roman Catholic Church at various times between the tenth and sixteenth centuries. One of them, I later found out, was supposed to have been gay, Number Four, who is said to have entertained a couple of his nephews as lovers. Sixtus IV is also credited with founding the Spanish Inquisition in the fifteenth century. I wonder if my grandfather's parents knew such things when they chose the name. I doubt it. The first Pope Sixtus achieved sainthood via martyrdom for the faith, and I presume he was my grandfather's namesake.

I've only ever heard the name in one other place, the beautiful, ritualized roll-call of the apostles and martyrs from the Roman Catholic Church's first Eucharistic prayer, declaimed just before communion; as an altar boy, I used to recite the prayer silently along with the priest. Something about the list intoxicated me: Peter and Paul, Andrew, James, John, Thomas, James (yes, two of him; I used to wonder if anyone knew which was which), Philip, Bartholomew, Matthew, Simon, and Jude, Linus, Cletus, Clement, Sixtus, Cornelius, Cyprian, Lawrence, Crysoganus, John and Paul (two more duplicates), Cosmos, Damian, and all the saints. Its lilt and mesmerizing rhythm were as heady as the pungent incense that smoldered in the censer on feast days.

Until the end of his life, my grandfather sparred with Catholicism, attending mass every Sunday but defiantly refusing to go to confession, something he hadn't done since 1950, as he bragged to me. I asked why he went to mass if he didn't believe.

"Who says I don't?" he said. "I just don't see the point in confessing my so-called sins to another mortal."

Once I had my driver's license, I got into the habit of taking him to church regularly. Watching him sit in the pew, solemn, his head bowed, his eyes closed, his hyperactive mustache—usually restive but here, still for a change—dressed in a white linen suit and pastel-colored shirt with a carefully-knotted tie, you would think you'd never seen anyone so devout. He dropped a generous envelope in the collection plate faithfully every week. After mass, he would generally take the priest to task over some point of contention from the sermon, respectful discourse that they both enjoyed. I wondered how my grandfather reconciled being queer with being Catholic, but that never seemed to trouble him. Come to think of it, why should being queer be at odds with *any* religion?

His true faith lay in the pages of a good book. Armed with sense of humor and a Ph.D. in literature, he was a popular and well-regarded full professor in the English department of our local university for more than forty-five years. During that time, he established a reputation as a Mark Twain scholar, one of the best in the country, with an encyclopedic knowledge of Twain's books, essays, and stories. Granddad regretted that he didn't have the talent to write fiction, but he could write *about* it concisely, with clarity and good humor, like no one else, with fourteen books to his credit and dozens of articles published in every major journal of literary criticism.

I couldn't wait to start college myself; I had devised a plan by the time I was twelve. I would major in literature too, under Granddad's tutelage, and upon graduation—with my degree and a commitment to Truth, Justice, and the Modern Language Association style guide for research writing—he and I would shake up academia as the scholarly equivalent of Batman and Robin, the Boy Wonder. My goals became a bit more realistic by the time I enrolled at the university, but I retained my optimism as well as a fondness for great books.

On the first day of my freshman year, a Monday morning early in September, I sneaked into Granddad's classroom and took a seat in the back, keeping my head down. One by one, he read the names from the computerized enrollment printout, slowly, making sure he pronounced them correctly. At the end of the list, he asked, "Is there anyone whose name I didn't call?"

I raised my hand, and he saw me for the first time. I could make out the grin he was stifling under his mustache. "You there in the back. Name, please?"

"Neil Graham. Middle initial F."

He chuckled. "What in blazes are you doing here? You're not old enough to be enrolled in college."

"You want to see my I.D.?"

"I'll take your word for it, Neil Graham, middle initial F. And why are you in my classroom?"

"I want to take your American lit course, Dr. Graham, but it's full. Will you sign a pink slip for me so I can get in? Please?"

He grinned big. "See me after class." Several other students were hoping to enroll in the class as well, and he agreed to take on all of us.

Anyone who saw us in the hallway after the session must have wondered why the old professor was embracing the young man so fondly. I was as pleased as he was. He hadn't even known I had been accepted for admission; I'd kept it a secret on purpose.

By the third classroom session, everyone knew the exact nature of the relationship between the professor and me. The class enjoyed our frequent and often intense jousting on points of plot, characterization, or theme. Clearly, I was well-informed and well-read, probably more so than any other student in the room. And my grandfather was clearly quite proud of me.

I never worked harder for an 'A' in my life, but I earned one.

My grandfather's office, tucked into a small corner of the building, featured a picture window that overlooked part of the campus green. A massive, ancient wooden desk, probably as old as he was, dominated the room, and a large globe of the world sat next to it on its own stand. His dog Central—named for Hank Morgan's baby son in Twain's *A Connecticut Yankee in King Arthur's Court*—had a cedar-chip-filled cushion in one corner and a water dish, and when my grandfather was in the office for the day, so was his faithful dog. He had been adopted as a pup, a hybrid of unknown lineage, and had been part of the family ever since. When I started college, he wasn't even a year old, medium-sized, quiet, and splendidly good-natured. Central made himself at home around the English department offices, and no one objected. He also saw to it that my grandfather got some exercise, as he demanded (and received) regular walks around the campus.

Three of the four walls in Granddad's office consisted of floor-to-ceiling shelves—crammed with books, journals, and file folders, haphazardly arranged. Yet Granddad could lay his hands on anything in a few moments. Prominent on the fourth wall was a large, elegantly framed portrait of Twain, taken when the author was nearing fifty, shirtless and grinning beneath his magnificent welcome mat of a mustache. In all his furry-chested glory, he revealed himself fit, trim, and damned attractive.

My grandfather agreed. "Why else do you think I have him hanging on the wall? It's quite nearly nineteenth-century pornography. Who says literature isn't as sexy as all nine circles of hell combined?" If more authors had posed shirtless, classic literature might have improved upon its undeservedly dry reputation, he said. Where were the pin-ups of such handsome men as Joseph Conrad? William Faulkner? George Bernard Shaw? Eugene O'Neill?

The perfect man, my grandfather used to tell me, was fifty years old. In his twenties, Granddad preferred older men, but as he aged, his ideal never changed. At fifty, he chased men his own age, and at eighty, he still kept his eye out for the perfect fifty-year-old. He steered clear of romantic entanglements, claiming he'd rather have fun with as many men as he could. Why limit oneself to a single cock, he said frequently, when every man had one? And they were so tantalizingly hidden most of the time. It was a crap shoot, a treasure hunt, with the potential for gold behind every zippered or buttoned fly.

I think flirting was second nature to my grandfather, regardless of the company. He aimed to seduce. It's one of the reasons, I believe, that his university courses were so popular, because what he sold in the classroom was the sensuality of a good book. He had more willing customers than he could handle. He even found himself elected "Professor of the Year" at the university four times during his last decade of full-time teaching, much to his amusement, embarrassment, and secret pride.

When he turned seventy-three, just before I started my sophomore year, he retired from his full-time post and eased into an emeritus role, remaining on call, teaching a course from time to time when needed, and serving as an advisor to the graduate students—and to me. He continued to stop by the English department every weekday to check his mail and make the rounds. At eighty, reluctantly, he gave up his office. I took a week's vacation to help him sort and move his books and forty-five years of memories back home.

He did not give up his daily walk around the campus with Central or his morning coffee at a local café with a group of friends, retired professors like himself. His enthusiasm for good books never waned, and he passed the torch to me. Thanks to his shining example, I majored in American literature myself, completing the program with honors. He fully expected me to follow in his footsteps.

I never intended for my part-time bartending job to become permanent, but when I took my shiny new bachelor's degree job-hunting after graduation, I was dismayed at the limited prospects. After mailing out dozens of resumes and undergoing several depressing interviews, the best offer I received came from a community college, a salary that equaled half of my bartending paycheck. I wasn't devoted enough to academia to make anything but the most obvious choice. I considered graduate school, and Granddad was rather forceful in his insistence that I apply immediately, but I put it off at first and then continued to do so. As the years passed, he stopped pestering me about it, but—to my regret—he never got over his disappointment. I convinced myself that I simply would not be able to equal (let alone best) his track record, so why bother?

"Granddad, Ranger told me you stopped by the Buick dealership and invited him to your house for dinner."

"I did. And he accepted. I fixed spaghetti and meatballs with Italian bread and a Caesar salad. We had a fine meal."

"With lots of wine, I imagine."

"He's not a wine drinker. Fortunately, I had a few bottles of beer in the fridge."

"I'll bet you don't have any now."

"I see what you mean about his drinking. He does drop his defenses rather quickly."

Along with his trousers, I suspected. "Did he pose naked for you?"

"Ranger is your young man, Neil. You know I would never interfere."

"He told me about your offer to trade a bottle of Johnnie Walker, but he wouldn't say if he took you up on it. He did. Didn't he?"

"Never you mind, Neil."

I sighed. "Where are the pictures?"

He played innocent. "He's damned sexy, even if he doesn't know it. You're a lucky man, Neil."

"If I could ever get him to kick down the closet door and settle down with me."

He nodded. "That's the secret of life, isn't it?" He paused. "You think you were the first man Ranger bedded down with?"

"Not the first. But he said he hasn't done it very often."

Granddad was most diplomatic. "And you believe him?"

"Why do you ask?"

He hedged. "Just an academic question."

But I began to wonder. A randy, good-looking man like Ranger with no inhibitions after a beer or five? I doubted that there was much that crossed his mind that he hadn't tried. How likely is it that a forty-two-year-old man with his guard let all the way down hadn't experimented—extensively and for the last couple of decades? The subject obviously interested him, and he certainly displayed a talent as well as a familiarity that would be unlikely in a novice.

"I guess it doesn't matter. I just want to be his last one."

Granddad wished me luck.

6

Even with the fourth wife out of the picture, Ranger proved an inconsistent suitor, if that's even what I could call him. I would certainly have never used such a term within earshot, as he continued to resist such categorization. The more we got together, however, the more my suspicion grew that he had racked up much more experience than he was willing to claim. I could not have been the first to be placed in the awkward position of being the lover-under-the-influence who reverted to the status of casual friend when the hangover sun crept over the horizon. I wondered how long I would have the patience to put up with it, put up with him, and I wondered if his previous lovers (and wives) gave up for the same reason.

But I yearned for more. I desperately wanted a man who would acknowledge me all day long, a man who didn't necessarily need a couple of beers before he'd let me put my hands on him. And how tightly could his closet door remain shut? After a few beers, he was far too willing to open it. How long could he keep his secret? In fact, *was* it a secret, or did he just imagine no one knew? If Ranger preferred male companionship in the dark, why would it matter to anyone but himself (except, of course, the various wives)? Yet I could no more persuade him that being gay was okay than I could persuade him that he didn't really need another six-pack.

He could do without me, however. Perhaps he became a little self-conscious about all the time we spent together, because he started limiting our dates (as I continued to call them) to once or twice a week. I didn't know what he did on the intervening nights. He may have had other partners, or he maybe he was drunk enough that he was better left alone. If he didn't see me every night, perhaps it was easier for him to pretend that he was straight, that he didn't need what I so willingly offered, that it was just something he chose to do from time to time, a casual interest or hobby. On those nights, I couldn't reach him by phone, and a couple of times, when I drove out to his house to look for him, he was gone, although the door was unlocked as usual.

On impulse, I left the country club early one soggy Tuesday evening, leaving one of my assistants to manage the thin crowd that had shown up for the afternoon tournament. I drove out to Ranger's house and waited for him to come home from work, but after an hour, I decided he'd made other plans.

Back home by seven o'clock, I browsed for bars within a ten-mile radius of his house and found eight listed. I started dialing and asking. It was a long shot, but it paid off after the fifth call, to a place with the unlikely name of Whiskey River. I remembered passing by the place occasionally, although I'd never gone inside.

"I'm trying to locate my friend Ranger Melusky. Is he there?"

"I'll check."

A pause; I could hear the bartending yelling his name, and then a familiar voice came on the line. "Who the fuck's this?"

"Hey, you."

"Neil? What d'ya want?"

"I got off work early, and I wanted to see if you wanted to get some supper somewhere. On me."

"I'm kinda busy." (I guess beer-drinking counts as an activity.) "How'd ya find me?"

I lied. "You told me this was your favorite bar."

"I did?" He laughed. "I don't remember. But this is the only bar I ever come to, so I guess it's my favorite. Why don't ya come down? Buy me a beer instead of supper. And meet my best buds."

Hmm, his best buds?

"I'll be there as soon as I can."

I hadn't been an actual customer at a bar for many years. Before I started working at Rumors, I used to hang out there occasionally, just to meet like-minded companions. But after Rumors closed, none of the other bars in town had become a gathering place for gay clientele as far as I knew. Maybe the perception was that gay bars weren't needed anymore. After all, we're so open-minded now (right?) that separate-but-equal facilities are no longer necessary, are they?

Or are they? Straight people may believe that the gay bar is a relic, but gay men will always need a place to go where the rules may be unspoken but also intuitive, at least if you're one of the family. You won't get into any trouble cruising another man in a gay bar. In a non-denominational bar, however, you never know what you might get.

I parked in the crowded lot. The exterior of the Whiskey River was unassuming and low-key. A couple of neon signs in the front window advertised beer, and a hand-lettered poster announced: "LIVE MUSIC EVERY TUESDAY FRIDAY + SATURDAY NO COVER." With some trepidation, I stepped inside Ranger's favorite establishment and adjusted my eyes to the dim light. The interior was laid out in typical fashion, a central bar with stools around it, a number of tables with chairs around the edges, a small bandstand, and a well-scuffed dance floor in front of it. A jukebox, lights flashing, offered a country tune. The bartender greeted me with a big "howdy, pardner," which I acknowledged with a wave.

"Neil!"

Ranger's voice cut through the clatter of conversation and the din of the jukebox. He came rushing toward me and greeted me as if he hadn't seen me in months, wrapping his arms around me in a joyous bear hug which I willingly returned. He couldn't have known how sexy he seemed to me at that moment, the perfect pistol for my bullets. My goal for the night would be to get him away from the bar as soon as possible and home to my bed, his clean white shirt, new jeans, boots, and Stetson in a heap on the floor.

"You son-of-a-bitch!" I thought he might kiss me out of reflex, but a second later, he let go of me as if he remembered men weren't supposed to engage in such public displays of affection in places like this.

I figured I might as well plant the seed early. "Suppose we get out of here right now? Come over to my place, and I'll show you a good time."

He frowned. "None of that shit, Neil. Not here."

Oh. Okay. This would take a little more time than I anticipated.

A bit self-consciously, he took a seat at the bar, and I sat next to him.

"Hey, Charlie!" he yelled. The man behind the bar shuffled over to us. "Charlie, this here's Neil. He's a bartender, too."

Charlie offered his hand. "Pleasure. Where do you work?"

"At the country club, actually. There's a bar attached to the men's locker room."

"Pretty fancy."

"I suppose. It's not much different than a regular bar, except no women are allowed."

"That ain't necessarily a bad thing." Charlie winked at me.

"And the clientele are a bunch of cheapskates. Tips are terrible."

"Why don't that surprise me? You worked there long?"

"About seven years now. I used to work at Rumors until it went out of business."

Charlie obviously remembered the place. While it was hardly notorious, it was undoubtedly well-known around these parts, by reputation if nothing else. Straight men and women, even the most adventurous, rarely frequented my old establishment because they were decidedly not welcome. Charlie's eyes narrowed, and I could see him recalculate his first impression of me. I half expected him to tell Ranger to watch out, because I was probably one of "them." Professionalism, however, won out.

"So what can I get you?"

"Uh, two beers, I guess."

Ranger spoke up. "I'll take two beers, too!" He laughed loudly at his joke. Charlie drew two drafts into frosty mugs and pushed them across the bar at us. "Seven bucks."

I pulled a ten out of my wallet and told him to keep the change.

"Thanks." He was pleased with the tip, a courtesy most of us in the service industry afford our fellow brothers/sisters-in-arms; he rang up the sale and stuffed the extra three dollars into his pocket. Country club members paid six dollars for a single mug of beer; I'd grown so accustomed to the ridiculous markup on everything, beverages and food alike, that I'd almost forgotten it wasn't standard operating procedure to gouge the customer.

I took a sip from my glass as Ranger downed half of his. He led me to a corner table where three men eyed me with some suspicion.

"Guys, this here's Neil. Old buddy of mine." He introduced his friends: Billy, Dave, and Tom. I was predisposed not to like Ranger's "best buds" for monopolizing more of his attention than I could. First appearances being what they are, I was willing to judge them immediately, and none of them passed muster. They appeared to be approximately the same age as Ranger, but other than that, there was little to suggest that they had anything in common beyond an affinity for alcohol.

Billy—short, fat, balding rapidly under a greasy comb-over, eyeglasses too large for his face—wore a T-shirt that announced, "I like your new girlfriend. What breed is she?" I wondered what went through his mind when he chose to wear it for the evening.

Mullet-headed Dave hadn't shaved in a day or two or, from the scent of things, bathed either. Slightly wall-eyed, he also had chosen a witty T-shirt for the evening, bright orange with blue letters claiming "Orgasm donor." It barely covered his gut; he looked to be about eight months pregnant.

Tom, tall and skinny, wore a precision haircut and a carefully sculptured mustache. He wore a T-shirt too, but it was tasteful and elegant, a brand-name logo on the pocket. Tom had tucked it into his designer jeans and worn a classy and expensive sport coat over it. He had taken the time to shave; his hair was stylishly cut, and his nails manicured. A splash of distinctly masculine cologne completed the picture. In no way did he fit the down-at-the-heel profile of the desperate hard drinker that Dave and Billy seemed to personify. I shook hands all around. Only Tom offered a wan smile and a greeting.

I wonder what they thought of me, still dressed for work in khakis, a pressed white shirt, and a company tie, as dictated by the country club. A little self-conscious, I loosened the tie and wadded it into my pocket.

"Neil's a bartender, too," Ranger said.

"Really? Where?" Billy wanted to know.

I told them. They were not impressed; the best way to handle something out of your league is to express disdain for it, I suppose.

Tom snapped his fingers a couple of times, drawing the attention of the waitress, whose name tag read "Della." I thought it was a demeaning way to summon anyone; it had been tried with me at the country club until I made it clear that I would come only when my name had been called, with "please" attached to the front or back. But Della didn't seem to mind.

"Bring us a round," Tom said.

"Sure thing, Tom." A moment later, Della was back with a pitcher of draft beer and three frosty glasses, which she set in front of Ranger, Billy, and Dave, and a shot of something amber with a small glass of ginger ale on the side for Tom. Billy poured his glass full, and Dave's and Ranger's, too. Tom tossed down his shot and sipped the ginger ale sparingly afterward.

Their focus shifted to me, as the interloper. I tasted my glass of beer and wondered what to say, and the best I could come up with was something to the effect that they knew about my job, but I didn't know about theirs. That observation animated Billy and Dave, at least.

Billy called himself a plumber's helper; I thought immediately of the wooden stick with a suction cup screwed to the end, used to unblock a toilet. He'd never passed the test required to get certified, although he claimed to have completed the necessary schooling. He worked as a non-credentialed assistant to a non-union plumber who was a dickweed, in Billy's estimation. Dave lived in a mobile home and drew unemployment, working various low-paying jobs only long enough to qualify for benefits. He related this without shame; instead, he seemed proud that he'd figured out how to game the system. Tom said he was a government contractor; what kind of contractor (or for which government), he did not say.

When he excused himself to visit the men's room, Billy and Dave told me that Tom was rich as fuck and didn't actually have to work at all, the lucky son-of-a-bitch. Tom was married, too, and his wife was a hot babe with impressive jugs, Billy and Dave said, but Tom (most likely a fudge-packing fag) mostly ignored her. The salacious talk ceased as soon as they caught sight of Tom returning from the restroom.

Having exhausted the conversational thread of employment, I asked Billy and Dave about their own marital status. Billy said he was divorced twice and wouldn't rule out additional walks down the aisle; he'd already lined up several potential candidates. He had two children by his first wife and was thousands of dollars in arrears on his monthly child-support payments, apparently a laughing matter. Dave, preferring to offer himself to many women rather than commit to a single one, had never taken the plunge himself.

"I got no kids that I know of," he said, laughing long and loud, as if he'd been the first to shoot that particular basket.

That prompted me to ask a question I'd wondered almost as soon as Ranger had shared his marital history with me. Coupled with his utter disdain for condoms, I wondered. "All those wives. How did you keep all of them from getting pregnant, Ranger?"

"He never fucked 'em," Billy offered.

"Bullshit," Ranger said. "I wore 'em out every night."

Quite possibly, but I doubted that the wearing-out had anything sexual to do with it. Still. "What's your secret?" I said.

He laughed. "Had myself fixed years ago."

"Fixed? I didn't know you was broken!" That was Dave, cackling at his own joke.

"You dumb shit. *Fixed*. A vasectomy."

"You let them cut off your tits?" Dave was mystified.

Ranger laughed. "Condoms are too much trouble when you're drunk. I didn't want to take any chances, so I had the surgery. Now I don't have to worry about it. Once I get the ol' freight train running, it don't stop for nothing, now."

"Yeah," Billy said. "Because if you had to stop even for a second, your dick would turn into Mister Softee."

Billy and Dave exchanged a high-five, suitable for a triumphant insult.

"Not me," Dave said. "Satisfaction guaranteed. I'll slip her my ten inches, and she'll be begging for more. Check this out." He pointed to his T-shirt.

"I'm sure somebody had to explain it to you before you bought that shirt," Ranger said. "Besides, it would take five of you to come up with ten inches of dick. I stood by you at the pisser enough times, and I seen it."

"That's bullshit. You ain't never seen me with a hard-on. I do *so* got ten inches, and I sure as hell know what to do with it. I could get me some pussy every night if I wanted."

"Not so damn loud, Dave," Tom said, irritated. He looked around, a little embarrassed, I think. I was startled to hear him speak at all. I suspect he did not want anyone to notice that he was with us, and I didn't blame him. He didn't really seem to be part of the group around the table, except as a funding source. I suspect it's why he'd been adopted by Ranger, Billy, and Dave. I couldn't believe Tom would have chosen them as his companions; I wondered why he simply didn't move to another table by himself.

I was seriously second-guessing my insistence about joining Ranger for a night out with his pals and vowed to myself I'd never suggest it again. I looked at my watch: eight-thirty, and nearly an hour had crawled by. At home, his or mine, we'd already be naked and rolling around the floor. It would have been much more fun.

The live music, as promised, would start at nine. A sign on an easel near the stage advertised the band, imaginatively named Horse Opera. The musicians, in colorful, exaggerated cowboy garb, started setting up their instruments. The lineup included the standard bass/guitar/drums with the addition of an accordion and a pedal steel guitar. A cheerful woman in a fringed turquoise suit and spangled hat approached the microphone and introduced herself as June.

"Good evening, ladies and gentlemen. We are Horse Opera. Thank you for coming to listen. And dance! We kick off our first set in half an hour, but in the meantime, we'll have our regular Tuesday dance lesson starting right now. You don't need a partner to participate in the lesson, so don't be shy! Beginners are welcome, so come on down."

Eight or ten men and women shuffled to the floor, looking a bit self-conscious that they didn't already know how.

"Do you two-step?" I asked Ranger.

"A little. I ain't great. But I'm better after a couple of beers."

"I don't dance," Dave said. "It gets in the way of drinking."

"The band is too loud," said Billy. "You can't hardly hear yourself talk." That would be a blessing, actually.

"Who wants to talk to you fuckers? I'm dancing," Ranger said. "Neil?"

Did he want to dance with me? I was pleased; this was a side-effect of the beer that I didn't anticipate. "I don't know how, but I might as well take a lesson, since she's offering a class."

"Do that. I gotta piss." He wandered off to the restroom. I joined the queue next to the stage.

I'm not a graceful dancer. I don't have much of a sense of rhythm. My efforts are workmanlike, not very skillful, but possibly amusing to anyone who would not be my partner at the time. I can't fake it very well, either. One of these days, I would like to take some real lessons, but then I wonder why. With whom would I dance?

With infinite patience, June guided us through some basic footwork and clapped her hands to give us a beat. I did my best to follow, as did the others who, like me, hoped the two-step was simple enough that a short tutorial would be enough to generate both confidence and skill. After half an hour, during which everyone's dreams of confidence and skill vanished, June told us we had all earned a passing grade and urged us to find a partner who knew the ropes. Practice makes perfect, she said.

The band members took their seats and June strapped on her accordion. There was general cheering and applause as partners paired off and staked some territory on the dance floor. The drummer counted off, and the band leaped into a song, tuneful and sunny. June and the guitarist shared vocal duties as the dancers scurried, stomped, swung, and kicked in a most energetic manner.

"Are you confident enough to go out there and try it?" I whispered into Ranger's ear.

Ranger's eyes narrowed and he whispered back. "With you?"

"Certainly with me."

"*Fuck*, no!" He seemed truly alarmed that others might think we were "that way." Not here, his home away from home. His whisper became a warning. "This ain't no fag bar. Don't queer it for me."

He was actually angry. It startled me.

I wanted to apologize when Billy cut in. "What are you two lovebirds whispering about? You gonna fuck later tonight?"

For a second, I thought perhaps I'd inadvertently given something away, but then I realized it was just a standard jibe. Gay slurs, impugning the manhood of all present, were part of the script.

Ranger flipped him the middle finger, emptied his—sixth? seventh?—glass of beer, and walked over to one of the tables where four women sat, clearly enjoying the music and just waiting for a man like Ranger to ask them to dance. In his cowboy boots and Stetson and pressed shirt, he looked endlessly sexy. I could believe he'd been married four times, and I believe any woman at the table would have been happy to be Number Five. The ladies giggled, and he selected one—no doubt with a promise that there was plenty of him to go around and each would get a turn.

Ranger led his first partner out to the floor, and a few moments later, I could see that he'd been too modest about his dancing ability. I was astonished to see how good he was, possessing all the grace and style and rhythm I lacked. All the beer he consumed couldn't have done more than lower his inhibitions. Had I drunk as much, someone would have had to scrape me off the floor, but Ranger seemed to show no ill effects from the alcohol. If anything, it seemed to energize him, rather than put him asleep.

Billy, Dave, and Tom remained glued to their chairs. I had decided, reluctantly, that they would be my only company for the rest of the night when someone tapped me on the shoulder. I turned to find a woman offering a coy smile as she batted her eyes. She wore more makeup than necessary and tight jeans, both obscuring a natural beauty. "You dancing, cowboy?" Her voice was a Southern caricature, honeyed and perfumed.

I was flattered. I don't believe I'd ever been asked to dance by a woman, and certainly not in such a charming manner. I followed her out to the floor, apologizing in advance for my limited skills. The music started and we bounced into it, along with a dozen other enthusiastic couples. The steps were tricky, and I hadn't really learned them at all. My partner had a good idea of what she was doing, but she couldn't teach me and have fun herself. I managed to step on her feet a few times and nearly topple us once, in addition to bumping into numerous other couples, who glared at us angrily.

At the end of the song, I apologized profusely for my clumsiness. "That's okay, sweetheart. Next time, maybe go a little easy on the beer. You'll have more fun."

My face burned. It would do me no good to say that I'd taken only a few sips. I made my way back to the table as the next song started. No one else asked me to dance, and I certainly didn't have the nerve to invite anyone myself. Billy and Dave were attempting to speak over the din. Tom knocked back another shot of whiskey and gave me a friendly nod.

"I hate beer," he said into my ear. It was the first thing he'd said directly to me since "hello."

"I'm not really drinking myself."

"I noticed. May I buy you a Coke or something?"

"I'd appreciate that. Thank you."

Tom snapped his fingers, and Della came over again. He ordered a soda for me, and when she brought it, he gave her a twenty and told her to keep the change. I no longer wondered why she was so prompt in responding to him. He was a good customer, and Della earned a couple more twenties from him over the course of the evening. He bought at least six pitchers of draft beer for the table, but he limited himself to whiskey with ginger ale on the side. He insisted that the empty shot glasses remain in front of him, and he lined them up in a neat row. Although Tom never grew sloppy, he became even more disengaged as the evening wore on. He did not dance, though he tapped his foot continuously, restlessly, to the music. Surely, he was aware that the present company was far beneath his dignity, but maybe he thought he got what he deserved. Alcohol can be a great equalizer, making a poor man king and a rich one a pauper, emotionally as well as financially.

At one point, he disappeared into the men's room. When he came out, he was significantly more animated and awake (if no more talkative), which suggested to me that he offset the tranquilizing effect of the booze with a stimulant of some sort, as his foot-tapping doubled in speed if not accuracy. His painful thinness also suggested that he didn't rely on food for his energy. He might have been handsome at one time; there were still vestiges of it, but his watery, bloodshot eyes and sallow complexion attested to the power of alcohol to alter irreparably. He was the only one of the group for whom I could drum up any sympathy, though why he should deserve it, I could not explain.

Ranger, meanwhile, was busy on the floor with a new partner, and he would stay thus occupied for much of the band's first set, pausing from time to time to dump a half-glass of beer into himself. He perspired accordingly, but he looked arrestingly attractive as he sired one lucky lady after another around the floor, the relative precision of his footwork belying the quantity of draft he'd consumed. If he grew a little loose by the second set, he'd established such goodwill with his dancing partners that they overlooked the effects of the intoxication.

I lost count of how many glasses of beer Ranger consumed. Ten? Twelve? He grew more friendly as the night wore on, wrapping his arm around my shoulder any time he came back to the table, at least until he noticed what he was doing. Then he jerked himself away as if he'd been burnt.

As much as he enjoyed dancing, the beer gradually won out. By the end of the second set, he was stepping on feet and crashing into other couples, frequently pulling his dancing partner with him. When the third set started, he found himself sidelined by popular demand halfway through the first number. After that, when he was approached and asked for a dance, he cheerfully announced he had retired from dancing for the night. "Sorry, darlin,'" he said more than once. "Ask sooner next time."

Finally, I asked if he was ready to call it a night.

"Ranger, I think your friend is a faggot," Dave said. "He keeps trying to get you alone. You better watch your ass."

"Shut up. He ain't either a fag."

I saw no reason to correct him. I'm not one to back down from an argument, but I suspected Billy and Dave rarely relied on logic as a basis for their discourse.

"I'm just looking out for him," I said. "I'll get him home. He's got to be at work in the morning."

"Hell," Billy said. "Everybody got to work tomorrow. No sense in letting your goddamn job get in the way of having a good time."

"I don't gotta go to work," Dave said.

"Ya lazy-ass bastard," Ranger said. "Who d'ya think pays your fucking unemployment? The rest of us dumb shits." By way of farewell, he flipped the middle finger to his best pals. Billy and Dave offered the same in return. Tom didn't even blink.

Leaning heavily on my arm, Ranger made it to the car and I poured him into the front seat and strapped him in. "What about my truck?" he said. "How the hell am I supposed to get my truck home so's I can get to work?"

"I'll take you to my place for the night. I'll fix you breakfast tomorrow and bring you back here for your truck."

"Sounds good to me. Must be some way I can say thanks." He unbuttoned his jeans and pulled out his dick and started to massage himself. "How 'bout a little of this?"

After all he'd consumed, how could he possibly manage to summon an erection like that? I asked him.

"Beer makes me horny. Want some or not?"

"You mean *now* you'll let me handle it?"

"I don't get ya."

"In the bar, you wouldn't even dance with me. Now you want me to suck your dick."

"Guys don't dance together."

"Yes, they do."

"Not at the Whiskey River."

"I noticed."

"Don't ya wanna suck my dick?"

I sighed. "Yes, Ranger. I want to. Anytime you'll let me."

"Good." He sounded relieved. As he was ready and willing and so was I, there was no reason to wait until we got to my apartment. Maybe Billy's crass comment about Ranger's not being able to get it up once he'd been distracted nagged at the back of my mind, since I'd seen it happen before. Maybe men didn't two-step together inside the Whiskey River, but there were two men engaged in a different kind of dance in the Whiskey River parking lot.

Ranger unbuttoned my jeans and reached in. "Ya got a beautiful dick, man. Goddamn. And a sexy ass, too. And I'm gonna fuck ya raw."

"How about a blowjob for starters?" I was fully aroused and eager for his immediate attention, and there was no time like the present. However, Ranger insisted that his heart was set on raw fucking first and a thorough cocksucking afterward. I could not dissuade him, so we headed for home.

Less than a mile from the bar, Ranger was snoring, and once we parked at my apartment, he didn't want to wake up. It took all my strength and ingenuity to get him out of the front seat, up the stairs, inside, and onto the bed. I sacked out next to him; in the night, unconscious, he wrapped himself around me, and his warm embrace made me feel absurdly optimistic in spite of the circumstances.

Ranger awoke to the smell of eggs and bacon frying in the kitchen, and he stumbled in, naked, sleepy, thoroughly mystified.

"How'd I get here?" he said. I silently recited his next observation in unison with him: "Jesus *fuck*. I was so drunk last night."

7

Not long after Ranger and I had spent the evening at his favorite bar, he turned up in mine. I came back from the beer storage cage in the back with a couple of six-packs to restock the cooler, and I found him leaning against the counter, grinning.

"Ranger! This is a surprise. What are you doing here?"

"You come and see me at work. I figured I would come and see you at work. How 'bout buying me a beer?"

I could tell he'd already bought himself one or two elsewhere. "I'd like to, but this is a members-only club, like I told you." I kept my voice down; a couple of guys sitting at the table nearest the bar tuned in, curious. Strangers rarely walked into this bar and were generally regarded with suspicion.

"Okay. How do I join?"

"You have to be invited."

"So invite me."

"It's not that simple. A long-standing club member has to issue a formal invitation, and then your name goes before the committee. If you're approved by majority vote, you will be sent an application. You fill out the application and submit it with a check for ten thousand dollars to claim your membership. That's just the initiation fee. On top of that, you'll pay six thousand a year to use the golf course, the pool, and the tennis courts, and you have a monthly restaurant tab of seventy-five bucks whether you eat there or not. Alcohol is extra."

Ranger shook his head. "Damn. Too rich for my blood. Do ya get to be a member for working here?"

"Hardly. We get to use the golf course or the tennis courts on Mondays when the club is closed to members, but since I don't play golf or tennis, that doesn't do me much good. And because I'm friendly with the chef, I get my meals on the house. I could offer you a glass of ice water at no charge, but that's about all, I'm afraid." I dropped my voice even lower. "Or you can come to my apartment after work. I've always got a six-pack in the fridge for you."

"Maybe I will. I'll bring dinner."

"Who's this, Neil?" one of the patrons asked me.

"It's okay. He's an old friend. He was just curious to see how things worked down here."

No one offered introductions. They eyed Ranger with distrust as well as condescension, and he gave as much back. Finally, one of them said, "Has he seen enough?"

I asked him.

"Yeah. Too much."

I ordered him out, quickly, before the situation could escalate into any kind of incident, and he left, cheerfully enough, with a wave and a "see ya later." Me? I had an erection most of the afternoon, probably because when he said he'd bring dinner, all I could think of was the Grade A prime beef he always carried with him. I doubt if I ever shut up the bar so quickly at the end of a work day. Ranger was waiting when I got home; true to his word, he provided all the dinner I could eat.

Granddad warned me to be cautious but offered no other advice, perhaps knowing I would probably ignore it. With alarming ease, I fooled myself into thinking I was indispensable to Ranger. He needed me, and not just for the sex (which we both enjoyed). I had gotten into the habit of buying groceries for him since his fourth wife had emptied the house. Without my contributions, the refrigerator would have been nearly empty except for cigarettes and Maxwell House; I couldn't let him go hungry! I'd fix a few days' worth of sack lunches and leave them in the fridge for him. After helping him furnish the place, I assumed he would want to keep it presentable. When he didn't bother, I started coming by once or twice a week and spent a couple of hours vacuuming, doing his laundry, washing the sinkful of dirty dishes, scrubbing the bathroom, and generally tidying up after him. He never commented, though he once complained that the laundry smelled a bit too fruity.

It finally dawned on me that he took me for granted. He knew how I felt about him and let me fall as far and deep as I chose without ever making any kind of commitment himself. I grew frustrated and impatient with his unwillingness to acknowledge that we were anything more than friends without the marinade of beer. On more than one occasion, we argued loud and long about it. He seemed particularly incensed that I (or anyone) might suggest that his drinking had become problematic. As the unpleasant times slowly began to overshadow the good ones, I wondered if we could ever tip the balance back the other way. What kind of future could we possibly share?

I had an answer sooner than I anticipated, not even two weeks after he'd visited me at the country club. When I arrived at his house around eight that particular Saturday night, he was ahead of himself, already two-and-a-half sheets to the wind, out of beer, and broke, and what was I going to do about it?

"Undress, for starters. Why don't you do the same? It's been a whole week since the last time. I'm hungry, and I want what's on your menu."

He snorted. "I'd rather have me a beer."

I suggested that he'd already had enough beer, so perhaps we could skip directly to what always came afterward. That was my mistake. I thought for a moment that he was going to swing at me; furious, he grabbed my arm, as close to violence as I had ever seen him. "Look," he said, hard and low and mean. "If you want anywhere near my dick tonight, ya better go get me a goddamn six-pack first. As I headed out the door, he followed me and yelled from the porch, "Make it two."

I drove to the convenience store, growing angrier by the mile. When I returned to Ranger's house with the beer, I could see his silhouette framed by the window, watching for the car. Damn him anyway; I knew what he was waiting for so anxiously, and it wasn't me. I shook up each of the six-packs vigorously before I took them inside.

The first can he opened spewed foam against the walls, ceiling, and carpet. When the second one did the same, he aimed it at my head. I dodged easily. He raged. "Fuck you, asshole."

I howled right back at him. "Is that an invitation? Come on, you drunken bastard. I'm ready, but I doubt if you can even get it up!"

I was wrong. He could. He was drunker than I had ever seen him before, and maybe nothing but white-hot anger kept him aroused. It was a long, vicious night of noisy couplings and climaxes, dizzying highs and unspeakable lows. Finally, and for the first time, I forced him to turn over and I mounted him from behind, despite his protests. I rammed every bit of my outrage into him at full bore, and he couldn't do much more than squirm and curse. For my part, I felt nothing but exhilaration. When we finally exhausted each other, and he passed out, I opened the last can of beer and dumped it over him in the bed. He didn't even wake up. I bolted, half angry and half ashamed of myself. But I'd be damned if he would find me there in the morning to nurse him through what promised to be a statewide hangover.

We didn't speak to each other for weeks afterward. And when we did, he called me at one o'clock in the morning from the local police station. He'd been arrested for driving while intoxicated after colliding with a telephone pole on his way home after a night at the Whiskey River. It could have been much worse; I had no idea how he'd escaped serious punishment or injury for as long as he did. The judge took away his license for six months and sentenced him to thirty Alcoholics Anonymous meetings in thirty days, or thirty days in jail.

How imaginative, I thought. Ranger chose the meetings, of course, confident that he'd gotten an easy pass.

It grew considerably more difficult when he started working out the logistics of it. For one thing, he could not legally drive and lived far enough outside town that no bus or taxi service was available. He had no friends who were interested in assisting him; most of them were drinkers who shared his problem, but none of them would be caught dead at an AA meeting.

Penitent, he came back to me.

I used up most of my accumulated vacation and sick leave that month driving him to every one of those meetings, sometimes two a day to meet the requirement. Since most groups in our area met but once a week, we covered hundreds of miles, tracking them down in distant towns I'd never visited before, big and small meetings, four people or forty at once. In church basements, empty storefronts, office-building auditoriums, peoples' garages or kitchens, we met hundreds of men and women, all with sad, hard-luck stories that started the same way his did: "My name is Ranger, and I'm an alcoholic."

"Hello, Ranger," everyone would say, encouraging, and when it was his turn, he would describe his craving with an articulate sensitivity that I'd never guessed him capable of, like the most yearning romantic poetry.

"It always lets me down in the end," he said at one of his first meetings. "But at the beginning, I can't wait to get there. That first rush. And after that? Tie me down, because nothing's gonna stop me." He described the moment as absolutely perfect, at the tail-end of the evening, when the room is spinning like it has a buzz on, that exact moment, just after he'd had enough and just before he'd had too much, balancing right on the edge, and the thrill, like a carnival ride, being at the top of the roller coaster, just before the car lets go, being suspended in space, his heart in his throat.

"Why can't I remember to stop right then? I don't want that feeling to end, but it won't stay. I can't hang onto it, so I have one more, hoping maybe it will stick around just a little longer, only it don't. But I'll try one more after that, just to make sure, and by then, it's too late."

Others nodded, and even I could understand. "I know when I had enough, so why can't I stop? Even the worst hangover in the morning, going to work with jackhammers pounding my skull, isn't enough to keep me from getting on the train the night before. It must've been worth it. Because otherwise, why'd I buy a ticket every goddamn night?"

He would smoke a whole pack of cigarettes during most meetings and drink cup after cup of black coffee. I don't know if the almost-imperceptible shake he developed was caused by the caffeine, the nicotine, or the fear of an alcohol-free life.

The AA people gave Ranger a medallion, about the size of a half-dollar, engraved with a prayer asking for serenity and courage and wisdom to recognize what he could change and what he couldn't, to have the strength to accomplish what was necessary. He carried this coin in his pocket as an incentive for ongoing sobriety. Or a taunt.

At the first meeting, he also received a blue hardback called the "Big Book" by AA members, the inspiring story of the group's founding in the late 1930s. It's packed with dozens of first-hand stories by men and women, old and young, professional and blue-collar, whose drinking ruined their lives before they chose to quit, and how they climbed back from the despair through the twelve steps of AA. It served as a kind of Scout manual for sobriety. I thumbed through Ranger's copy once. I'd never known him to be a reader, but he finished the book and then started it again, underlining phrases and circling paragraphs. He carried it with him most of the time, and he'd even spend his lunch hour with it while he ate his sandwich.

I helped him change the things he could by staying up with him a lot of nights at his favorite truck stop, lousy scrambled eggs and toast, and then coffee and cigarettes in the parking lot until nearly dawn. I wonder what people thought, seeing us sitting next to each other, our shoulders touching, his mustache against my ear as he whispered that he was afraid to be by himself because he couldn't stand the company.

How could I leave him alone?

I don't know how he managed with so little sleep. I was fortunate; I could drop him off at work and then go back home to crash for a few hours before starting my shift at the bar, but Buick expected him at eight sharp, five days a week.

Alcohol may be a monkey on a man's back, but reluctant sobriety is another one. In the whole of his adult life, Ranger had never spent time getting to know himself. Now, with the bottle taken away, he had no place to hide. What if he truly couldn't face the man in the mirror watching him shave?

I have been forced out of closets too.

But somehow Ranger made it through his workdays, past the first week, then the second. A month—and a new red AA medallion for that landmark—then two months (a gold medallion), a day at a time as the instruction book outlined, climbing the twelve steps. All his concentration steered him toward sobriety; slowly, he gained confidence like some old-time religion. His co-workers proved supportive, and he discovered a whole tribe of new friends who had something in common with him.

I tried hard to defeat my creeping resentment. I had little use for the revised edition of Ranger. I desperately needed one thing from him— validity, proof that we could be more than convenient pals when he was sober—but it wasn't forthcoming. At first, I gave him room to concentrate on sobriety without pestering him for intimacy. I figured it was temporary; surely, before long, he'd miss my attention.

Surely.

During the six months that he was without a driver's license, he was essentially stuck at home in between the after-work drop-off at night, courtesy of a co-worker, and the morning pick-up (me). As he had never cultivated hobbies apart from drinking, he had to find other ways to fill his free time. He was surprised to discover how much disposable income he had after eliminating alcohol from his budget. Six-packs alone cost him upwards of four hundred dollars a month, he told me. He'd been putting an additional hundred dollars a week into the gas tank of his old truck, but not with his license suspended. Even with the extra money, he didn't bother upgrading to new furniture, though I tried to persuade him he should buy a sturdy table and a comfortable mattress. But he couldn't see any reason to do it.

"It ain't like nobody ever visits," he told me, as we sat at the card table in his kitchen. "And I ain't got nobody to sleep with, neither."

I was speechless. I had the presence of mind to stop buying his groceries, at least. He could afford his own TV dinners. And he could certainly figure out how to operate the washing machine, so I let him do his own laundry. No one did the housecleaning.

After the accident, his vintage Ford had been towed to his yard with a smashed front end, broken headlights, a punctured radiator, and deep scratches in the cherry-red finish. The damaged truck sat in the yard, accusing, and I'm sure it didn't help his mood. I proposed that he tackle the repair as a practical activity to keep his mind off other things.

When I suggested he might clean out the garage as well to make room for the truck (and who knew what he might find in there, up to and including pirate treasure?), he told me quite simply that I was nuts. But after a couple of frustrating days of trying and failing to find some of the tools he needed to begin the work, he started filling heavy-duty trash bags, thirty-seven altogether, and hauling junk out to the road for the garbage collectors to take. He built himself a solid workbench out of scrap lumber he had stacked behind the garage and added some shelves against one wall. He mounted a pegboard above the bench and arranged his tools in neat rows so that he could find anything he wanted, and then he moved the truck inside.

When he finished the repair and reconditioning (and added a hot wax, chrome detailing, and a product that shined the tires), I marveled not only at the care and attention to detail he lavished on the truck but also at the quality of the work. It looked better than new. Gently, as he was still a couple months away from regaining his driver's license, he covered the Ford with a soft blanket.

From start to finish, the project engrossed him for nearly two months and gave him something to fill his time between AA meetings on many nights and working at Buick. He would, he told me, do anything to take his mind off the beer that called to him like a siren, crooning its love song, promising sweet release and kisses if he would only pop that first top.

He could not let her win, he said.

All the remainder of the summer and into the fall, he hung grimly onto his sobriety with no backsliding. Three or four times a week (sometimes more), he could be found at one meeting or another. He had his own sponsor and any number of fellow alcoholics-in-recovery who were more than happy to provide his taxi service, and he transferred his loyalty to them. I was relieved to give up that little chore; word got around about my job, and I felt a little resentment from some of the meeting attendees, as if I represented some kind of temptation by proxy merely because I tended bar. Possibly, they were envious that I could face the enticement of alcohol every day without fear that I, too, was headed down the path of drunkenness and damnation.

I remember congratulating a man who'd announced eleven months and twenty-seven days of sobriety. "You'll have a whole year in just a few more days," I told him.

To my surprise, he scolded me for looking ahead. "You've got to take it one day at a time. Live for the moment! You make a pledge to stay sober for one day, not the next three. Who knows what's going to happen tomorrow or next week? I can't say I'll never take another drink for the rest of my life. The temptation is always there, but it's easier if I only have to concentrate on keeping out of trouble twenty-four hours at a time. Tomorrow can take care of tomorrow, but I won't jinx anything if I make a promise just to make it through today."

"I'm sorry. I never thought about it like that, but it makes sense. So how about congratulations on eleven months and twenty-seven days?"

He was all for that, and thanked me profusely.

Five months after his arrest, Ranger enrolled in a safe-driving course, another requirement set by the judge. The class consisted of four sessions over two weeks at the Department of Motor Vehicles. Ranger completed them without incident. On the day the six months were up, he was first in line at the license bureau when it opened in the morning. With his reinstated credentials, he was as proud as any sixteen-year-old earning the right to drive legally for the first time. He took his red truck to the highway, where he promptly earned himself a speeding ticket. But he couldn't have been happier.

On the other side of the (sobriety) coin, Ranger resisted my ongoing attempts to be intimate, sometimes quite angrily. I was perhaps almost comically desperate, but nothing—cajoling, bargaining, bribing, coaxing, teasing, threatening—could persuade him. I don't know if he simply didn't believe we'd ever had anything between us (perhaps he truly had been so drunk, last or any night, that he couldn't remember a thing), or maybe such intimacy reminded him too much of drinking. If he needed beer to be in the mood for love, there might be no way to separate the two. I didn't know. I had no experience with such things.

He quit relying on me for close council as well. His new friends were always available when he needed someone to listen or issue an empathetic pep talk to overcome a craving. My services were no longer required in any capacity, apparently. From time to time, usually at my request, we'd meet at his favorite diner for breakfast, and every blue moon or so, he'd actually call to see how I was doing.

As sobriety tightened its grip, perhaps predictably, he turned his judgmental eye to me and began criticizing my source of paycheck.

"Bartending is no kind of job. A smart guy like you can do better."

"And what would you suggest instead? Want to hire me as your personal housemaid, cook, and bedmate? I could move in immediately."

That shut him up.

As sobriety became habit, Ranger became a different man, but the man he became had little interest in me. Since I had little interest in that particular version of him, I guess we were even.

8

I poured my aching heart out to my grandfather, who offered a sympathetic shoulder. He agreed that Ranger could not have continued along the road to ruin he'd set for himself, bottle in hand. Granddad could not, however, understand why Ranger denied himself the pleasure of my company in bed and elsewhere.

"When he took the pledge, he seems to think it included every other kind of fun, too," I said.

"He's a fool. There's nothing like a little romance—or at least a little sex—to take your mind off other unpleasantness. I would think he'd be offering himself to you all the time."

"It hasn't happened since he quit drinking. And I'm not very hopeful at this point."

"What do you want from him, Neil?"

"I want the let's-go-to-hell-and-back Ranger that he used to be, but I want him to want me without having to fortify himself with a six-pack first."

"You think it's possible for him to be that man?"

"I have to believe it."

"Have you asked him?"

That stopped me. I hadn't. I had hinted, but I'd never come right out and stated my case. Granddad suggested inviting Ranger for dinner again for just that purpose, perhaps a romantic, candle-lit dinner to relax him, and maybe (maybe) he'd be open to the idea. If not, at least I would have my answer.

I was optimistic enough to think that perhaps my grandfather's charisma and persuasive abilities might influence Ranger in my favor, so I agreed to my grandfather's tentative suggestion that we hold the event at his house. I phoned Ranger and offered the dinner date, and he agreed to join us in spite of a little suspicion. Perhaps he thought the pair of us might overcome him, break down his guard, and molest him. He arrived half an hour late and had little to say after being seated in the living room. He seemed more than a bit nervous, as if he'd been warned to be on his best behavior.

The tantalizing scent of oven-fried chicken and biscuits wafted in from the kitchen, and Ranger sniffed appreciably, but we didn't even make it to the dining room table. Out of habit, Granddad mixed himself a whiskey and soda and thoughtlessly offered one to Ranger.

"Fuck you," Ranger said. "I see your game. The pair of you."

My grandfather apologized profusely, insisting he had simply been forgetful, but Ranger would have none of it and used the pretext to scram, leaving us with dinner enough for three.

"Careless of me," Granddad said as we ate some of it. "I'm sorry, Neil."

"It's not your fault. He's the one who should apologize. It's your house."

"He's not very interesting when he's sober, is he?"

"No. He isn't. He doesn't have any kind of social life these days except Alcoholics Anonymous meetings, and reformed drinkers as a whole aren't the most magnetic bunch, in my limited experience. They've only got one thing in common, so it's all they talk about. At the next meeting, Ranger will probably claim that we tried to seduce him with Demon Alcohol. It'll give him a good story to tell, and he can pat himself on the back for resisting temptation."

If nothing else, it gave him something he could feel superior about. We all need such things against one another, and I suspect he doesn't have many.

Granddad and I shared a quiet dinner *and* a glass of wine. Afterward, we rolled up our sleeves and washed the dishes together, and I caught sight again of the tattoo on his arm.

"Granddad, who's Sam? Ever since I was a kid, I've wondered, and you promised to tell me the story when I was old enough. I think I've racked up enough years to qualify."

He considered. "I guess I owe you that. But I'll need another glass of wine or two myself. Let's finish the dishes first."

As the twilight fell, we sat on the porch together with the bottle and our wine glasses, and I let him speak at his own pace.

"Once upon a time," he said, "I was so indecisive that I believed it would be my undoing. But I learned, the hard way, that when we're forced to make choices, it's best to act quickly. Do what the heart believes is right, and never look back."

He offered his right forearm. "I did that sixty-one years and five months ago, fortified by a couple shots of bourbon and sheer panic. With a razor blade and a safety pin, I carved that name into my skin so deeply that I thought I might die from loss of blood. I honestly wanted to. Obviously, I didn't, but it gave me something to carry for the rest of my life—a reminder of my stupidity."

It seemed foolish when he was just around the corner from the light of day and wet-crack sober, he said. But it was non-refundable; even after the external wounds healed, it remained incorrigibly legible, the letters lined up neatly. The 'S' must have been tricky because of the curves. The 'A' and the 'M' would have been much easier—all straight lines. The outline of it turned purple in extreme cold, like litmus paper, he said, a reminder that the past is an acid to etch and burn.

"I don't regret doing it. I needed the souvenir. It keeps me honest. Not that it's any consolation."

He gulped the rest of his wine and poured himself another glass.

"I still dream about him. It's always late September in 1962, that day we met. I'm dancing with him—this handsome, handsome man, skinny and folded like a pair of scissors and old enough to be my father. He's wearing a dark suit with a white shirt, a tie, suspenders, wing-tip shoes gleaming like mirrors. He dressed up for me. Can you imagine someone doing that just to please you? The music is drowsy, a lazy sort of waltz, and he's holding on and whispering my name. 'Just follow me,' he says, and we turn and glide, so gracefully. As if we're floating above the floor. But even in the damn dream, it always ends the same way."

"Is he the man you left Grandma for?"

"This was years before I married. Sam and I spent a single day together. Twenty-four hours, and then I never saw him again."

He fell silent. I knew he needed no prompting from me; he'd continue when he was ready. Slowly at first, picking up speed gradually, he unfolded the story of the Sam who'd prompted the indelible souvenir. I could see as if it were a film: a long shot first of a man in the morning sun of an early fall, standing outside a downtown hotel, his hands in his pockets. He's dressed in memory of the summer just gone, in khaki trousers and a pressed white shirt. He's standing, restless, scanning the crowd as if he's waiting for someone. Across the street from him is a young man on his way to the university, a full day of classes ahead of him, waiting for the light to change. Chance had put him at the intersection just at that moment.

A medium shot reveals a little more of the older man, his approximate age (fifty), and the skin-and-bone leanness of his frame and how well he wears it, and how unbearably handsome he is with that swarthy complexion, severe haircut, black heading to gray, and his intimidating pitch-colored mustache as big and wild as Wyoming. Then a close-up: his eyes, shining brown as Easter chocolate and deep as Socrates, and his black eyebrows, animated, one of them raised just slightly, rakish. Then cross-cutting from the older man to the younger man as their gazes meet, an immediate spark, wonder and disbelief and excitement and a little fear.

My grandfather was all of twenty-one, still naïve but not so innocent that he didn't cross the street to the corner where the man waited.

"Hello," Granddad said.

In response, the man folded Sixtus into his arms and kissed him, hard and long, a kiss full of lust and fire, debt, gratitude, and burning need. It was bruising and tender at the same time, dominance and utter submission in one.

When they separated at last, the older man said, "I don't even know your name."

Breathless, the younger man answered.

"I should have permission asked first. I'm sorry."

"I'm glad you didn't. I might have said no."

"Think of all you would have missed," the man said. He introduced himself, Sam Arlington, passing through town on business, spending a single night at the hotel. He led Sixtus inside, passing through the lobby and up the stairs. A brief pause outside the door as Sam Arlington inserts the key into the lock, a few seconds when Sixtus could still change his mind (as if he ever would). The frantic, hungry, eager coupling that transpired inside lasted the rest of the morning and into the afternoon,

Sixtus's first time with a man and the best forever after, the yardstick by which every other encounter would be measured.

A woman could never compete with a man who could make you slice his name into your arm—a man who invites you to an elegant dinner in the hotel dining room later that evening where a blue-shirted-and-tuxed band played polite music for an empty dance floor, while the same man grins at you, like a promise to keep, over a glass of champagne, iced perfectly.

"A waltz," he said as the band counted it off, one, two, three. "I love a good waltz. May I have this dance, Sixtus James Graham?"

"I don't know how to waltz."

Sam refused to listen to such nonsense; offered his hand and led Sixtus to the floor, gently folded him into the music, spiraling in three-quarter time with the night and the rhythm colliding and champagne coursing through their veins, like the dream it would become years later. Anyone watching who might have considered it shocking, offensive, *queer* for one man to be waltzing with another, could be damned, because instead, it was everything necessary, mercy and forgiveness, fear and renaissance, and love consuming like buildings in fire.

They shuffled around the floor, the older man graceful and confident enough for two, laughing at the absurdity and improbability of it all. After a wondrous night dissolved into the next morning's blue sky, on the same corner where they met, Sam asked the young man to come with him. "Be with me. Be my lover. My partner, my companion for the rest of our lives."

How could Sixtus respond with anything but yes?

How could he?

Yet he said no.

"He cried," Granddad said. "I can hear him saying 'why?' and 'please' over and over again, but I was too stupid and afraid and practical, and it just seemed too risky. What about school? How would I explain to my parents? I couldn't be swayed. He kissed me one last time and walked away. He didn't look back. An hour-and-a-half later, after I wised up, I ran back to the hotel to tell him yes, and he was gone. Checked out. No trace, not even a hometown. I tried bribing the people at the front desk to give me some information. They wouldn't budge."

My grandfather sat next to me, sobbing. I collected him into my arms and held onto him, tight, until he quieted down.

"I'm sorry," he whispered. "So sorry."

"Shh. There's no reason to be. None at all."

He untangled himself from me and sighed. "I've never told that story to anyone. *Anyone.*"

I embraced him again. "Thank you, Granddad. I'm honored that you trust me enough to share it with me."

He shook his head and absently traced the letters on his arm.

"He promised to teach me everything I didn't know. Trigonometry. Canasta. The foxtrot. Golf. The French horn. Ice skating. Spanish. How to find constellations in the night sky. And I said no. I should be damned to hell for all eternity. I said no, and I never got another chance after that, with anyone. I lost him for being careless and stupid and afraid. I will tell you that a day doesn't go by that I don't think about Sam and wonder what happened to him, wonder if he sometimes thought of me. If he met someone else. Made the same offer to a man who accepted.

"Sam is long gone—probably died years ago—but in my mind, he's still fifty years old and the most handsome man on earth. We're still waltzing together, *one*-two-three, *one*-two-three. I would trade the rest of my life for just one more day with him. Don't," he ordered me, stern, "let that happen to you. Ever. Carrying such regret is pointless. Useless. A waste."

"So why did you marry Grandma?"

He shook his head. "Once I figured out for certain I was gay, I knew I'd never change, but I also realized that two men settling down together wouldn't exactly go over very well in the academic community at that time. I was still too goddamned concerned about what other people would think. I wanted to be a teacher—it's what I was cut out to do, and all I ever *wanted* to do—and in the 1960s, you didn't take out an ad in the paper to announce to the world that you preferred fucking other men."

He paused. "Your grandmother is an amazing woman. When we married, I didn't think about the fact that I was deceiving her. I truly hoped the affection I had for her would make it possible for me to conquer my natural bent."

"Grandma must have seen your arm."

"Of course she did."

"What did you tell her?"

"A lie." He didn't elaborate.

"While you were married, were you meeting men on the side?

"Not at first. I was teaching. I loved it. I had a full schedule at the university, so I threw myself into the work. Your dad was born less than a year after we married, and I was thrilled. Took some persuasion for your grandma to agree to the name I picked out, but she knew how devoted I was to Mark Twain, so she finally allowed it. Besides, I was determined to have a Sam in the family, even if it could never be the right Sam."

He confessed that, after seven or eight years, being a husband and father weren't enough. He started getting together with a like-minded history professor for some discreet activity. He was older by a decade. After Granddad's divorce, they moved in together; it lasted a couple of years.

"I suppose I was desperate to prove to myself that it was possible to find a little happily-ever-after with a man. At least until he abandoned me too, after allowing himself to be seduced by one of his students. He apologized, but it didn't stop him from leaving me. And that was the last time I tried."

Night had fallen around us by then.

"I never learned trigonometry. Or the constellations, apart from a few of the basic ones. I can't speak Spanish. I love the sound of the French horn. It's so incredibly beautiful. So elegant and mournful. Yearning, and full of a promise never given the room or the chance to come true," Granddad said, and after a minute, "I still look for Sam everywhere I go."

Long after my grandfather's confession, I kept replaying the story of the tattoo in my head, and the more I analyzed the details—however I might choose to cast Ranger and myself in a similar tale—the question of true love seemed even more remote, more incongruous.

9

Marlene knew Ranger from the time she started waitressing at the Blue Plate Diner nearly a decade back. When she told Ranger that she'd recently been divorced too, he offered his sympathy. One thing led to another, including a first date. It didn't go well. He called me up afterward and ranted about her for half an hour in the most unkind words possible. Their planned movie-and-dinner outing got off to a bad start because she refused to see any film that wasn't rated G, and there were none playing at the local multiplex. She criticized his first choice of restaurant (his favorite pizzeria), which didn't sit well with him either. He suggested they rent a DVD and go back to his place, and she seemed to think he was bent on seducing her.

Marlene was the opposite of Ranger in nearly every aspect, being quiet, refined, ladylike, non-smoking, non-drinking, non-swearing, and churchgoing. To hear Ranger describe them, none of these were virtues.

So why did he ask her out again?

Perhaps she asked him and he was too polite to say no, or perhaps because she was rebounding from an unhappy marriage that had ended about the same time Ranger sobered up. That alone would've snagged his sympathy up front. Marlene seemed to be looking for someone to fix everything. And Ranger was a mechanic, after all.

AA guidelines recommended waiting at least a year before a recovering alcoholic became emotionally involved with anyone. It was distracting, and it could be a source of stress at a time when climbing the Twelve Steps provided all the stress that was necessary, and then some. I learned this from Ranger's AA sponsor, a polite, well-mannered and soft-spoken older gent I knew only as Philip. He sought me out, as Ranger's friend, hoping I might talk some sense into him.

No luck. Ranger merely scoffed. What was the harm in a little romance, particularly one's first sober attempt at it? Not to mention all the pussy he could eat....

"One thing about Ranger—you can count on him to speak his mind," Philip said.

I agreed. "And he never forgets to add salt."

"Yes. But you always know where you stand with him."

And exactly where Ranger stood himself. I couldn't wait to ask him why he'd discussed cunnilingus with his sponsor.

"Cunny-what?" he said when I called.

I explained.

"He was the one brought it up. Said I shouldn't date."

"Is that the only reason you're seeing Marlene? Because AA says you shouldn't?" I barely stifled a laugh.

Injured, he said, "I like eating pussy. Does that make me a bad person?"

"I like sucking cock. Does that make *me* a bad person?"

"To each his own, Neil." His smug tone infuriated me. "All I gotta say is I done without it since the divorce. Now I can get it whenever I want. What's wrong with that?"

"The fact that you'd much prefer bedding down with a man?" I offered. "Even if you're too much of a coward to admit it now? I hope she's returning the favor, since I know first-hand how much you enjoy a good cock-sucking. Getting *and* giving."

"That wasn't me. That was the beer."

"Your beer certainly gave great head."

"Fuck you, Neil."

"Happy to oblige. You still have a key to my apartment. Stop by any time, Ranger."

He hung up.

It was some time before I actually met Marlene again. I hadn't seen her since the one time she'd served us at the Blue Plate months before, and I hadn't bothered to notice much about her at that time. Ranger was very particular about introducing us outside of the restaurant, a rare instance of his being concerned about possible consequences. Marlene and I were both cautious when we finally connected face-to-face on a sunny morning at his place. I wanted to be polite, but I couldn't get past my own jealousy. She seemed equally suspicious of me.

For the first time, I really looked at her. She stood about six inches shorter than Ranger, slender and pretty, though she wore perhaps a bit more blush and lipstick than necessary. She didn't need such a mask. Ranger had told me she was thirty-five, but she looked younger next to his shaggy, skinny carcass. She had dressed up for our meeting, too, which surprised me. Perhaps she wanted me to like her, though (I admit) I was predisposed toward the opposite. Or maybe she just wanted to make sure there was a clear difference between the waitress and the woman.

"You want to go for a walk?" she said. "Just us?"

I admit it disarmed me right away. Ranger didn't like the idea, but Marlene shushed him, and off we went down the gravel driveway, leaving him to worry on the porch.

"It's nice to meet you again. I mean, officially. Away from work. Ranger talks about you all the time."

I wondered what he might be saying about me and, in particular, about us. I suspect his recitation was very selective.

"He says he could never have sobered up if it wasn't for your help. That was really nice of you."

So, at least he'd told her about that part of his life. "What are friends for?"

"I know. Right? Anyway, I want to thank you for everything you did for him. It was very helpful. We appreciate it." I felt as if I was being given the pink slip, as if she would be taking over from now on and my services would no longer be required.

"He's not really a project. I can't really hand over the reins to you to pick up where I left off."

She laughed. "Don't be silly. I don't think of you like that."

Then how did she think of me? *What* did she think of me? And, even more to the point, how and what did she think of our Ranger?

She outlined her agenda to improve him, and her aims would have given the Twelve Steps of Alcoholics Anonymous money for their run. Her goals were wholesome enough but extremely ambitious. She wanted him to quit smoking and swearing. To attend church with her. Pay a little more attention to the housekeeping and a lot more attention to his personal grooming. Regular haircuts, polished boots, and pressed sport shirts instead of faded T-shirts and dirty jeans. I'm sure she left out a few when she ticked the items off for me.

What she wanted was well-meaning, and hard to argue with if you wanted a long life and heaven afterward, but she was working against four decades of habit. I wondered if she'd reached consensus with Ranger before drawing up the blueprint. Since there was very little of him that would be left untouched once the renovation got underway, I wondered what parts of him attracted her in the first place. Or maybe he led the charge, and she'd allowed herself to be swept away.

He could be charming. I'd seen it.

"It's for his own good," she said. "Am I being too hard on him? Be honest."

I was at a loss. Where to begin? She'd never met the drinking Ranger. The after-dark Ranger. How could I make her understand that sobriety for him wasn't a sure thing yet, that it might never be, that he needed whatever consolation he could get right now, be it cigarettes and swearing or hell and dirt? That when we're forced to give up one vice, we must find solace in another to fill the gap?

"You need to let him know that you love him for who he is, not what you can make him into." I winced at the greeting card sentimentality of my statement, but it was the most polite way I could put it.

"Oh, he knows that," she said, dismissing my concern. I couldn't think of another thing to say, and I was feeling a little guilty myself. There were some things I would change about Ranger too, given the chance, and I had certainly tried to reinvent at least part of him.

As we walked back up the driveway, I could see Ranger anxiously pacing on the porch. Marlene liked the house all right, she said, but it was crying—just crying, mind you!—for a woman's touch. I'm sure her mothering instincts were aroused by the card table and folding chairs in the kitchen, the TV dinners in the freezer, the dearth of matching towels and any kind of window treatments. She had a few things of her own that she would contribute to spruce up the interior. As for the outside, wouldn't the yard look so great with a luxurious green lawn where currently crabgrass and dandelions thrived, and a bed of pansies (fitting or ironic? I couldn't decide) around the mailbox, and maybe a wishing well over there, and a little goldfish pond, maybe, and for the porch, a cement goose with some perfectly darling outfits?

Ranger was visibly relieved when we climbed the porch stairs again. Perhaps he thought we would kill each other. Or that I would tell on him. Which would he consider the greater catastrophe?

She sent him to the kitchen to fetch a glass of iced tea for her: "You know how I like it."

Dutifully, he scurried inside. I could hear the radio blasting from the living room, tuned to his favorite station. Marlene covered her ears. "What an awful racket!"

I gathered that country music was also on the endangered species list. Poor Ranger. He liked his honkytonk blues as much as he liked his cigarettes and, until recently, beer.

Marlene moved in with him almost immediately. She must have been hoarding a fully-furnished house in her hope chest, because she brought it all with her. I was appalled when I visited for the first time after the great unboxing. I was relieved that Ranger didn't ask me to assist. Moving her things into his house and unpacking would have required a degree of effort that I could never have mustered.

She wasn't home when I stopped by, but her presence overwhelmed the place. Furniture was crammed in until the rooms were weary and out of breath—and what to make of the frilly lace curtains, knick-knack shelves filled with creatures made from seashells and pinecones, little baskets of artificial flowers, wall plaques of big-eyed children, a kitchen motif of Bible verses? Ranger sat in the middle of it, sullen, looking lost at a kitchen table far too large for the room. If I were decorating the place, it would at least look like a man's house, not some nightmarish queer-kitsch stereotype, and I told him so.

"I know," he said, grim.

"This isn't you."

"I *know*." Perhaps he thought it didn't matter.

"Don't lose yourself."

"I don't know what the hell you're talking about."

I think he did. He kept drinking more coffee, more coffee. I left. He didn't see me out.

Marlene wasted no time in putting the Ranger Melusky Improvement Plan into action, and there were immediate results on the surface, anyway. Due to her insistence, he got a haircut regularly and let her choose his clothes. He started going to Sunday services with her—this from a man who used to wisecrack that he broke nine of the Ten Commandments regularly and was saving only murder for later. He attempted to quit smoking. Perhaps most tellingly, he made a genuine effort to delete the offensive words from his vocabulary when she was around.

Without profanity, Ranger seemed almost inarticulate. He used to wield vulgarity like a fencer; I never knew the word "fuck" had so many nuances until I heard him struggle to express himself without it, as if he'd been disarmed. He reminded me of a child warned to be on his best behavior or no candy.

Ranger, of course, never mentioned our past, as Marlene was always there to chaperone, smiling as if nothing could be wrong. I couldn't be sure if Ranger simply wanted to please her, or if he only wanted to convince himself that our own sexual exploits—not our friendship, for I never doubted that—had been little more than a side effect of the alcohol. They emphasized their coupledom whenever I came around, kissing and giggling and whispering to each other, but it struck me as humorless; it had quotation marks around it. Marlene held tight to Ranger's arm as if he might escape if she weren't careful. She may have thought she had good reason to be cautious. Perhaps she had already recognized that there was a certain ambivalence about him, that he might be hungry for something she couldn't whip up from her Betty Crocker cookbook.

How could she even guess?

I asked her if she attended AA meetings with Ranger to support him, but she refused to go. She couldn't understand why he still needed them or why he ever did in the first place.

"What's so hard about quitting drinking? Just stop." I asked if she was a drinker herself, and she said she'd never tasted liquor in her life. She was also concerned how it would look if she attended the meetings. "People might think I'm the one with the problem. No-siree-bob. He picked up that bad habit all by himself, and he can just go to those darn meetings by himself, too."

I wondered if he only took up with Marlene because he needed company at night. And—sober—he couldn't convince himself that mine would do. But in spite of his new love interest, Ranger seemed reluctant to let go of me entirely, though I wasn't sure how to take his attention. Did he truly think we could be any sort of pals now, given our history? Or was he merely sure of his hold on me and determined to exploit it?

What did it say about me that I let him?

Being near him was difficult; I had to wrestle with a constant urge to reach out and make contact with him. I stopped even trying to like Marlene; everything about her grated against me. I resented even her virtues—she was, for example, an excellent cook and an immaculate housekeeper. Being merely polite took all my exertion, so I avoided or ignored her as much as possible—which meant I rarely went to his house.

With Ranger reinvented to her satisfaction (at least on the outside), she focused her energy on the house. She insisted that Ranger repaint the interior, a different color in every room. He managed that little project on his own; when he called to tell me about it, he complained at the hours involved as well as the backbreaking nature of it. And speaking of backbreaking, he said, Marlene had already outlined her next project: a full landscaping of the yard. Her detailed sketches included flower beds with decorative edging and chipped bark, annuals along the path to the front porch, a tractor-tire planter for the driveway, flowering vines climbing the mailbox, and half an acre of vegetable garden in the backyard. I'm sure Ranger would spend a month's wages at the garden center.

"This damn project will kill every weekend for the next three months if I got to do it all myself."

Was he requesting for my help? I played stupid until he finally asked.

I wasn't in the mood to assist. "What's in it for me? Something tells me Marlene wouldn't let you come over to my place to help me with a project of *any* kind."

"It ain't up to her."

"You sure about that?"

"Fuck you."

It wasn't an invitation, but I pretended it was. "Anytime you want. I miss all the fun we used to have at night, now that Marlene has taken my place. I hope your cock is getting the attention it deserves." He was silent. Maybe he felt a bit nostalgic himself.

Whatever.

"Okay, Ranger. I'll ask for one Saturday off so I can help you plant your garden, but if Marlene is there to supervise every move we make, I won't stick around for long."

"She won't. I promise."

Ranger may have promised, but Marlene didn't. From the moment I arrived, she took up her overseer's whip. When I suggested that she give us a hand instead of merely directing the labor, she offered a sticky-sweet smile, and I could hear the nauseating dimple in her voice. "You big, strong men can handle the heavy work without me."

Coyness didn't suit her.

Late in the afternoon, she moved to the porch, out of the sun, sipping iced tea and sewing something or other. Ranger lost himself in the work, focusing on the digging and edging. For all the conversation we exchanged, I might as well have stayed home. At the end of the day, I felt bitter, angry, and well-used. I returned to the country club on Sunday and for the weekends following, leaving the rest of the yard for Ranger to landscape by himself (under Marlene's watchful eye, no doubt).

I would receive but one more invitation into their home. It, too, involved a chore that Ranger could not do by himself, and perhaps no one else would come when he called. It seems that Marlene had picked up an entertainment center—assembly required—at the local Home Depot. The directions with the kit suggested that two people build it for safety and convenience. Marlene insisted that Ranger get a friend to help. He called me, perhaps as revenge against Marlene's insistence—or was it possible that he just wanted to see me?

I had a bit of experience with such furniture, having built several similar pieces for my own apartment, a stereo cabinet and a kitchen hutch. At any rate, I offered to assist only if he would schedule the job at my convenience—any Monday, my only regular day off. He actually agreed to take time off from work himself to accommodate me.

The following Monday found me knocking on their door. Marlene let me in. Ranger was already in the living room, furniture cleared out of the way, wood pieces and hundreds of parts spread out on the floor. I doubted that the finished product would look as good as the photo on the box, which showed an elegant, polished piece of furniture in a spacious living room, a happy family sitting enraptured in front of a television shown off to its best advantage by the cabinetry.

"You ever built furniture from a kit?" I said.

Marlene snickered. "Tell him, Ranger."

He glared. "You tell him, if you're so goddamned anxious to." He muttered something else under his breath as she scolded him for bad language.

I learned that this was the second entertainment center they'd purchased. The first lay in a pile of broken pieces behind the house. Ranger had attempted to put it together himself, supremely confident in his skills as a mechanic and his male intuition about construction. The composite wood, never very sturdy in these kits, didn't hold up to the stress of his refusal to consult the directions and his mounting anger.

Marlene shared the story in detail and with relish. With effort, I didn't laugh, though she did.

"Well, we won't let that happen again," I said. "It's really not so hard once you decipher the instructions."

Like most things, I guess.

Assembling the unit was more time-consuming than difficult. Ranger and I inventoried the parts and then worked side-by-side, passing the lone specialty Allen wrench (included) back and forth. He grew warm enough from our exertion that he removed his T-shirt, after giving me a hard look that I couldn't decipher. Was he warning me not to make any comments? Daring me not to get aroused, as he knew the sight of his furry belly always made my trousers itch? Or was he asking for just that, as a taunt?

It took us nearly three hours to get through all the steps on the instruction sheet, but we finally tipped the unit upright and muscled it into place against the wall. It fit with an inch to spare, and it would merely make the overstuffed room look even smaller and more cramped. Ranger was relieved that it was done.

"All we need is a decent TV," he said. They'd been using the same ancient, fat portable set that he'd found beside the road months earlier, and the new fixture wasn't deep enough to accommodate it.

"We've already picked out our new one," Marlene said. "We're going to get it tomorrow. Wait 'til you see it—a sixty-inch flat screen and a sharp picture like you wouldn't believe. And the store offers buy-now-pay-later, so we don't have to wait."

"What a great way to plan for the future," I said, doing my best not to sound as sarcastic as I intended.

"You're very handy with tools," Ranger said.

"It's nothing." And I thoughtlessly added, "It's all in the wrist, if you know what I mean," as I mimed jerking off. He laughed. But he stopped when I said, "I've had lots of practice, these last couple of months."

I don't know if Marlene followed the bent of the conversation. She knew she didn't like it.

"That's enough of that dirty talk. There's a lady present."

Ranger, perhaps emboldened, said, "Where?"

Marlene was livid. She glared at me, perhaps searching for something in my face. Clues? She wouldn't find any in the insouciance I wore at times like these, a kind of willful, placid ignorance. She stomped out of the room; Ranger muttered "fucking hell" under his breath and followed. I grabbed my jacket and headed out, but I stopped by the door when I heard them arguing, loud, from the upstairs bedroom.

"He's a... *homosexual*!" she said, as if the word itself tainted her mouth. Had he told her, or had she figured it out all by herself?

"He's my friend."

"That's beside the point," she insisted, even louder. "Don't try to tell me you don't notice it. And you parading around in front of him with your shirt off! I don't like the way he looks at you."

"He don't mean any harm."

"How do you know? Unless you're like that too."

"The hell I am!" What a surprise.

Marlene persisted. "What do you want to be around someone like that for? I certainly don't."

"I told you. He's a friend of mine. I owe him a lot."

Why was I surprised to hear him stand up for me?

"But," and she pronounced each word distinctly, irritably, as if she were addressing a foreigner or a stupid child, "he is a *homosexual*!"

I slammed the door on my way out, hard enough that the house shook.

When I stopped by a week later to admire the new TV, Ranger met me on the porch and did not let me inside.

"Marlene don't want you to visit anymore."

"What? Why not?"

"She don't approve of your lifestyle."

I'd never heard Ranger use such a word; I would have been as surprised to hear him use some French idiom. I was incredulous. Seething. "My *lifestyle?*" What the hell does *that* mean?"

He was embarrassed. "You know. That gay shit."

"I can't think of any gay 'shit' I've done that you haven't done too, unless you've conveniently forgotten to mention that to Marlene."

"Neil, *shut up,* for fuck's sake! She's right inside!"

I lowered the volume on my voice but couldn't ratchet down the anger. "And what did you say when she told you I couldn't visit anymore?"

He hung his head.

"Thanks a lot. What happened to your balls, Ranger? You used to have some in your pants—big ones that hung nice and low down here, under this dick you liked to shove down my throat." I groped his crotch and squeezed hard enough that he winced.

"Jesus *fuck!* Let go of me, goddamn it. That hurts."

I let go. "Oh, right," I whispered. "I forgot. You don't make it with guys anymore. I'll bet Marlene just loves having a man around who likes to eat pussy as much as you love being around a woman who likes to suck your cock."

He glared. Having spent a bit of time with Marlene, I suspected that Ranger's tongue never got anywhere near that part of her anatomy, even if he actually wanted to put his mouth in the vicinity (which I also doubted).

"And I'll bet she just loves returning the favor." I kept my voice low.

I would have bet my car that Marlene didn't permit that part of Ranger anywhere near her mouth, either. In this or any parallel universe, I could not imagine oral sex being on their list of activities mutually enjoyed. That didn't leave much in the way of sexual activity that the two of them were both likely to appreciate.

"Does she let you fuck her up the ass too? Maybe I'll just ask her myself." I raised my voice. "Marlene!"

I heard her footsteps.

"What are you doing here?" She kept the screen door shut between us.

"Hello to you, too. You invited me to come see your new TV. Don't you remember?"

Maybe Ranger simply wanted to avoid a confrontation. He desperately wanted to change the subject, at least, and he knew me well enough to recognize that I was capable of making good my threat to bring up the topic of oral (or anal) sex. In the seconds that followed, I imagined that he reviewed the scenario and didn't care for any of the possible consequences.

A desperate man takes desperate measures. "I got a joke for ya!"

I waited, but not for this: "So, this fag walks into a bar, right? Which is really kind of stupid, because don't ya think he woulda seen it first?"

Given her distaste for anything vulgar, Marlene startled me by laughing, loud, as if she'd never heard anything funnier. When Ranger unexpectedly joined in (relieved, perhaps, that he'd averted disaster), I blazed.

"Okay, smart guy. Here's one just for you." For once, I found a proper audience for one of my grandfather's smutty jokes, and I retrieved the perfect one for the moment. "What's the difference between your dick and your paycheck?"

He and Marlene quit laughing.

"Give up? You don't have to beg your wife to blow your paycheck."

One of Granddad's finest. Marlene stood there with her mouth open, and so did Ranger. I suspect the joke may have hit a little closer to home than either would ever admit, and neither said anything as I walked off the porch. I drove away, convinced I would never see Ranger (or his dick) again.

But I could not convince myself that I didn't want to, and it hurt.

Since I was no longer welcome in their home, I saw less and less of him and none of her into the late fall and past Thanksgiving. His phone call on December 25th caught me by surprise, but I remember exactly what he said and how he said it: "Guess what?" like a child with a secret. I couldn't imagine, so he helped out: "Marlene and I got married today."

Well. Merry Christmas, asshole, I said to myself. And hung up on him. And I wrapped up a case of his favorite beer as a wedding gift because it was the meanest thing I could think of and left it on their doorstep for him to find when they returned from the honeymoon (which, I discovered, amounted to three days at the Holiday Inn in Indianapolis). On the "thinking of you on your wedding day" on the card, I crossed out the "th" in the sentiment and wrote in "dr." Which had been true enough; after his phone call, I'd gotten thoroughly soused for the first time in my life. I was hung over for two days.

Maybe I wanted to see how it felt, just once, to walk in Ranger's shoes. It certainly was instructive.

If you are inclined to bend, it's a talent to act straight for a straight world. It isn't easy; you become ever-vigilant and stay that way. The laws of motion may be strict on rest as well as progress, but there is no respite, no cure for self-consciousness. Tending bar seems safe enough; mixing Manhattans and martinis can be an art if you let it, and it's kind of a public service, in a way. No one brings anything small into a bar—didn't I hear that in a movie once? Everyone confides in the bartender. But when it's his turn to need solace, where does he find it? In the eyes of someone like Ranger, a mustanger who hasn't ever been self-conscious, even when driving around naked except for cowboy boots, singing loud along with the radio?

He must have felt speechless and handcuffed, confined and repressed not only by Marlene but also by sobriety. Temperance is such an odd word for a movement dedicated to wiping out alcohol. It better suits the process for testing steel in fire. Not for sobriety. But if Ranger could quit beer *and* me, the least I could do was return the favor and quit him, or at least make the effort. I had to let go or drown. Why I couldn't continue to see him is the same reason an alcoholic can't have just one drink: the memory kills.

I didn't expect to hear from him and wasn't disappointed. Only in my fantasy could he have pined for me late at night, missing the intimacy we once shared. The scars you acquire in your life are a map of how you got where you are and all the places you stopped along the way. They're souvenirs. Postcards. Having a fine time. Wish you were here.

With Ranger out of the picture, I had plenty of time on my hands. His absence left a gaping hole in my life, and I couldn't remember what filled my nights before he came. I split my free time between my parents and my grandfather, and I became convinced that my dad and his dad needed to make peace with each other. My grandmother wasn't interested; I could not persuade her to meet her ex-husband under any circumstances, and she finally asked me to stop trying. She and I were on good terms, as she was with my parents, and she saw no reason to meet Granddad again, a half-century after their divorce. The Roman Catholic in her was still bitter, and she would not be reconciled. Reluctantly, I agreed.

My father, on the other hand, could not talk me out of it. I was convinced that he needed to settle the account; if something happened to his father without some attempt having been made at compromise, Dad would regret it. And, perhaps selfishly, so would I. How could I hope to be successful in a relationship (with, say, someone the approximate size, age, and appearance of Ranger) if my family remained broken? At first, my father refused to accommodate me, even when I corralled my mother into applying some gentle pressure.

"I appreciate what you're trying to do. Really," my dad said. "I'm glad you have such a good relationship with your grandfather, if that's what you want. You're a grown man, and you're welcome to pick your own friends. But he and I will never be pals, and that's that."

"Dad, you don't need to be friends. It would be nice, but it's not necessary. But you do need to be father and son."

"We are. Accidents of disorder have seen to that."

"You don't even know him! And you *could*. It's not too late. I can't imagine what my life would be right now if you hadn't been there for me when I was growing up. I can understand that you have some resentment toward your dad because you think he abandoned you. If only Grandma hadn't been so—"

"I won't have you say a single word against your grandmother! She did what she believed was right, and your grandfather did everything he could to make our lives impossible." He took a breath and calmed himself down. "That's all water over the dam. It was a long time ago."

"He's eighty-three years old, for God's sake! He could drop dead at any time. What if something happened to him? You'll never be able to shake that guilt."

Perhaps weary of my argument (or maybe I caught him at a weak moment), Dad finally agreed to meet with his father. I suggested a restaurant in town, neutral territory, so that neither would feel he were at a disadvantage. A meal would give us something to do should conversation prove difficult. My mother, thankfully, approved of the plan—she had always liked her father-in-law—and she took my side, doing her best to encourage and convince Dad that he was doing the right thing, and what a magnanimous man he was to take the high road, to put his grievances aside. Granddad, of course, was thrilled.

We set a date and time, and as the day approached, my anxiety increased accordingly. My state of mind alternated between absurd optimism (they'd become best friends) and the blackest pessimism (a combination of patricide and filicide). On that fateful Tuesday, I picked up my dad first, who claimed the front seat next to me, and then my grandfather. He attempted some lighthearted conversation, and I tried to assist, but my father refused to participate. We drove the rest of the way to the restaurant in silence, the longest fifteen minutes I've ever spent in a car.

The restaurant I chose, family-owned, had been in business for decades. My parents and I had eaten there often when I was growing up, and my grandparents might very well have eaten there when they were still married. The fare covered a broad range, well prepared with a minimum of fuss and no gourmet pretension. I announced that lunch would be my treat. Our waitress was indifferent, young, her neat skirt and apron offset somewhat by several scary tattoos and metal hoops and such that pierced her head. She handed us menus, sloshed water into our glasses, and recited the day's specials from a note she had in her pocket.

"I'll give you guys a minute," she said and took off.

When she returned to take our orders, my father chose meatloaf and mashed potatoes. I opted for a chicken cutlet and pasta. My grandfather selected Polish sausage with fried potatoes. In advance, I had requested that he not order a cocktail, and I was pleased that he obeyed for a change, asking only for black coffee. So far, so good.

I can't remember what I talked about to fill the time after ordering our meals. My father—still sulking like a schoolboy in detention—chose to answer all my queries in monosyllables. Out of exasperation, my grandfather took the cue from his son and followed suit. By the time our waitress reappeared with our meals, I was weary, exhausted, and talked out. She handed the chicken to my father and the meatloaf to me. We traded.

"I got one right, anyway," she said as she slid my grandfather's plate in front of him. "You guys want anything else?"

We didn't. She disappeared.

I examined Dad's plate; at least he couldn't complain about the portions, a generous slice of meatloaf and a mountain of potatoes, slathered in aromatic gravy. Then I looked over at Granddad's meal.

Uh oh.

I ignored the steaming heap of fried potatoes and zeroed in on the two suggestively large sausages glistening on the plate. In their size, color, and gentle curve, the sausages resembled but one thing. My grandfather's eyes met mine instantly, and I knew we thought along precisely the same lines. His mustache began quivering, and he grinned and then snickered. I bit my lip. My father, who had been busy salting and peppering, looked up, first at me, then at his dad.

"What?" my dad said. "What's wrong?"

"Nothing," I said. "Not a thing. How's the meatloaf?"

He eyed me strangely. "I haven't even taken a bite yet."

He didn't seem to have noticed, or perhaps his train of thought simply didn't run in that direction. I prayed that Granddad would stifle any of the hundred inappropriate remarks that were doubtlessly coursing through his mind as he examined his entrée. To my immense relief, he squirted ketchup on his potatoes, picked up his fork and dug in.

For a few minutes, hunger took over. We attacked our plates with relish; if we were silent, at least it was for a good reason. I began to relax a bit myself. If we exchanged no meaningful discourse, at least we were eating together, and that had to count as progress—didn't it?—or at least a step toward reconciliation.

I believed this fiction until my father set down his knife and fork and cleared his throat.

"Do you have any idea how hard you made things for Mom?" he said to his dad.

Wait…what? Granddad was as startled as I was, since this was the first comment of any consequence that my father had contributed thus far.

"Um, Dad?" He might at least have waited until dessert.

"You were the one who said we needed to talk," he said to me, accusing. "All week long, I've been wondering what the heck I'm supposed to say to him. Did you expect me to apologize?"

Come to think of it, perhaps that is exactly what I expected, for Dad to admit he was sorry for ignoring his father, and for Granddad to apologize to my dad for—what? Divorcing his mother? Being gay? I wasn't sure. Perhaps I hadn't given the matter enough thought, simply hoping. But my grandfather accepted the ball lobbed at him and returned it with a strong backhand.

"I provided very well for your mother, and for you too. She received a check every single month until you were eighteen, and I seem to recollect that I paid your tuition for college, too. Every nickel."

"Money had nothing to do with it," my dad said.

My grandfather was exasperated. "You can't blame me for disappearing from your life. That was your mother's doing. I tried. God knows I tried. I sent you birthday cards. Letters. All those books. You never responded. Not even a thank-you note. I begged her to let me see you. She refused. She didn't even want me to speak to you."

"That's not true. We talked on the phone sometimes."

"Only when you happened to pick up the call yourself. If your mother answered, she'd tell me you were out, or too busy, or that you just didn't want to talk to me."

"Did you even know that?" I asked my dad.

He shook his head. "That's neither here nor there."

"I think it's both," I said.

"This isn't about you, Neil!" He turned to his father again. "Do you have any idea of the shame that Mom had to live with after you left us?"

"Don't be melodramatic. Your mother didn't have to do anything of the kind. If she felt that way—*lived* that way—it was her choice. Do you think I should have stayed with her? Would that have been fair to her? Or to you?"

My father ignored these practical questions. "You didn't even have the decency to move out of town! And a week later, you let that professor move into the house. My mother's house! *Our* house!"

I was lost, thoroughly, but not in any position to request a study guide or background paper on the situation. My dad and grandfather, however, knew exactly what they were talking about. It was not my place to interrupt, to say, "Wait a minute!" or ask for an explanation so that I could catch up.

"Look, son. We separated because I thought it was best for you and your mother at the time."

"You mean it was best for you."

"All right, maybe it was best for all of us. But I put you first, and your mother."

"What a load of bull!" my father said, contemptuous. "Best for me and Mom? Hah! Can you imagine the indignity of such a thing? And didn't your precious 'boyfriend' run off a couple of years later?"

"You sanctimonious prick." My grandfather blazed right back. "So I was a fool for love. There is nothing else worth being a fool for, besides love."

"Love." My father spat out the word as if it were venom sucked from a snakebite.

Granddad was suddenly gentle. "You should try it sometime."

This was territory we'd never crossed. I sat with my mouth open, unable to contribute a word, as if there were some need for me to speak at all. The dam broken, I found myself in fear of drowning. I sat between them, petrified, but it was instructional nonetheless; I learned, as the whole history of my father's immediate family was laid out for me. Gradually, the pieces came together, like a film of an explosion being shown in reverse slow motion, until the original whole was revealed with all its shards intact. My father reached for his version of the truth, things he had not discussed in my presence before. Slowly—being given, for the first time, the raw materials to do so—I began to rebuild the foundation of his youth, and with the construction came an understanding I'd never believed possible.

What could life have been like for a thirty-year-old woman and her nine-year-old son, suddenly and unexpectedly cut loose from their moorings, a woman who had never even thought about homosexuality, could never have imagined that such an ugly thing could swallow someone she thought she knew and knew she loved, until her husband—

after a full decade of apparently congenial marriage—came to her and explained that he was leaving her for someone else? Not a woman, mind you; she could have fought for her status and position if her adversary were another woman—fought and perhaps won. But a man! How could a woman combat another man, whom history and genetics and society and culture had labeled the stronger in all things?

My grandfather, never one to be physically violent toward another human being, had directed his anger where he could, punching his fist at the living room wall, not once but three times, leaving three holes in the plaster and himself with two broken fingers on his left hand. My father, a boy of nine, could only watch in wide-eyed silence, understanding little of the argument and the violence but recognizing that it would have catastrophic consequences for him, his father describing what he liked doing in bed with other men, his mother promising to forgive, if he'd only stop for a minute and think about what he was doing to them all.

His father saying, "I'm sorry. I can't stop."

His mother saying, "You mean you won't!" with something like hysteria against this evil that had infiltrated and smashed their home and their lives.

And finally, his father saying, "I mean, I don't want to." She raged, cried, yelled, calling him the worst names she could conceive, calling him filthy, a freak, an abomination. She broke one of the good dinner plates over his head before he could move back in self-defense, stunned, and she threw others at him; he dodged, and they shattered against the wall. I'd never known why the china service in Granddad's dining-room cabinet was a complete set otherwise—cups and saucers, bread plates and bowls for eight, serving dishes and platters—minus most of the dinner plates.

My father would spend that night and many nights to come at the home of his own grandparents on his mother's side. Never thereafter would he be permitted to return to his father's house after they left it that night, the longest taxi ride across town. His mother would return every day during the following week while Granddad was away at school, packing my dad's belongings and her own. A month later, they would be living someplace else by themselves, in a strange little house with all new furniture and different pictures on the walls. He would be transferred from public to parochial school and endure the shame of being the only

Catholic boy in the third-grade class of 1977 whose parents were divorced, not to mention the only child whose father was living openly with another man. The priests and nuns shook their heads and clucked their tongues. Everyone knew.

Though my grandfather never wanted to shut off contact with his son, it happened. The things they'd shared—treks to the library for books they would read together, secret trips to Dairy Queen for chocolate-dipped vanilla cones, star-gazing, swimming excursions to the lake (like the one he and I had shared)—ended just as abruptly. My dad never found anyone else to pick up where his father had been forced to leave off; no other adult male role model was permitted.

By the time my father reached his late teens, Granddad quit trying. He continued to send generous support checks every month that were cashed but not otherwise acknowledged. Granddad paid my father's college tuition, even when he chose an expensive school out of state. Why, I wondered, had Dad returned to his hometown after completing his pharmacy degree and hired on at a local drugstore? Simply for his mother's sake? Why hadn't *she* left?

Now, years later, as they traded—I might say hurled—accusations back and forth, I pieced together the whole story. I knew they were not sharing it for my benefit but for their own, perhaps a desperate need for understanding coupled with the compulsion to testify, to make the case for exoneration, to expel the anger and injury built across half a century. However, with each being the other's judge and jury, there was no chance for a fair trial on either side. The couple at the table next to us had given up all pretense of minding its own business and tuned in avidly. We offered, I realized, something juicier than the rarest of steaks.

"I've spent most of my life apologizing for you and for everything you did to us," my father said.

"Listen, son. You're not responsible for me. I've never asked you or anyone to apologize for anything I've done. I'll deliver my own 'sorry' when it's necessary and pay my own debts."

My father had climbed on the highest horse I'd ever seen him ride, and his voice rose accordingly. "Some debts can't be paid. Ever. You marked Mom for life. And me, too."

"Horseshit." Granddad's anger matched my father's. "Challenge makes us strong. Look at the independent woman your mother became. If we had stayed together, she would have been content to remain as she was—a housewife and mother. As for you—you're a grown man. Stand up for yourself. Where's your salt, son?"

"Why did you even get married in the first place?"

"That was my mistake. At least I had the courage to recognize it—to let your mother go."

"Maybe she didn't want you to let her go. Maybe I didn't either."

"And was I supposed to pretend to be straight? All three of us would have been miserable. I wasted a lot of years trying."

"You certainly made up for lost time after kicking us out. All those ugly stories."

"I never went to jail." His attempt at humor was lost on my dad.

"Only because you were lucky. I heard what happened with the chief of police that one time. Probably everybody in town heard about it, how you escaped arrest by—servicing him."

"Rumors. No truth in them," Granddad said, before amending himself: "At least not much."

My father pushed harder. "Those stories made me sick. I did what I could to protect Mom, but she heard them, too. I used to pray that they were lies, but by the time I got to high school, I couldn't pretend any longer that I didn't know what you were up to. It's not easy when your father's a—a—"

"Cocksucker?" my grandfather supplied in the same clarion tone of voice. If my father ever could have convinced himself that my grandfather deserved to be called a son-of-a-bitch or worse, this was one of those times, but my father would not bring himself to say such a thing under any circumstances.

The couple sitting next to us gasped, and my father exploded. "Watch your filthy mouth!"

"Cocksucker! Cocksucker!" My grandfather repeated it like a taunting schoolboy. "Heroic deeds demand heroic words to describe them. 'Cocksucker' is so perfectly descriptive of the task in question. And a most pleasurable task it is, too."

Our little play had attracted the attention of the restaurant manager (quite clearly of the same persuasion as my grandfather and me), who minced over to our table, outrageously outraged. "Excuse me!" He placed his hands on his hips and pursed his lips, every inch the prissy queen. "Excuse me, gentlemen, please, but I must remind you that this is a family restaurant."

"Oh, yeah?" My grandfather eyed him. "We are family. The father," he said, pointing to my father; "son," pointing to me; "and"—indicating himself at last, "the Holy Ghost, before too long, I'm sure. The good Lord may damn us all to hell, but we are family."

The manager didn't seem to understand. "Be that as it may. Keep your conversation polite—and tone it down—or I'll have to ask you to leave the restaurant. There are children present."

"We're terribly sorry," my grandfather said. "It won't happen again, believe me." The manager crossed his arms and glowered at us, a final warning. As he turned away, my grandfather goosed his ample backside, and he let out an involuntary startled hoot. With a fiercely disapproving glare at Granddad (who stared back, all innocence), the manager walked away.

"Damn fruitcake," my grandfather muttered under his breath.

I noticed that he had not even touched his entrée, in all its obscene glory. Perhaps he hadn't had time to eat it before my father had started the argument. Whatever the reason, the sausages had grown cold. Granddad poked them with his fork and seemed lost in thought.

"Something wrong with your supper?" I tried not to sound as alarmed as I felt.

"Not at all. Just saving the best for last." Carefully, he set down his knife and fork.

I froze. He looked at me. I shook my head. No. Please, no. But as my father and I watched—my father suspicious and I terrified—my grandfather picked up one of the sausages. Something awful was imminent, and I could do nothing to stop it. He would go in whichever direction he was headed.

He was, after all, a grown man too.

He leaned his head back, positioned the sausage carefully, and slid it suggestively into his mouth. Whole. All the way. (The capacity of his throat both surprised me and made me envious.) My father nearly choked. To his utter horror, my grandfather serviced the sausage a few times before removing it from his mouth and setting it back on his plate. "Mmm, mmm!" He addressed the sausage: "Did you enjoy that as much as I did?" My father's face had turned the color of cherry cough syrup.

"Do you have a cigarette?" my grandfather asked me.

My father would have willingly sunk into the floor at that moment if such a thing were only possible; he watched, struck dumb. Considering the situation—utterly abysmal—I could only do precisely the wrong thing. My grandfather sat placidly and, for all I knew, pleased with himself for devising his little stunt—and I started howling. The couple at the table next to us had not witnessed my grandfather's beautifully vulgar performance, but my laughter drew immediate attention to our table. The man and woman gawked.

My father kicked me under the table. "That's just about *enough*, Neil!" The waitress, likewise drawn by my distinctive caterwauling, rushed over to the table, concerned.

"Is everything okay, guys?"

I was crying, gasping, from laughing so hard; I could not help myself.

"Fine," my father said, his teeth clenched.

I couldn't manage a word, only a nod. Yes, I was fine, considering that my unrealistic and downright ridiculous dream of reuniting my family had crumbled before my eyes. This would be the final act of our tragedy. But what a scream.

The waitress studied my grandfather's plate. "Something wrong with the sausage? Didn't you like it?"

My grandfather got another gleam in his eye. "I loved it, as a matter of fact." For a second, I thought perhaps he'd explain exactly to what extent he had loved it. The waitress seemed confused, and my grandfather pressed his advantage. "I've rarely had the opportunity to enjoy a meal so—so well-endowed," he said with a straight face.

I lost control again as my grandfather smirked. The poor waitress opened her mouth to say something, but nothing came out. She backed away, probably convinced my grandfather was senile or something. My father looked as if he would kill both of us with his bare hands, but such an act would only draw more attention to our little play.

In the split-second after that, we could have been a still-life painting. Call it, maybe, "The Sins of the Fathers" as we sat, the three of us, in a freeze-frame. By then, we were utterly exhausted. How foolish of me to think that fifty-plus years of pain, anger, and mistrust could be assuaged with a single meal under my blundering but well-meaning guidance. What could cauterize such wounds as these? I knew of nothing, no hot knife to sear the flesh, no salve to cool the sting.

We looked at one another; my grandfather grown weary of his outrageous game, my father weary of his accusation, and me of my pretentious Salvation Army soldiering. We'd reached the climax, the orgasm (if I can call it that), and there was nothing left to do but turn away from each other, embarrassed at the things we'd said at the moment of passionate release, ashamed of dirtying the sheets with the sticky byproduct of something that could have—should have?—been love.

In the tense silence that followed, my dad and I watched as Granddad, penitent, cut the sausage into tiny bites and ate them one at a time. After an eternity, the waitress crept back to clear the table, asking us if we wanted a take-out box for the leftovers. I told her she could put what remained into one and give it to Granddad for his dog.

We did not order dessert.

She brought back the scraps in a tidy bag with the bill. As I stood in line at the cash register, my father and grandfather waited in the lobby, separated from the dining room by swinging glass doors. I watched the two most important men in my life talking, gesturing in the largeness of anger, in quotation marks, the fury clearly resurrected again on both sides. I could hear their muffled voices without making out the words; I saw my grandfather—his mustache working furiously—in final desperation, shutting my father up in mid-rant the best way he could, crushing his mouth against my father's in a stinging Judas kiss, my father shoving him away angrily. I thought for a minute they would come to blows, but an instant later, they embraced each other as if both of their lives depended upon it—each grasping tightly as if to a life preserver. But only for a second; they realized what they'd done and they disengaged, unable to trust themselves.

By the time I pushed open the glass doors and walked into the vestibule, they'd retired to opposite sides, both silent, arms crossed in defense, not quite seeing eye-to-eye, just as they'd stood their whole lives. In the parking lot, I helped my grandfather into the front seat of the car while my father climbed into the back. I dropped him off at home first.

"I'll call you later, Dad. I'm sorry."

He shrugged and sighed. "Whatever. Thanks for lunch." I wonder if he was simply being sarcastic. After he slammed the car door, he stood on the sidewalk for a moment, hands in his pockets, as Granddad rolled down his window. I hoped they might shake hands and apologize, at least. It didn't happen.

"Take care of yourself, son. In spite of yourself—or perhaps I should say in spite of *my*self—I love you. With all my heart, I do, Samuel Langhorne Clemens Graham. I wish—" and the rest of the thought left unsaid.

My father remained silent. I wanted to yell at him. "Say something! Tell your father you love him even if you don't understand him! Give him some hope!" But he only turned and walked into the house, and he didn't look back.

Though none of us knew it, they would not see each other again.

At my grandfather's house, he and I went inside, and he poured himself a shot of whiskey and downed it in one gulp, and then a second. He put the bottle away in the kitchen cupboard and then brewed a pot of coffee. Silently, we watched and listened as it perked, chugging and gurgling like a steam engine on the stove. He poured two cups, and we headed to the living room to drink it, bitter and black.

Casting about for something, anything to talk about, he defaulted to one of his old jokes: "Hey, Neil. What's most useful when it's long and hard?"

I shook my head.

"A college education!"

I did my best to chuckle.

"What's long and hard and full of seamen?"

Again, I shook my head.

"A Navy submarine!"

His heart wasn't in it. We sipped our coffee.

I inquired about the large framed oil painting hanging on the wall above the sofa, a quaint image of a mill by a stream, the kind of sunny and optimistic image that represents nothing that ever actually existed anywhere in America. It had always been there, hanging lower than it should have been and off-center as well, and I'd never thought to ask him why.

"Look behind it."

Carefully, I lifted the frame from its nail on the wall. The canvas hid three holes in the plaster.

I asked why he never had them fixed.

"They remind me to be true to myself," he said.

II

The man with whom my grandfather was sharing his bed on the night he died left the sticky evidence of his satisfaction all over my grandfather's furry chest, in his mustache, and in the sheets. Before this stranger left, he thoughtfully stole my grandfather's wallet, watch, and the inlaid-wood box from his dresser that held his cuff links and tie tacks—nothing of real value except sentimentally, perhaps. My grandfather kept no credit cards and rarely carried much folding money, so the thief probably got only a few dollars for his efforts. In fact, a week later, the wallet was returned to me, its contents intact except for the cash, having been found in a trash bin at the park near the courthouse.

Perhaps my grandfather met his last conquest in that same park. Such things happened rather regularly there, though the town turned a blind eye to these transactions. The stranger may have been a professional for hire, or he may have been just another lonely man. I suspect he was not my grandfather's fifty-year-old ideal, but I hope he was close, or at least handsome and friendly, for my grandfather's sake. I wanted his last experience to have been pleasurable. Certainly, the stranger used my grandfather most thoroughly that night, but I suspect my grandfather returned the favor. He'd been engaged in nothing he hadn't done before, and often.

One of my grandfather's friends—a quiet old fellow named Bill Sarver, a retired professor of economics—grew concerned when my grandfather didn't show up for the daily coffee klatch the next morning. Bill stopped over at the house, discovered the front door ajar, and found my grandfather in his bed. He'd probably been deceased for many hours.

Bill called 9-1-1 first, then the others in their coffee-drinking club, then the parish priest, and finally me. I contacted my parents and my grandmother.

An autopsy (which I requested, given the circumstances) indicated that no foul play had occurred. Granddad had apparently suffered a heart attack, brought on by strenuous activity, sometime around midnight. It was likely to have been very quick. As sorrowful as I was for his passing, I was relieved that he likely didn't suffer, and particularly glad that he left this life while engaged in something he found pleasurable.

I'm sure, however, that his bedmate from that evening will never be quite the same.

My grandfather received no Last Rites. There was no viewing, as dictated by his will, and no casket, as he had chosen cremation. But his priest—who recognized in him some greater good, for all his waywardness—held a dignified mass in his memory. Quite a few of his colleagues from the university attended, and I recognized a number of the professors from my undergraduate days. My parents came, of course; Mom had always been on good terms with him. My father showed up primarily at my mother's insistence, but I was glad she persuaded him. Even my grandmother came, which surprised me most. None of my grandfather's friends even knew who they were. To my surprise, Ranger was there too, sitting in the back, looking very uncomfortable with the whole funeral ritual. I don't know how he even knew about the service.

I sat in the front pew with the family and served as the lector for the mass. The priest gave an honest eulogy, choosing to highlight the best of my grandfather's character—his generosity, his broad knowledge of literature and life, his dedication to teaching, his ongoing search for faith. At the end of the mass, Ranger slipped out before I could get a chance to speak with him.

I could not cry. I surprised myself at how level-headed and clear-eyed I could be when accepting the sympathy of well-meaning friends and my grandfather's colleagues. My mom was not as strong, and she wept as we embraced.

"I know how much you loved him," she said. "I'm so sorry."

"Thanks, Mom. Thanks for coming, and thanks for insisting that Dad come, too. I tried to make him see that Granddad meant well. He did the best he knew how."

"I couldn't agree more."

My father and I had no words to exchange. I think he was a little ashamed that he'd never managed to overcome his anger about the past. A son should be big enough to forgive his father, especially when his father had made every effort to earn such forgiveness. I could feel my dad's sorrow and regret, but I could find nothing to say to him. My grandmother and I shared a quick, dutiful hug. "I'm sorry for your loss," she said, but I knew it was none of her own.

A wake of sorts took place in the church hall afterward, including a luncheon prepared by the women's auxiliary. I was the only family representative present.

Granddad had named me as his executor, and I had the immediate responsibilities of the estate to carry out, providing proof of his death to close bank accounts, settle bills, and cash out a generous life insurance policy that named my father as beneficiary—much to his shock. Apart from a stipend earmarked for a scholarship in Granddad's name that the university agreed to match, I was the sole recipient of the rest.

While my grandfather would not have considered himself a wealthy man, he certainly lived very comfortably. He owned his home and car outright, had no debts of any kind, deposited his pension in the bank, and left a sizeable investment portfolio—enough for me to live comfortably, too. I could quit working for a while and just enjoy myself if I chose. I could travel. I could start a new career in anything, even if it were not particularly lucrative.

Go back to school.

I sat down with my parents and grandmother at home after I'd examined the will.

"I'll be moving into Granddad's house immediately, mostly because of Central."

"What in heaven's name are you talking about?" my grandmother asked.

"Granddad's dog. Central. Named for—"

"Hank Morgan's son in *A Connecticut Yankee in King Arthur's Court*," my father said.

I was startled. "How do you know that?"

"I read the book, Neil. The same books he sent you for Christmas and your birthday when you were young, he sent to me. Every one." I was surprised but enormously pleased to learn that my father and I had this shared literary experience.

"Did you read them all?"

"Of course I did." As if there could have been any doubt.

"Did you enjoy them?"

He nodded; it was all the answer I needed.

"Isn't Central staying with you at your apartment?" Mom said.

"Yes, but it's not his home. He's an old dog—must be about fifteen years old now—and he should be in a familiar place. I love Granddad's house, and I'm looking forward to moving in, but I don't expect to keep all of his things. I'd like to know if there's anything you'd like to have."

"No," said my grandmother, immediately. I think she'd taken everything she wanted when she left, years before. As for the rest, she'd either forgotten or made the conscious choice that she could do without it.

"No," my father echoed.

"Nothing at all? Some kind of memento? Furniture? Photographs? Why don't you come and take a look, just to make sure?"

My father considered. "Well," he said, softly. "I always liked the painting that used to be on the wall in the living room. The old mill by the stream. Is it still there?"

"Yes. It's yours, Dad."

My grandmother seemed displeased, perhaps even insulted that my dad wanted the painting, as if it were some personal affront, or a rejection of the choices she had made so many years before. She said nothing, only set her mouth in a thin, uncompromising line. After she left, my dad admitted that there was one more thing he might want: the rusty, ancient Buick under the grey blanket in the garage. I was surprised. I'd figured on selling it to a scrap metal dealer eventually, not believing it could possibly be worth anything in its present condition.

"It's a pile of junk, Dad. You're welcome to it, but why do you want it?"

"One of these days, I think maybe I'd have a go at restoring it. You don't mind?"

"Of course not." Like his own father, he knew nothing about auto-body work or engine repair and, in fact, wasn't very handy at any kind of household chore, but I saw no reason to point out these shortcomings. If he wanted the car, it was his. "Do you want to leave it in Granddad's garage until you're ready to start the work? It's not in the way."

"If I left it there, I'd never get around to it. You know what they say. Out of sight, out of mind. Maybe we could tow it over here and put it in the backyard. If I have to see it every day, I'm a lot more likely to get inspired to start the project—and I think I can count on your mother's gentle reminders. That's probably the only way I'll ever get started."

"That's fine. Just let me know when you want it delivered, and I'll arrange it."

Later that week, I removed the blanket from the Buick. In spite of the rust, the peeling paint, the dry-rotted seats, flat tires, and mossy engine, the bones and heart of a beautiful car could still be seen, and it held together when the tow truck hauled it out. My mother was none too pleased to see the heap parked in the yard and covered with a blue plastic tarp, but she kept her tongue, at least initially. I also gave Dad the painting of the old mill, and he promptly hung it in their living room, in the spot of honor above the couch. It looked as if it belonged there.

In its place in Granddad's living room, I hung the portrait of the grinning, shirtless Samuel Clemens that had decorated his office at the university for so many years. It had been relegated to the guest bedroom after Granddad retired, but it deserved to be seen and admired. In his memory, I positioned it just off-center to cover three holes in the plaster.

Granddad's will specified that his ashes should be scattered over Mark Twain's furry chest, which gave me something to ponder. After the cremation, I put the ashes in a tin box and used it as a bookend for his first-edition complete works of Twain. Granddad was always a restless soul, and I knew that he wouldn't want to stay in the box. I would see to it that he did not, though I hadn't quite figured out the best way to fulfill his last request.

As for my own relocation, I decided to ask Ranger if he'd be interested in repaying me for all the help I'd given him in the past by assisting in the cleanup and clean-out of my apartment. I called; Marlene's voice greeted me on the answering machine. I left him a message but he never returned the call—no surprise. Mom and Dad helped me out when they could, and we hauled most of my furniture and housewares to the local Saint Vincent store (though I stored the best pieces in Granddad's basement just in case Ranger might need them someday). After a cursory cleaning, I turned in my keys.

I also sold my own old Buick through an online advertisement. As I watched the new owner drive away, I realized that not even a car connected me to Ranger and his life any longer. Granddad's bright red Mazda X-7 offered a sportier ride; it was a decade newer than my car and got significantly better gas mileage—a sensible trade, although practicality offers little consolation to the lonely man.

I was still putting in forty to fifty hours a week at the country club. But if sorting my grandfather's belongings would take months, there was no hurry. Every time I swore to be ruthless about getting rid of things I didn't want or need or that had no value, I'd find myself hedging, bargaining, trying to change my own mind. At least I had little incentive to rush; what else did I have to do with my spare time?

Fortunately, Granddad wasn't much of a hoarder. There was no question I would keep his books and records and the souvenirs he'd collected throughout his life. I packed up his clothing for donation, though I kept most of his shirts, since we wore the same size, his socks, and an elegant wool overcoat. And one of his white linen suits, because it was distinctly his (though I had no plans to wear it), and his pipes in a rack on the mantelpiece—and, next to them, his tobacco blend in the same old tin. Every now and then, I'd lift the lid for a whiff of his fragrant rum-and-maple.

I found four packages of condoms (flavored!) in the drawer of his nightstand by the bed, and a stack of gay pornographic magazines in the closet—some fairly recent ones, in addition to a pile going back forty years. I marveled that he'd kept such things. An archive, perhaps, but likely an aphrodisiac on occasion, if no one else were handy. I hung onto the magazines, too, even if the contents didn't interest me much, but I didn't hide them. Instead, I spread a selection of them out on the coffee table in the living room.

In a flat cardboard box in an old bureau in the attic, I discovered his wedding ring, clipped apart with a pair of wire cutters, probably, and twisted so that he could remove it. I recalled my grandfather's story about punching the wall after his argument with Grandma, when he broke two fingers. There might have been no other expedient way for him to shed the ring and all its significance.

The box contained a batch of old photos that I'd never seen, including several formal portraits from the wedding and a stack of snapshots from a honeymoon on Cape Cod. My grandmother was a startlingly beautiful woman at twenty, and my grandfather already handsome (and majestically mustached) at thirty. I doubt that they had any idea what they were getting into. There were early school pictures of my dad, and the only photos I'd ever seen of him with both parents. I wondered who had taken them, these three posing, smiling for the camera, self-conscious, oblivious of what was to come.

In Granddad's sock drawer, I found a beautifully matted and framed picture of a man who was clearly the Sam of the tattoo—the man leaning against a brick wall, casual and sure of himself in a light-colored suit and tie. The photo suggested some of the beauty and fascination Granddad had described to me; I assume he had taken the snapshot, and I could only imagine how he might have felt when the film had been processed and he held the image in his hand.

I stood the picture on the fireplace mantel beside my favorite portrait of Granddad. I'm not specifically a believer in heaven or any kind of afterlife, but if there is such a thing, it exists for people like my grandfather and his Sam. I hoped fervently that they were somehow together again at last.

I also found an old Pentax camera in its leather case. There was a roll of film still in it with a couple of exposures left. The drug store where my father served as chief pharmacist still offered a photo processing service, so I dropped off the roll, curious as to the contents. When I picked up the prints a week later, I found proof that my grandfather had indeed made a deal with Ranger—who grinned a bit sheepishly in the photos with his shirt off and his jeans around his ankles. Until then, I'd forgotten that Granddad had promised to share the naked pictures. They were good ones, too, in sharp focus and well-lit (as Ranger himself probably was at the time they were taken). My first impulse was to toss the whole packet into the trash, but I retrieved it a moment later.

Perhaps I needed a souvenir as well. It wasn't a tattoo, but it would suffice.

On impulse, I accepted Bill Sarver's invitation to join the coffee club as an honorary member and my grandfather's proxy to complete the quartet. I had no interest in meeting the group every day, but Bill said I was welcome anytime, and I did enjoy their company on occasion. In particular, I appreciated the opportunity to hear from a trio of men who quite possibly knew my grandfather—or at least a side of him—better than I did.

As I became fully acquainted with them, I discovered that they, too, shared some common ground with my grandfather apart from their connection to the university. All three were gay, for one thing, which didn't surprise me in the least. But the fact that my grandfather had bedded all of them at one time or another, unbeknownst to the others, did surprise me a little. (I learned this as each, in turn, privately, swore me to confidence.) Yet each one thought himself special, that my grandfather had chosen only him and asked him to keep the trysts a secret.

Bill was the oldest, in his late eighties but spry and animated, completely bald, short and stout, and still married to the same woman after sixty years, though they had little to say to one another by now. They also had no children and zero in common. Bill claimed he was straight, though his friends scoffed at such a notion. "I'll bet your missus is still a virgin, Bill," my grandfather told him—as related to me by Murray Nicholas—more commonly called Nick—retired from the chemistry department, divorced, and the father of three daughters and two sons who were united only in their unwillingness to recognize their dad's fondness for other men. Thus, he kept quiet about it.

James MacGowran, whom my grandfather called Scotty because of his lineage, was my favorite, tall and furry and the youngest of the trio, about fifteen years junior to my grandfather and a retired mathematics professor, with a neatly-trimmed-and-squared beard, still shaded with black, as if you'd added dark streaks with a charcoal pencil. Scotty was clearly my grandfather's favorite too, I imagined, based on the number of times they'd shared a bed (according to Scotty's estimation). I wondered if it had something to do with the fact that only he and my grandfather were actively out of their respective closets, comfortable with themselves and content in their affinity for like-minded men.

I'm sure my grandfather admired most Scotty's unwillingness ever to marry. He'd been drafted during the Vietnam War. During basic training, he'd discovered—much to his surprise—that he preferred the company of men. In two years of Army service, he found a dozen soldiers, officer and enlisted alike, to share his foxhole at one time or another. He retained a fondness for men in uniform, but he liked my grandfather best.

"Hung like a horse, was your granddad," Scotty told me. (I already knew this, but I got a kick out of hearing him say so.) "Damn. And he made the most of it. Could that man fuck." He shook his head.

"We used to meet nearly every Sunday night without fail. Lately, it's been less frequent, but still once or twice a month. I wanted more, but he said it wouldn't be as special if we did it too often. Hah! I'm sure he was screwing other men Monday through Saturday. He had no business picking up strangers. For years, I badgered him to move in with me, or let me move in with him, but he never was interested." He shook his head again and repeated himself, wistful and sad. "Love of my life. I honestly believe that, but he couldn't see it."

The fact that he had in Scotty at least one regular partner several times a month meant my grandfather was more sexually active than I was at the moment. I also had to admire his prowess; I hoped I would still be able to enjoy the company of a handsome man if I reached my eighties—though who the man might be, I couldn't imagine.

Ranger was so far away and so distant that I felt no compunction to fidelity—he was, after all, spoken for at the moment—so there is no sorrow in my confession that I spent a most pleasant night in my grandfather's old bed with Scotty, who'd disarmed me by confessing that he found me incredibly sexy. I was flattered. Except for Granddad, Scotty said, he wasn't much more than a tourist these days, but I found him to be a kind and considerate partner. Early the next morning, over a leisurely breakfast, I asked if he would come again another time.

"Any night but Sunday," he said.

Granddad's old dog attached himself to me in my grandfather's absence. Central was mystified as to his master's disappearance, and he remained restless. He was, I think, despondent; you only have to look into a dog's eyes to see how deeply he feels. Every evening, just before sleeping, he made a thorough search of the house, nosing around each room, sure that he'd find Granddad but disappointed time after time. Central was fond of me, but he belonged to only one, who would surely be coming back for him any day. But how can you tell a dog something?

Barely two months after my grandfather's death, I awoke at four o'clock in the morning, sudden, as if someone had shaken me violently and ordered me to get up. I could just make out the sound of Central whining, ever so quietly, from his bed in a corner of the kitchen. The sound was so faint that I almost didn't hear him at all. I made my way downstairs and found him stretched out, clearly in some discomfort. When he saw me, he struggled to get up and could not.

"Easy, Central. Good fellow." His tongue caressed my hand. I lifted his head and tried to get him to drink some water. He refused.

"You rest, old man." I sat next to him and stroked his gentle head, talking to him, slow and soothing. I told him everything I could recall about Granddad. I never stopped talking. I think Central just needed company, the hum of a familiar voice, even mine, giving him permission to go. An hour later, he slipped away, peaceful, and joined his master again. I sat on the floor and held him in my arms and wept as if my heart had cracked in two. I hadn't been able to cry at my grandfather's funeral, but now I couldn't stop.

The house seemed even emptier without Central. I knew the only true way to honor his faith and dedication was to adopt another dog, and I resolved to do so—someday soon. I discovered a place in town that offered pet cremations, and I decided it was only fitting. After I picked up Central's ashes, I put them in the same box with Granddad's, on the bookshelf in the living room.

The time had come to make my pilgrimage to Elmira, the New York town where Samuel Langhorne Clemens was buried with his family. One way or another, I'd figure out a way to spread my grandfather's ashes there. It was the only proper solution. I wouldn't be able to ask anyone's permission, but I reasoned that I could be discreet about it, and no one would be the wiser. I confided the plan to my mom (though not to my father). She agreed that Granddad would have loved the whole elaborate scheme, up to and including the scattering of ashes, as nearly as possible, on Mark Twain's furry chest.

I called the country club and quit my job. I'd had enough, and it was time to move on. I could almost hear my grandfather cheering. I determined that my pilgrimage to Elmira would be a turning point, a new direction toward a more meaningful life. My boss at the country club, however, was less sympathetic to such pursuits.

"What the hell am I supposed to do now?" he howled. "The bar opens in two hours, and you're the only one scheduled to work today!"

Bridge-burning is not by name or nature diplomatic. I told him it was no longer my problem. I told him I had someplace I had to go; my quest was urgent and couldn't wait. He asked what the hell I had to do that was so important I couldn't even give him the courtesy of two weeks' notice.

"Bye." I hung up.

I packed light; I wouldn't need much. I threw some clothing and my favorite framed photo of Granddad into a suitcase, grabbed the old Pentax, my backpack library, a road atlas (which seemed more in keeping with Granddad's adventurous life than the GPS application on my phone), and the tin box of ashes. I locked up the house and headed out of town.

I stuck a random CD in the player and turned the music up; it was something Ranger had chosen for me, a collection of country music's biggest recent hits. He had no patience for anything else, and to placate him, I'd made a minimal effort to like it, but I could never conquer my ability (or my misguided sense of superiority) to listen without prejudice, my ears attuned for the clumsy rhyme, the grammatical error, the ludicrous analogy, the clichéd storyline that prompted my ridicule.

Its lowest common denominator was manufactured with him in mind, and millions like him, everyday-average guys who worked for a living, took home a minimal wage, drove pickup trucks, drank a lot, and were often unlucky at love. The genre embodied (embalmed?) a proud redneck sensibility that Ranger could identify with. Even though I derided it endlessly—which he usually countered with a cheerful "go fuck yourself, Neil"—there was something about it that occasionally brought a lump to my throat. The right song could catch me at just the right wrong moment and make me cry.

Why, I wondered, did I continue to listen to the stuff?

My mind wasn't on the road, because I was halfway there before I realized I was heading toward Ranger's place.

What?

I hadn't seen him since the funeral and hadn't even talked to him on the phone in months. I hadn't been to the house since delivering that case of beer as a wedding gift at Christmas. (No thank-you note had been forthcoming.) But once I realized where I was bound, I decided—why not? I was curious to see how the place had changed.

I didn't expect to find anyone home in mid-afternoon on a Tuesday. Both vehicles were gone. Ranger would be fixing Buicks at the dealership, and Marlene probably had a shift at the restaurant. The house, as usual, was unlocked—apparently, she had not been able to break him of that old habit—but no one answered when I hollered inside. The only greeting I received came from Spot, who came running when he heard my voice. He was thrilled, leaping all over me, licking my face, and barking. No creature shows pure pleasure the way a dog does, and Spot could hardly contain himself.

When I opened the car door to leave, he immediately jumped into the front seat, eager, as if he expected to come along with me. I knew he loved car trips, and on a whim, I decided—why not? It was only fitting. If I would testify for my grandfather, then Spot could provide the same proxy for Central.

I grabbed his water dish and leash from the porch; we backtracked into town and made a quick stop at a supermarket for kibble, a box of biscuits, and a rawhide bone. I also stopped by Dad's drugstore to say goodbye and pick up a couple rolls of film, which—surprisingly—the drugstore continued to stock, in limited quantity. And then I and Spot turned the car toward Elmira, New York, some six hundred miles away. I'd never visited the state of New York, and it was high time.

12

He didn't look like a hitchhiker, standing at the edge of the highway, dressed in a rumpled black suit, white shirt and tie, hands in his pockets, looking up and down, bewildered, as if he were trying to figure out where he was, like a dog just dropped from a car. Behind him, off to the side, was a large suitcase, open and empty, its contents scattered along the road and blowing in the wind.

I wasn't sure if the things were his or not; if they'd been mine, I would've been running around frantic, collecting them before the wind spirited them away. But he didn't seem to notice. I drove past, but on impulse, a short way down the road, I made a U-turn and backtracked, U-turned again and pulled up a short distance from him. I leaned over and rolled down the passenger window. He didn't pay any attention until I hollered "Hey, bud!"

He walked over to the car and peered inside. His sandy brown hair was thinning, and he wore the clearest blue eyes, except one of them had been blackened and was nearly swelled shut. It looked recent and ugly. And he hadn't acquainted himself with a razor in a day or two. And, I confess, he struck me as startlingly handsome.

"Need any help?"

"I guess." He glanced up the highway again. "How about a ride? If it's not too much trouble."

"Sure." I reached over and opened the passenger door.

He slid inside and slammed the door shut.

"Is that your stuff out there?"

He looked out the window and nodded.

"Don't you want it?" I said.

"If you're in a hurry, forget it."

"No hurry at all. I've got all day."

He shrugged. "All right, then."

I pulled a little further off the road and parked the car. He sighed deep, paused a second, his fingers gripping the door handle. He seemed utterly exhausted. "Ready."

First, he picked up the suitcase and set it near the car. We headed in opposite directions for the rest of it. I collected two shirts still in their packaging, socks, a windbreaker, a pair of trousers, a bath towel, jockey shorts. One running shoe. I found a gay porn magazine, too, and wondered if it were his or if it had just happened to be tossed on the side of the road by someone else before his suitcase had been dumped near the same spot.

When we met back at the car, he had the other shoe, a shaving kit, and a similar armful of clothing. He looked a bit hangdog when he saw the magazine, but I put him at ease.

"I see we've got similar taste in men."

His outlook brightened considerably. "How did I get so lucky?" He offered a rueful smile as he stuffed the magazine into the suitcase with the rest of his things and shut it.

"I don't think we got everything." I pointed over his shoulder at something blowing in the distance. "What's that? A T-shirt or something?"

He shook his head and lifted the suitcase. "Close enough. I've held you up too long as it is. Let's go." And quickly apologetic: "I mean, if you still want to take me with you."

"Don't be ridiculous. Of course, I do." I took the suitcase from him and put it in the trunk. "That's Spot in the back seat." As always, Spot was pleased to make the acquaintance of a new friend, especially a man who knew how to scratch behind the ears.

There's something highly personal and secret about what we hide in our luggage, and seeing someone's suitcase dumped out feels like an invasion of privacy. I felt as if I knew him almost intimately, and I hoped he could relax. He took off his jacket and threw it into the back seat. His carelessly knotted tie had been yanked down a few inches so he could undo the top shirt button.

I put the car into gear. "Where are you headed?"

"Wherever you're going." He offered a pale grin, friendly but a little rusty. Probably he hadn't used it much lately.

"Elmira, New York, in fact."

"What do you know? I get up that way all the time. It's a nice area."

"This will be my first visit. Actually, my first time in the state of New York."

I had a long trip ahead of me, and if he wanted to stick it out for a while, I didn't mind. I tended to get bored on long car trips anyway. The first couple of hours might be tolerable, but it gets old when all you've got is the unrelenting sameness of broken white lines, mile after mile. Company would help. My cohort looked as if he'd been up all night, judging from his two-day beard and the weary condition of his suit. Underneath the surface, however, lurked a very attractive man.

"I've got to get some sleep. You mind?"

"Make yourself comfortable." And he did, sinking deep into the seat and leaning against the door. He was out within minutes.

I'd never picked anyone up along the highway. I'd passed plenty of willing people—holding cardboard signs with destinations written on them, or just with a thumb in the air—but I'd been indoctrinated by my parents long ago: even the most innocent-looking person could have a gun in his pocket to kill you, steal your money, and hijack your car. Hitchhikers almost *promised* mayhem and murder.

So I wondered, as I headed down the highway, if I'd made a mistake. But I kept glancing over at the sleeping man next to me and doubted it. I'd had enough of the tired comfort of a sad song and all the clichés that went with it. Maybe I needed this; such Samaritanism would give me a reason to feel good, and this man was handsome enough that my grandfather would have heartily approved. I could almost hear Granddad whisper in my ear that I wouldn't be a Graham if I didn't invite the guy to spend at least one night with me.

I'd been watching the billboards and the exits and finally turned off one of them to get some gas. I'd gone several hundred miles and the tank registered empty. I filled up, washed the bugs off the windshield, got myself a cup of coffee, and let Spot run around for a minute. My passenger remained asleep.

Not long after I'd pulled onto the highway again, he woke up, sudden and scared, the way you do when you're not in your own bed and can't immediately recall where you are instead.

"Oh. Right," he said when he remembered. He rubbed his face, yawned and stretched as well as he could in the seat. He'd been soundly asleep for about three hours.

"That was some nap. You feel better?"

"Much." His voice was gentle. "Thanks." We drove in silence for a couple miles, and I thought maybe he'd gone to sleep again when he said, "Jesus. I don't know where my manners have gone. My very proper mother would chastise me thoroughly." He held out his right hand and I shook it. "Rex Baker."

"Neil Graham. Pleased to meet you."

He was, he said, from Bensalem, a town I'd never heard of, in Bucks County, Pennsylvania. I'd certainly heard of Bucks County.

"High-end."

He sighed. "A bit."

I was curious to know how he'd ended up so far from there, unceremoniously dumped along the highway with his suitcase. He didn't say anything about his eye, either, but I figured he'd share the story when he was ready. I also realized I had yet to eat this day and suddenly felt ravenous.

"I could use some breakfast, even if it's afternoon. What about you?"

"I haven't eaten a thing since dinner last night. Breakfast sounds great. And it will be my treat."

I wondered if he could afford it, but I appreciated the gesture. We kept an eye out for any kind of restaurant, and I pulled into the lot outside the next one we came to. There were a couple of trailer trucks in the lot, and my dad had told me you could identify a good place to eat along the highway if there were trucks parked outside. This was one of those pre-fabricated crackerbox buildings, dubbed the Country Kitchen. A large figure of Humpty Dumpty sat on the edge of the roof above the door, smiling and beckoning. Spot snoozed in the back seat of the car; I cracked open the windows and left him a couple of biscuits in case he woke up.

The waitress, large and motherly, aggressively cheerful, showed us to a table—there were half a dozen empty ones in the place—and handed us ice water and menus. She rattled off the lunch specials and eyed us expectantly.

"Can we still get breakfast?" Rex said.

"All day long, hon. I'll give you boys a minute to look at the menu. Coffee?"

We nodded. She returned with two steaming mugs, and we both ordered eggs scrambled with wheat toast, bacon, and hash browns. Minutes later, she brought two steaming platters, and we dug in.

"I was a little out of it when you picked me up this morning," he said between bites. "My recollection may be a bit hazy, so forgive me for asking, but are you—?"

"Am I—a stamp collector? A politician? Left-handed?"

He laughed. In a stage whisper, he said, "Do you...like men?"

"In general, or do you mean in *that* way?" I was enjoying myself.

"*That* way, of course. I thought maybe I'd dreamed it. For the record, I do too."

"Good."

"Two like-minded men, traveling together." He wagged his eyebrows. "Who knows what we might get up to?"

"I'm open to suggestions."

"I have several. Further information available upon request."

"Careful, Rex. I have a distance to drive yet, and it won't do for you to distract me. At least until tonight."

We shook hands across the table. With our pact sealed, we gave our full attention to breakfast. At his urging, I explained why I was headed to Elmira. I told him about my late grandfather, his curious name, his magnificent mustache, his love of literature, his brilliant teaching career, his lust for handsome men (which I shared). About the circumstances of his passing, the family schism, his unresolved relationship with his son. About his faithful dog, Central, and how he'd gotten *his* curious name. About the tin box on the car seat between us and what it contained, and my grandfather's disposition instructions. About my job as a bartender and my doomed romance (or what have you) with a recovering alcoholic.

Rex offered a compassionate ear; as I listened to myself tell the story, it sounded hopelessly absurd, but he understood. I spilled all of it, how

Ranger and I had met, how we'd gotten entangled, the blow-by-blowjob of our early nights together, and my mixed feelings about everything since.

"Ranger has been sober for almost a year now. And it's been almost a year since we last bedded down together. Cocksucking was good enough for him when he had a six-pack or two of beer inside him but not anymore. Since he quit drinking, he's decided he can also do without me—and men in general. And he's gotten himself married again. To a woman. His fifth go-round, as if it will stick if he tries it often enough."

"What a shame. Seems like he'd enjoy being with you all the more, now that he's sober enough to remember how much fun it is."

I agreed. Could what I felt for Ranger be true love? I wondered, but Rex demurred, gentle. "No, it couldn't. There's a difference between love and merely fucking and sucking."

Listening to myself talk about it to a disinterested but empathetic third party seemed to put it into new light for me.

Two hours passed. We had four cups of coffee, provided by our cheerful waitress. When we finally said, "no more!" she brought the check to the table.

"Pay at the register. You boys have a nice day, now!"

"You sure you can cover this?" I asked Rex.

"I insist." He produced a credit card, paid the bill, and held the door for me on the way out of the diner. I thanked him for the meal and, in particular, for the door. He liked that.

Breakfast relaxed both of us; we'd slipped comfortably into that place usually reserved for close friends. I realized I had done all the talking at breakfast, and I apologized. He laughed. I promised him I would keep quiet for the next three hundred miles so he could tell me his life story.

"So, for starters, what's your profession, Rex?"

And he was off.

He called himself a freelance writer, which made him sound significantly more gifted as well as important than he really was, he told me. But he claimed to be a fairly accomplished wordsmith, and he enjoyed the job. He wrote a weekly column on running for an online fitness magazine, his only regular assignment. In fact, he admitted, he didn't even get paid for it, but he told me I could find the publication online if I wanted to search.

"I'll take a look. For some reason, I suspect you're a very good writer."

He seemed kind of sheepish. "I don't know why I feel as if I need to justify myself. I always wanted to be a writer, from the time I was a kid, but the truth is, I haven't had to work for a living in a long time. I guess it embarrasses me a little to say so."

"Why should it? You're lucky."

"Maybe. And you're a bartender. Is that what you always wanted to be?"

"Oh, of course. Isn't that every kid's dream? There's nothing like ambition. If my motto was 'aim low and fail to achieve,' I would be a complete success. My grandfather was terribly disappointed that I never used my degree to get a respectable job."

"What did you study?"

"American literature. Useful, huh?"

"It could be. It all depends on what you want to do with your life. It's probably not necessary for a bartender, but if you want to teach or write or research or all three, it could be essential. Why would you pick tending bar instead?"

I shared an abbreviated version of the story with Rex, and he wondered if we were both in the same boat—wasting our potential. We determined that the subject was too depressing for continued discussion at the moment.

"So why don't you just follow in your grandfather's footsteps? Seems like you could, and it sounds like you should. I can't think of a better way to honor his memory. I can tell he means a lot to you."

"I could never accomplish what he did."

"You don't need to. He's already done that. Start there and take it further, or take it in a different direction."

"These days, to get a decent teaching job, you have to have a master's degree at least. Maybe a doctorate. I don't."

"Get one. Or both. This is too easy, Neil."

"Graduate school isn't cheap nowadays."

"Good-quality stuff never is. Suppose you go to school during the day and bartend at night? Lots of people do both." He grinned. "Sorry. Throw any obstacle at me, and I'll tell you how to get over, under, or around it."

He was right, of course. I knew I could probably get an assistantship to teach while I earned my master's, which would minimize the cost (not that I had much to worry about, thanks to my inheritance); all I would have to do is inquire at the English department of my alma mater. My own academic record and my grandfather's reputation would probably be a sufficient passport. But just because Rex was right didn't mean I was in the mood to agree at the moment.

"Let's talk about something else."

Rex shrugged. "You're the driver."

"Tell me about this column you write."

He laughed. "It's not much. Really. First off, I should tell you that I'm a long-distance runner. Committed, for the past twenty-five years or so. Track star in high school and all that."

In the past decade, he said, he'd been running eight to ten miles almost every day, with over thirty thousand miles logged so far. He'd set up his courses carefully, driving from home and through town, measuring the distance on the odometer of his car: five miles exactly along a dozen different routes for variety. He ran three or four full marathons each year, regularly placing in the top five percent of finishers and occasionally taking first place in his age group, the forties. He trained almost every day, and he preferred running very early in the morning or very late in the evening. He could hide in the dark, he told me. It took his mind off things.

"I have the qualifications to write about running, at least. In my column, I cover all kinds of things. Marathons and other races in the area. Stretching exercises. Diet and nutrition. The challenges faced by the middle-aged runner. The importance of good shoes."

"You've piqued my curiosity. I'll be sure to check out your column online. You might even persuade me to do some running myself."

"You've got the frame. It would be easy for you. Start slow and build."

I nodded. We lapsed into silence that wasn't the least bit uncomfortable.

A while later, he said, "Thanks for picking me up back there, Neil. Not everyone would take a chance with a hitchhiker these days."

I felt responsible for him by then. Nothing matches that feeling of being needed. "The pleasure is mine, Rex. I should thank you for waiting for me."

13

A quarter of an hour later, he said, "I'll bet you're wondering what happened. How I ended up on the side of the road this far from home with a black eye and all my worldly possessions scattered along the roadside."

I couldn't deny my curiosity. I told him I was a good listener if he wanted to share the story, but he shouldn't feel compelled.

He wanted to tell.

"His name is Sparky. He's my—lover, I guess. He hated that term, but I don't know what else to call him. 'Housemate' doesn't tell the whole story, and 'bedmate' seems a little impersonal. I don't know. Last week, I would have said that we shared more of a commitment than you and Ranger do, but now I'm not so sure."

He started at the beginning, so I'd get the whole story. Sparky—born Lyle Francis Rogers—picked up the nickname as a junior officer in the Air Force because of his explosive temper. The name suited him even now, Rex said. He described Sparky: compact, lean, impatient, proud, as fiery as a box of Roman candles. Black hair cropped short, a trim mustache, and sexy as all get-out, he said.

I learned more about Sparky over the next hour as we headed through upstate Pennsylvania. He was Granddad's ideal age, fifty, six years older than Rex. Sparky had retired from the Air Force, a full colonel, with twenty-eight years of service and a full pension, and now he broke and trained horses in Bucks County.

"How about that for a masculine man's job?" And Sparky was an expert, quite in demand.

Sparky's wife (heterosexual marriage having been an occupational hazard for a senior military officer in the old days) had left him several years back; he'd lost track of her, and his teenage son and daughter, too. They didn't cotton too much to his being queer. But even after retirement from the Air Force, Sparky felt unable to come out.

"He's too hard on himself." The unspoken other half of his remark was that Sparky was no doubt hard on Rex, too.

Rex pointed at a blue "Rest Area One Mile" sign as we passed it. "Can we stop there? That coffee wants to escape."

"I'm with you. It's about time for Spot to have a run, anyway."

I pulled into the empty lot a mile down and parked. It was a small rest area and vacant at this hour of the day except for us. Rex rummaged in his suitcase for a towel, and we went inside. At the urinals, standing side by side, we made an elaborate attempt not to look at what each of us held in his hand, but we finally gave up and dissolved into laughter.

"You show me yours..." Rex began.

I finished. "...and I'll show you mine!"

We showed. The initial stirring of arousal was very clear.

"Damn," Rex said. "I'm tempted to invite you into the nearest empty stall."

"You better not, because I'd accept. And we'd never reach Elmira before dark. Besides, I think we'll have more fun in a nice, soft hotel bed."

He nodded. "Okay. I promise to keep my hands to myself until we get there."

"Likewise."

We attended to our business. The evening promised to be provocative, and I was looking forward to it. I believe Rex felt the same.

Afterward, at the sink, Rex shrugged out of his shirt and handed it to me. "Any port in a storm." He pumped green soap from the dispenser into his hands and wet them under the faucet before lathering his face and his belly and under his arms, washing briskly. He rinsed himself off as best he could and rubbed himself dry with the towel, shivering a bit.

"God, that felt good. It'll do, at least until I can get a shower."

I enjoyed the view, and he was fully aware that I did. His six-pack of abdominal muscles (liberally furred with dense brown hair) not only put my scrawny chest to shame but attested to his commitment to fitness, and I told him so. He shrugged. "I've got to work at it pretty damn hard. It doesn't get easier with the onslaught of middle age. I'm forty-four, and there's only so much I can do." He looked down at himself and sighed. He said having a bellyful of hair when it was inexorably thinning on top made him self-conscious. "Kind of like I don't have my priorities straight." He scratched his belly. "Itchy, too. Damn it. But Sparky sure likes to get his hands into it."

"So would I. There's nothing sexier than a furry man. Granddad used to say, 'All the best playgrounds are covered with grass,' and I fully agree." Ranger fit the bill as well, but he was far and away from me, from us, from this place, not just in distance but in ideological miles too. And I had to admit I hadn't been up close to a man as attractive as Rex in a long while.

He grinned. "I'm pleased to meet your specifications. And right now, I'd rather please you than anyone I know." He took my hand and rested it against his chest. He wagged his eyebrows. "Grassy playground, eh? That's a new one."

Reluctantly, I pulled away; we had miles to go before we could... er, not sleep.

"Will you let me take some photographs?" It was an impulsive question. Perhaps I already suspected that Rex would disappear from my life and I'd never see him again. I had no intention of tattooing his name on my arm, as Granddad had done with Sam, but I knew I would want something more than a memory.

"Of me? Why?"

"Why not?"

"Well, I guess, if you really want to. Now?"

I nodded. And retrieved Granddad's camera from the trunk of the car.

"You want me to strip?" He watched, amused, as I loaded a new roll of film and adjusted the shutter speed and aperture.

"Not yet. But leave your shirt off, if you don't mind."

He laughed. And patiently posed while I clicked off a couple dozen shots of him in the sun and shadows around the rest area. The camera liked him. When I finally, reluctantly, put the camera away, he said, "No one has ever taken so many pictures of me at once. I'm flattered."

"You're handsome enough to appear in the pages of GQ. Maybe you'll let me take some more pictures tonight after you take your pants off."

"I'll be happy to oblige, as long as you take off your pants too. But I predict you'll be so distracted that you'll forget all about the Kodak moment."

"No doubt you're right." He slid back into his shirt as we walked back to the car. I let Spot out to run free for a while, since we were the only ones in the parking lot. He raced around at warp speed, circling us at a dizzying rate.

"I envy him," Rex said. "I could really use a good run myself. It's been five days. You get into the habit, and it's hard to break off."

When Spot tired himself out, we climbed back in the car, buckled up, and hit the road again, and Rex continued his tale. Sparky didn't run— he hated such things—but he was one of those men who never had to make time to exercise anyway; it was built into his work with the horses. He stayed hard and fit and didn't need to do anything "artificial. That's what he calls it, anyway," Rex said.

"So, where did you and Sparky meet?"

"We started hooking up while he was still in the service, about fifteen years back. I was twenty-nine when we met and a full-time newspaper reporter. He was a lieutenant colonel. You won't believe this, but we actually met at church. We both sang in the choir." Sparky, Rex said, had a masculine and tuneful baritone voice.

"The first time I showed up for rehearsal, the director put me next to him in the back row because he knew the parts, so I'd have someone to follow while I learned the music. Before we got to the first 'amen,' Sparky had his hand on my crotch. I had a raging hard-on, and so did he. After practice, he led me into the men's room in the back of the church and told me he was going to suck me off whether I wanted him to or not. Damn. I *definitely* wanted. Then I returned the favor, and then it was his turn again, and so on. We were in the restroom stall for over an hour, and I came three times."

Since Sparky was married with children, however, there was no question that their relationship could be anything but clandestine, sporadic—and exclusively on Sparky's terms.

"For months, the only contact we had was in that church, him feeling me up discreetly during the hallelujahs, and swapping blowjobs with me in the men's room after rehearsals on Thursday nights. And endless promises from him that things would change. Would get better."

"And after he retired?"

"He moved the family back to Bucks County, where he'd grown up. I followed him, of course. Got myself a little apartment and a job on the staff of the local newspaper." Sparky joined the choir at the same church where he'd been baptized and received his First Communion. He ordered Rex to do the same, but Rex balked. It had nothing to do with the notion of profaning the church by using it as a place of sexual assignation, Rex told me, and everything to do with the fact that he had nothing else to use for leverage.

"At least it forced Sparky to come and see me at my apartment two or three times a week. Every now and then, when he could count on his wife and kids to be gone for the day, he'd sneak me in through the back door of his house. I think it gave him a little extra kick for us to fuck in the family home."

Rex grew tired of the promises that things would be different soon, but Sparky had no incentive to change, since he had his cake and could eat it too, several times a week. He continued stuffing his face happily until he took one chance too many. "His wife came home unexpectedly from her bridge club. Caught us bent over the kitchen table with his cock up my ass." Rex chuckled. "That was awkward for him, but I confess I enjoyed watching him squirm."

The wife left that same night with the son and daughter. One expensive divorce later, Rex moved into Sparky's home, quietly, but even with the inconvenience of the wife out of the way, the relationship took place exclusively behind closed doors. Sparky insisted that Rex quit his job at the paper so that he could concentrate on Sparky.

Rex acquiesced. "He can be a little domineering."

"Are there compensations?"

"The sex is mind-blowing."

"I've learned the hard way. That's not quite enough."

Rex nodded. "You're right. Sparky still calls me his housemate when anyone asks. He won't even let me put my arm around him in public, and I have to keep reminding myself not to say or do anything that would give away our secret. It's hard."

"I'm sorry. You deserve a better man. Love is something to shout about, not to keep in a kennel."

"Mmm hmm." He was silent for a long moment. "Listen to me go on. And I still haven't told you why I was standing at the side of the road with a black eye." He sighed. "Sparky's planning to get married again."

"And you will not be the groom, I gather."

"You're right about that. There's another woman."

Startling news indeed, a page from Ranger's own playbook.

"*What*? Why?"

"He's got a lot in common with your Ranger, except Sparky isn't much of a drinker." Sparky's intended bride was a woman he'd met while working at a local stable. They did have horses in common, Rex admitted, but still—she was young enough to be his daughter. She'd thrown herself at him, and who could blame her? He was handsome, well-off, apparently available, and her parents disapproved. But she'd gotten Sparky to think about respectability again. And she would make the perfect trophy wife for a retired colonel.

"I guess my presence complicated matters somewhat. Sparky said I'd have to leave, and I said where am I supposed to go? I asked him why *we* couldn't just get married. It's been legal for years now, so why not? We had a big fight. He said he didn't need me, and I said, oh, yeah? Who else would be stupid enough to put up with you?"

"Is that when he socked you in the eye?"

I could tell Rex was embarrassed; I'd guessed some time ago where the black eye had come from, and I'd wondered if Rex would manufacture some sort of story, like bumping into a door, to explain it. He shook his head.

"But he did it. Didn't he?"

Unexpectedly, Rex started to sob. I steered the car to the side of the road and stopped and pulled him into my arms. "Shh, Rex. It's all right. Shh."

He quieted down after a couple of minutes and, haltingly, finished his story.

"I asked Sparky to introduce me to her. I told him he owed me a chance to defend myself, or at least throw my hat in the ring to compete for his attention. But he refused, so of course I saw to it that she and I met by accident."

Rex had followed them into an upscale restaurant and boldly sat down at their table. Sparky was seething, but he'd been forced to introduce Rex to the young woman—as an acquaintance, per his custom. "Really? That's the best you can do, after we've been sucking each other's cocks for the last fifteen years?"

"Congratulations. Well done."

"Maybe. In retrospect, it was not the most civilized thing I might have said." In the scene that followed, he and Sparky had exchanged more angry words. One thing led to another, and Sparky had thrown a punch that landed just below Rex's left eye. So that was it.

"I hope you hit back."

He shook his head. "It happened so quickly that I didn't even think of it. Besides, the stakes would have to be pretty high for me to resort to violence."

"If you're being dumped for another woman, I'd say the stakes were pretty high."

"Maybe I'm too civilized, then. There's nothing like a brawl in a restaurant to attract attention to yourself—and it's exactly the kind of attention that Sparky detests. I don't blame him." The management ejected them from the restaurant with a stern warning never to return. (I was reminded of the scene with my dad and granddad in the diner back home....) The young woman disappeared without a word.

"You think she's out of the picture for good?"

Rex shrugged. "I don't know. I think I scared her away, but what's to stop him from going after someone else, just for spite? Once he sets his mind on something, he doesn't stop until he gets it."

"If he doesn't set his mind on you, then you're well rid of him."

Rex was glum. "Am I?"

"What happened next?"

"Back at home, I start throwing stuff in a suitcase. Sparky's yelling at me the whole time. 'Where the fuck do you think you're going, and how the hell do you expect to get there?' he says, and 'If you take the Prius, I swear I'm going to call the cops and have your ass arrested for car theft.' And on and on. So I tell him to shut the hell up. I'm going to walk. And

I do. Right out of the house. Ten o'clock at night. My eye is swollen shut, and it hurts like bloody hell, but I walk."

He chuckled. "He conveniently forgot to ask me to empty my wallet, so I've still got his credit cards. I don't think he'll shut them off, but who knows? He bought us breakfast today, so he hasn't canceled them yet. But even if he does, I'll manage. I did fine before I met him, and it will do me good to rely just on myself again."

The telling of this sad tale seemed to make him stronger.

After leaving the house, Rex had hiked a couple of miles with no particular plan in mind before meeting an accommodating college kid who offered him a lift to Allentown. Rex accepted. He spent the rest of that night at a hotel. And the next morning, he solicited another ride, not really caring about the destination. He'd been dropped off at a rest area where he spent half of the previous night before persuading a trucker heading north and west to take on a passenger. A few miles into the ride, the preliminary introductions and one very wrong assumption out of the way, Rex had gotten a little too familiar with the man.

"So I made a mistake. Can't blame a guy for that. I just wanted to thank him for the ride. I would have put money on him being gay. Good looking, too, but he sure didn't like the come-on, and he definitely wasn't in the market for a blowjob. He came to a screeching halt and ordered me out of the cab, pronto. He threw my suitcase out after me. Before I could grab it out of the road, a car plowed right into it. It broke open and everything scattered, hell to breakfast." The wind hadn't helped.

"I was a little dazed. It happened so unexpectedly. And I was too tired to move, actually. And then you stopped and saved my life."

"I'm glad I could be of service."

"I am, too."

I was more than willing for Rex to travel with me to Elmira and beyond. He could return to Indiana with me, if he had the interest. I asked if he had any idea where he wanted to end up. He thought about it.

"I guess I might as well go visit my folks."

"Where are they?"

"Rochester. That's my hometown. It's not too far from Elmira." He thought about it for a mile or two of silence and then said, "Yes. I didn't have any specific plan when I left Bensalem, but since I'm nearly halfway there, I think I'll head to Rochester and spend some time with Mother and Dad. Haven't been there since last Thanksgiving. They'll be glad to see me. I could catch a bus from Elmira, I think."

"I'll drive you there instead."

"I couldn't ask you to do that."

"You aren't. I'm volunteering. It'll be my pleasure—I can't imagine better company for a road trip."

"Flatterer. I'll take all you've got."

"Do your parents know about you and Sparky?"

"They do. He comes home with me all the time, and my folks just love him. I know they're expecting a wedding invitation any day. I don't blame them, actually. Once Sparky's out of Bucks County, he's a totally different person. I like him a lot more away from Bensalem."

"Then you shouldn't live there."

"It's his home."

"But not yours. You should get some say in the matter."

"Maybe. Right now, I think we just need a little time apart. I thought Sparky would phone me, but it's been two days and not a word. If he doesn't call—"

He left the thought unfinished.

"You'd really go back to him?"

The forlorn look in his eyes told me more than his words could, but he rallied nonetheless. "I don't know why I should! The goddamn son-of-a-bitch makes me feel like a fag joke." I will never forget the way he said it, resignation, weariness, and pain.

"Don't say that, Rex. The only one with the power to make you feel *any* way about yourself is you."

He nodded. "Sage advice, Neil. Do you follow it yourself?"

He had me there. I had to change the subject, and all I could think to ask was if Sparky shared his passion for running.

"Sparky equates running with one of those horses they used to park outside grocery stores, the kind where you put in a quarter and go up and down for two minutes. You don't accomplish anything, but you pay for the privilege."

Rex could be just as stubborn. He rebuffed Sparky's requests to teach him how to ride horseback. Come running with me first, Rex would reply when the subject came up, and they'd argue endlessly about it. What are you running for? Sparky would ask. Where are you trying to get to?

"Have you figured that out yet, Rex?"

"No. But if I keep running, maybe one day I'll get there."

I was a little relieved for the confirmation that romantic heartbreak and its attendant empty ache were not specific to me. It felt liberating to speak with a man close to my own age, a man who could understand the challenges of navigating a gay life.

The combination of exhaustion and a full belly finally caught up to him, and Rex was talked out. I had nothing left to say either, but by then, I knew him better than some people I had called friends for years.

I wasn't aware that the car stereo was still playing until we stopped talking. Since I'd picked up Rex, the music had been little more than background noise. In the absence of conversation, the songs demanded attention, and I couldn't help but listen more intently because I could tell that Rex was doing the same. A redneck anthem poured from the speaker, extolling the fiction that smart, beautiful women secretly lust after beer-drinking, tobacco-chewing hayseeds with pickup trucks. Its predictable, ungrammatical lyrics—delivered via a twang as phony as a spray tan—suggested that the performer himself was little more than a simpleton. It ended, and another followed of similar stripe but for the point-of-view—female this time—proclaiming her allegiance to a beer-drinking, tobacco-chewing hayseed with a pickup, punctuated with the occasional "hell, yeah."

"So, who is this we're listening to?" Rex said.

"I don't remember." I felt more than a little self-conscious. "Some Top Ten country song, I think. It's pretty lame when you listen up close."

"Or even from a distance." He picked up the stack of CDs from the seat and examined them, one after another. "I'm guessing these belong to Ranger."

"How'd you know?"

He read a few of the song titles aloud and snickered. "Come on, Neil. What kind of music do *you* like?"

Ranger had never asked me such a question.

"Jazz. Another gift from Granddad, who taught me to appreciate Billie Holiday. Ella Fitzgerald. Chet Baker. The Dave Brubeck Quartet. Miles Davis. Weather Report. Duke Ellington. Even some of the really old-school stuff like Jelly Roll Morton and Bix Beiderbecke."

"I don't see any Billie Holiday here. Or Duke Ellington or Miles Davis or anything even remotely jazzy. Why are you listening to this crap? Ranger isn't here to pass judgment—and why in hell should you care what he thinks anyway? This is your car. You're the driver."

I had no answer. Perhaps I *was* trying to remake myself in Ranger's image, as if such a thing could make me more attractive to him. He'd probably never even noticed, so what was the point? I ejected the CD from the player, rolled down the car window and tossed it outside, along with the rest of the stack. In the rearview mirror, I could see the plastic cases and the shiny discs bouncing along the highway.

"Good call!" Rex said. "I'm not in favor of littering, but I applaud your decisiveness." He fiddled with the radio tuner until he found a jazz station broadcasting from somewhere close by. "That's more like it. Will that do?"

John Coltrane's "A Love Supreme"? It certainly would—and what a good omen.

"I could use a man like you, Rex. You're good for my morale."

"Glad to help. Anytime." He stifled a yawn.

"You need some more nap?"

He nodded and grinned. "Gotta rest up for tonight."

"Fine. Put me at a disadvantage. But help yourself."

He chuckled. Settled down in the seat and was asleep almost immediately, and I had the pleasure of some good music for company as the miles sped by. I stopped for gas again late in the afternoon, but Rex didn't wake up until we pulled into Elmira early that evening. At his insistence, we checked into a very high-end hotel; I protested, but he waved away my concerns. He slapped Sparky's credit card on the counter and requested a single room with one king-sized bed for three nights—for starters, he said. "We can extend our stay if you want to."

"Fair enough. We'll see how it goes."

While Rex took our suitcases upstairs to our third-floor digs, I took Spot for a run on the hotel grounds. I heard my name being called and looked up to find Rex watching me from the outside balcony of our room, a crooked grin across his face. The nap had refreshed him and he seemed altogether a different man from the one I'd picked up that morning. Except for the black eye, I couldn't even see that edition of Rex. He leaned casually over the railing, splendidly relaxed, shirtless, and in the twilight, he may have been the most beautiful man I'd ever seen. Spot and I bounded inside and up the stairs—I didn't have the patience for the elevator—and I joined Rex on the balcony. For the eyes of the whole world, he took me in his arms and affixed his mouth to mine. We took ourselves inside and hung the "do not disturb" sign on the door.

14

What Rex and I occupied ourselves with that evening, he called making love. It was something I'd never actually done on his terms with Ranger. I'd become so accustomed to his salty terminology and blue-collar approach (with orgasm the primary goal, and as quickly and often as possible) that I'd forgotten there was even supposed to be a component of genuine affection and respect and mutual satisfaction in the complex interaction between two men, the dance that unfolded when there was no hurry, the slow escalation that convinced me the journey was as important as reaching the destination. Rex proved himself tender, considerate, and communicative, but above all, sensuous and passionate.

It was easy to respond in kind. We started with a long, hot shower together. We took our time, and when we moved to the bed, there was no fury, no anger, no fear, no revenge, no pain, only exquisite pleasure. If this was love, I could stand a regular diet.

The furthest thing from my mind was Ranger, back in Indiana, and I hoped Rex could say the same about Sparky. I didn't even ask; I didn't want to remind him, or perhaps I simply didn't want to know. I wondered if Sparky and Rex made love together or if—like Ranger and me—they merely sucked and fucked too. Perhaps Rex was as starved for the warm embrace of human interaction as I was.

I didn't take any more pictures. I didn't need to.

We took a break for a leisurely late dinner in the hotel restaurant and a long walk together with Spot. We let him off the leash, and I found a stick to throw. When he tired himself out chasing it, we headed back to the room. Rex and I watched the moon from the balcony, our arms draped around each other.

"Would you like to go running?" I said. "You know I'm not a runner myself. You'd find me pretty sorry company around the track, but you're welcome to go off by yourself if you want. You said you hadn't been for a run in a week, and it's nice and dark out there for you."

He shook his head and grinned. "Funny. There's nothing here I want to run from. Besides," he said as we went back into our room and climbed into bed again, "don't you think we're getting plenty of exercise?" We fell asleep that night with Rex's arms wrapped around me, and the relaxed, steady rhythm of his breathing provided the most exquisite lullaby I might have ever heard. I slept better than I had in years, probably.

In the morning, I woke up only when Spot's nose nuzzled the back of my neck. Rex and I stretched and yawned, and it was a genuine pleasure to find him next to me.

"Good morning, sexy man," he said.

"Good morning yourself. I've got to take Spot outside for a quick run. Stay put. I'll be right back."

"Mmm. You better be."

Reluctantly, I dressed and left our room to take the patient Spot around the back of the hotel and let him tear around the yard for a few minutes. I picked up the Elmira *Gazette* in the lobby as we headed back upstairs. Rex had already brewed a pot of coffee and ordered breakfast through room service (charged, again without incident, to Sparky's credit card).

As it happened, the waiter who brought our meal was gay too, as well as friendly and talkative. He said we made a lovely couple and wondered how long we'd been together. "Our whole lives, practically," I said. Rex laughed and didn't contradict me. After the waiter left, I said, "You know, Rex, I really *do* feel as if I've known you my whole life."

"I couldn't agree more. It's funny, isn't it? Yet, except for a happy collision of our two planets, we would never have met."

We shared waffles with strawberries and whipped cream and the most agreeable conversation I could remember at any breakfast table. Afterward, I set the tray outside the door, and we stretched out on the bed to read the paper and work on the crossword puzzle together. Spot napped.

Rex quickly lost interest in the puzzle and directed his attention toward making me lose interest in the puzzle as well. I surrendered without much struggle. We spent the rest of the morning in bed, with me exploring the plains and peaks and valleys of Rex's splendidly furry terrain as if he had been sculpted and landscaped exactly to my specifications and solely for our mutual gratification. He responded in kind.

"You're spoiling me, mister," I said, later, when we took a break for another cup of coffee.

"No apologies. You deserve it."

"Thanks. So do you. I have a proposal for you, by the way."

Rex laughed. "You want to make an honest man of me?"

"Quite possibly. Suppose we find out? Come back to Indiana with me for a while, and let's see what happens. I know you well enough to know that I want to know you better. Let my house be yours too. There's plenty of room. And we have a decent daily newspaper that could surely use a sports columnist. Central Indiana isn't Bucks County, but it doesn't need to be."

He looked at me for a long minute. "That's just about the most generous offer I've ever had. Thank you for asking. Maybe I will."

I was elated. Maybe he—we—could start again, with something new and good and right.

Last evening's spectacular sunset had given way to a hazy morning that only grew more cloudy as we headed into the afternoon. Rex eyed the sky and checked the forecast in the paper. "Looks like we'd better get over to the cemetery now. Once the rain hits, the forecast says it'll stick around for the rest of the week—and as much as I'd love to stay inside with you all day, I think you want to put your grandfather to rest. Then we can figure out what we're doing next."

I agreed. We showered and dressed, and when my cell phone rang for the first time since I'd hit the road, I was surprised to see Ranger's name come up on the display.

"Guess who?" I said.

"Not Ranger!"

"I don't even remember the last time he phoned me." I took the call.

"Where in goddamn hell are you at?" he barked. Not even a how-do.

"New York. A little town called Elmira."

"Is Spot with you?"

"Yes. Don't worry. He's fine. He doesn't seem to miss you at all. And," I said, "come to think of it, for the first time in well over a year, neither do I."

"Fuck you."

"That's being taken care of, believe me. Would you like to say hello to him?" I almost said "your replacement," but it would not have been fair to Rex, even if it might have shot a dart into Ranger. Instead, he was silent. I thought perhaps he might be jealous, even furious. Maybe a little nostalgic or regretful. But quite possibly he was none of these. Quite possibly, he had not changed at all. And I realized at the moment that I didn't care.

But a beaten man said one thing more. "Sorry about your granddad, Neil. I didn't get to tell you before. Take care of Spot and bring him back one of these days, okay? I miss—him."

"I will. Don't worry. He's having a great time with us."

Ranger muttered "Jesus goddamn fuck" under his breath and hung up. I tossed the phone across the room. Rex graciously bore the brunt of my anger as I spouted off. "Not even a word about how I'm doing. Or what I'm doing here, or why I borrowed Spot in the first place. Not a word! That sorry son-of-a-bitch!"

Rex wrapped his arms around me. "Calm down. Just settle. *I* know how you're doing. *I* know why you're here and why you borrowed Spot, and what's more, I'm here. I'm not going anywhere, and there is no place I'd rather be just now."

That stopped me, calmed me down, shut me up. A contest between Ranger and Rex would be no contest. He kissed me gently, then pulled me in tight for something long and deep. When we separated, we were both grinning.

"That's better," he said. "Now, suppose we get going?"

The desk clerk gave us directions to Woodlawn Cemetery and assured us that we would see the signs directing us to the grave of Samuel Clemens.

"You should do a tombstone rubbing while we're there," Rex said as we backed out of the parking lot.

"What's that?

"Oh, come *on*. You've never done a tombstone rubbing? You put a piece of newsprint paper against the gravestone and rub the side of a crayon against it. You get an image of the inscription on the paper. You never did that when you were a kid?"

"I didn't hang around graveyards much as a boy."

Rex insisted that we needed such a souvenir, and I let him lead the charge. We stopped at a drugstore and picked up a box of crayons, but he couldn't find paper suitable for his purpose.

"We need a few sheets of white newsprint. It's the best thing. Let's head over to the *Gazette* office."

We asked the clerk where to find the newspaper building and headed there next. I dropped off Rex at the door and parked across the street. While I waited for him, I picked up the box containing the ashes and had a necessary chat with my grandfather.

I asked Granddad if he liked Rex as well as I did. Was Rex anything like Sam? I'd waited my whole life to meet a man like Rex—never mind Ranger, who wasn't Rex's caliber and could never be. I spoke of my anger toward Sparky, whom I never expected to meet, for not realizing what he held in his hands and for treating Rex so shamefully, and wondered if Sparky's carelessness could be my salvation. Perhaps I could win Rex, in spite of the cards being stacked against me, if I could but say the right words, do the right things and thus relegate Sparky to the cellar of Rex's memory, where he belonged. And Ranger to mine.

"I miss you, Granddad. Did I ever thank you for all you did for me? For teaching me how to be a gay man?"

I'd learned so much from my grandfather, and I was indebted to him in many ways. He had certainly taught me about being gay in the twentieth century, about navigating the waters with grace and aplomb. But he could never teach me to be a proud gay man in the twenty-first century. My grandfather couldn't imagine a world where being out was not considered vaguely criminal, or at least somewhat unsavory. While Granddad relished his reputation and did all he could to feed it, there was in him, I think, still a remnant of shame, that he had somehow let his wife and son down. I don't think he could quite accept the notion that being gay was perfectly normal because he'd been indoctrinated so thoroughly that it was not. Once he headed down the path toward that imagined hell, he didn't look back, and he enjoyed every step.

But what did it cost him? He died without ever finding a faithful and lasting partner to walk through the world with him, only a distant memory of the Sam he lost. Died without reconciling with his son. I'm sure Granddad was angry about that until the end, and perhaps rightfully so, but I could see my father's side of it too. Had anyone in my life ever betrayed me as he believed his dad had betrayed him? I was deeply sorry that Dad missed out on everything his father wanted to share with him. I didn't know if Dad would ever change his mind about homosexuality, if he would always remain suspicious, but I remained grateful that we had a better relationship than he did with Granddad.

What a long and strange and wonderful trip we'd shared, and soon we would reach his last stop.

Rex returned to the car, jubilant, with an end roll of white newsprint paper.

"It took a little shameless flirting, but I talked my way into the newsroom and found a sympathetic reporter. The guy liked the angle about your grandfather's ashes, but he agreed it wouldn't do to publicize it. He said to wish you good luck."

We made our way to Woodlawn under a thickening sky. I hoped the storm would hold off long enough for us to complete our quest. The cemetery was easy to find, as was the Clemens family gravesite, and we were able to park close by. Spot seemed content to snooze in the back seat, so we left him there. The scent of rain hung heavy in the air as we got out of the car.

The Clemens plot was larger than I expected, including markers not only for the author and his wife Olivia but also for his daughters Jean, Clara, and Susie; his baby son Langdon; Olivia's parents; and several other relatives whose names I didn't recognize. Mature trees shaded the graves, landscaped with grass and clipped bushes. I was relieved to find so much vegetation. Spreading my grandfather's ashes would be easier than I anticipated, and the rain would ensure that they became so much fertilizer for the trees. There was, however, a small group of hovering tourists, gravely reading the stones.

"How fast do you think we can get them out of here?" Rex whispered. "Maybe if we start making out."

I agreed; it might be a useful arrow for our quiver (in addition to being a pleasure), and I knew my grandfather would heartily approve of such tactics. Under the circumstances, however, we decided to keep that strategy in reserve.

One overly stout man clearly was the leader of the expedition, as he let forth nonstop prattle about the life and works of Mr. Clemens. The others hardly even seemed to pay attention, probably more embarrassed by the man's spectacular gall and lack of situational awareness than they were interested in the (frequently inaccurate) information he imparted. I tried to ignore him; perhaps he'd run out of gas or simply deflate, and he and his party would vacate the premises. Maybe the impending storm would chase them away.

In the meantime, Rex took great delight in showing me the finer points of tombstone rubbing. First, he measured off sheets of newsprint and scored them with his pocketknife. Then he experimented with different crayons before choosing the best colors, and finally, he made half a dozen of Samuel Clemens's stone. "Some for you to keep and some for me. Do you think the old windbag would take a photo of us standing by the gravestone?"

"I'd rather ask one of his minions."

The woman we spoke to was happy to oblige, and we posed for a couple of snapshots.

"Your friend certainly likes to hear himself talk," I said.

She rolled her eyes. "He's not *my* friend. I'd have been long gone, but unfortunately, he drove us out here, so we're hostages."

With nothing else to do until the group left, I positioned myself close to the orator and eyed him. He seemed pleased to have a dedicated listener, and if anything, he puffed up even more. If I thought his lecture would have to end at some point, I had clearly underestimated his ability to blather on. Ordinarily, I would have kept my mouth shut, but I was impatient to beat the rain, and Rex and I could not carry out my mission until they'd gone. Thunder rumbled ominously in the background; it could well have been Clemens himself offering editorial comment.

Finally, when the stuffy pundit made a remark about *The Gilded Age* being Mark Twain's personal favorite of all his books as well as a true classic, co-written with his best friend William Dean Howells, I felt I had to interrupt or my grandfather would surely haunt me from the other side, whatever or wherever it might be. I spoke up.

My first impulse was to announce, "You're full of shit," but I opted for the more democratic "You don't know what you're talking about."

The man turned to me slowly and glared with piggy eyes.

"What did you say?" He was incredulous; perhaps he had never been thus challenged in his adult life. "What on earth do *you* know about *The Gilded Age*?"

"Apparently, more than you." I turned to his group, each member of which had quickly tuned in, possibly eager for the challenge. Or perhaps my butting in was infinitely more interesting than his monologue had been on its own.

"Look, folks. I wouldn't exactly call myself a Twain scholar, but I've read most of his books, and you don't need a Ph.D. in literature to know that *The Gilded Age* appeared not in 1892 but in 1873. It was subtitled 'A Tale of Today' because it satirized the greed of post-Civil War America, which would still have been a current event. And his writing partner was Charles Dudley Warner, his next-door neighbor in Hartford, not William Dean Howells, who was living in Massachusetts at that time."

I explained that Mr. Clemens and Mr. Howells were friends, but Mr. Howells had already published his own first novel and was working on a second, as well as editing the *Atlantic Monthly* and lecturing at a Boston college, so he would have had neither the time nor inclination to co-author a book with Mr. Clemens in 1873 or any time. What brought about *The Gilded Age* partnership was this: Mr. and Mrs. Warner were having dinner with Mr. and Mrs. Clemens one evening, and the husbands were complaining loudly about the quality of fiction being written at the time. Their wives challenged them to write a better book, and they accepted the dare. The result was Mr. Clemens's first published full-length novel, though he had to share the byline.

In no way did he consider it his best book—in fact, he was inclined to agree with the many critics who rank *The Gilded Age* among his weakest, in part because his style was so different from Mr. Warner's, and—excuse the pun—never the twain shall meet. Mr. Clemens was actually proudest of one of his least well-known books, *The Personal Recollections of Joan of Arc*—rather astonishing, if one considers how he felt about Roman Catholicism and the saints in general, a point made repeatedly in his travel books (*Innocents Abroad,* say, or *Following the Equator*). He used to say his *Joan of Arc* took twelve years to research and two years to write. It was serialized first in *Harper's Magazine* in 1895, anonymously at his request because he was afraid it would not be taken seriously otherwise, or that readers would expect it to be funny. It was published in book form the following year—with his name on the cover. In spite of the beauty and heartfelt nature of the prose, it wasn't a success.

As a postscript, I threw in the fact that in 1892—identified by our inflated pedant as the year of publication for *The Gilded Age*—Twain actually published its sequel, entitled *The American Claimant*, without the assistance of Charles Dudley Warner.

I could have kept on for hours. The Twain history and arcana that I'd accumulated as a young reader stuck with me because I honestly loved Twain's writing. Even years later, I could call the details easily to mind.

"I *could* be wrong," I concluded, "but I'm not. Look it up for yourself."

The windbag, as offended as I'd hoped, collected his acolytes (most of whom were snickering behind their hands or busy checking the accuracy of my remarks on their phones) and departed, glaring daggers in my direction. The woman who'd taken our picture gave me a high-five as they left. I'll bet their return trip, whatever the destination, was interesting.

When they had gone, Rex kissed me long and hard. "That was magnificent. Absolutely incredible! I'm blown away! Why the hell are you wasting your life serving booze and beer when you could be standing in front of a classroom?"

Hmm....

"Have you ever read Mark Twain?"

"*Tom Sawyer*. Years ago. That's all I can remember. And that story about the frog in the jumping contest."

"Not enough! I insist that you further your education in that respect, or my grandfather will surely haunt you. *A Connecticut Yankee in King*

Arthur's Court is a must. And *The Adventures of Huckleberry Finn* after that, and then *Pudd'nhead Wilson*. Promise?"

"Promise."

We retrieved Granddad's tin box from the car and opened it. The ashes that used to be a human being and a dog don't take up much room. But no box could ever contain the spirit of the man whose dust I cradled in my arms, and it was time to set him free, with his beloved pet.

Rex, gentle: "Are you ready, Neil?"

Carefully, discreetly, I scattered the ashes among the grass and shrubbery that marked Sam Clemens's resting place as Rex kept lookout. The first drops of rain hit as I finished. Rex put an arm around me.

"Peace on you, Sixtus James Graham," he said.

I liked that. "Peace on you, Granddad. And Central, too. May your spirits soar. Thank you for everything."

By the time we tumbled into the car again, we were drenched, laughing improbably at the whole unbelievable adventure and shivering uncontrollably in our sopping suits. In the back seat, Spot lifted his head when we slammed the doors and then promptly went back to sleep.

"Thank you for helping me with this, Rex. I don't know how I could have done it alone."

"It was an honor and a privilege. I wish I'd known your grandfather. He sounds like a fascinating man, and I'll always be grateful to him for introducing us."

"He would have been pleased to know you, too. Intimately, I might add. He would have asked your permission, very politely, before roundly seducing you. You wouldn't have been able to resist his charms, and I never would've had a chance."

He laughed. "I'm sorry I'll never have that experience, but I'm perfectly content with his grandson."

15

Returning to the hotel, we showered—together, and I hate to think of how much water we wasted in the process—and changed into dry clothes. I took my grandfather's framed photo with us to the restaurant for dinner and gave it a position of honor at our table, complete with a votive candle and a small bouquet of roses that Rex purchased at the gift shop. We raised a toast to Granddad and enjoyed a fine meal. He would have appreciated the food, company, and especially the conversation and laughter as I shared anecdotes of his exploits and our shared history.

"So you saw your granddad jerk off when you were fifteen." Rex was awed. "That must have been educational."

"You have no idea. And I'll bet no other kid in my school had a grandfather who cracked dick jokes at the dinner table. Here's one of my favorites: what's the difference between a man and a roll of Lifesavers?"

"Hmm...I don't know."

"A man can't come in five flavors."

Rex proved a most appreciative audience.

"What's the difference between jam and marmalade?"

Rex shook his head.

I lowered my voice to deliver the punch line. "You can't marmalade your cock up a hot man's ass."

Rex cackled. "You really got those from your grandfather?"

"And dozens more. He always had a new one, every time I saw him. I asked him one time how he came up with so many great jokes about his dick, and he said, 'It's... hard.' I wish I could remember them all. I should have written them down."

Back at our room, warm in bed as the rain sheeted against the window, we were deep into some leisurely foreplay with an ecstatic climax or two being our general direction at some point when Rex's cell phone rang for the first time since we'd been together. Immediately we separated, guilty, maybe, as if the mere sound of the ringtone were accusing Rex—both of us—of infidelity.

Rex grabbed the phone and identified the caller before placing it to his ear. "Hello, Sparky." There was a pause. "Elmira." And another. "A hotel." Again. "No. With...a friend." I could imagine Sparky barking out the interrogation, and I could fill in the questions between the pauses: What town are you calling from? Where are you staying? Are you alone? Under the grilling, Rex seemed to shrink. He huddled on the edge of the bed, shivering a little. Abruptly, he stood up and went into the bathroom, slamming the door behind him. Perhaps he wanted to spare me the discomfort of having to listen to the third-degree Sparky gave him. Or perhaps Rex was embarrassed because he let Sparky get away with it.

In bed, I wrapped the sheets around me and settled in. I couldn't make out what Rex was saying through the door, but he seemed to be talking as much as he was listening, and that might have been a good sign. When he came out, forty-five minutes later, I could see that he'd been crying, but now he was clear-eyed and resolute. He tossed the phone onto the table and climbed back into bed next to me. He put his arm around me, protective.

"I should be holding you," I said.

"Suppose we hold each other." He sighed. "Sparky wants me to come back home."

"Hah. I'll bet he does. What about the bride-to-be?"

"She's gone. Out of the picture completely. He even apologized."

"Big of him."

"He says he never really intended to go through with it. He just wanted to make me jealous."

"Why? Did you ever give him any cause?"

"No."

"I didn't think so."

He was quiet for a long time. "He's coming to get me."

"Right now?"

"He probably hit the road as soon as he hung up the phone."

"How far is the drive from Bensalem?"

"About three hundred miles. At this time of night, with no traffic, it will probably take him five hours at the very most."

I checked the time. "That means he'll get here around three a.m. Why doesn't he wait until a more civilized hour? At least you could get a decent night's rest."

"I won't be able to sleep anyway."

"You don't have to go with him."

"He says things are going to be different. Better."

"Oh, sure. And he's never made *that* pledge to you before." I was sure Sparky had sworn to change, and more than once. Weren't abusive people always penitent, full of promises that they would never strike again?

"Rex, listen. Come with me. Please? Let's pack our stuff, check out, and hit the road ourselves. Right now. We can go to Rochester so you can spend some time with your mom and dad. You don't even have to introduce me if you don't want to. I'll stay in a hotel." If they genuinely liked Sparky, I suspected I would not fare well in comparison. "Hell. Let's get married ourselves. We can go to Niagara Falls on our honeymoon."

"He'd come after us."

"You make him sound like a stalker! If he's that violent, or you're that afraid, I won't *let* you go with him."

It was too late.

I wanted to be rational and deliberate, even if I wanted to yell. Throw things. "Do you really think anything will change? I mean, do you? Honestly?" Rex only held onto me more tightly. Somewhere between midnight and sunrise, between his anxiety and my concern, we managed some restless sleep.

A loud, urgent, no-nonsense knock jarred us awake. The bedside clock read 5:45. Either Sparky had gotten unavoidably delayed, or he'd decided to give Rex a break. I suspected the former, but I kept quiet.

I reached over to turn on the light, and we leaped out of bed.

"Should we be dressed?" I whispered.

"Probably." He grabbed his running shorts, and I slipped into a pair of boxers and a T-shirt. The knocking continued, uninterrupted. Spot, uncertain about this turn of events but positive that it signaled some new game or at least a little excitement, started racing around the room, jumping on the bed and barking. I shushed him.

Rex opened the door, and Sparky stepped inside.

He was compact and trim, shorter than I had imagined, black hair salted with white and trimmed with military precision, a forbidding mustache almost comically large, steel-grey eyes, as tense as a cocked pistol. We stared at each other. Minus the anger, his face would have been extraordinarily handsome, someone even a straight man might enjoy finding in his bed. He wore a burgundy-colored cashmere sweater over a crisp white shirt, black denim jeans, and black cowboy boots polished to a mirrored gleam—and masculinity, like cologne. He pushed me aside and stepped inside to survey the room, the only place Rex and I would ever share.

Sparky's sweep of the room took in our suitcases, untidy on the floor, at our clothing (shucked as soon as we'd come inside the room after dinner and cast aside as we tumbled into bed), at Spot (who'd positioned himself between Sparky and us, head cocked and ears back, a growl percolating in his throat, looking very alert and watch-doggish), at the single bed we'd shared and its tangled sheets, at my grandfather's framed portrait, the box of condoms on the dresser. At Rex, afraid but clearly in love. At me, my arms crossed defensively, in love myself with the man standing next to me.

Sparky parked his gaze longest on me, a look that could have burned through reinforced concrete, but I was not in a mood to cower. I felt as fiercely protective of Rex as Spot did of the pair of us, and I would do more than growl if necessary. "Don't give me that look," I barked at the man who held Rex's heart in his hands. "I don't like you any more than you like me, so we're even. If you can't be civil, then get the hell out of our room before I call the manager."

"Neil, please," Rex whispered.

"Nice guy you picked, Rex," Sparky said.

"For your information," I said, "I picked *him*."

Unexpectedly, Spot stepped forward and went to Sparky. To my surprise, he bent down and immediately scratched Spot behind the ears and set his tail wagging.

"Who's a good boy?" Sparky said, roughing up Spot's fur. He wriggled with delight, the little traitor. "What's his name?"

"Spot."

Sparky gave him the once-over and determined that he was, in fact, spot-free. "What a great disguise," he told Spot. "We can all use a place to hide now and then. Good boy. *Good* boy." Spot couldn't contain his joy. His tongue washed Sparky's chin.

He stood up. "I'm sorry about your eye, Rex."

"It's all right."

"No," I said. "It's *not* all right. You should be arrested."

Rex protested. "It's getting better. It hardly even hurts now."

Sparky sighed. "Pack up your things, Rex. Now."

"He's not in the military anymore, Rex, and you never were. He has no right to issue orders, and you certainly don't have to follow them." And to Sparky: "Rex hasn't decided if he even *wants* to go back with you. What kind of home life can you possible have if you punch him in the face every time you get mad?"

"Neil, that's enough." Rex was calm, resigned perhaps. "You haven't even been introduced. Sparky Rogers, Neil Graham. Neil, Sparky."

We did not shake hands.

"You want to help me pack my things, Neil? Suppose you wait in the car, Sparky. We won't be long."

For a moment, I didn't think Sparky intended to leave. Finally, muttering under his breath, he turned and took himself outside, slamming the door behind him for punctuation. Only Spot seemed sorrowful when he left. I helped Rex collect his clothes and fold them neatly, his running shoes, his shaving kit, and two rubbings of Samuel Clemens's gravestone. I offered him the condoms.

"Sparky doesn't use them."

I shrugged. "Neither does Ranger. As if I'd ever have to worry about him again. Tell you what. Let's split the box. Maybe we'll both get wise and find a man who's smarter. Look. You're making a mistake. Can't you see that? I realize I've only just met Sparky, but after all you've told me, I feel as if I already know him too well. He hasn't learned a damn thing since you walked out. Nothing has changed!"

"Maybe you're right. But I have to believe he's going to do better, that *we're* going to do better. That things will be different."

"How many times has he told you that?"

He was silent.

"How many times has he blacked your eye?"

Silence.

"Rex?"

"I love him. I think he loves me too, in his own way."

"That's a pretty violent thing to call love, in *any* kind of way. How's that stack up against fucking and sucking as a substitute for intimacy?"

That riled him a bit. "How much better off are you and Ranger? You're not even welcome at his house anymore. He has a wife! You haven't seen him for months, except for a minute at your your granddad's funeral—and he didn't even stick around long enough to offer condolences."

"And Sparky introduces you as his housemate and socks you in the face when he gets pissed off at you."

"There's more to our relationship than that."

"Not from what you've told me. Is he even worth fighting for?"

"Yes. Is Ranger?"

I sighed. "I honestly don't know."

"You don't think he's really in love with that woman he married, do you?"

"Of course not. My guess is he just wants to fix her, like she's a broken toy. That's the way he rolls through life. Fixing things. I mean, he's a mechanic, for God's sake. He can fix her life, and his at the same time. Prove to the world that he's not *really* gay now that he's sober."

"So why not give him a chance to fix you?"

"I'm not broken. At least not from his point of view."

"Don't you think he needs to believe that there is something about you that is less than perfect? Something that needs a little tune-up, at least? Because how demoralizing is it to be around the perfect guy all the time?"

I didn't know. I'd never been around the perfect guy myself—though I wonder if my grandfather wouldn't qualify. He was handsome, literate, urbane, sexy, gentle, fun, an enormously entertaining conversationalist. Although I found Ranger to be sexy and handsome (and unreliable and unpredictable, both of which could be charming as often as they were damned annoying), what wouldn't I change about him if I could? Was I any better than Marlene, with her twelve-step program that would result in the perfect Ranger?

I gave up. "I can't stop you. Good luck, Rex."

"Thanks."

"Call me?"

"I will."

"You'd better." We took a minute to load each other's contact information into our cell phones. Rex scrawled his address on a page of hotel stationery and I did the same with mine.

"Have you got everything?" I said.

"All packed."

"You've got a piece of my heart in your suitcase too."

He embraced me. Kissed me for a long time, hard, passionate.

"And you've got a piece of mine. You always will."

I retrieved my backpack and rummaged in it for my copy of *A Connecticut Yankee in King Arthur's Court* and handed it to Rex. "Here. You need this more than I do." I opened the book and showed him the inscription, "Happy tenth birthday with love from your old Granddad."

"You never had the pleasure of meeting my grandfather, but I hope you've come to know him a little through our great adventure these last three days. You need a memento of him besides the tombstone rubbing. He'd want you to have this, and I do too."

It was, I told him, my most preferred Twain novel and my all-time favorite book. This particular edition was one of the first gifts I'd gotten as a boy from my grandfather, and I'd read it at least eight times. "No matter how often I revisit it, I find myself laughing out loud. The last chapter makes me cry. For a man to do that with just words placed in the right order, one after another, is brilliant."

Rex examined the book, its well-worn dust jacket scotch-taped together and its pages dog-eared from rereading. "Thank you. I'll start it tonight. And I'll always treasure the gift—and the memories." He placed the volume in his suitcase, zipped it shut, and then turned to face me.

"I think Sparky's been cooling his heels in the car long enough. He's going to kick the door down in a minute or two if I don't get out there."

"Yes. Doesn't that concern you?"

He shrugged and sighed.

"What do you say we get some breakfast before you hit the road?" I said.

"I don't know if Sparky would go for that. We can ask."

I figured I would never see Rex again, and I was desperate to extend the little time together we had left, even if it meant including Sparky. Maybe I wanted to give him a chance to redeem himself, for Rex's sake.

"We can go to the diner across the street and get a quick bite."

We went outside. Sparky got out of the car—a classic silver-grey Porsche, sleek and stylish—and took Rex's suitcase and put it in the trunk.

I half expected Rex to ask Sparky's permission, or pose it as a question—"May I please get a bite to eat, sir?"—but Rex said, "Sparky, I'm hungry. We're grabbing some breakfast. Want to join us before we head out?"

I was proud of Rex; when Sparky shrugged and said, "Okay," my resistance did not exactly erode, but it was the first flicker of hopefulness I'd felt.

We crossed the street to the diner. Rex slid into the booth and Sparky followed. I sat opposite. Rex ordered waffles and sausage, juice and coffee; I followed suit, and Sparky made it three. The waitress brought our plates in short order. Throughout the meal, Rex made a point of catching my eye and smiling, and I couldn't help but smile back. If Sparky minded, he pretended not to notice. None of us could think of a damn thing to say, though, and it was the quietest breakfast I'd ever had with two other people, such a marked contrast to yesterday's morning meal and the bright promise it contained.

After clearing away our plates, the waitress brought the check. I reached for it, but Sparky took it out of my hand. "It's on me."

I didn't press. "Fine. Thanks."

We traipsed across the street again. Rex excused himself to use the bathroom before they hit the road. Sparky and I stood by the car.

"Thanks for picking up Rex and looking after him these last three days."

"You're welcome. He deserves someone who'll look after him all the time."

"I'll take care of it."

"Maybe you're not the guy."

"I am, Graham." His tone was even, but I could tell it was an effort.

"You almost lost him."

He gave me a disdainful glance. "To *you*?"

My heart sank.

Rex returned, and we stood in the parking lot for a minute, awkward, looking for the words to say goodbye. He checked his watch. "We'd better get a move on. You're working today. Aren't you, Sparky?"

"Nope. I canceled the rest of the week and called your folks. Told them we were coming up for a few days. We should reach Rochester in time to have breakfast with them, too."

"It's about a hundred miles further," Rex told me. Clearly, this unexpected turn of events pleased him, and I admit to feeling a bit more optimistic as well. If Sparky were a better man outside of Bucks County. Rex could only benefit.

I offered my hand to Sparky, with some misgivings, and he took it, a businesslike shake that ended in a draw.

Then I turned to Rex. Again, I offered my hand; it didn't seem enough, after all we'd been through, and he seemed to feel the same way. We embraced, and Rex—perhaps not wisely—attached his mouth to mine and kissed me long and hard and deep. If he undertook it for Sparky's benefit at first, its conclusion was between Rex and me alone.

"I'll miss you," I whispered.

"Likewise. Call me. Please. Anytime."

"I will. You do the same. Let's get together again one of these days."

"We'll have to."

"Is it possible to fall in love in three days?"

"Of course."

Sparky cleared his throat. We separated.

"You want me to drive? You must be tired," Rex said.

"You're not driving my Porsche."

Rex shrugged. "Okay. I'm not driving your Porsche."

Sparky opened the car door for him and stood by as he got in and buckled up. Then Sparky climbed into the driver's seat, gave me a last inscrutable look, and backed the Porsche out. I followed to the end of the parking lot and waved at the car until I couldn't see it anymore. I thought Rex would open the window and wave back, but he didn't. Perhaps he didn't dare.

I worried for Rex all morning as I showered and packed. I wasn't in a hurry and hung out until the required checkout time at noon. The rain had returned, and I got drenched just putting my suitcase into the car. Spot napped in the corner of the room until we left. If he felt concerned about the sudden absence of Rex (or Sparky), he gave no sign.

I was glad that we'd asked the woman at the cemetery to take a couple photos of the two of us together, and glad I'd taken those of him at the rest area a few days earlier. I'd try calling him in the evening. Maybe.

Would Sparky change? Could he? Was their relationship as wrong as it seemed to me? I would never tolerate physical abuse from Ranger or anyone. How could that be anyone's definition of love? But they are grown men. As I am. As is Ranger. We are responsible for the choices we make, and old enough to assume the consequences.

16

The trip back to Indiana was significantly less exhilarating than the trip to New York. With little mid-day traffic, I made good time, but I decided to stop for the night even before I hit the Ohio border. I felt exhausted, and no amount of coffee could force me to drive any further. I'd found no likely hitchhikers to relieve the ache I felt for Rex and not even any decent jazz on the radio.

I passed a restless night in a lonely motel room and took my time the next morning, reluctant to hit the road. Spot did his best to console, but I think even he missed Rex. I was in no hurry to get home. A vacation's end always depressed me, but this had been a monumental and emotional journey for me.

At mid-afternoon, I reached Ranger and Marlene's house. It was quiet; they were probably at work again. I hollered inside the front door, just to be certain I was alone. Spot was pleased to be home. I let him inside, and he raced through the place, upstairs and down, making sure all was right before heading back outside to explore the yard.

A hand-painted slate tile hung by the door. I hadn't noticed it before, and I stopped to look: in large letters, it proclaimed "THE MELUSKY'S" at the top, and I almost didn't read further. Like my grandfather, I had a profound dislike for this common punctuation mistake, the misuse of the apostrophe to indicate plural rather than possessive. Under this egregious error, I found an even more egregious bit of doggerel. I doubted if Marlene had asked for Ranger's opinion before hanging it by the front door.

MARRIAGE TAKES 3.
2 Lovers Come Together
Ask The Lord To Enter
Marriage Never Fails
With Jesus At It's Center.

I wondered if she had composed it. Apart from the excessive and pointless capitalization, there was another misused apostrophe in the last line. I recalled being taught in elementary school that the correct possessive was "its," but clearly, not everyone had a teacher as insistent as Sister Maria Dolores. For a quick moment, I took comfort from the pathetic charge I got from basking in my superiority, but reality kicked in. All right, I told myself; you can use punctuation marks correctly, but Marlene gets to sleep with Ranger, and you're alone.

Who wins?

On the other side of the door, more inspiration: "Keep Our House Neat. Take Your Shoes Off Your Feet." I was confident that at least one-third of their domestic threesome (possibly two-thirds; would Jesus take off his sandals?) ignored the policy.

I knew I shouldn't go inside, but curiosity got the better of me and I crossed the threshold. I convinced myself there was no harm in exploring. Besides, the door was unlocked! Perhaps I wanted to see if anything remained from the time I spent with Ranger in the days before Marlene. Did they, I wondered, still use the plates and glasses and pots I had purchased for him? The bath towels and blankets? Would I find any evidence of me—of us—at all?

The house was tidy, which surprised me not in the least. Marlene was a dedicated housekeeper, and I'm sure she kept Ranger aligned in that respect. The rooms seemed smaller than ever, and Marlene's overstuffed furniture seemed larger—would it have been possible to cram even one more thing inside? I had my first look at their gigantic flat-screen television; like the furniture, it was out of proportion to the space. I passed into the dining room and then the kitchen. I peeked into the cupboards and drawers but found nothing familiar. Marlene had purged the place pretty thoroughly.

From the kitchen, I went down into the basement and discovered that Ranger had acquired a workout contraption, a combination of cables and weights attached to a bench designed for total fitness with minimal effort. I'd seen the ads, promising results that seemed inflated even by TV's reduced standards. I wondered if he had actually made a commitment to exercise. Possibly the purchase seemed like a good idea at the time. I knew it hadn't been cheap. Its primary use at the moment seemed to be a clothes rack for Ranger's shirts and coveralls, pressed and neatly hangered.

Back upstairs, I headed to the second floor. The master bedroom interested me most, because a cursory glance told me that the only one sleeping in it was Marlene. The bed was made with hospital corners, covered with a beautiful patchwork quilt and matching pillows. Two Cabbage Patch dolls, relics from the early 1980s, sat in the middle of the bed. Marlene's babies? I wondered. Above the bed, a giant lacquered wood plaque proclaimed more inspirational verse:

We Made A Promise
To Have And To Hold
The Love That We Share
Is More Precious Than Gold

Someone in the house certainly had an affinity for clever couplets. Two big-eyed, naked, sexless cartoon children held hands underneath the words. The boy wore a top hat, and the girl a bridal veil. Another wall displayed a carefully stitched sampler, "Marlene and Ranger Happiness Is Being Married To Your Best Friend." Had Marlene done it, or was it a well-intentioned gift? I marveled, once again, at the use of capital letters to add conviction to the text. On the nightstand, I found a neat stack of four romance novels. I'm sure they provided cold comfort on chilly nights.

The closet, picture-perfect, contained Marlene's dresses, blouses, and pants, arranged by color. A dozen shoe boxes were stacked underneath the clothes. The other half of the closet was empty. The dresser top was tidy as well, everything placed just so, a comb and brush, face creams, perfumes, and lotions in a row, a hand mirror, a glass jewelry box full of rings and bracelets. A photo frame, with room for six pictures, trumpeted "All because two people fell in love" across the top, but it was empty. It made me sad.

Ranger, clearly, had moved into the other bedroom, down the hall. The furniture in it—probably Marlene's as a child—had been neatly painted a light pink with a red heart motif, and it all matched. There was a twin bed, unmade, a dresser heaped with old magazines, several ball caps, a pair of broken sunglasses, a dozen or so empty and crushed soda cans, a pile of matchbooks, a roll of smokeless tobacco cans—a trade-off for the cigarettes Marlene had insisted he give up, I imagine.

The floor was strewn with laundry, soiled as well as clean; a couple of damp towels, mud-caked boots, and sneakers. The closet door was open, revealing nothing inside but empty hangers. A kid-sized chair stood in the corner, and on the seat, in a neat line, were Ranger's sobriety tokens, in their various colors—a day, a week, a month, two months, and so on, up to eleven. I marveled. Nearly a year!

A lamp with a crooked shade sat on the nightstand, and a battered copy of the Alcoholics Anonymous "Big Book." A poster thumbtacked to the wall advertised a brand of muscle car with absurdly large wheels and a young, buxom bikini-clad woman draped across the hood. There was nothing in the picture that would have titillated Ranger, except possibly the certainty that Marlene would have been supremely irritated by it.

I sat on the bed for a minute and could almost smell Ranger in the sheets. And I felt as if my intrusion had crossed an unforgivable boundary, as if I'd stumbled across the dirty secrets of a crumbling marriage.

I left Spot sunning himself on the porch, content. And I felt guilty all the way home. As much as I disliked Marlene, I felt sorry that both of them were sleeping alone, whether by choice or force. Even by Ranger's yardstick, the romance had ended quickly. Who had grown exhausted first, Marlene for trying to enforce her high standards, or Ranger for trying to reach them?

Having nothing better to do after I unpacked again at my grandfather's house, I fixed myself a rare whiskey and soda, my grandfather's go-to drink, and kept an eye on the clock. I knew Ranger got home from the Buick dealership around half past five, and as I expected, the phone rang a few minutes after.

"When did you get back?" he said, elaborately casual.

How about "hello" or something? Not Ranger. "This afternoon."

"Spot's glad to be home."

"He was a good traveling companion. Thanks for loaning him to me."

"Did you bring him back with you?"

"Spot? Obviously."

"No!"

"Who?'

I could hear his exasperation. "Jesus Christ, Neil. The guy who was fucking you in New York. Did he come with you?"

"Why the hell should it matter to you, Ranger? Thanks for calling. Ring me again sometime when you can be civil. Bye, now." And I hung up.

I'd been looking forward to his call. Hearing his voice, even for a minute, brought back the old yearning, as strong as ever. Maybe my adventure with Rex made me feel somehow that Ranger and I, too, could work things out. But after our aborted phone call, I wondered: could our relationship ever work any better than Rex and Sparky's? Nothing seemed even remotely possible that evening. I desperately wished my grandfather were around to provide a sympathetic shoulder and some needed advice.

I thought about calling Rex and decided against it. I didn't want to interfere, as much as I longed to hear the comfort of his voice and his laughter. Of course, what I most wanted was for him to say that things hadn't worked out. He was catching the next flight to Indianapolis, and could I meet him at the airport?

Rex did call, a week or so later, but not to say that he was heading for Indiana. He and Sparky were back in Bensalem, following a relaxing visit to Rochester.

"I'm glad we didn't head straight back to Bucks County. It was good to spend some time with Mother and Dad. Sparky, of course, was on his best behavior."

"Really?"

"We needed a little time together. I think we've reached an understanding."

"That was quick. And this happened in bed, I imagine."

"Well, not entirely." An awkward pause. Then: "I gotta say, Neil. He really *is* remarkable in bed. And, if you'll forgive a little bragging, he's hung like a jackass."

"Which serves as a model for his behavior, based on my recollection."

"I suppose on occasion. But when he's standing in front of me naked, I've got only one thing on my mind. He knows how to use what he's got in ways that satisfy both of us."

Jealousy poked its hole through my belly.

"You're the one who said there had to be more to a relationship than sex."

"And there is." He didn't elaborate. I didn't want to hear it anyway.

"But when you picked me up along that Pennsylvania highway, there wasn't anyone in the world I needed more than you. You saved my life, and I'm not exaggerating."

"You're welcome. I needed you just as much at that time." I might have added that I *still* needed him just as much.

"I read *A Connecticut Yankee in King Arthur's Court* while I was in Rochester. Twice over. Laughed my ass off. It's brilliant! I never would have discovered it, if you hadn't been so generous. Do you want me to send the book back? Your grandfather's inscription and all—I'm sure it's got real sentimental value for you."

"Keep it. Really. My grandfather has a first-edition set of the complete works with his annotations penciled in the margins, so I've got his copy."

"I'm honored. Thank you. I can see why it's your favorite, and now it's one of mine too. I just started *Pudd'nhead Wilson*, and I couldn't resist picking up *The Gilded Age* and *Joan of Arc* at a secondhand bookshop in Rochester. Are you home again?"

"Yes, back in Indiana."

"And Ranger?"

"We spoke on the phone once, briefly. He knew when I got back because I'd delivered Spot to his house. Ranger was dying to hear about you and about the trip. But he couldn't bring himself to ask, and I didn't volunteer anything."

"Probably a smart move. So what's next?"

"I have no idea. Ranger doesn't seem to have any interest in meeting me, so that's where we stand. After he quit drinking, it was easier for him to concentrate on pretending to be straight, because he didn't have the alcohol as an excuse to let his guard down. As far as I know, he's still not drinking and still pretending he wants to be married to a woman, even if he and Marlene aren't exactly having an easy time of it. That's the way it goes. I won't have anything more to do with him until he's untangled from her. If I can stop myself."

"You've got the willpower. Do it."

I changed the subject. "How are things between you and Sparky now that you're back in Bensalem?"

"Better, actually. And I really mean it."

"He's not talking about marrying a woman again, is he?"

"No. I think you scared him a little—I doubt if it ever occurred to him that he could lose me. He's actually making some progress in coming out now. It's slow, and he's very cautious, but he's introducing me as his partner now, instead of his roommate. We just started some couples counseling this week—at my suggestion—but he admitted that it could be useful, and the first session went well. I'm hopeful. He's even hinted that we might get married ourselves one of these days. I'm not rushing him. But I have you to thank for that, too."

Great. "I hope things work out the way you want, Rex. But you know my offer still stands. If you ever need a place to go, you're always welcome here, no questions asked. Just let me know when and where, and I'll even drive straight to Bucks County if you need to escape."

"I'm grateful. I don't think you'll need to do that, but it's a good thing to have in my back pocket just in case. Thank you."

"Even if you just need a vacation. Come on out. I'll be happy to show you everything our fair state has to offer."

"Which is—?"

Hmm… "Hoosiers, mostly."

He laughed. "In my back pocket. Thanks, Neil."

"Anytime. Thank you for calling, Rex. Please keep in touch."

"I will. You do the same."

Both of us were silent for a moment. I was reluctant to hang up, to sever the connection, and maybe he was too.

"I'd guess I'd better get along," I said.

"Yes. Me, too."

"Take care of yourself, Rex. If it means anything, I love you."

"Of *course* it means something to me. I love you, too."

Maybe he did, but not in any way that was useful to me at the moment. We traded goodbyes. And I had a good old-fashioned pull-out-all-stops cry afterward.

I missed him, yearned for him. Or—Ranger, maybe? Or just a man's hands on me?

After an idle and frustrating couple of weeks, and with no other handy options, I contacted my former boss at the country club, who was eager and willing to offer my old job back. I fell into the old rut with surprising, depressing ease. Without enthusiasm, I resumed my occasional trysts with a couple of patrons from the country club, who were thrilled that I had returned. But I found nothing satisfying in them beyond the seven minutes leading to ejaculation. I met with Scotty from time to time. And missed Granddad more than ever.

Before I became a homeowner, my free time was truly free. I could read, see a movie, hang out with a friend, sleep in...but after Granddad left me his property, my leisure time evaporated under the severe glare of responsibility. The exterior brick of his courtly and spacious two-story house enclosed three bedrooms, an expansive living room and dining room, a large kitchen and den, a finished basement, and the two-car detached garage in the back. A full porch stretched across the front with a comfortable, creaky porch swing, just made for morning coffee and the newspaper. The house sat on a charming lot, painstakingly landscaped with style and skill. But behind the appealing facade lurked the reality of homeownership, of maintenance indoors and out, of gutters to clean, flower gardens to weed and tend and water and fertilize, a yard to mow and trim, an attic and basement and nine rooms separating them to keep clean.

My one-bedroom apartment had been easy to maintain; at most, I'd probably spent about half an hour each week on cursory upkeep. But the house presented a whole different challenge. Although my grandfather was a tidy man, he was also old enough to recognize that mopping and vacuuming deserved to be low on his priority list. When I'd point out that I could write my name in the dust on the dining room table, he reminded me that no one on his deathbed ever wished he'd spent more time housekeeping.

I commiserated regularly with my parents, who'd learned the same lessons thirty-five years earlier when they purchased their home. They proved to be a generous source of inspiration, and, occasionally, assistance in the yard, though my dad stopped short of actually entering the house.

Homeownership is not for the faint of heart; I confess there were times I cursed my grandfather for naming me his sole heir because I felt a responsibility to keep the place up in a way that would make him proud. I wanted anyone who walked down the street to be surprised to discover that Granddad no longer lived there; I wanted the transition to be that seamless, as a kind of homage to his life.

A month or so after returning from New York, I sat on the porch swing with my morning coffee and the newspaper. On page two, there were pictures of a mangled vehicle and a headshot of a man who looked vaguely familiar. I couldn't quite place him at first. Thomas J. Traynor had been killed in a single-car crash at about one o'clock, two mornings previous, slamming his silver Corvette into a guard rail on a curve while being chased by the police. He'd been seen leaving a bar, obviously impaired, and someone had called to report him. His speed at the time of the crash had been clocked at nearly ninety miles an hour, and he'd probably been killed instantly. He left a widow and a grown son.

I examined the photo again, a handsome man with a thin face, and realized that I'd met him once, at the Whiskey River, Ranger's old haunt. Tom Traynor had bought me a soda.

Ranger called out of the blue to report that he was but days away from the anniversary of his first full year of sobriety. In spite of the jinx of looking ahead, his primary AA group wanted to throw a little party with a cake and a single candle to present him with a shiny one-year medallion for his pocket.

Would I attend?

He'd asked Marlene, but she refused, maintaining the position that polite (non-drinking) citizens shouldn't be seen at such events because people would talk. But Ranger wanted to be sure I could be there the following Thursday night.

Of course I could.

Nervous, I waited for him outside the designated meeting place, the back room of the local Knights of Columbus hall, about twenty minutes before seven o'clock. For an absurd moment, I wondered if I would have trouble recognizing him and promptly scoffed at such idiocy. It had only been a few months, I told myself, not twenty years.

Out of the shadows he appeared, wearing a clean and pressed white button-down shirt, faded blue jeans, well-worn white sneakers, the same battered Stetson. He looked wondrous; he took my breath away and my heart with it all over again. Damn him for the effortless power he held over me and for his complete dismissal of it. In the warm dusk, his eyes glinted, hopeful perhaps; he'd jammed his hands deep into his pockets— lest he might reach for me with them, put them on me, around me, and draw me to him, perhaps? A tantalizing shock of chest hair escaped the top button of his shirt.

In short, he was as sexy as all fuck, the dirty, ass-grinding, cum-stained, cock-sucking, exquisite throbbing orgasm summed up in his favorite four-letter word. He peered out from underneath the brim of his Stetson, and a shy grin hid beneath the mustache, as welcome (and nearly as large now) as a mat on your front porch.

"Neil! Hey!" He sounded relieved, as if I might have stood him up.

"Hey, yourself."

"Thanks for coming."

I almost responded with the punchline from one of Granddad's old jokes (has the milkman come yet? No, but he's breathing hard) but thought better of it. Instead, I merely said, "You're welcome."

He nodded. "You hear about Tom Traynor?"

"I saw it in the paper."

He shook his head. "What a fucking waste."

I agreed.

"That would've been me one of these days if I didn't quit."

I agreed with that, too. "Did you ever see him, or those other guys from the bar?"

He shook his head. "Not for a long time. Ran into Billy at the grocery store about six or eight months back, maybe. He looks like shit. We didn't have nothin' to say to each other." He looked at his watch. "We can go in anytime."

"Okay." I followed him into the hall. I wanted to take his hand, put an arm around his shoulder, maybe—something, anything to show everyone who might see us that he was with me, that I was here by his express invitation. With *me*, so step back; leave him be, and no one will get hurt. But he didn't reach out and didn't give me any signal that such a gesture would be appreciated, let alone tolerated.

He grabbed a cup of coffee and headed for the front row of chairs. I sat far behind, against the wall. There was a good-sized crowd, perhaps twenty-five people or more, men and women, young and old, because Ranger was well-known around the AA scene by then and well-liked, I suspect. I'm sure many of those attending were as eager as he was for him to reach the one-year point. I hoped Ranger would volunteer to testify this night in honor of the occasion. I longed to hear some kind of story from him, even if it were only some memory from his drinking days that I'd already heard half a dozen times. I'd settle for a nursery rhyme. But beyond giving his name, claiming ownership and responsibility for his alcoholism, and saying he had accumulated a year and three days of sobriety thus far, he said nothing.

The meeting chairman presented Ranger with his newest medallion, the bronze one-year coin embossed with "To thine own self be true." I knew it would be the last relatively easy one for him. For the first year, he'd collected a different color every month, the gratification of a new token earned every thirty days to carry as a sign, as proof not just of membership in the club but of a certain rank or status within the organization. But after this, there wouldn't be another coin until he reached eighteen months, and after that, just one per year.

How bad, I wondered, was the craving tonight? Would tomorrow be the day he gave in, or could he show the demon who was boss for another twenty-four hours?

After the meeting came the refreshments, neon-pink lemonade, and a sheet cake offering congratulations in fancy script for a year of sobriety, a day at a time. I'd brought Granddad's camera to document the encouragement and cake-slicing, and I took as many pictures as I felt I could get away with. But I also took a snapshot of Ranger afterward, focusing my telephoto lens on him, unaware, sitting by himself, the one-year coin on the table in front of him. When my flash went off, he was startled, pasting on a smile too late. In the resulting picture, I would find him looking utterly beaten, wearing every one of his forty-five years like a bruise and a year of sobriety like a scar.

But as the guest of honor, he was not permitted to dwell on his thoughts for long. He was pulled back into the circle, to the socializing that is at least as important to the meeting as the testament. He accepted the envious congratulations of the relative newcomers who could claim but a couple of weeks or months of sobriety, and the condescending claps-on-the-back from the elder statesmen who carried six- or ten- or twenty-year coins in their pockets. Could they ever let go of the thought that it could all end tomorrow with a single sip of wine or whiskey?

I did not envy any of them.

After taking pictures of the main event, I had little to do. I was already conspicuous as the one guy who didn't offer the ritual introduction, and

I'd learned a long time ago that meetings were not considered spectator sports for non-alcoholics. So I sat at the back of the room in the shadows.

As the crowd thinned a bit, I noticed Ranger talking to an effervescent blonde who looked to be close to him in age. Willowy and attractive, she wore her hair cut short and styled, and she dressed in snug-fitting black jeans, an equally snug bright-yellow top, and knee-high black boots. She and Ranger were taking turns whispering in each other's ear and laughing. I couldn't tell who was flirting with whom, but I was certain it was taking place.

I fumed. Not again. He and Marlene had barely been married seven months. Was Ranger lining up Number Six before Number Five had even filed for divorce? I wondered if it was a new record. I was also plenty pissed off, and I decided to interrupt their cozy little tête-à-tête and see if I had any sort of snowball's chance (in any sort of hell) to short-circuit the situation before it went too far.

"Ranger?"

He turned to me, guilty, and the woman faced me too—only *not* guilty. Not at all.

"Oh. Hey, Neil."

"Hey." Since no introduction was forthcoming, I stuck out my hand. "I'm Neil Graham," I said to the woman. "Ranger is—a friend."

"I don't doubt it." She laughed. as bubbly and musical as ginger ale. Her blue eyes sparked and sparkled. "Laura Melusky." She took my hand in hers and shook it firmly. "Pleased to meet you, Neil."

Another Melusky? I looked sharply at Ranger, who was busy studying his sneakers.

"You seem to share a last name."

Laura laughed again, as if I'd just cracked the funniest joke she'd ever heard. "Aren't you the observant type?" She lowered her voice conspiratorially. "We're all over the place. You better look out."

I was slightly confused.

"Don't worry, hon. I just never went back to my maiden name after we divorced. When you grow up with a last name like Vercingetorix, can you blame me? I didn't even learn to spell it correctly until I was in the second grade." She laughed again. "I married the first guy who asked me, and guess who it turned out to be? I probably should have waited for the second guy, huh?"

Ranger had turned the color of his pickup truck. He was still staring intently at his sneakers, apparently memorizing them in case he'd be tested later.

"So you two were married before."

"Small world, huh?"

I was sure Ranger, for one, wished it had been significantly smaller at this moment, or at least reduced by one. "Five whole years. Good God. I still can't believe we lasted that long."

I'd never thought to ask Ranger if any of his ex-wives were still in town. I knew the fourth, Marlene's predecessor, had left Indiana, but the others might live down the road from him, for all I knew. What, I wondered, might I learn about him if I cornered these women? Laura might prove to be a valuable fount of information.

"Remember the reception at the V.F.W. hall, Ranger?" Laura said. "You did that striptease, waving your pecker around for everyone to see." She laughed again; Ranger looked as if he wanted to sink into the floor. "I hate to admit it, Neil, but the only thing we ever had in common was that we both liked beer and Willie Nelson records."

I remembered that she'd introduced herself at the meeting and announced that she'd been sober for twelve years plus. I asked if memory had served me well.

"Yup. Very good!"

"Congratulations."

"Thanks. One day at a time—and all that 'Big Book' crap!" I suspected that Laura hadn't fought quite the same battle as Ranger since she quit drinking. Perhaps she'd been stronger, or not as dependent upon the alcohol fix as he was. She'd also had a eleven-year head start on him, and perhaps that too made the process a bit easier.

"I hardly ever go to meetings anymore. But a friend of mine told me about the party tonight, and I wouldn't have missed it for love or money. I mean, who'd have thought Ranger would quit drinking at all? And for a whole year so far! That is just *so* amazing!" She grabbed him around the neck and gave him a big, messy kiss on the cheek. He squirmed like a little boy.

Then she turned her attention back to me. "We got rip-roaring drunk celebrating our fifth anniversary, see, and I woke up the next morning with the mother of all hangovers. I decided then and there I was just plain sick of it, and I wasn't going to let it happen again. So I sobered up, starting on that day, all by myself."

After eliminating beer from her diet, she'd taken a good, hard look at their marriage, she said, and realized that they didn't have much going for themselves. Ranger had gotten pretty upset when she quit drinking because it was the only social life they had together.

"The last thing I needed was to come home from work every night to a drunk husband who could never get it up." She laughed again. "I have my needs!" She slapped me on the back. "Ranger got thrown out of the Air Force right about then, and he was sitting at home with nothing to do but chug down one six-pack after another. It was time for me to fly. And I did, thank God. Smartest decision I ever made. I never got a cent of alimony, but I got a better last name as a souvenir, at least! And we had some laughs. Didn't we, Ranger?"

Ranger muttered something under his breath, but I couldn't hear it. Laura didn't seem to notice. She continued chattering, and I—if not our companion—was all ears.

"Were you the first Mrs. Melusky? The second?" I asked. "Or maybe the third?"

"That's a good question. There's a bunch of us around. I think I came third, actually, but I can't keep 'em all straight—" and she cackled, patting me on the arm—"so to speak! You know what I mean, right? Did Ranger ever tell you about that time I came home from work and found him buck naked in the back of that red truck of his?"

"That'll do, Laura." Ranger hastened to intervene. "Neil don't want to hear about all that shit from back when I was drinking."

Except Neil did want to hear about it. Very much. And to my satisfaction, I don't think a freight train could have stopped Laura from continuing her story.

"So I came home from work—I was a secretary for a real estate office in those days. Now I'm a licensed agent myself."

"Congratulations."

"Thanks. Are you in the market for a new home, by any chance?" She pulled a business card out of her purse and presented it to me.

I was willing to humor her, because I knew I'd hear the rest of the tale. And perhaps I derived a bit of perverse satisfaction from Ranger's discomfort too. "Not at the moment. I own a house already, in fact, thanks to my late grandfather. I inherited the family homestead when he died in the spring."

"Sorry to hear about his passing."

"Thanks. We were really close, so it's been tough. He spent his whole life in this town. A university professor. Even Ranger knew him."

Laura laughed again. "And why would Ranger be hanging out with university professors?" She giggled and lowered her voice. "Unless they were really well-hung."

I whispered back. "He was, in fact."

Laura hooted. Ranger clearly wished he were anywhere on the planet but here, in this building at this moment, and I'm sure he would have traded his whole year of sobriety if only Laura (and I, being a part of this humiliation too) had never been born.

"I won't even ask how you know that about your own grandpa," she said.

"It's probably best that you don't."

She remembered that her story had been interrupted. "Oh! Ranger in the back of the pickup truck! So, anyway, so I come home from work late this one night. It's getting on into the fall, right around mid-October, with a little chill in the air and dark by five o'clock. I park my car, and I'm walking into the house, and I hear this weird sound. No idea what it could be. Sounds something like two *animals* going at it, hot and heavy.

"So I listen real close, and I figure out it's coming from the truck bed, which doesn't make a whole lot of sense to me. I walk over there, real quiet, but I could've had a brass band with me, because I don't think Ranger and his buddy would have noticed. I tell you. What I saw in that truck! It was like some gay porno flick—not that I've seen any of those, mind you," she said with a wink and more laughter. By this time, I was laughing right along with her, as if it were contagious. Perhaps I felt as if I had nothing more to lose.

Ranger seemed to have resigned himself to the situation, or at least he figured out that he could do nothing to stop a runaway train. He muttered "Jesus fuck" and backed away from us, grabbed himself another cup of coffee and a second piece of cake. He stood by himself, clearly seething, eating the cake in savage bites and then blowing across the Styrofoam cup to cool the hot liquid. He had nothing left inside himself for the people who approached him with handshakes and congratulations for reaching his milestone.

Laura gave me the rest of the details, how she'd stood by and watched until Ranger had climaxed and then extracted himself, how he'd finally noticed she was standing there and couldn't think of a thing to say except to ask her if she wanted to join them. How she'd filed divorce paperwork the next day. How she'd always had kind of a suspicion he might be that way and finally had some proof.

I recalled the story Rex had told me of Sparky's wife coming home to find them similarly engaged on the kitchen floor. For a moment, I wondered how Rex and Sparky were doing ....

"You guys just make the cutest couple, Neil," Laura said, jarring me from the memory. "I can tell you two were just made for each other. And I'm glad he's finally being true to himself."

I was too surprised to say a word. She gave me a hug, and then gave Ranger one too. With a "see you guys around sometime," she was gone.

The meeting broke up with some reluctance. Who likes to see the end of a satisfactory party? Ranger and I stood outside the K of C hall as the rest of the group filtered away, one or two at a time, congratulating him again as they passed by. He smoked a cigarette and then lit a second, apologetic, saying Marlene didn't know he was smoking again, even though he'd endured the nicotine patch for months. I didn't care. I was reluctant to disconnect from the scene myself, scared for the moment he'd actually walk away from me because I didn't know when (if) I'd see him again. I wanted to tell him not to worry about anything Laura said, that I would keep his secrets forever, and that—improbably—what she'd told me hadn't harmed him in my estimation but only bumped him up a notch or two: at last, I had proof that Ranger the gay man wasn't an illusion.

Having him out of my sight all these months had been difficult enough, but having him so close to me that I could smell him—reach out and actually put my hands on him now, though the contact might sear us both—was torture. The exquisite ache, the craving I felt for him might never wane. Was it anything, anything at all, like Ranger's desire for drink? Were there any twelve steps I could take to help me recover?

Could Ranger ever feel the same again about me, or were we both doomed?

I wondered if he was looking for clues of some sort, proof of how I felt about him, or trying to sort out how he felt about me. He flicked the cigarette butt into the bushes; I watched the glowing end arc through the air and disappear.

"Laura thinks we're a couple," I said. "Isn't that funny?"

He merely sighed and seemed to deflate. Was there regret in that sigh, or merely resignation? He crossed his arms in front of him, protecting himself—from me, perhaps. Or from himself.

"Whatever. Thanks for coming."

"You knew I would, Ranger."

"Yeah. I can always count on ya." I wasn't sure if he intended a compliment. It did not sound like one.

He pulled another cigarette from the pack. It gave his hands something to do. He lit it and inhaled again. Checked his watch. Marlene expected him home, I imagine. I wondered if he told her that he'd see me this evening and immediately wondered why he should.

"Congratulations," I said. "I didn't get a chance to tell you inside."

"Yeah."

"Um, I shot a whole roll of film. You want copies of the pictures?" I wasn't in a single frame, so he could take the photos home and Marlene would not have any reason to be upset—not that she'd have any interest in seeing them.

He shrugged. "I guess."

"Okay. I'll get an extra set of prints for you."

He nodded.

I was desperate to keep him, even for a couple of minutes. Why? I asked myself. What did I have to prove? That I could do it, that I still had some hold over him?

"Um, how are your mom and dad?"

"What?"

"Your parents. How are they?" I'd never met them. I knew nothing about them beyond what Ranger had told me almost two years ago on our first lunch date, as he'd never mentioned them since.

"Why the hell would ya ask about them?"

I sighed. "No reason, Ranger. I'm stalling. I couldn't think of anything to say, and I just want to spend as much time with you as you'll let me."

He seemed surprised. "Oh. They're okay, I guess. I called them—I don't know. A couple months back."

"When did you last see them?"

He shrugged. "Not since I quit drinking."

"Do they know about that?"

"Yup."

"So they've never met Marlene. Do they even know you're married?"

He shrugged. "Probably not five times." Abruptly, he said, "I gotta go," and he started walking away. Suddenly angry, I stood in the light by the door and willed him to turn around and look at me. He did not, and, desperate, I had to get his attention.

"I miss you, you son-of-a-bitch," I yelled after him.

He turned then and looked at me with haunted, hungry eyes, and until that moment, I was positive he did not feel the same way at all.

In the space of five seconds, he retraced his steps, wrapped his hands around my neck and pulled my mouth to his in a bruising kiss that might have seemed like punishment from anyone else, all the dirty magic of hell's fire and redemption rolled into one. He turned and loped away without looking back.

All the way home in the car, I could taste his mouth, and something else—the exquisite longing in him that I thought nothing I could say or do would ever bring back.

Early the next morning—as in two a.m. early—I was awakened by a banging on the door. It jerked me from sleep into wide awake, initially from fear. I reached for the clock and tried to focus. Only something evil could be knocking at this hour.

I wrapped myself in a bathrobe and reached the door in a fog. The hammering didn't let up, and as I opened the door, Ranger tumbled inside and then stood up, laughing.

"Neil!"

He was shirtless, wearing only blue jeans, sneakers, and his old Stetson. I hadn't seen his furry chest exposed in so long I'd forgotten how much pleasure I gained from it, but he wouldn't stand still to let me enjoy the view. He didn't have to tell me that he'd fallen rather spectacularly off the wagon. He carried the remains of a six-pack, one can still hooked to its plastic yoke. He was lit up, glowing from the inside, and he didn't say anything as he unbuttoned his pants and let loose a rampant erection, of which he was particularly and justifiably proud.

It was certainly arousing, I must say, under my robe, I responded in kind. Immediately.

"Looks like you were expecting me," he said as he untied the sash and revealed my excitement as well. "Whatcha waitin' for? It's all yours."

"Ranger, wait. What's going on?"

"Wait, *hell*. I been waitin' too long. What the fuck do ya think's going on? *This* is what's going on. My dick could punch through solid concrete." He wrapped a fist around said dick and stroked himself.

"I think you've had a couple of beers."

"I think yer right." He popped open the last can and offered it to me. "Les' drink a li'l toast—to sobriety!"

"No, thanks. It's a little early in the morning."

"Sure as hell ain't gonna waste it." He brought it to his mouth and downed half of it. He stopped to gulp in air, then emptied the can and crushed it in his fist, tossing it on the floor.

"What about AA? Your one-year anniversary?"

"*Fuck* AA! And now I wanna fuck your sweet ass."

So there was a connection. After relieving himself of the inconvenience of sobriety, he had other appetites to satisfy. And I (Neil of the Sweet Ass) came to mind, of course.

"What happened?"

"Shut up, Neil." He wrapped himself around me, and when he put his mouth over mine—making speech not only pointless but also impossible—I surrendered. I wanted to. I didn't question further. If I were glad I had nothing directly to do with the violation of his sobriety (beyond wishing for it), who could blame me for taking advantage of the pleasure of his company this early morning?

Who, indeed?

As he pulled me toward the couch, he said he wouldn't stop until we'd done everything we used to do twice over.

"What brought this on, all of a sudden? What happened?"

"Nothin' happened. If I wanna have me a beer, I'll have me a goddamn beer."

"Just one?"

He grinned. "Yeah. One at a time."

"How many times over did you have just one?"

He snickered.

"Is that your first six-pack or your second?"

"First, second, third. Who the hell knows? Jus' shut th' fuck up. If ya can't think of nothin' better to do with yer mouth, lemme show ya."

He kicked off his sneakers and shucked his pants and we pulled me onto the couch, but his virulence dissipated as swiftly as if someone had flipped the "off" switch. Within a minute, he was snoring, and I couldn't even rouse him enough to stop the noise. I rounded up a pillow for him, wrapped a blanket around him, and took myself upstairs to the bedroom. At least I could shut the door and block out the snoring.

I checked the clock; barely twenty minutes had passed since he arrived. He was due at the Buick dealership by seven, and I knew he would be in no condition to make it after a few hours of drunken sleep. I grabbed my alarm clock, set it for 6:30, and settled into the sheets, but my eyes would not shut.

I wished so many things. I wished Ranger hadn't fallen asleep. I would have happily engaged in any kind of sexual play that he asked of me, in spite of Marlene and my vow that I'd have nothing more to do with him while they were still attached. I was so damned lonely for his company, for the feeling of his mouth against mine, his skinny, hairy legs wrapping around me, the urgency of his cock telegraphing his arousal, the lusty comings and goings. I missed using his chest for a pillow when we were done. But for his sake, I found myself wishing he hadn't fallen off the wagon. He wouldn't like himself in the morning, and I knew he would hurt in more ways than one.

For months, I'd longed for the old Ranger to come back to me, the drinking Ranger, the guy who could (almost) guarantee a little rowdy fun anytime he spent the night, but how selfish was that longing? He'd only have killed himself, or someone else, if he'd continued to drink. His system had gone a year without alcohol, and that first beer tonight probably charged him like a thousand volts of electricity applied to his testicles, rocketing him across the moon. After going that far, why not aim for Saturn, or the outer reaches of the Milky Way? So he went for a second, and a third, a fifth, a ninth, who knows how many? Beer made him feel bulletproof, he used to tell me. But it wasn't bullets that would do him in.

And what about Marlene? Surely, she would be wondering where he was, perhaps afraid or at least anxious when he didn't turn up. I felt ashamed of myself.

I watched the clock go from three to four and five and six, and at half-past, I went downstairs. I opened the blinds and let in a little light, enough to see him. He was still sprawled on the couch, naked, uncovered, quiet. I wanted nothing more than to climb on top and fold myself around him. But the last thing he'd want after a night of drinking was that kind of attention; he'd told me more than once to leave him the fuck alone when I dared to approach him on a hungover morning.

And there had been too many of those. He'd learned long ago to function with a hangover, and most people probably wouldn't even notice because they were so accustomed to his aloof nature. Fixing cars was ingrained in him now, and I suspect he could have done it in his sleep, so why not when he was hungover as well? Based on evidence from his trash bin in the old days, I'm sure on more than one occasion that the thermos he took with him to work held a little tomato juice and Tabasco and a lot of vodka to get him through a rough morning.

"Ranger?" I shook him very gently.

"Neil?" he whispered. He sounded a bit bewildered. "Is that you?"

"Good morning, Ranger."

"Is it?" he whispered. He sat up a little too suddenly and fell back against the pillow for a moment before swinging his feet over the edge of the couch and sitting more slowly. "Jesus fuck. How'd I get here?"

"Don't tell me you were so drunk last night that you can't remember."

He held his head. "Fuck. Fuck. Fuck. Fuck. Fuck. Fuck. Fuck."

"We didn't get around to anything like that, actually. You were very interested at first, but you passed out as soon as you hit the couch. So your precious virtue is still intact." Although I was tempted, I didn't complete the thought: even if your sobriety isn't. And I suppose there was no call for me to be snide.

"What time is it?"

I looked at the clock. "Twenty-five to seven."

He muttered again. "Fuck. My head hurts."

"I would suggest that you're the slightest bit hung over."

"Ain't nothin' slight about this. Goddamn. Don't wanna do nothin' but lose consciousness and sleep for a week."

"Then you should. You want to call in sick?"

He thought about it for a moment. "I better. Yeah." His boss had known about Ranger's sobriety and wasn't likely to think there was anything amiss other than some kind of actual unexpected illness, an upset stomach, or virus. I handed Ranger my phone, and he called the garage to make his excuses. Ranger said he was sure he'd feel better the next day, and he thanked the boss for being understanding.

Ranger handed the phone back to me.

"Do you want to call Marlene? She's probably worrying about you."

He considered. Shrugged. Shook his head. "I gotta get to a meeting. When d'ya have to be at work?"

"One o'clock. Same as usual."

"Could ya take me? I don't know if I should drive."

"I know you shouldn't. Is there a meeting someplace close by?"

"What day is it?"

"Friday."

"Methodist church at noon."

"I'll take you. Why don't you sleep for a while? I'll wake you around eleven so you can shower."

He nodded. Carefully, he positioned himself back on the couch. I wrapped the blanket around him and closed the shades. I called one of my assistants at the bar to let him know I might be a few minutes late. After breakfast, I found I was able to catch a quick nap myself, waking in plenty of time to get him into the shower. I would like to have joined him, but this wasn't the time. The additional four hours of sleep didn't appear to have done him much good.

I loaned him a shirt, socks, and a razor. He emerged from the bathroom looking as tidy as possible under the circumstances. His eyes were still bloodshot and his skin, usually swarthy, had taken on a sort of pallor. I warrant he felt as sick as he looked. I fed him a little dry toast and black coffee, but he didn't keep it down for long.

He was silent during the drive to the church. Before we went into the meeting, he handed me the one-year AA token from his pocket. "Twelve months of sobriety right down the shitter," he said, downcast. I expected him to make some sort of flippant comment like "easy come, easy go," but he couldn't summon anything. "Goddamn it," he muttered. "God-fucking-damn it."

He eased himself out of the car slowly and headed for the church basement door. After a few steps, he turned back. "Will ya come in with me? Hate to ask, but I can't face this alone."

Without a word, I followed him.

Ten others sat in a circle of folding chairs, and at first, he took a seat behind them, outside the circle. Most of them recognized Ranger from previous meetings. Many of them had been at the party last night, and all encouraged him to join the rest. He moved his chair but didn't look anyone in the eye. They waved me forward as well, and I thanked them but stayed in the back. The man who chaired the meeting wore a three-piece suit. Impeccably groomed, he could have been a bank president, surgeon, CEO of a big corporation, or just a grocery clerk who liked to dress well.

"I know we've got places to be, and some of us are on our lunch breaks, so let's get to it. This meeting will come to order. Hi, everybody. My name is Frank, and I'm an alcoholic."

"Hi, Frank!" Everyone responded, aggressively cheerful.

"I haven't had a drink in eight years, three months, and eleven days." I could tell how proud he was. He had kept an exact count, and he wanted full credit. Maybe it's all he had. Everyone clapped.

Around the circle, each person went through the same ritual. They gave their names, admitted their sins, and stated how long they had been sober, from a couple of weeks to sixteen years. I marveled at the fact that the woman who had gone that long without alcohol still felt the craving and still believed in the power of an AA meeting every week to reinforce her resolve.

When Ranger's turn came, he gave his name and said he was an alcoholic. Everyone said hello, and his courage failed him. "Ain't had a drink in...'bout ten hours," he whispered, and then he seemed to crumple like a fender in a car crash, and broke down in sobs. I hadn't expected such a reaction, and my heart went out to him. If others in the group were surprised or shocked at his confession—his year of sobriety had been much discussed and greatly admired the previous night—they showed no sign. Immediately, ten people surrounded him with comforting hands and comforting words.

Gently, Frank asked Ranger if he wanted to talk about it.

He shook his head.

Frank handed an aluminum token to Ranger. I knew it spelled out "One day at a time" on it, the sobriety coin given to those just beginning the long and arduous journey. Ranger clenched his fist around it and sat quietly for the rest of the meeting. Others testified, sharing stories of their humiliation at the mercy of drink, their struggles to overcome, the challenge of it, the need to remain focused on today, not tomorrow or next week. Ranger sat in their midst as Exhibit A. Or Brand X.

Coffee and cookies were served at the end of the meeting, but Ranger slipped out as soon as he could, and I trailed after him. We returned to my house, and I helped him undress and put him in my bed. When I left for work a few minutes later, he was already asleep, but by the time I came home that evening, he and his truck were gone. I wished I could call Granddad for consolation.

He'd ask, "Did you get lucky, at least?" And when I'd say no, he'd remind me that I wouldn't want Ranger on those terms anyway. And he would have been right, but being right is lousy company and pale shelter when you're lonely.

And Ranger was many miles distant, his head still splitting, no doubt in need of comfort and sympathy and possibly trying to appease Marlene. I couldn't help him now. And I couldn't come up with any way he could help me at the moment, either.

18

Four weeks later, early one Saturday and a rare day off—following a very late-night wedding reception at the country club, which I'd agreed to work—my phone rang, waking me a few hours into a sound sleep. The noise startled me so much that I knocked the phone and the lamp off the nightstand. In the dark, as I climbed out of the sheets and fumbled for the lamp on the floor, I managed to kick the phone under the bed. When I finally retrieved it, I groused before I even knew who was on the line: "This had better be good."

Ranger's laughter greeted me. "Wake up, ya son-of-a-bitch."

I fumbled for the clock, a quarter past five. I'd been planning to sleep until eight or nine at least. "What do you want, Ranger?"

"Rise and shine."

"You can get a rise out of me any time, but it's too early for shining. I wasn't sure I'd ever hear from you again. I think you blame me for what happened after the party last month." I had not, in fact, seen him since the day after he fell off the wagon.

He laughed again. "I don't know what the hell you're talking about."

"You do, too."

"Fuck you."

"Ranger, anytime you want. Just say the word."

He laughed again. "You're shameless."

"I don't care if I am. But don't offer if you don't mean it."

He was silent.

"Come on over. I got the day off. I'm in bed. Naked, and I'm getting a hard-on just thinking about what we could accomplish under the circumstances."

He said nothing for the longest time, and I wondered if he, too, wasn't growing aroused. The silence finally became uncomfortable. "Okay, so why are you calling me at this hour on a Saturday?"

"Why don'tcha come over here instead?"

"What for? Don't you think Marlene might object if we have sex at your place? Maybe that's not what you want at all."

"Or maybe—"

"Maybe what? Maybe you *do* want sex?"

He didn't reply.

"Ranger, I'm going back to bed right now, unless this is an emergency. Is it?"

He sighed. "Look, I'm sorry I called so early. I couldn't sleep. I been up since four o'clock, and ya been on my mind. Ever since the party, I— I can't—"

He fell silent again. What was the rest of his unfinished sentence? What was the thing he couldn't do? Did it have something to do with what I couldn't do either, as long as he wouldn't let me get close to him, wouldn't let me touch him, wouldn't let me unbutton his shirt and put my hands against his belly and wrestle him out of his pants? Did his unfinished sentence hide the same ache that I felt?

Or maybe I read too much into it. Even though a month had passed, maybe he was concerned about the story his gregarious ex-wife had shared at the party. Maybe he wanted to make sure it didn't get back to his current wife, though if I wanted to tell Marlene about Ranger's being caught with a man, I wouldn't share an unsubstantiated second-hand tale that included a stranger in the back of a pickup truck. Not with all the juicy first-hand stories I could share about Ranger and me ....

I began to doubt as Ranger remained silent; a serious change of heart since the party might stretch credulity, and I didn't want to take any more chances. "Look, if all you want to do is confess your sins, let me sleep for a couple of hours. I'll call you back and give you penance later."

"It ain't that. Marlene's gonna be gone most of the day. Her and a couple of girlfriends are going to them outlet stores up north. She figures I'll weed the garden and cut the grass while she's gone."

"It's August. Who has any mowing to do in August? Everyone's grass is dead."

"You ain't seen mine, on account of Marlene makes me water it every goddamn night. If I don't spend the day in the yard, she'll bitch at me all week. Ya wanna come over and help me? We'd get it done quick."

"And then what?"

He chuckled. "I got a couple ideas."

As did I. I didn't want to press him too much; it was the closest thing to an invitation I'd gotten from him since he quit drinking. Perhaps that kiss we'd shared had awakened some sleeping dogs, and possibly they'd been growling and barking ever since I'd seen him at the Knights of Columbus hall. My erection snapped to full attention.

"Are you sure Marlene will be gone?"

"Her friends are coming to pick her up at seven-thirty. I'll call you when the coast is clear."

"This is your last chance, Ranger."

"That's the only one I need." I could almost hear him grinning when he said goodbye.

The clock said half-past five. I was wide awake and wouldn't be able to sleep anymore, so I showered and dressed and headed over to the diner, the same one we used to frequent, only a few miles from his house, where I could have breakfast and wait for his call. From there, I could reach his place within ten minutes.

By the time Ranger called again, I'd finished my breakfast and was sitting in the car at the parking lot, trying to concentrate on the newspaper. Seven minutes after he hung up, I pulled into the driveway. He was a little startled by the speed at which I appeared.

"You fly over here, or what?" He pulled me close to him; he seemed to be a little agitated himself, and the optimism of my own arousal seemed justified by his own.

"Something like that. Let's just say I was close by, loitering with intent. But don't worry. Marlene didn't see me."

"She's gone and you're here, and that's all I care about." The first thing I wanted to put anywhere was my mouth on his, and he seemed to agree. I brushed my fingers against the nape of his neck, into the short hairs, still bristly from the recent haircut. His eyes closed slowly and he muttered under his breath, a kind of low growl of satisfaction, allowing himself to be lulled by my proximity, by the warmth of the sun on our backs. "You taste good," he said, when we finally stopped to catch our breath.

"Thanks. You do, too."

Now that we were together, under the warming sun with the promise of a whole day to spend as we pleased, I think both of us felt a bit little timid. Ranger was suddenly almost shy. It had been more than a year since we'd been intimate, before he was forced to sober up. I don't know if he recalled the last time, but I certainly did. It had been memorable in all the wrong ways.

As far as I knew, however, he had never done any of those things when sober. I don't know if that thought occurred to him. I pushed out of my mind the fact that he was married (still) to a woman (again), and I didn't like to think of myself as a homewrecker. But how many times had I shared my bed with married men from the country club, with no thought of the fact that they owed commitment to others? And felt no guilt for accommodating them as they cheated on their wives, in spite of my grandfather's disapproval?

The difference, I supposed, is that I'd fallen for Ranger, and that put him into an entirely separate, elite category. I don't know if I'd ever claimed to be truly in love with anyone. But—Ranger. Damn him for mixing me up. I still couldn't quite believe his change of heart. I wondered what had brought it on after a year. What brings any of us to the breaking point?

Maybe, I thought crassly, he was just horny, and he knew I'd accommodate him. And I was angry with myself, not only for his certainty but for the weakness in me that would likely do what he asked. Eagerly.

I'd been dreaming about this moment for so long that I could hardly realize it was within reach. We could tear off our clothes and molest each other right there in the front yard, and it would be done. But I knew it would not satisfy me. Our encounter, so long in coming, had to be special, memorable, and I didn't want it to end too abruptly—whatever happened today might have to last me a long time, possibly even forever. I'd been perfectly willing to meet Ranger as often as he chose while he was married to his fourth wife. I'd never met her; the lust and love I felt for Ranger was enough for me to ignore her, to disregard her feelings entirely. But I knew Marlene, even if I didn't like her. And I wouldn't like myself if I let Ranger make me his boy on the side, his down-low solace from another disastrous marriage.

Why couldn't Ranger just divorce her and marry me instead?

He rescued me from my sudden crisis of conscience. "What d'ya say we finish the yard work first? Then we got plenty of time to do whatever the fuck we want." He grabbed my crotch. "Which might include whatever the fuck. Or, hell, we could just fuck instead and to hell with the yard."

My eyes snapped open and I pushed him away, not roughly but forcefully enough to serve as a warning.

He laughed. "What's the matter, Neil? You want me to suck your dick instead?"

How romantic. Instantly I recalled what Rex had pointed out to me: getting one's rocks off—mere fucking and sucking—had little to do with actual love. I supposed I had as much right as anyone to know Ranger's intent, if he even knew it himself. Even if he might, at some point, willingly admit to being gay, would that version of Ranger necessarily be any more faithful than the presumed straight one had been? Given the imprecise nature of our encounters up to this point, what chance would we have?

I hadn't managed to sustain a partnership myself, regardless of how many times I'd convinced myself I'd found Mister Right. But I'd never met a man like Ranger, either, and he made me feel improbably, absurdly confident that we could forge a lasting bond. And all he would have to do is commit.

And untangle himself from his current wife.

And not opt to marry any more women.

It would never happen. In a moment of crystal clarity, I laughed at the absurdity of it all.

"What's so funny?"

"Me. You. I've been carrying this crazy notion in my head for nearly two years, ever since I met this naked, drunken guy in his pickup truck, singing at the top of his voice at two o'clock in the morning. He invited me into his truck, and I accepted his invitation. After that, I made a fatal mistake."

He was mystified. "What the hell ya talking about?"

I shook my head. "Never mind. You wouldn't understand."

He spat, disgusted. "Gimme a goddamn chance. I ain't as ignorant as ya think."

I hadn't meant to suggest that, and I apologized.

"All right. I fell in love with that guy. Okay? Line and sinker and both hooks. How stupid is that? I don't know what the hell I even mean to you, Ranger, if I mean anything at all. You invite me here because you're so desperate for a blowjob that you can't think straight, and I'm the only one you can think of who's dumb enough to fall for your come-on. Right? And I race right over here because I'm desperate to be the guy who'll give you that blowjob. Or anything else you want. Maybe that will satisfy you today—and I can't tell you how much I need to wrap my arms around you and put my mouth on yours and the rest of you. But I get the feeling that all you need is a blowjob from a guy—any guy—and some nameless ass to fuck. And I'm sorry, but I don't think I can do that right now."

He meant too much to me. Perhaps if he'd invited me to his truck after the party, I might have been more inclined to give him what he wanted—when it was just the two of us in the warm dark. But in the unforgiving light of day, now that I'd had time to think about it, I decided it wasn't going to happen. Not now. Goddamn it. And him.

He didn't expect such a storm. He took a step back from me, a little uncertain about what I might do. He also couldn't think of a thing to say, but I had no problem filling the gap. I had plenty of words and a captive audience.

"What the hell *do* you want, Ranger? Where do you see yourself in ten years?"

"Sober. I hope." He sounded doubtful.

"I agree that sobriety is important, because I don't know if you can accomplish anything else without it, but what else do you want? Have you ever figured out that you have the right to establish goals, to make plans? To dream? But if those dreams don't also include a step-by-step process for how-to, they'll remain nothing more than wishful thinking. Are the things you're doing now helping you reach the goals you set?"

If not, he needed to remake or remodel the present so that he could reach those dreams. Or downsize, settle for diminishing returns. It wasn't up to me to say which he'd do, but if he didn't actively strive to accomplish the former, he'd achieve the latter by default.

The same prescription might well cure me.

If I saw Ranger and me together in ten years, what was I doing now to ensure it? Was there anything I actually *could* do? Planning one's future as a couple requires a certain buy-in from the intended partner.

At the end of my tirade, I also wasn't sure I had accomplished anything apart from purging my system of the toxin that had plagued me for so long. But I admit it felt good. Whether Ranger understood what I said and why was another story. I had heaped question upon question and didn't even wait for his answers, assuming he would have none. Perhaps I should have been more open-minded, given him a chance to respond as I worked through my argument, because I was no better off when I shut my mouth than when I opened it.

When he was sure I was done, he said, "You've been saving up for a while."

"I'm sorry, Ranger. I didn't mean to go off like that. I'm just mixed up, I guess. It's just...." I stopped. I didn't even *know* what it just was.

Neither did he. He shoved me into one of the porch chairs, yanked open the screen door, stomped inside.

Moments later, glaring, he returned with two mugs of coffee and handed one to me. He sat opposite, avoiding my eyes. He sighed and took a deep breath.

"Neil, I don't rightly know what to say. You make sense. Mostwise, anyway, if I follow ya. I think maybe ya just kind of hit me with a little more than I can rightly manage at one time. Kind of like one beer too many, the one ya had after ya should've quit."

"I can't figure you out," I said. "I want to be with you more than anyone I've ever known, but I don't know if you feel the same. You need to tell me, because I have the rest of my life ahead of me, and I can't waste it sitting around wondering if you feel the same. Wondering if we might ever be together. Tell me, for Christ's sake!" Then I could map out a course—if it's together, then we'd work out the logistics. If it's apart, then I'd have to untangle from him once and for all, and get moving on my own. I'd miss him like hell, but the sooner I knew, the sooner I could start building my *own* future.

I finally looked him in the eye. "Well?"

"Well, what?" he said, savage. The best he could do was pull a cigarette out of the pack in his pocket. He lit it and sucked in as if he hadn't had a smoke in a year and exhaled with the deepest, most complicated sigh I'd ever heard from a man.

"Goddamn it. Ya spoke a mess of words there, and I reckon I don't know what to say back. I've been thinking about some of that same stuff! Ya think I haven't? That there in the parking lot after the AA meeting last month. Where did that come from? I never done nothin' like that. I come home and couldn't sleep the whole damn night. Ya sure do mix me up, Neil Graham. I get to thinking all kinds of crazy shit sometimes, and I don't know where the Jesus *fuck* it comes from."

I settled back with no intention of interrupting him once he got going.

"It just always seemed to me that two men was never supposed to— well, was never supposed to do that stuff we did. And maybe I was drunk—okay, there weren't no maybe about it. But maybe I had it figured out *anything* is okay when you're drunk, so I always had a readymade excuse. For anything. For waving my dick around at my own wedding, like Laura was nice enough to tell you about. Jesus fuck! For breaking up the furniture or kicking down the Christmas tree, or skipping work. Not showering or shaving or wearing a clean shirt."

"Fucking a man?" Crude, yes, but I knew he'd grab my point instantly.

He nodded.

Being drunk, he said, was the best excuse in the world, but now he couldn't use it anymore. Anything he did or said now, he was responsible for it and the consequences. For the past year and twenty-eight days (so far, except for one slip-up), he'd been responsible, and he'd have to make every effort to ensure the responsibility continued.

"Do you like fucking men?"

He scowled. But he said yes.

"Do you like fucking me? Sucking my dick?"

He sighed and said yes again, impatiently, as if there were no question.

"Do you like it well enough to want to do it without the beer for a crutch?"

In response, he heaved his cigarette butt against the ground and took me around the neck and rammed his mouth against mine and held on as if his life depended on it. As the kiss went on, he ground his crotch against mine, a move that was as erotic as it was unexpected. A minute—an hour? A lifetime?—later, he pushed me away as if I might be a bad memory.

"Jesus fuck. Enough of this bullshit. We got work to do." I would get no more answer from him in words, but at the moment, I needed no more words. Other issues (Marlene, for instance) would have to resolve themselves in some way, but I was content for the time being—considering that nothing at all had been settled. What kind of man was I if it took nothing more than one passionate kiss to make me shove aside all my misgivings?

"What shall we do first?" I took a close look at the garden. The plot, maybe fifteen by twenty feet, was perfectly positioned to take advantage of the summer sun. Yellow squash, zucchini, tomatoes, peppers, and fat beans loaded the vines, nearly ready to harvest. Potatoes, onions, cucumbers, and carrots competed for space, too, and a variety of salad greens. The garden was the finest I'd seen that year, and it certainly beat mine by a long shot.

"Wow. Marlene certainly has a green thumb."

That aroused his hackles. "Marlene, hell. She don't work in the yard." He swore he'd done it all, from staking the plot and tilling it to planting, watering, weeding and otherwise tending to it. He outlined his elaborate, backbreaking effort in detail, but the neatness and attention to detail in the tidy plot suggested that Marlene participated at least somewhat in its success.

"She's gonna can or freeze anything we can't eat. Tomato sauce and pickles and relish and all that shit." For a change, he sounded actually proud of something she could do, instead of critical. He sighed. "Mow or weed?"

"I'd rather mow."

"In there." He pointed to the garage.

I hadn't been inside the garage since Ranger had cleaned it out to make room for repairing his truck. In the intervening months, the tidied space had reverted partially toward its earlier condition but not entirely. The work bench was still organized, the tools mounted neatly on the wall. There was enough room for him to park his truck, but the other half had gradually been filled with assorted junk. I found the old mower right away, but I was curious, so I poked around a bit and found boxes containing the pots, pans, dishes, towels, sheets, and other housewares I'd provided after his fourth wife had emptied the place. The bed and dresser from the Saint Vincent store had been stored in there as well, under a blue plastic tarp, with the beat-up couch, the card table and chairs, the lamps, the rugs, even the old TV.

I was surprised that he'd hung onto all the stuff, as careless as he was with things. Maybe he had the good sense to be aware that he might need them again one of these days. Maybe he was already hedging his bets. I wonder what Marlene thought of his stash.

Ranger poked his head into the garage. "You get lost?"

"You could toss all this junk and make enough room for Marlene to park her car in here too."

"She's been on my ass for the last six months to do that. I been too busy, I guess." He grinned. I suspect he had no intention of making room.

Clearly, the yard had been tended as carefully as the garden. The grass seed had taken root and grown in lush and dark green. As I pushed the mower around the house, I marveled at the transformation of the property. It had certainly become a showplace under Marlene's supervision—not only the grass but also the flower beds and planters. However resentful Ranger may have been of her grim determination, he must also have recognized the positive results. I hoped she found people to admire it—her own friends, if none of Ranger's.

I wondered. Did he even have friends anymore?

Before long, the morning's coffee got to me. I powered down the mower and headed behind the garage. A moment later, to my surprise, Ranger followed me. "Whatcha doing?"

"Too much coffee. I'd use the bathroom in the house, but I'd hate to spill any of my lifestyle on the tile. Don't tell Marlene I defiled your grass."

"Like I would."

I unzipped my fly to do what I had to do, and to my surprise, Ranger did the same.

"What?" he said, when he noticed I was staring. "I drank just as much coffee."

"Oh, come on, Ranger. Leave me alone."

"I gotta piss, too. It's my yard, and I can piss anywhere I want."

"Do you have to stand on top of me to do it?"

"Maybe I just want to see your dick again. Brings back some happy memories."

"I'm not showing you my dick. Please. I really need to piss, and I can't if you're watching."

"I really need to piss too, but I can't because I'm getting a hard-on."

He shifted so I could get a better view. He was right about the erection. He let his pants slip down to his ankles, and I could see that he still didn't trouble himself with undershorts. "What d'ya say, Neil?

I could have exploded.

He leaned against the garage and started stropping himself.

"Ain't nobody around to see. Wanna help me out?"

I confess I wavered. But I was determined, for once....

We didn't even notice the sound of wheels coming up the gravel driveway.

Both of us were startled when we heard a car door slam and Marlene's voice calling goodbye as the same car turned around and headed off.

Moments later, she called for Ranger. She'd seen the mower and garden tools, most likely, and expected to find him outside somewhere.

In a panic, he yanked his pants up. I buttoned my own jeans as he whispered, "What in fuck is she doing home?"

I shrugged. We'd find out momentarily.

I think we shared the same immediate thought: suppose she came behind the garage to look for him? "Should I hide until the coast is clear?"

Ranger thought about it for a second. "She's already seen your car."

"It was Granddad's car. She doesn't know it's mine."

"But she knows somebody's here!"

"Raaaan-gerrrr!"

My first thought was that he had he deliberately planned the day, knowing that she would interrupt us. My second thought was something like relief that she had. Initially, we both anticipated that there would be time to play when the work was done, and clearly, Ranger had been determined. He hadn't noticed, from all our conversation, that I had become just as determined not to.

The sudden turn of events made me smile. Ranger found nothing funny in the situation, however.

"She'll head back here looking in a minute," he whispered.

"Yes. And you've got about ten seconds to come up with a good story about why we're behind the garage together. And why you have that tell-tale bulge in your pants."

I pushed him around the corner of the garage to confront Marlene.

"There you are," she said.

"Uh…yeah. I was, um, looking for the gas can."

"Behind the garage? You always keep the gas can under the porch."

I knew Ranger well enough to realize that he wouldn't tell Marlene the truth if he could help it. If it weren't for my car, he'd probably choose to keep me hidden behind the garage until nightfall, when I could sneak away under cover of darkness. I was suddenly disgusted with myself; I had no business being here, doing chores for Ranger (no matter what initially tempting offer he'd made). I had a yard and garden of my own at home that desperately needed attention, and I knew he wouldn't be helping me.

As Ranger stumbled to devise a plausible excuse, I solved the problem for him. I trotted out from behind the garage, and Marlene was stunned.

"This is a surprise."

Not a pleasant one, apparently. She crossed her arms.

"You got a new car, I see."

"Yes." I didn't feel obligated to explain that I'd inherited my grandfather's car along with everything else of his, that I'd gotten rid of my old sedan when I moved out of my apartment.

"What are you doing here?" She glared at both of us.

"Giving Ranger a hand with the yard work." An explanation should have been Ranger's responsibility, and Marlene looked to him, but he had nothing to offer. I thought for a moment that the two of them might get into an argument right there, but Marlene swallowed hard and sighed as Ranger merely looked away. She focused on me again.

"I hardly expected to find *you* here."

I decided Ranger wasn't going to offer any excuse at all, so I came up with the most plausible story I could think of at short notice. "Ranger asked me to help. I had the day off. I just assumed you knew about it and told him it was okay for me to come over. I thought you'd be here."

She scowled. "I went shopping at the outlet mall up north with my girlfriends."

"You said you'd be gone all day," Ranger said. "It ain't hardly even noon."

"We found everything we wanted, so there was no reason to stick around. We'd just spend more money. Besides, one of the girls had to be home by twelve-thirty because her son has a Little League game." Then, accusing: "You didn't tell me he was coming over." Perhaps she would have canceled her shopping trip.

"I'm almost done mowing," I said. I aimed to short-circuit her growing irritation with a sincere compliment. "This is the finest garden I've seen this summer. It's fantastic. Ranger is doing a great job, but I doubt if he could have done it without your help."

My praise deactivated her somewhat. And, besides, I meant it.

She wasn't entirely convinced, however. "Well, I wanted the garden to be twice as big as this right from the beginning, but you know Ranger." He glared at her.

I expected more uncomfortable questions. Why had Ranger suddenly decided, today, that he needed a helper to weed and mow? Why couldn't he have done it himself, as he'd been doing all along? Why did he call me, of all people? But she didn't ask. She gestured instead with her shopping bags, momentarily sidetracked, excited about her purchases.

"I found some really nice things at the outlet mall, Ranger. The cutest yellow sundress and a handbag to match. And a pretty blue-striped jacket and skirt. On sale for fifty percent off! Come see."

"No. I want to get this goddamn garden finished. It's hotter than shit out here, and I'm hungry enough to eat a fucking horse. Why don't you make yourself useful and fix us some lunch?"

"What's the magic word?" she said, like a mother scolding a child.

"Make us some fucking lunch." Marlene was taken aback by his rudeness. We both were. I was inclined to think it wasn't her fault if all his machinations came to naught, and I was willing to let her off the hook.

"Please? We'd appreciate it." My politeness, a startling contrast to Ranger's vicious response, caught her by surprise. "Can I help?"

"No, thanks. I can manage."

She and Ranger stared each other down for a moment; I wondered if such scenes were typical and decided, sadly, they probably were. Each conceded at the same time. Without a word, Marlene turned and headed to the porch. Her shoulders sagged. I could see that she was deflated, since Ranger had denied her the crowning moment to show her prizes and receive praise for the beautiful outfits (and good value) she'd found. She looked as hot and cross as he did.

After she went into the house, Ranger muttered "Who in fuck ever heard of a woman coming home early from a goddamn shopping trip?"

"It's just as well."

"What the hell does that mean?"

"It means you weren't going to get lucky even if she didn't come home early. Did you hear anything I said before?"

"About what?"

Was he being deliberately opaque? "Forget it. I don't know what I was thinking."

He spat in the dirt. "I do. You fucking cockteaser."

I shrugged. "I just had to pee. You're the one who tried to turn it into a scene from a gay porno flick. Marlene came home early. So that's that. It's not her fault that she interrupted your little scheme, and it's no excuse to be so rude to her."

He stared at me. "It's my house. I can do whatever the fuck I want."

"It's her house too. Remember?"

He turned his back to me and yanked the starter on the mower. Once it roared to life, further conversation was impossible. I went back behind the garage to urinate at last, unmolested. As long as Marlene was fixing lunch, and as long as I would be permitted to share it, I'd stick around long enough to eat and head out after that. Ranger could not be philosophical about his bad luck. He spent his rage on the mower, handling it more roughly than he should have. When it stalled, he was unable to get it started again. Kicking it several times didn't reactivate the thing, but he hurt his toe and filled the air with blue.

A few minutes later, Marlene brought a big tray to the porch and called us. "Lunch is served!"

"About fucking time," Ranger grumbled as he limped toward the porch.

"Oh, come on, Ranger. Why don't you just say 'thank you'?" To Marlene, I hollered, "Thanks. I'm starved." I was, in fact, suddenly ravenous, and she had set out a generous spread of ham and cheese sandwiches, potato chips, sliced watermelon, and a pitcher of iced tea. I dug in most appreciatively and heaped my plate.

Ranger complained about mayonnaise on the sandwiches. "Then go make your own," she retorted. He didn't. I settled on the top step. Ranger climbed past me and sat at the bottom.

Marlene didn't share the meal; instead, she stood by the screen door and nibbled a plate of lettuce, cottage cheese, and carrot sticks. The fact that Ranger and I seemed no longer to be on speaking terms probably cheered her, but for once, I felt inclined to take her side. I was angry at him for being so impolite, and I could think of no better way to express it than to be more courteous toward her.

"This really hit the spot, Marlene," I told her when I had finished. "Thank you."

She seemed surprised. "You're welcome." As an afterthought, she added, "And I appreciate you helping in the garden. It's a lot of work for one person."

"If you helped, it would go a hell of a lot faster," Ranger said.

"You take care of the outside, and I take care of the inside. That's the deal. Remember? I cook and clean and do the laundry and keep the house tidy—*and* work three days a week at the restaurant. The least you can do is the watering and weeding. And who's going to do all the canning this fall? It won't be you, but I bet you'll eat what I put up. I'd say you get the best end of the trade-off."

Ranger didn't respond. He set his plate down and approached the mower again, shucking his T-shirt as he prepared to tackle the recalcitrant machine again. As much as I loved the view of his naked furry chest, I was startled to discover that he had the beginnings of a gut that bulged over the waistband of his jeans.

"What've you got there, Ranger?"

"Where?

"Looks like you're carrying a spare tire."

"So fucking what?" He wasn't in the mood for any kind of playful joshing on my part, so I merely shrugged; I would have preferred a flat-bellied Ranger, but what difference did it make? He didn't belong to me.

The mower roared to life with the first yank on the starter; apparently it had only needed to cool off a bit (Ranger might have taken note). Instead, he channeled the rest of his anger into the long grass and made good progress. Leisurely, I poured myself some more tea and sat down with a second piece of watermelon. Ranger glared every time he rounded the bend and caught my eye.

"Get your lazy ass back to work," he hollered once. I pretended I couldn't understand over the roar and clank of the mower. The noon sun baked the ground, and I made myself comfortable in the shade of the porch.

A short time later, Marlene came outside with a sewing basket and settled into a chair.

"Thanks again for lunch. I was really hungry."

"You're welcome." She busied herself with her project, a patchwork quilt with various colored print fabrics arranged in an intricate design. She stitched by hand, quickly but carefully. It seemed tedious as well as time-consuming to me, but her fingers flew. I couldn't imagine having the patience to complete an entire quilt.

"That looks like a lot of work," I said.

"Not a bit. I love it."

"You certainly do it beautifully."

"I've been quilting since I was a girl." We all enjoy talking about the things we enjoy and do well, and Marlene seemed to forget her distrust as she explained how she learned the skill from her grandmother and how they'd sew together for hours.

"I finished my very first quilt when I was only twelve years old, and my grandma only helped me a little bit. It was a pretty simple pattern, and the stitching came out kind of crooked, but I was so proud of that thing. My mom still has it. I've made fourteen more since then, and each one turns out better than the last. And every one is different."

She unfolded the section she had been working on, more than a full square yard of swatches arranged into a pattern that suggested a multicolored flower garden, each triangle fastened together patiently with infinite tiny stitches.

"Do you invent your own designs?"

"Sometimes. At first, I copied patterns I found in magazines, but then I started making up my own. This one is based on a traditional design, the 'window box,' but I've changed it some. I'm giving it to my mom and dad for Christmas, if I can get it done in time. The colors match their bedroom. I've got a long way to go, but I work on it at night while I'm watching TV."

She told me that she'd made a quilt for Ranger as a gift when they were married, a special one for their bed, a classic design from the pioneer days, the double wedding ring. She described the pattern, interlocking rings against contrasting colored squares of fabric, and I realized it was the quilt I'd seen upstairs, spread over the bed she now slept in alone.

Ranger finished cutting the grass, dripping with perspiration and radiating resentment. He came up to the porch, grabbed a bottle of water, and downed it in one long gulp, his throat pumping furiously.

"Ya just gonna sit on your ass all afternoon?"

"Maybe," I said.

"Them weeds ain't gonna pull themselves."

"No doubt you're right."

Marlene asked if I would like to see the wedding quilt.

"Certainly." For a minute, I thought she was going to invite me inside and take me upstairs to look, but a second later, I think she realized I would be able to tell immediately that they no longer shared the bedroom. So she said, "I'll bring it down and show you."

Ranger stomped off the porch. I sipped my tea. Marlene was gone only a minute, and she was so excited when she spread the quilt out for me that I had to make a fuss. I told her it was perfect, and it was; intersecting rings arced perfectly against multicolored squares. She appreciated the praise.

"I made pillows to match. And I quilted some smaller pieces for us too, a throw for the couch and some placemats for the kitchen table. Most of the big quilts I made, I gave away as gifts. There's only so many you can use in your house."

"It's just beautiful, Marlene. Remarkable! Thanks for showing it to me."

Who doesn't enjoy being praised for a special skill or talent? Marlene positively glowed. I doubted if Ranger had ever made much of a fuss, and he reinforced my opinion with his next remark, yelled from the garden where he leaned on his hoe: "If you ladies could stop talking about that goddamn blanket for a minute, we got work to do over here."

We ignored him. I thanked Marlene again for showing me her work. Her eyes looked brighter than I had ever seen them, full of gratitude, and it gave me something to think about for the rest of the afternoon. Her skill made me painfully aware that I had no similar talent for which she or anyone might flatter me—I could make no music, sketch no portrait, write no novel, quilt no double-ring. Ranger could brag about his ability to repair and restore cars. And, if swearing could be considered an art form....

I could mix a decent Manhattan and dry martini. Hah.

I thanked Marlene again for lunch, and to my surprise, she offered me a handshake before I left. Ranger offered nothing, just a middle finger aimed at me as I backed the car around and headed out of the driveway.

A day or two later, I was looking through the newspaper on the porch with my morning coffee. I saw an ad for the state fair, opening on Labor Day weekend. There was still time—the ad said—for interested folks to fill out applications and bring in their art, handicrafts, photography, produce, jams and jellies, baked goods, and more. One of the photos in the ad showed a smiling woman holding up a quilt, and on impulse, I reached for the phone.

"Hi, Marlene. It's Neil. I'm fine. Say, I was looking through the newspaper this morning, and I saw an ad for the state fair. It opens next month. Have you ever considered entering one of your quilts for competition?"

19

Ranger got right to the point when he called. "Marlene put one of her quilts and some of her other shit in the state fair. She wondered if you wanted to come along since it was your idea. Thanks a whole fucking lot, by the way. She hasn't shut up about it since you told her."

He didn't mention the garden fiasco; perhaps he'd forgiven me—as if it had somehow been my fault. Or perhaps he'd forgotten already.

I was pleased to hear that Marlene had acted on my suggestion, and pleased as well at the prospect of attending the state fair, something I hadn't done since my early teens. My parents had taken me every year until I felt I'd grown out of it. And I guess I had, for a while, but maybe I'd grown back into it again, recalling those old days with some fondness—arriving in mid-morning and spending the next ten hours neck-deep in livestock, crafts, and produce, music performances, and the rodeo. And a whole day to gorge on junk food, deep-fried and otherwise, funnel cake and French fries, candy apples and corn dogs, sno-cones and popcorn and sodas. And, just after dark, riding the roller coaster and the Tilt-a-Whirl and the bumper cars and the Ferris wheel, everything, while my patient parents waited on an endless succession of benches.

"Are you sure Marlene really wants me to go along?"

"It's her idea. Seeing as how you're to blame for getting her into the goddamn thing."

That sounded promising. "Are you going, too?"

"Hell, yeah. Marlene don't like the weekend crowds, so we're going Monday. Ain't that your day off too?"

He actually sounded eager.

"Yes. I haven't been to the Indiana State Fair in thirty years."

"When we were kids, Dad took us to the fair in Kentucky. I reckon it's the same old shit here."

"Probably, but that's what makes it fun, because it never changes. Livestock and produce and arts-and-crafts exhibits, lots of food, and a carnival with rides and games."

"Sounds good to me. I'm the biggest sucker for them games. I know you can't beat the fucking things, but that don't stop me from trying."

"You can win me a teddy bear."

"That's a promise."

"Bumper cars and the roller coaster?"

"You damn betcha. Anything that goes around, upside-down, backwards, or fast, I'm on it."

"Does Marlene like the rides?"

"She says even looking at a merry-go-round is enough to make her lose her lunch." I could hear his satisfaction. "We're gonna have to ride by ourselves."

I wondered how Marlene would feel about that. But what kind of trouble could we get into strapped into the seat of a machine that tossed us into the air and whipped us around with enough force to snap a neck? I agreed to go, but upon later consideration, I wasn't convinced it was a good idea. Not for the first time, I missed my grandfather's wise counsel. *He'd* know what to advise.

Ranger suggested that we ride to the fair together, as there was no use in taking two cars. I showed up a good half hour before the scheduled departure time and was admitted (presumably, Marlene had decided I would not taint the premises too much). I sat in the kitchen and watched them together over the last of their breakfast, Ranger complaining about the toast and Marlene saying he wasn't helpless; operation of the toaster should be easy enough for a guy who's a mechanic anyway, if he weren't so lazy, and so on. I noticed that, while Marlene still wore her wedding ring, Ranger no longer sported his. How long after the ceremony had her decided he didn't want to carry around that symbol of commitment?

None of us wanted to cram three people into the front seat of Ranger's pickup. I offered to drive, but Ranger kicked up such a fuss that we took Marlene's car instead so that he could man the wheel. They rode in the front seat, and I in the back. The breakfast-table bickering morphed into road-trip bickering, as Marlene complained about the speed at which Ranger was traveling (too fast) and the time we had gotten on the road (forty minutes later than she had planned). Their wrangling spilled over into other concerns, Marlene's general unwillingness to cut anyone some slack and Ranger's general untidiness that made housekeeping even more of a chore. His swearing. As their argument grew more heated and I grew more uncomfortable, Marlene remembered that I was in the back seat with nothing to do but listen. Abruptly, she stopped talking and turned on the radio.

Country music may have been too earthy and impolite for her, or perhaps she made her selection knowing it would set Ranger on edge. She tuned into a contemporary Christian station, playing not hymns or gospel music but glossy, smooth songs in the modern pop style, tricked out with electronic beats, synthesizers, rap breaks, and autotune. Only the lyrics differentiated the music from standard Top 40, but you had to translate carefully to recognize they were love songs aimed at Jesus. Some of them sounded downright salacious—and could almost have been about having sex with your boyfriend if you changed a couple of words. I'd never spent much time listening to it, but I had two hours' worth on our way to the fair and decided it was unctuous stuff, as off-putting to me as country music with none of the occasional minor reward. Marlene turned up the volume loud enough that further conversation seemed useless until we reached the fairground parking lot.

We hiked toward the entry gate. Marlene reached it first and bought a single admission for herself. Ranger bought mine and his, and we each grabbed a program on the way inside. Marlene immediately looked at the map to find the pavilion for the arts and crafts, and we headed there first to see if she'd had any luck. She was thrilled to discover that her quilt had not only won a first-place blue ribbon but special "judge's choice" and "people's choice" awards as well. She clapped her hands like a little girl at a surprise party and hugged everyone, including Ranger and me and the women who were overseeing the display. Her quilted pillows took another first-place prize, and a cross-stitched wall hanging placed second.

I took dozens of photos with my cell phone and then with hers to document her moment of triumph.

We spent a good hour in the pavilion, looking at the various quilts and other sewing and needlework projects. Marlene, the only one of us in a position to do so, offered observations about other works on display, as well as succinct criticism of some of the work that was not up to scratch, by her estimation. She announced that next year, she would bring not only a new quilt she had in mind to stitch, but several other needlework projects that were underway. We walked by endless glass-fronted cabinets displaying crocheting, knitting, macramé, embroidery, and sewing projects of all kinds. There was a demonstration on how to spin sheep's wool into yarn and another for making lace, and Marlene took the time to watch and ask questions.

To be honest, some of the stuff fascinated me, as it had when I was a kid, but you would have thought that Ranger was undergoing some kind of textile-arts torture. He parked himself on a bench and refused to budge, sighing and glowering.

The craft pavilions sat next to the food displays, and we headed there next.

"Why bother?" Ranger said. "Ya don't get to eat none of it." He tagged along, grumbling, as we walked through the displays. Taking in the cakes, cookies, pies, jellies, and pastries on display—and the ribbons that had been awarded to them—Marlene swore that next year she would enter her whole-grain bread and bran muffins, as well as her peach salsa, watermelon pickles, and blackberry jam.

"Just see if I don't come home with a whole basket of blue ribbons next year."

"You'll be queen of the fair," I said.

"If you don't beat her to it," Ranger shot back. I was startled—and pleased when Marlene whacked Ranger with her purse.

"Kidding! Sorry! Jesus. Ya don't gotta attack me." He glared at me as if I were at fault.

"I would've. But she beat me to it," I said. "Thanks, Marlene." She gave me a thumbs-up.

After the food, Marlene wanted to see the floral displays, but Ranger drew the line. I suggested that we take a look at the schedule for the day, choose some shows and other entertainments, and plan the day around those. I tried to be diplomatic, but they found fault with each other about everything. Ranger wanted to see the Country Gents; Marlene wanted to see the Pop Tarts. (Neither asked me for my preference.) If Marlene wanted to check out a particular exhibit, Ranger vetoed it. The tension would simmer all day if neither of them would compromise. My proposal that we split up—and meet again at the gate at the end of the day—met with stony silence from Marlene, even as Ranger expressed his enthusiasm for it.

"I expect my husband to show me a good time, not have to wander around here all by myself."

"Ya got a map," he said.

"That's not the point," she snapped.

"Then quit belly-achin' so much. I let ya drag me through the goddamn quilts and cookies and jelly and all that shit. I want to see the draft horses compete, and if ya don't, you can sit outside and fucking wait for us."

"Language!"

She followed us into the equestrian arena, and while we watched the contests, she made a deliberate show of sighing loudly and reading a romance novel that she'd stuck in her purse. The initial elation about her prize-winning quilt had faded quickly in the face of Ranger's indifference, and I suspected her day would get no better.

I assumed I'd feel some elation about seeing first-hand that the marriage was clearly showing stress fractures with no assistance from me; thus, I would not have to shoulder the blame or the guilt as it cracked apart. I would only have to wait. But I didn't feel as pleased as I thought I might. I wondered why I'd bothered to come at all. Did I really want to tempt Ranger into offering me a blowjob in a men's room stall just so I could turn him down?

I was better than that.

True to his word, Ranger allowed himself to get suckered into the games. And true to his word, he won a teddy bear for me, popping a succession of balloons with darts, trading small prizes for larger ones. When he finally presented me with the bear, I didn't have the heart to tell him he'd paid about twenty dollars for it. He was proud of himself, and I didn't want to spoil the moment. Marlene, however, was a bit miffed when he didn't offer the bear to her.

"What about me?" she said, indignant.

"I didn't promise you." He offered to buy her some darts to try her own luck, but she sniffed and said she didn't care about winning some cheap prize anyway.

The day was sunny and warm but not too hot. We wandered around the livestock barns because Ranger wanted to see the cows, sheep, and goats—while Marlene groused about the smell. We all enjoyed the Grange and 4-H exhibits and the trade show. We attended the lumberjack competition, which was little different and just as cheesy as it had been when I was a kid, and watched an Elvis Presley impersonator who had the look but proved surprisingly pitch-poor. We caught a program featuring three precocious sisters who sawed away at violins while performing Irish step-dancing, and another show improbably called an international circus, a group of eight young acrobats who performed impressive feats of balance with a low tightrope and bicycle.

In between, Ranger and I stuffed ourselves with hot dogs, funnel cakes, caramel popcorn, and candy apples. Marlene criticized every single thing we ate and refused to share with us. Ranger finally asked her to pick out something for herself so she'd quit being such a bitch about everything. At that, she set her mouth and said no more about our snacks. She had brought a sliced apple and some carrot sticks from home for herself, and she purchased nothing but a cup of coffee from one of the vendors. Perhaps as payback, she insisted that Ranger chase down the endless row of food stands for artificial sweetener in the blue packet instead of a pink or yellow one. She made such a fuss that he finally stomped off to look.

Marlene and I sat at a small table, waiting, as her coffee went cold.

"I'm sorry," she said.

What? "Why?"

She shook her head. "I'm sure you must think I'm awful contrary. Seems like everything I want is different from what Ranger wants. I'm not really like that."

I didn't know her any other way, come to think of it. But he was just as contrary.

"I guess it really doesn't make much difference if the sweetener is yellow or pink or blue. I just think the blue one tastes the most like real sugar. And I love sweets so much." She appeared so forlorn that I thought she might cry, and I hastened to comfort her.

"I don't think you really need to worry about it one way or the other. Why don't you just use real sugar? One little packet won't hurt."

"I don't need it," she said firmly.

I shrugged. "Well. While we're waiting, want to check out the pictures I got of you and your quilt?"

She was eager, and we scrolled through them. Ranger came back at last, finishing yet another funnel cake, licking confectioner's sugar from his fingers and wiping them on his jeans. He dug into his pocket and threw some pink packets on the table. "Couldn't find that blue shit anywhere. Use these. What the fuck."

Without a word, Marlene tore open a pink packet and dumped it into her cold coffee.

"Marlene, let me buy you a hot cup, at least," I said.

She was surprised. "That's okay."

I insisted, and she was appreciative. Ranger couldn't understand why I should waste my money; the coffee had gone cold because of her stubborn refusal to make do. It was her own fault, he said.

"You hush. I can afford it." I presented the steaming cup to her with a flourish and a "thy coffee, milady," and she giggled.

In the twilight, the lights of the carnival glowed to life, the rainbow incandescence that looks so beautiful from a distance you never want to get close enough to break the spell. We walked down the midway. Ranger stopped at a food stand and ordered a pink cloud of cotton candy on a paper cone. He offered to share. I took a handful, but Marlene declined.

I asked if she was interested in trying any of the rides, but she refused, as Ranger had predicted. Even watching some of them, with their cars being slung around in circles and jerked back and forth, was enough to make her feel queasy, she said.

"Do you mind if Ranger and I go on a few?"

"I guess not. You ought to have some fun while you're here."

"I'm going on the rides whether she minds or not," Ranger said.

"Here's an idea. Marlene, why don't you go back to the pavilion where the crafts and the flower arrangements are displayed? You can take all the time you want, and browse to your heart's content." She liked that suggestion and said she would head to the bingo tent after that. We agreed to meet her there at half-past nine, which gave us about two hours. I suspect my courtesy helped her think better of me, and she even agreed to hang onto my prize stuffed bear so I wouldn't lose it.

The lure of the carnival lights was strong, and I fell under the spell. Ranger grabbed my hand and said we'd have to hurry as we ran to the ticket booth. If the rides couldn't be as violent or impressive as their names suggested, they sometimes came close enough: the Twister, the Whip, the Hurricane, Zipper, Cliffhanger, Rock-O-Plane, Slammer. Each ninety-second voyage promised a dizzying, churning, twisting, edge-of-seat, hash-and-mash, and Ranger and I got in line for each of them, one after another. We enjoyed ourselves as little boys might, hurling ourselves against each other and yelling our heads off. Even before we finished the ride, Ranger would holler "We gotta do this again!" and we'd rejoin the queue for a repeat performance. The end of a ride usually found us breathless, laughing so hard we couldn't stop.

After begging off a third excursion on the Zipper, I asked Ranger how he managed to keep his head and keep the contents of his stomach inside himself. "Neil," he said, "ya can't keep up with an ex-drunk when it comes to spinning and flipping upside down and backwards. That's how we operate. Vertigo is my old buddy. I can't reach him the way I used to. This is as close as I can get these days, so you bet yer ass I ain't quittin' until the lights go out tonight."

I didn't know what to say in response.

After a memorable turn in the bumper cars—Ranger's got stuck and couldn't move, and I looped around and around, bashing him repeatedly—half-past nine was upon us. He was reluctant to leave the rides and even suggested that we ignore the time; what could Marlene do but wait for us until we were good and ready to meet her? But I demurred, and we headed for the bingo tent.

We found her with a dozen sheets spread in front of her, but she'd had no wins, only come close a few times. "A miss is as good as a mile," she said. We stood by until the end of her game, when she wadded up her game sheets and tossed them in the trash. Her lack of good fortune had not improved her mood.

"What a waste of time. I'm never lucky."

I had to sympathize with her. Ranger went off in search of something to eat, claiming to be hungry again, although I didn't see how he could be. Maybe it was simply for Marlene's benefit, or mine, that his cast-iron stomach permitted him to indulge in the most conspicuous consumption of the worst kind of food and still throw himself around and upside down on the Slammer or the Hurricane with no ill effects. Marlene and I left the bingo tent and found a bench outside.

"You haven't gone on a single ride, Marlene. It's not the full state-fair experience if you don't go on at least one! What about the merry-go-round? That's pretty gentle, and it doesn't go too fast."

She shook her head.

"Ferris wheel?"

"Nothing that goes around. I get dizzy."

"What about the bumper cars?"

"I never could understand why anyone would want to bash into somebody else."

I was running out of ideas. "The giant slide?"

"That's for babies."

"We could go back to the fun house. We can walk through at our own pace."

There were no other options. Reluctantly, she agreed, but I could see that her heart wasn't in it.

Ranger returned with a plate of onion rings, dripping grease and ketchup, and offered to share. I took a couple, but Marlene just rolled her eyes and shook her head. For our benefit, and in spite of our vocal protests, he ate half of them as we continued our walk, but I noticed that he tossed the rest into a trash can.

We wandered to the fun house, garish in colored lights. The exterior was elaborately spray-painted as if it were some giant graffiti artist's canvas, with SUPER FUN HOUSE LAUGHS GALORE splayed across the top. Slightly menacing clowns and harlequins danced around the edges. A mechanical woman's face, giant and grotesque, with oversized rubber lips that opened and closed, revealed crooked yellow teeth as a maniacal screeching laugh emitted from a speaker.

I've always found such "fun" houses to be totally incongruous. Even as a kid, I wondered what was supposed to be fun about them. They were seedy and scary with nothing particularly amusing about them at all; I wondered who had come up with such a concept. I could understand a house of horrors, tricked out for Halloween, since we all have fears—and we can all be startled by unexpected ghosts. Who doesn't enjoy a good scare? There is something liberating about screaming when you're suddenly made afraid, caught completely off guard by a monster leaping out from behind a door. A collective shriek unites the participants in an elemental shared experience that is somehow satisfying, even comforting.

But what is unexpected about fun? Laughter is as completely mystifying as fear, but significantly more idiosyncratic and personal. What constitutes fun, anyway? Is it comedy, something that makes us laugh? Or merely the feeling of pleasure or enjoyment? Is it happiness? The whole notion of a house of any sort being an encapsulation of the feeling is utterly absurd. Certainly, the dismal, forced presentation of this experience defied anyone's perception of fun. I'll take ninety seconds in a turning, twisting cage or a speeding car racing around a track. The thrill of acceleration, of being thrown for a loop (literally), was something easier to understand on a more fundamental level than an abstraction of "fun."

Such thoughts for the state fair! Just enjoy the experience, I chided myself. We traded our tickets and the gate opened for us to enter. We climbed a flight of stairs that started jiggling when we were halfway up. Marlene almost lost her balance, but I caught her. She offered a tight smile of thanks. The irritating maniacal-laughter soundtrack repeated itself like a record needle stuck on a scratch.

We walked on, Ranger first, then Marlene and me. Ahead of us loomed a giant tumbler, a good nine or ten feet in diameter, slowly rotating, and we were required to walk through it, navigating on a bias to accommodate the revolution that contrived to waylay us before we could reach the safety of the other side, to reach the solid ground we all want for our lives. There was nothing to grab ahold of to assist in the trip through it. Only balance and resolve could keep us upright.

Perhaps I am simply accustomed to accommodating the twists and turns of life. I didn't even have to think before I stepped confidently into the rotating tumbler, and a few steps later, I emerged from the other side. Ranger crossed, confident. We turned to welcome Marlene, who hesitated.

"Come on. There's nothing to it," Ranger said. To illustrate, he walked through it again, back to her side, and then a third time as he rejoined me. "See?"

She wasn't convinced.

Ranger lost patience. "Goddamn it. We don't got all night. Just walk through the fucking thing."

"I will! Don't rush me."

Ranger sighed. We could do nothing until she walked through the tumbler, and she knew it. She closed her eyes and took a hesitant step into the rotating barrel, and then a second step before she lost her balance and fell. She screamed as she tried to regain her footing. She could not. She tried to crawl on her hands and knees, but the rotation kept turning her onto her side. Ranger laughed, but it was in no way funny; I sprang into the tumbler to assist. Somehow, I managed to get her through the barrel and safely to the other side, but by then she was crying, nearly hysterical. She might have been injured; at the very least, she was embarrassed.

Still, Ranger laughed, taunting her for falling down "like an old drunk," he said. He finally shut up when I gave him the evil eye. (*"What?"* he said. "What did *I* do?" The answer, though I didn't tell him, was nothing. He'd done nothing at all, and that was the trouble.)

I embraced Marlene and could feel her heart beating fast against the speed of panic. "Shh," I whispered. "You're out of it now."

She seemed more human at that moment than she had in all the time I'd known her. She clung to me for a minute until she could catch her breath and stop crying. When she felt strong enough, she let go. Ranger stood by, scowling, but at least he was quiet.

"Thanks, Neil. I'm sorry," Marlene said, her voice shaking. "I was so scared. I lost my balance and I just couldn't get it back." She took a few deep breaths. "Fun house. Hah. I hate these darn things."

"I'm sorry too." I meant it. "Why didn't you say so? We could have skipped it."

"You guys were having such a good time. I felt left out. I only wanted to be part of it. I didn't want to spoil everybody's day, but it looks like I did anyhow."

"You didn't. Don't even think like that." I caught Ranger's eye and made an I'll-cut-your-throat-if-you-say-a-word gesture, and he could tell I wasn't kidding. He grumbled but kept quiet.

The last element of hilarity, just before the exit, was a row of wavy mirrors, reflecting some warped versions of ourselves in various combinations, with elongated or shrunken heads and torsos and legs. I hoped Marlene might at least get a chuckle out of that. One mirror made us appear morbidly fat. Marlene stared at her reflection, lost in thought for a moment. Ranger stood beside her and laughed at his own image.

"You keep eating those funnel cakes, you're going to look like that for real someday. Mark my words. You got a good start already, in case you haven't noticed."

"This?" He cupped his hands around his rounded belly. "Hell, Marlene. That just means there's more for you to love."

I don't think any of us believed that statement. I had certainly noticed that his T-shirt fit him a lot more snugly than it used to, and the slight paunch hanging over his belt wasn't likely to shrink, given his appetite for junk food. He blustered on. "What's the point of coming to the fair if you ain't going to eat your way through it?"

She took a deep breath and seemed to make up her mind. "I'll tell you."

We waited, expectant. She pointed at the grossly obese figure in the mirror. "I used to look just like that."

Of all things that she might have shared, that was the last one I would have guessed.

In a small voice, she said, "I used to weigh more than three hundred pounds. Three hundred and twelve, to be exact."

My mouth dropped open. I could not imagine anyone as petite as Marlene ever being such a size. Ranger, too, seemed startled.

"It's true. It was gross. Disgusting."

She required no comment from us, or even encouragement. She needed only listeners, and as the tale unfolded, I felt nothing but compassion for the scared, overweight girl still trapped inside her. As for Ranger? I'd go broke trying to read *his* mind. But he hung on every word.

"I hated being fat. I'd get home from school and cry to my mother about the mean things the kids said, and my mother would say, 'You're not fat, Marlene; you're just big-boned,' she'd say. Hah! Nobody's bones are bigger than anyone else's. And my dad would say, 'You're just pleasingly plump.' I hated those words. I wasn't plump, and it wasn't pleasing. I was just plain fat and getting fatter all the time. I hated being fat, but I didn't do anything about it but eat more."

Her mom would make her a hot-fudge sundae to cheer her up; she ate every bite and sometimes sneaked a second one, she said. The problem grew even worse in high school, with no friends and constant bullying because of her size. It was, she said, a nightmare.

"The kids used to say I was five feet tall and five feet wide. I hated shopping for clothes because I could never find anything that really fit— certainly nothing that was in style. Even the teachers would make nasty comments about my size. When it was time for graduation, I couldn't get a gown that was short enough for someone my height and wide enough that I could get into it."

She had no choice but to select a gown designed for someone much taller to gain the required girth, and her mother opted to fold up the hem and seal it with masking tape. Somehow, Marlene managed to catch her shoe heel in the tape and tear it away as she crossed the stage to pick up her diploma. She tripped on the loose fabric and fell, and the auditorium erupted in laughter. She picked herself up, collected the huge gown, and ran offstage as quickly as she could. The school mailed her the diploma later in the summer because she was too embarrassed to pick it up.

"After that, I just decided enough was enough. I was going to lose weight if it killed me. And it nearly did."

She shuddered and turned her back on the mirrors.

"Can we please get out of here?"

I led the way, and we stepped into the relief of the cool night. She took in a deep breath and seemed to settle a little. We walked down the midway, leaving the house of fun behind, as she continued her story. But there was an undercurrent of urgency, as if she needed to tell it before she lost her nerve.

"The first twenty pounds were the hardest. My mom didn't help at all—I'd remind her that I was on a diet and she'd turn around fix fried chicken and biscuits for dinner, or something. I spent a fortune buying every new diet book. I went to Weight Watchers every week. I was hungry all the time, and I prayed a lot, asking Jesus for willpower not to eat junk food."

"Did that help?" I said.

"No. Jesus didn't seem to care much. So I learned to depend on me. I started eating better and eating less. I joined an exercise group with other fat women, and we helped each other out. I got a job at Sears in the mall, and I used to go early in the morning so I could walk around before it opened, when no one was there to stare at me. I got to know a lot of the old folks who walked every day, and they sort of became friends of mine. I bet I logged a thousand miles around the mall."

I put a protective arm around her—to my surprise as well as hers, but she didn't push me away.

"Just look around here. Most of these people are twice as big as they should be." I did look; tons of humanity streamed by us, most of the people being overweight to one extent or another, straining the seams of their stretch pants or spilling over their belt buckles—and most of them had something deep-fried or sugar-coated in their hands that they were shoveling into their mouths. "They're killing themselves. You'd think they would look in the mirror and see that they have a problem."

Ranger, for one, looked distinctly uncomfortable.

We passed a shooting gallery. The operator, a tattooed twenty-something, waved us over, urging us to try our luck.

"Show the little lady what you can do, gents! Shoot out the center and win a prize for her!"

"Hmm," Marlene said. "I used to be pretty good at this."

Ranger and I exchanged puzzled glances. He shrugged. Marlene paid her money and picked up a rifle. She took aim at the target and fired. Bullseye. Even the operator was impressed.

She continued telling her story, bluntly, matter-of-factly, punctuated by the ominous shots from the rifle, each blowing away part of the center circle.

"I didn't think I would ever find anyone who wanted to marry me because I was such a fat pig, but guess what? I did. I started dating this guy I met in Weight Watchers."

Bang.

"He said he loved me. I didn't think I would ever hear that from anyone. I was twenty-four and still living with my parents. So when this guy proposed, I jumped at the chance. We could lose weight together, him and me. Kind of support each other, I thought. Boy, was I wrong."

Bang.

In no time, Marlene regained half the pounds she'd lost, she said, thanks to her husband's encouraging her to eat, to her surprise. It might have continued, except she accidentally discovered some photos on his computer.

Bang. Bang.

"Turns out he has a thing for fat women. I mean *really* fat women, which is why he hung around Weight Watchers in the first place. You wouldn't believe some of those pictures. He had hundreds. Naked fat women doing...things. I puked when I saw them."

Bang. Bang. Bang.

She set the rifle down. "That's some impressive shooting, lady," the operator said. He handed her a pink teddy bear, twice as big as the one Ranger won for me.

She offered the bear to me. "You want this one too?"

"I'd be honored. But you should keep it. You've certainly earned it.

"Why would I want a souvenir from today?" She scowled at Ranger.

I did my best to salvage something from the day. "Because look at you. Not only are you an expert marksman, but you get to take home two blue ribbons for your beautiful creations. And you're the People's Choice. Who else can say that?"

She offered me a quick, unexpected hug.

We walked away from the shooting gallery and she continued her story. She redoubled her efforts to slim down, and apart from a few slip-ups here and there, she reached her target weight loss of a hundred and seventy-five pounds. Every time she dropped a dress size, she celebrated by picking out a new outfit for herself—she went down eight sizes in eight years. Her husband turned mean, threatening divorce if she didn't fatten up again. He did all he could to trick her into putting the weight back on, leaving chips and cookies and candy where she couldn't miss them. Sometimes she succumbed to the temptation.

"We finally had kind of a showdown. He told me I was half the woman he married, and I guess that was true in terms of my size, but I was twice the woman in terms of my self-confidence. For the first time in my life, I *liked* myself. But he didn't care about any of that. He started getting mean. Smacking me around. He said I could either start eating again or get along without him, and guess which I picked? He finally walked out about four months before I started going out with Ranger. But the marriage was over for years before that."

She admitted that watching her diet was still difficult, but she knew she could never get lazy or complacent, or the weight would pack right back on. She'd already gained five pounds since marrying Ranger.

"Sometimes I think all I have to do is look at a piece of cake and I'll put on weight. Everything I eat, I worry that it will go right to my hips and my bottom. It's always a trade-off. If I have a cookie at lunch, then I won't have any bread with dinner. If I have potato chips, that's two miles of brisk walking. I've learned how many calories are in everything."

She did the math at every meal, adding up to ensure she didn't eat too much. "You never notice that I cook real healthy, balanced meals, do you?" she said to Ranger. He shook his head. "Because I make sure they taste good first."

He also didn't notice—or, more likely, care—that she ate small portions and rarely had dessert, she said.

"I could put a little packet of sugar in my coffee instead of sweetener. But it's a spoonful of sugar I don't need. I'd rather save up for a couple of days and reward myself with a fudge brownie. I hate to see you two eating all this junk food—not because I want to fuss at you like some old schoolmarm—but because I can't do it too. I'd like nothing better than to pig out on cotton candy and French fries and pizza, but I can't. If I eat a funnel cake today, it will take a week of exercise and no sweets to make up for it. And it's just not worth it to me."

She couldn't help herself; the tears came. She took a handkerchief from her purse and wiped her eyes. "Besides, if I eat a funnel cake, what's to stop me from getting a plate of those onion rings, and a giant soda pop to wash them down? And maybe a candy apple or a waffle cone after that? Everything looks and smells so good. But I'm afraid if I start, I won't be able to quit, and in a little while, I'll be as big as I ever was. Bigger, even. But I won't let myself. I will *not* be that fat girl ever again, for anyone. But most of all, for me."

She fell silent after her story, as if she were exhausted. I didn't know what to say, how to respond. I would never have guessed she hid such a secret. She had every right to be proud. I watched Ranger to see how he'd respond, but he offered only a poker face that communicated nothing.

She addressed Ranger: "Now you have one more thing you can throw at me. Make fun of me for."

I hoped she was wrong. Ranger must have been surprised, as I was, to learn that she had conquered an addiction of her own. Surely, he could relate to her struggle. Perhaps it might give him a little compassion, too. As for myself, I could relate to her feeling outcast as a result of being fat; I'd felt similar alienation as a gay teenager.

Wait a minute, I told myself. Whose side are you on?

"Can we go home? I've had my fill of this place," she said.

We headed toward the main gate. I was ready myself. It was nearly ten o'clock, and the fair would be closing soon anyway. She was subdued on the drive, saying little, and she didn't even comment when Ranger dialed in a country station on the radio.

The helplessness and fear she must have felt inside the fun house tumbler gave me something to think about, and for the first time, I looked at the situation from her point of view. Despite the fear, her readiness to follow Ranger and me into that place suggested that she was unwilling to give up on him despite recognizing their general incompatibility. I suspect she regretted tangling with a man like him, who regularly proved more than she could handle. If she were used to people being polite and using their company manners, what could she do with Ranger and his aggressive, mean-spirited vulgarity in spite of his rakish grin?

I couldn't shake Marlene's story, and I realized that she and Ranger had addiction in common, the same fear that one slip-up could undo months or years of careful attention. I wished Marlene could hear Ranger tell *his* story about his own war. They might both recognize that each of them had demons to fight, demons that wouldn't sleep tonight or possibly ever. It could give them a reason to bond, something on which they could agree instead of fight. Why were they both so stubborn? If the marriage was beyond repair because of the lie underneath it, they might at least establish a truce. Respect each other.

I felt guilty myself, as if I were mostly—even partly—to blame. If I had just let Ranger alone as he coped with sobriety, had quit trying to lure him back into my bed, perhaps he wouldn't have felt obliged to find another woman to marry. By insisting that he be true to himself and come out, I merely scared him, and Marlene paid the biggest penalty. The turnabout had come: Ranger was chasing me, and I had to wonder. Was it worth it?

The ride home seemed interminable, quiet except for the radio. I could not think of a thing to say, and Ranger offered nothing, which didn't surprise me. Marlene was talked out. I felt sorry for her in a way I had not even thought possible. I couldn't forget the details she'd shared about battling her weight and the monumental self-control required to keep it in line.

When we arrived at their house, I helped Marlene out of the car and walked her to the porch. "You know, the same thing happened to me once at a carnival when I was maybe twelve or thirteen years old, only there was no one to rescue me. I was going through the fun house by myself. I tried to walk through the rolling barrel, and I fell. I don't know how much time went by before the guy outside noticed that I never came out. He had to turn the thing off before I could get out." She shuddered under the memory. "No more fun houses for me."

No fun houses. She might have been talking about this place that she and Ranger shared as well. Fear can drain the vinegar out of anyone. Facing fear, from childhood or otherwise, is never easy; most people never even make the attempt. Suddenly, I didn't want to be considered a threat. The fact that Ranger chose her (however spectacularly inappropriate) wasn't her fault. The fact that she had accepted spoke more of her optimism than anything. She certainly didn't marry him out of spite, to get back at me. She had nothing against me except she understood that my feelings for Ranger matched her own. So perhaps we were in competition in that respect, but because he married her, she had won. It was up to me to bow out, if I were a gentleman.

Was I? I could be.

I gave her another hug, willingly returned, a handshake to Ranger, and bade them good night.

20

A month passed, not very different from so many months in my recent life. I continued to log too many hours at the country club, in spite of the guilt I felt every time I caught sight of Granddad's photo on the mantelpiece. I continued the occasional casual hookup with a couple of the patrons, but the experiences were empty. My life would continue endlessly thus unless I could force myself out of the lethargy that threatened to undo me. I needed a catalyst, and I finally got one. Out of the blue, I got a call from Ranger inviting me to join them for a three-day camping trip in late October.

I was mystified. "Why?"

"What do you mean, why?"

"Since when do you go camping? You don't even have a tent."

"We borrowed a camper from Marlene's folks."

"Whose dumb idea was that? Why would we want to spend three days together in a camper? What are we going to do all day long?"

Clearly, my questions irritated him. "Jesus fuck, Neil."

In the background, I could hear Marlene say, "Language!" I wondered how many times a day she said it and if she was even aware of it. It probably was a reflex by now.

"Here," I heard him say as he handed off the phone. "You tell him."

A second later, Marlene's voice came on the line. "Hi, Neil."

"How are you, Marlene?"

"I'm all right, I guess. But I think it's time we all had a talk."

I had to agree. Perhaps it might, finally, clear the air. "Why don't we just meet at your place? Or mine? Or have dinner at a restaurant in town? We don't need to go on a camping trip."

"I just want to get away. At home, there's always chores to do. Housekeeping and cooking and laundry. I need a break from the routine if I'm going to take a few days off. It'll be nice to get out of town, and the fall colors are so beautiful this time of year."

Camping would undoubtedly be a break from routine. I had a lot I wanted to say to Ranger—refined from the tirade I'd delivered in his backyard in late summer—and maybe I'd have the chance. I had a lot I could say to Marlene as well; my own experience as a gay kid perhaps couldn't compare to hers as a fat one, but I believed she needed to know at least some of the truth about the past that Ranger and I shared. If we could be honest for a change, if the details were all in the open, perhaps our little triangle drama could be concluded. I wanted Ranger, Marlene wanted Ranger, Ranger wanted—what? Who? Any, all, none? Perhaps once and for all, choices could be made, and I could move on from him. Or with him, though I doubted the latter.

Ranger took a few vacation days from the Buick dealership, and they took off for a K.O.A. south of Indianapolis. I looked up the campground online. The place redefined the sport; "roughing it" meant guests had access to full water and electrical hookups, restrooms with hot showers and flush toilets, an internet connection, and a laundromat. A general store on site sold groceries, beer, tobacco, and firewood. Who could ask for more from the wilderness?

They drove down on a Thursday morning. I claimed I couldn't get off work until late afternoon, mainly as an excuse to drive my own car. That way, I wouldn't be dependent upon them for transportation in case I needed to make a quick getaway. I packed light, a change of clothes, a shaving kit, and my backpack library. As an afterthought, in case the weekend proved too much to bear, I grabbed a pint of whiskey from Granddad's liquor cabinet and put it in the glove compartment. It might come in handy to prove a point or—something.

I had two hundred miles to think about Ranger, me, and us, and a hard-crack blue day to travel in. I wondered if he missed me or merely the services I had provided so willingly, once. I made a point to ask for clarification on that issue. But I recalled how I used to feel driving from my house to his, the breathless anticipation at the prospect of seeing him. I glanced at the speedometer and discovered I was traveling fifteen miles over the posted limit.

I wondered if I'd be able to survive three whole days next to him in cramped quarters, or if I'd have to escape, guilty. Although I felt considerably more sympathetic toward Marlene, I couldn't quell my attraction to Ranger or my conviction that he and I—rather than he and she—were destined to be together in a romance novel scenario. But I was determined to do the right thing, even if it meant bailing early.

I found the park where the campground was located, but I got lost not long after entering the gate. Ranger's directions, unsurprisingly, were vague and incomplete. I tried calling him, but his phone had been turned off, so I drove on, looking for signs to point the way. The darkness had sunk in when I finally chanced across their campsite. I parked the car and grabbed my things. The camper was clumsy and uncomfortably large for towing behind a pickup, but Ranger's truck obviously managed the trick. Ranger and Marlene were exchanging angry words inside as I approached the door, their voices thankfully muffled. I didn't have any idea what topic fueled the argument. It went silent as I knocked and waited to be admitted.

Ranger opened the door and eyed me from the other side of the screen. "About damn time, Neil." He stepped outside.

"Your instructions were lousy. I've been driving around the park for forty-five minutes looking for this campsite, and the GPS kept saying, 'You have arrived.'"

"They must've been good enough. Ya made it."

I offered my hand, but instead of taking it, he grabbed me around the neck and kissed me on the mouth. He could certainly behave unpredictably; although I liked the trait, I wondered how smart he was to exercise it just at that moment. I was thankful Marlene wasn't watching. He did, however, taste very good. When we stood apart, he grinned.

"Got to keep you off guard some way, you son-of-a-bitch."

"That particular way works wonders." Through the screen door of the camper, I said hello to Marlene.

"Hi, Neil. Come on in."

"Good to see you again."

"Likewise." Spot couldn't have been more welcoming. He came to me, expectant, tail in motion, and my fingers remembered where he liked to be scratched.

"Dinner's been ready for a while. I turned off the stove so it wouldn't overcook. I just have to heat it up. Won't be but a minute." She turned her attention to the skillet, picking up a fork and stirring something that smelled wonderful, and I realized how hungry I felt.

"About damn time," Ranger said again.

"We had to wait for Neil. It's your fault that he's late, so just you do us all a favor and keep quiet."

I'd never heard her talk back to Ranger like that before. He definitely deserved it, but I suspected that her new-found confidence was lost on him. It also made me wonder if she hadn't simply had enough herself. Maybe she was planning her own exit strategy. She could win blue ribbons; why should she be content with Ranger, his lack of appreciation for her talent, his vulgarity, his obstinacy?

A transistor radio sat on the counter, blaring more Christian pop, and she turned up the volume so that additional conversation was impossible. Since no one offered, I gave myself a tour of the camper. It was designed to sleep four, but only two could get any privacy. One end contained a double bed, separated by a curtain from the rest of the space. The tiny kitchen took up the middle, with a small fridge and a two-burner stove that ran off a compact propane tank. The bathroom fixtures didn't work; that cramped space was filled with junk stacked nearly to the ceiling. The far end of the camper contained a table and two benches that folded down to make a second bed. The interior was faded and well-worn, but it was clean and tidy.

"The toilets and showers are a little way up the road," Marlene said. "Not very far. Pretty nice, too."

"When do we eat?" Ranger said.

"It's ready. Would you set the table, please?"

Ranger ignored her.

"If you tell me where the plates are, I'll do it," I said.

"Thanks. In there." She pointed to a cupboard crammed with dishware, and I sorted out the necessary pieces. As I stood next to Ranger and laid the table, he reached over—unseen by Marlene—and gently squeezed my crotch and wagged his eyebrows, suggestive. I frowned, though I admit he got a rise out of me.

Marlene brought the skillet to the table, an aromatic concoction of cubed beef, vegetables, potatoes and gravy. "Campfire stew. Of course, we don't have an actual campfire to cook it on." She spooned a generous portion onto my plate and Ranger's and a small serving for herself.

"You couldn't cook over an open fire anyway," Ranger said.

"I could if I had the right kind of pots." She set a pitcher of iced tea and a tub of low-calorie butter substitute on the table and a pan of hot cornbread from the oven before sitting down herself.

"Ain't there any real butter?"

"I didn't bring any. This tastes just like real butter."

"The hell it does." He crumbled a chunk of cornbread over his stew and stirred it in. After a bite, he shook his head, grabbed the salt and pepper, and doctored the stew heavily. For my part, I found the meal precisely to my taste; hunger is the best sauce.

"This is just about the best stew I've ever had. It deserves a blue ribbon all by itself."

"Thank you."

"You're very welcome."

Ranger offered neither criticism nor praise, and indeed, there was no more conversation as we continued eating. For a moment, I flashed back to the disastrous last meal that my father and grandfather had shared with me; the silence here was equally uncomfortable. I wondered what the next three days here would hold. Though I'd agreed with Marlene that we should talk, I had deliberately avoided thinking about the content of that conversation.

The state fair experience had only reinforced my feeling that Ranger wasn't quite the man I'd built him up to be. Absence—separation—can make the heart forget and forgive the inconsistencies and the weaknesses of the one out of sight. When Ranger was drinking, he could be an exciting lover just as often as he could be casually cruel, and I never got to pick which one would show up on a given night. The good may have outweighed the bad, and even the bad didn't seem so terrible after Ranger left my bed. But he left me hungry, thirsty, and the small morsels he'd doled out recently neither satisfied nor settled the argument. Did I want Ranger more because he seemed unattainable? If he hadn't met Marlene, would he eventually have come around, come back to me? And would the new thing, the rebuilt thing, have been strong enough to last?

I did not—could not—know, but I suspected not. The physical attraction I felt for him would be difficult to resist. But he wasn't the first man who aroused my shameless cock, and he likely would not be the last.

After dinner—and Ranger's complaint about the lack of dessert beyond fresh fruit—I offered to wash the dishes. He insisted I come outside and help him make a fire in the pit instead.

"Let's clean up first," I said. "Marlene fixed such a fine dinner. It's the least we can do."

"Go on." She shooed us away. "I washed everything up before we ate. All that's left is the plates. I'll have it done in no time."

Outside, Ranger made a fire amid a circle of stones: crumpled newspaper, slivers of wood, and thin, dry branches first and then the logs once the flames took hold. He tended it carefully, and it responded with love. Fire can be mesmerizing, wood burning like need, stinging your eyes. There is something honest, authentic, about fire.

Unexpectedly, he turned to me and put his hand on my neck, pulling my mouth to his, and kissed me again, hard and deep. The violence gave way a moment later to aching need as he pulled me against him and wrapped himself around me. Unlike his kiss when I'd arrived—which felt like nothing more than a stunt, in case Marlene was watching—this one was serious. But as much as I wanted to remain attached to him, I couldn't forget where we were. His rudeness during dinner seemed repellant, but faced with his sudden vulnerability, I could almost forget and forgive.

We stood with flames between us and the cold night tapping at our backs. He lit another cigarette; he said Marlene hadn't figured out that he was smoking again, but I doubted as much. She probably had just given up complaining about it, as she had about everything else on her list. At the start, Ranger did his best to conform, but not for long. He clearly hadn't eliminated or even significantly reduced the swearing that punctuated his conversation. He quit taking any more care with his appearance than he had before they'd met. He'd quit accompanying her to church on Sundays. He had not in any way turned into the kind of man of whom *Reader's Digest* would approve.

I knew these things not because Marlene had shared any further confidence with me, but because Ranger had told me, proudly, when I'd asked him how things were going between them. His answer didn't surprise me, but his bravado evaporated almost as quickly as it had flared.

Like a quick sketch artist, he filled in the rest of the picture: financial worries from the last divorce, looming layoffs in the Buick service department, his mother in ill health from some undisclosed ailment, Mistake Number Five inside the camper, the utter loneliness that even AA couldn't fix. He colored in the details between deep drags on the cigarette, interspersed with a menacing, strangled cough. He'd kept ahold of sobriety with grim determination, but the cost seemed to be everything else in his life.

Anything I could say seemed so appallingly inadequate that I kept my mouth shut. I didn't know if things would or even could be different if he were mine; I didn't know if I could save him from himself. I used to think I could, but everyone feels such misguided omnipotence sometimes.

He heaved the cigarette butt against the fire. "I need a drink so bad."

It was quite an unexpected confession.

Did he really mean it? Perhaps I could help him after all. Impulsively, I walked over to my car and grabbed the flask from the glove compartment. Ranger saw what I had in my hand; knew exactly what it was, what it contained. I saw his eyes shining, moist, and greedy in the light from the fire.

"Whatcha got there?" Hoarse.

"You know what it is."

After a long pause, he whispered, "Ya bring that for me?"

I looked at him, frozen, scared that I might actually hand him the flask and scared that I might not, and I realized how selfish I'd been all these months to want that Ranger back.

Ashamed, I shoved the flask in my back pocket.

"No, Ranger. It's nothing. And I'm sorry. I'm so sorry."

He embraced me again, tight. "Thanks," he whispered, his mustache against my ear. However despicable my impulse, he chose to consider it but a test, and he had passed, no small triumph, emerging stronger as a result. I felt the sandpaper of his beard against my neck, and he started to sob, quiet, and I let him. I held onto him and let him. There was nothing else to do.

For all his faults, I wanted him. Desperately. We'd never before used the "L" word, and it certainly seemed inappropriate now. But it was a true thing, a fact.

When he spent himself, quieted down, I pushed him away, reluctantly.

"Ranger, I've got to tell you something I think you should know."

He squeezed my shoulder. "I already know it. Maybe that's why I invited you."

"So you could rub it in?"

He shook his head.

"You going to tell her? You have to. You're not being fair."

And maybe it was just the smoke making our eyes water. He buried his head against my neck again, but only for a second, before his mouth searched for mine again and found it

After a minute, reluctant, he pushed me away. "Jesus," he said, weary. Beaten. "What's the fucking point? Let's go in."

We carried the memory of the smoke inside with us.

Marlene had already retired, and there was nothing else for us to do this night, so we turned in as well. Ranger disappeared behind the curtain that separated the front end and his wife from the rest of the camper, and I finally figured out how to fold down the dining table to make a narrow bed at the back end. Marlene had left clean bedsheets and a towel for me. When I undressed, I found the flask again in my back pocket. Without thinking too deeply, I gulped down half of the contents, thinking it might help me get to sleep.

It didn't.

I wondered about cultivating a drinking problem myself at some point, weaving it into a red cape, or waving it like a white flag. Would it arouse in Ranger some sympathy? Anger? Disgust? I'd do almost anything to capture his attention because he would surely come to my rescue—wouldn't he? How could he resist such a semaphore? Yet I wondered if I'd have the courage to stand in front of a group of strangers and confess my name and my weaknesses even if he were there next to me, encouraging. I did know that developing a drinking problem would be difficult, time-consuming, inconvenient, and singularly unpleasant, as I had little predisposition toward it. There simply had to be some other way.

An old space heater warmed the place against the coming November. As it heated, it sounded like drops of rain hitting a tin roof, slowly at first—you could count them—and then faster until finally it hummed to life for a few minutes before the thermostat turned it off.

Repeat until daylight.

I never quite got to sleep, though I fell into something of a stupor in the dark. Nor did Ranger sleep. I heard his cough all night, and his restlessness too. He'd been out of the habit of sharing the bed with Marlene for some time, I expect. I wondered if he were wishing me next to him this night.

21

The rain came by morning, the steady and leisurely kind that threatened to stay around all day and confine us indoors. I wasn't at first sure why my head throbbed so, but the half-empty flask reminded me. I hoped Ranger wouldn't notice—or ask any questions about it.

To my surprise, he asked me to fix breakfast; Marlene couldn't make scrambled eggs for shit, he said, loud enough for her to hear, and no one except me could fix his fucking bacon right, he said.

"Language!" Marlene said, resigned, as she had probably said it a million times in the past year. How easily we fall into habits, however useless. I'm sure he didn't hear her reprimand; possibly she was not even aware she had issued it.

Carefully I prepared everything just how he liked it, toast dark with no butter, bacon medium-rare, eggs soft-scrambled but not runny, ketchup over everything—as if I had never been gone. Marlene complimented me too, even though she ate little of the eggs and no bacon. Ranger said he was heading for the showers, and did I want to join him? Marlene rolled her eyes. I begged off and said I'd help with the dishes. Angrily, Ranger grabbed a towel and bar of soap and slammed the door behind him. As wet as he would have gotten en route to the facility, he might just as well have stripped and stood outside the camper for a minute or two.

"You don't seem to be yourself this morning," she said.

"You're right. I confess I'm a little hungover."

She was shocked. "I didn't know you were a drinker."

"I'm not, usually. I brought a flask with me and had a couple of shots last night, hoping it would put me to sleep."

"Did it?"

"No. And now I feel lousy."

"I've got some aspirin in my purse. Would that help?"

I nodded, and she fetched a packet. I swallowed two with the last of my orange juice.

"I don't think it's a good idea to bring that stuff around Ranger, I wish you'd put it away." Her loyalty startled me because it was so unexpected. What makes us stick up for those we used to love as if we still did? But she was right, though she didn't scold or accuse as much as I deserved. "He still has a hard time not drinking. He goes to those meetings three or four times a week."

In response, I retrieved the flask and poured the rest of it down the sink.

"Thanks. That's one less thing we have to worry about, anyway."

"How was your night?"

She sighed. "I couldn't sleep either. Ranger did, though. I don't know which was worse, his snoring or the sound of that darn heater."

I dried the dishes in silence for a few minutes.

"Why would anyone pick to be gay?" she said, thoughtful.

I was startled. "Where did that come from?"

"I was just thinking. Like I said, I couldn't sleep. But I couldn't keep my mind from going all over the place."

Mine had been galloping too.

"Well, it's not a matter of choice. You don't pick to be gay. It's just how you are. How you're born. I never made a decision when I was a kid that I would like men instead of women. No one recruited me. I had a good relationship with my mom and dad when I was growing up, and I still do. I think they would have preferred me to be straight, but they know it wasn't their fault that I'm not. And they're fine with it now."

"Wouldn't it be easier?"

She had me there. It would be, most definitely. It would, for example, exempt me from all such scenes as the one in which I'd currently found myself. "Yes. I guess it would, at that."

"You know, you can change things about yourself that you don't like. Look at me. I hated being fat, and I did something about it. It was hard, and it took me a long time, but I did it."

I agreed that there were certain things one could change if one had the fire inside.

"And look at Ranger, staying sober. It's been hard for him, but he made a commitment, and he's sticking to it. See? Don't you think you could be...not gay if you wanted to?"

"Look at it this way. Do you think you could decide right now that you were attracted to women instead of men? I mean, romantically attracted. Like you could fall in love with a beautiful woman. Could you?"

She was shocked. "Of course not. What a question."

"That's exactly how I feel. If I get excited about a handsome guy with a nice, um, physique, there's not a whole lot I can do. It's a physical reaction. I don't control it. I certainly just can't decide that I won't prefer men anymore. I can't make myself feel attracted to women any more than you can."

"Hmm...I never really thought about it like that."

"Besides, what makes you think I don't like being gay?"

"Do you?" She sounded surprised.

"Yes. I'm perfectly content. I can't imagine being any other way, nor would I want to be. Besides, I'm not the only one in my family. My dad's father—my granddad—was gay too. He was a professor of literature at the university. He just died earlier this year, eighty-three years old. Ranger met him a couple of times."

"How do you know he was gay?"

"He told me. He and my grandmother got divorced because of it, when my dad was nine years old."

"Did your grandfather have a—whatever you call it?"

"A partner? Yes. That's one reason why my grandparents split up. His partner was another professor at the university. Granddad was hopeful it would last, but after a couple of years, the guy dumped him for one of his students. And that was the end of it."

"Well, even if your grandpa was gay, he got married. To a woman. And had a kid."

"Yes, he did, but he shouldn't have. It would have been a lot easier on my grandmother and my dad."

"Your dad wouldn't even be around to care. And neither would you."

She had a point. "I can't argue with that. I'm not sorry that my grandfather was gay. At the same time, I can't be sorry that he got married, or I wouldn't be here to tell the story, as you've pointed out. Lots of gay men marry women."

"Why?"

"In my granddad's case, he didn't have much choice in the late 1960s. He was a schoolteacher, and people expected schoolteachers to be straight—and to be married. Even though more gay people are out today, you still find a lot of them who marry someone of the opposite sex just for the sake of appearances. It can be an occupational hazard to be gay in a lot of career fields. Look at professional sports. And politics. Unfortunately, when a gay man gets married to a woman, there's always a risk that he'll cheat. Get caught with another man. People get hurt. My dad and grandmother had a very hard time after the divorce, and I don't think my dad ever got over it."

"Your grandpa just died this year?"

"In April. I miss him."

"I'm sorry." Marlene dumped the dishwater down the drain and crammed the dishes and skillet into the little cupboard. "Is Ranger like that?"

"Like what?"

"You know. Gay."

"Marlene, that's not a question I can answer in his place. You have to ask him."

"I know. I think I know the answer, but I'm afraid to ask him. But I'm going to have to, huh?"

I nodded. Marlene's question made me wonder if Ranger had told her anything about me—us?—as their marriage started to unravel. It might have been ammunition for the battle, maybe, or just sheer spite. Or longing. Perhaps she had simply opened her eyes and taken a good look.

We poured ourselves another cup of coffee and had just sat down when Ranger returned, his clothes and towel sopping wet and clearly in ill humor. Without ceremony, he kicked off his sneakers, and stripped off his soggy shirt and jeans. Naked, he rummaged in a duffel bag, glaring at us as he did so.

"Ranger, please. Cover yourself up."

"Why? You seen me buck naked before. And what makes ya think Neil never saw my bare ass?"

His comment startled me. It was a bold statement for him to make to her. She chose not to ask any of the follow-on questions that I could not have resisted if presented with such a provocative opener—such as "when?" and perhaps "how often?" or maybe even "how recently?"

"Good grief. I don't care if Neil has seen your bare—bottom. Get dressed, for heaven's sake. Be civilized. Or at least decent."

"Ya knew I wasn't fucking decent when you married me."

She didn't even bother to chide him with "Language!"

Taking his time, he fished dry pants and another T-shirt from the backpack and got dressed. When he finished, Marlene thanked him, sarcastically, for the performance.

"Let us know in advance when the next show will be. We'll take some pictures and put them on the internet."

He muttered something under his breath and poured himself another cup of coffee as well. Spot, still outside, woofed and scratched at the door, and without thinking, Ranger opened it. Spot bounded in, dripping wet, and promptly shook himself, anointing all present.

"Jesus *fuck*," Ranger yelled. Poor Spot cowered and slunk off, hiding himself under the bed. We wouldn't see him for a while, but—the scent of wet dog being so pungent—he made his presence known. I wondered if Marlene would finally confront Ranger, but in his current bad mood, she apparently decided to postpone it. When she finished her coffee, she excused herself and went to get her book, a romance novel with a steamy cover: a buffed, muscular man in a torn white shirt and a voluptuous woman crushing each other in an embrace. A chasm lay between the picture and any reality she had ever known. Or I, or Ranger.

Taking a tip from Marlene, I pulled *An American Tragedy* out of my backpack, a little light reading I'd been slowly wading through for weeks. Theodore Dreiser wasn't a favorite, but the title might seem prophetic, if a little exaggerated, for our own little drama. Marlene gave me an approving nod. Ranger, left out, turned on the transistor radio to a country station. Both Marlene and I said "no way" at the same time.

"I sure as hell ain't gonna listen to any more of the Christian shit."

"Well, I prefer jazz, myself. Since that's not likely to fly either, let's find something we can all agree on for once."

He settled for an oldies station playing innocuous '60s tunes, overly familiar but inoffensive all the same. More than once as the afternoon crept on, one or another of us—occasionally all three—hummed along or tapped our feet to the Beatles, the Miracles, the Byrds, the Supremes, Mamas, Papas, and others. And when Connie Francis came on, singing "Where the Boys Are," was I the only one of our trio aware that it could have been our very own theme song? For three minutes, anyway, we shared common ground.

Marlene fixed a lunchtime salad for herself and for me while Ranger pretended to take a nap. Though none of us believed he actually slept, we appreciated the break. His glowering presence hung in the room like the scent of the wet Spot. If Ranger remained sullen, there would be no chance of civilized discourse between us, and I wasn't sure I would stay another night.

The rain quit in mid-afternoon, and gradually, the sky cleared. After several valiant attempts, the sun came out to stay and brightened things considerably. Marlene opened the door of the trailer and the light spilled in, cheering all of us. She pulled two folding chairs out of the truck, and even though the temperature stayed in the upper fifties, we bundled up and moved outside.

"It's so nice here," she said. "It's good to get away from home once in a while. The light this time of year is my favorite, just like gold. Look at the leaves changing color in the sun. It's so magic."

I agreed. I was surprised at how effortlessly we fell into companionable conversation, peppered with easy laughter as we traded our stories—none of which involved Ranger. At last, a little too late, possibly, but a relief nonetheless, we could take the time to get to know each other in a way that would have served us well a year earlier. I shared the blame, however; even if Ranger had not sabotaged any chance of friendship the three of us might have had, I'd been too jealous of Marlene for stealing Ranger away.

He did, however, make his own choice. If he were unhappy with the results, only he could fix the situation. Marlene seemed to understand, which may have been the only reason she, too, was now willing to let our troubled past go. In this campground, far from my own home, a mug of hot cocoa in my hands, I was grateful for her condescension.

Perhaps sick of his own company—or maybe feeling utterly left out—Ranger finally joined us, setting up a chair for himself. If he expected us to shift the conversation toward him or make an effort to include him, he was disappointed. He continued to sulk, but neither Marlene nor I took much notice.

The fading sun seemed to bring benediction, and it did not surrender to the night without a struggle. The entire sky glowed with color, and from our chairs under the campground trees, we watched the show until dark crept in.

I think we all seemed to recognize that something was ending. The chill in the air seemed to add its own sardonic postscript.

"It's going to be a cold night," Marlene said. "I don't guess there's any dry firewood, huh?"

"I covered it with a plastic tarp last night because I knew it was fixing to rain," Ranger said, clearly proud of his foresight—and the first remark of any consequence he'd made since joining us outside. Unprompted, he built a blazing fire in the pit, and we were grateful to move our chairs around it. For dinner, Marlene brought out hotdogs. On skewers fashioned from wire coat hangers, we barbecued them over the flame. She added sodas and homemade coleslaw for an impromptu picnic, the perfect conclusion to the afternoon.

We ate in silence until Marlene spoke up. "Ranger, let me ask you something."

I knew precisely what would follow. And it came. "Are you gay?"

Her question caught him unaware. He'd just taken a big bite of his third hotdog and started coughing, choking on the mouthful. I pounded him on the back until he caught his breath again.

Marlene remained calm. "Well?"

"Well, what?"

"Are you?"

"Am I what?"

"Come on. It's time we talked about it. Long past time. Are you gay?"

"Jesus, Marlene." He threw a log on the fire and poked at it. He glared at me. "Did you put her up to this, Neil?"

"No. But why don't you answer the question?"

"Okay, fine." I could see he was working himself up into a proper lather. With an effort, he controlled his response. "No, Marlene. For your information, I ain't gay."

I was speechless.

"Because if you are, it's okay," she said. "You can be honest with me for a change. It would be kind of nice, actually. Neil and I had a long talk this morning while you were out taking a shower, but he wouldn't say what he thought. He told me I needed to ask you."

"You and yer big mouth," he said to me. And to Marlene, he again issued a denial.

"I saw how you kissed him when he got here. What was that about? You never kissed me that way, Ranger. Even when we first got together, when I used to think you liked me. You never did."

Ranger muttered something under his breath.

Marlene continued. "All you had to tell me was that you liked guys. Why did you even ask me out the first time? You could have saved us a lot of trouble."

"Goddamn it, I ain't no fucking faggot!"

"Speak a little louder, Ranger. I'm sure everyone in the campground wants to know. I think you're protesting a little too much. It's kind of hard, after we've been married for ten months, to find out. It explains a lot."

I wondered what it did explain for her. I'd never had a clear picture of the kind of sex life Ranger shared with Marlene. For all I knew, it could have been lusty and vigorous or virtually non-existent. I rather suspected the latter.

Ranger lowered his voice to a more conversational level. "Shut the hell up, Marlene."

"So much for having a real adult discussion. I'm going inside." She did, and she locked the door to the trailer.

"Fucking bitch." Ranger heaved the rest of his hotdog into the fire, and his can of soda too. "Goddamn fucking *bitch.*" I'm sure the whole campground heard him the second time.

"Hush up. There's no reason to be nasty. She asked you a fair question. And you lied to her."

"Did not."

I wasn't about to get into a schoolyard argument with him.

"Okay, have it your own way. You're a straight man who happens to prefer sucking cock. Why are you angry at Marlene? It's not her fault that you're stuck. You had no business marrying her. You have no business marrying any woman if you would rather have sex with men."

"I never said that."

"You don't have to say a word. You put your tongue in my mouth and grab my crotch. Actions speak louder and faster. I don't know, and I surely don't care if you and Marlene had sex every night or if you never had sex at all. It doesn't matter to me. But she married you in good faith, and she deserves a man who wants her. You're not that man."

"That's for damn sure."

"So what are you going to do about it?"

He shrugged. "Give her the divorce if she wants it."

"Don't you want to get out as well?"

He shrugged.

"What about me?"

"This ain't about you."

"You've been throwing yourself at me ever since the party."

His eyes glinted in the firelight. "And now ya can have me. I got a blanket in the truck. We can spread it out in back."

His abrupt shifting of gears startled me. I flashed back briefly to the story his ex, Laura, had told me at his one-year sobriety party, about her catching him in the back of his pickup, having noisy sex with a man he'd picked up somewhere. I didn't like the similarity of the situations.

"Marlene is inside."

"She won't come out. Fuck her."

"No!" I was angry at him for mixing me up again. "That's *your* responsibility. It's part of the marriage contract. If you don't want to, or if you can't get a hard-on for a woman, or if there's even the tiniest possibility that you might actually be queer even though you won't admit it—then you need to tell her and give her a chance to get out of this mess."

"Jesus Christ, Neil. Ya think too much. Ya want that blowjob or not?"

I wanted to explode—and take him out at the same time. "*No*, Ranger. I do not."

He seemed genuinely mystified.

"You made your own bed! Even if you choose not to lie in it anymore, you still have a wife in it. That's not my fault. Now you're desperate for some attention from a man, but that's not my fault either. Let me introduce you to your right hand. It will never let you down. I speak from too much experience."

"I had a wife when ya met me. Ya didn't seem so worried about *her* when ya was sucking my dick."

"That's true, and I'm ashamed to admit it. I didn't think about your wife. It was a lapse in judgment. I didn't care. I never met her, and I never wanted to. It was so easy to pretend she didn't matter. Or even exist because, for me, she didn't."

"So what's so damn different now?"

"One crucial thing. The difference is that you could have come with me. Picked *me*. You had the chance, but you chose Marlene instead. I can't forget that."

He was, I told him, careless with people. He used them for his convenience, and when they were no longer expedient, he dumped them. Only he was in such an all-fired hurry that he picked people up and started using them before he really got to know them, and by the time he grew bored and ready to move on to the next one, they'd fallen in love with him. And he was already gone.

"I'll bet every one of your ex-wives will agree with me, and Marlene too. It's no wonder she didn't like me, and I didn't like her—how could I, the way you jammed her in between us all the time, as if you wanted me to compete with her for your attention?"

Having gotten to know her better recently, I realized she wasn't the evil witch Ranger wanted me to believe. She never had a chance. He'd treated her despicably. Come to think of it, he'd treated me the same way, not only before he quit drinking but since. He'd been willing to let me do his laundry, clean his house, buy his groceries, drive him to and from meetings, and assist with tedious tasks because two could get them done faster than one. There had been nothing in our interaction for me except my time and expense. He gave nothing—only took.

The trip to the state fair was, in a way, the last straw. Instead of making it an enjoyable outing, a chance to make peace or at least declare a truce, he'd only made Marlene even sorrier that she'd married him, not even allowing her to enjoy her achievements. That was just plain meanness, I told him. Nice guys didn't do that. And because I'd been stupid enough to go along with it, I wasn't a very nice guy myself.

Throughout my tirade, he'd remained silent. It wasn't the first time my mouth had gotten away with me, and I'd overwhelmed him with my stream-of-consciousness.

"Neil, simmer down. It's whiskey under the bridge, okay? So I ain't been the best husband to Marlene. What the hell. Can't do a damn thing about that now. But that don't change what we got."

"You and me? What do *we* have? You won't even admit to anyone that you're actually gay. And now you expect me to believe it's me you wanted all along?"

He shrugged. Nodded.

I was determined that he would not seduce me this time. I wasn't proud of the role I'd played in his manipulative game. Perhaps it wasn't too late to remove myself from it.

"Ranger, I've been waiting to hear you say that. Ever since we met—but you know damn well you don't really mean it. You finally figured out I could be very useful to help you get rid of Marlene. You knew how convincing I would be, playing the part of the other man, because you knew I loved you. Now, thanks to me, Marlene is angry enough to dump your sorry ass. That's exactly what you want. And you're feeling magnanimous, so why not let me give you a blowjob in the back of your truck to show your appreciation?"

"Ya think too much. Who gives a goddamn? Marlene sure as hell don't, so what difference does it make? How come yer gettin' so all-fired hot about it? Let's you and me roll around in the back of my truck for a while. I'll cool ya down." He unzipped his jeans and lowered them enough to show he was fully aroused.

"Have you listened to a single word I said?"

"Every one. A million words. But what the fuck? Talk's just talk. I don't know what the hell yer goin' on about." He stropped his cock, and it responded eagerly to his touch.

After the party at AA, I would've already been undressed and on the blanket, blissfully enjoying all the Ranger I could eat. Tonight, I'd been lambasting him for ignoring Marlene's feelings—and mine—and the only response he could offer was this?

"Pull up your pants, Ranger. At this point, I'm not actually interested at all."

I felt exhausted, but I knew I would not be able to sleep. I knocked on the trailer door and identified myself. Marlene let me inside. I hadn't brought much with me, and it only took me a couple of minutes to collect my things.

"What will you do about Ranger?" I said.

"I'm through. Do you want him?"

"No. There was a time I would have said yes, but I didn't know him very well then."

"So you wised up, too, huh? Good for you. Well, he can just sleep in the truck tonight. I won't let him back in here. Tomorrow, we'll go back home. I've got a lot of thinking to do, and some plans to make. It will take some time, but I guess there's no hurry. I'll manage."

Marlene gave me a hug.

"Call me one of these days," I said. She promised and let me outside. I didn't see Ranger as I headed for my car. I threw the duffel bag into the back seat, fired up the engine, and backed out of the parking spot. As I shifted into first gear, he suddenly appeared in the shine of my headlights, walking toward me, naked except for his cowboy boots and shapeless Stetson—skinny, vulnerable, scared, every breath a cloud in the chilled night air. I paused for a second to look and as I watched, the air simply went out of him. He seemed to crumple for a second, and then he straightened up and stood tall.

I rolled down the window.

"Hey, good-lookin.' Whatcha got cookin'?" he whispered.

"Most people are asleep at this hour."

"Eat me, pal."

Alice had gotten a similar directive in Wonderland.

Ranger shivered, as much from the cold as—I think—fear. I could see it in his eyes. But I could not do it. I reached over and locked the passenger door in case he had ideas about joining me.

"Ranger, you don't belong to me. Until you and Marlene are all done, and until you can tell me that you want me—publicly, not just for ten minutes in your pickup truck—I can't. And I won't."

His eyes narrowed. "Ya been throwing yourself at my ass for the last two years, Neil. Now I'm ready to fuck and ya change your mind. Goddamn cock-teaser. Well, all I got to say is—" and I watched him trying to come up with the worst possible insult, the most withering remark he could summon, and it was this: "Fuck ya, ya fucking fucker!" I couldn't help but laugh, even if it wasn't exactly funny. Weary, I eased the car out of the lot and onto the main road leading out of the campground.

I got home around four o'clock in the morning, but by then, I was wide awake. I'd left Ranger with plenty to think over, but he didn't seem inclined to want to think or to accept any responsibility. If he wanted to get in touch, however, he knew how to reach me. I wondered if I'd ever hear from him again.

I let my parents know that I'd returned early, and Mom invited me for dinner. I happily accepted, as I still had two days of vacation left. We spent an enjoyable evening together, and it proved the perfect antidote to the empty feeling in the pit of my stomach left over from the camping trip.

"Your father has finally agreed to do something about that heap of rusty junk in the backyard," Mom said over chocolate layer cake and coffee.

I laughed. "I'm sure you had nothing to do with his decision, huh, Mom?"

As my dad had told me, nearly five months previously when I delivered the Buick to their yard, he could count on my mother to make sure he either started the project or got rid of it. She finally gave him the ultimatum; it was his choice, but he had to exercise one of the two options.

"When it got swallowed by the weeds over the summer, he probably thought I'd forget all about it. Didn't you, dear?"

"Hmm...well, maybe," my dad admitted.

"So what's the plan?" I said.

"Well, I don't know the first thing about restoring an old Buick, so I started at the library to see what I could find."

"Which was approximately nothing," my mom said.

"That might be a little specific for the public library," I said.

"There's all kinds of stuff online, but I spent a week sorting through websites, blogs, videos, and who-knows-what, and I still didn't have a clear notion of how to begin. Then I had a brilliant idea."

I waited, expectant.

"I stopped by the service department at the Buick dealership in town and asked if they knew anyone who could help. And guess what? I found a guy there who's actually done some restoration work. So I introduced myself and told him about the car. He came by to take a look and says it's doable! And he's already got most of the tools. Offered me a reasonable hourly rate. Of course, I'll buy all the parts and supplies, too. Says he might be able to start next weekend."

He was clearly proud of himself and his good fortune.

"I'll believe it when I see it," Mom said. "I hate to sound like a skeptic, but it seems a little too good to be true."

"Not a bit," my father said. "I'm a good judge of character. This fellow's on the up-and-up."

My mother clucked her tongue and rolled her eyes for my benefit.

"I know a guy who works in the service department at Buick, but he can't be the same one," I said. The man I knew would never offer to help a total stranger tackle such a project. "What's his name?"

"It's an interesting one. Hang on." My dad took out his wallet and pulled out a business card.

"Ranger Melusky," he said.

22

Now that I'd been handed the man I wanted on a plate, with the soon-to-be-fifth-ex-wife's permission, I knew one thing: I honestly no longer wanted him. He was selfish, careless, mean-spirited, sanctimonious. Life is hard enough; why saddle yourself with someone who'll deny himself—and, directly or indirectly—you, too?

There was no reason. Just no reason whatsoever. But despite the brave face I showed Ranger at the campground and my eloquent argument, I still missed him. Not seeing him again, ever, would hurt. The heart wants what it wants; no logic can penetrate or short-circuit it. But I would have to figure out a way to manage. If a man could quit drinking alcohol in spite of continuing to crave its blissful escape, I could quit Ranger.

I still yearned for a sober version of him who would kiss me as lustily as the six-beers-along version used to, whose raging hard-on could conquer foreign lands as efficiently as any sword. His loud, appreciative monologue as our various tabs and slots slid into and out of each other. But I wondered if, in Ranger's mind, fucking could ever be transformed into making love.

How different would sex be for him since he quit drinking? Alcohol loosened his nuts and bolts; without a drink or five, would he still be able to relax and enjoy himself?

I might never find out.

Apart from the sobriety, which was essential, I didn't care if he smoked and cussed and put his feet up on the coffee table and wandered around the house stark naked. I didn't care if he went to church, wore pressed shirts and clean boots, or got a haircut every month. I wanted him to fix cars as long as he desired, and I wanted him to want to come home to me at the end of the day. I would happily cook and keep house as necessary, as long as he let me pursue my own career as well. If we kept two residences (he'd never give up the home he built, and I'd never be able to part with my grandfather's place), that would be fine, too. But he would have to accept himself. Me.

And, most importantly, us.

November gave way to December, and I couldn't shake the nagging feeling that maybe I should have grabbed him when Marlene offered and taken my chances. Perhaps he and I could have worked out a deal of some sort, if he'd have agreed to—well, what, exactly?

I remembered Marlene's multifaceted improvement program for Ranger, and how I'd told her it was doomed to failure. It did. He didn't want to change, or he would have made the effort himself. His success with Alcoholics Anonymous was proof that it was possible for him to eliminate destructive behavior and aim his life in a more positive direction, but only if he chose.

Maybe if I changed. If I promised to quit bartending and if I promised to quit drinking entirely (neither of which would have caused me significant heartbreak). Maybe I could accept Ranger's refusal to commit himself to being gay and simply be patient, knowing he would come to me at least on occasion when he got desperate.

Oh, hell, no.

I called Rex. I hadn't heard from him in so long that I felt the need to touch base with him. With my grandfather gone, there was no one else who could understand, sympathize, relate. In the back of my mind, I even entertained the dim notion that I might persuade Rex to leave Sparky in Bensalem and fly to Indiana to be with me. We could, I believed, start all sorts of fires between us, slow-burning embers and forest-destructive conflagrations in turn. Maybe he could make me forget Ranger altogether if I could do the same for him and Sparky.

Maybe.

I didn't expect Sparky to answer the phone, but he was civil, even amiable, asking what was new and how life was treating me. In return, I inquired about his health and his horse training, but he knew why I'd called.

"He's right here," Sparky said. "Hang on."

Rex's enthusiastic greeting brought tears to my eyes. I hadn't realized how much I'd missed him. For his part, he couldn't have been more thrilled that I had reached out.

"All this time, I thought you were missing in action," he said. "It's been a long time, and I should apologize for not calling, too. I've thought about you often, wondering how you're doing. So you'd better tell me everything, starting with a progress report about Ranger."

Where could I begin?

"The short version is that his wife Marlene decided she was done with him. She actually offered him to me, and after careful consideration, I turned the bastard down flat."

Gentle, he said, "So what's the full-length version? You need to tell someone, and I've got nothing on my calendar today. Find yourself a comfortable chair, pour yourself a cup of fresh coffee, and tell me all about it."

We were on the phone for nearly three hours. Rex proved himself to be a compassionate listener, offering sympathy as well as support, mercifully without prescription. At the end of it, I felt better. I no longer wished for Rex—or anyone—to come and rescue me, as if I were trapped in some slightly-fractured fairy tale, wherein one handsome prince awaited another handsome prince. I would find my own way, alone if necessary.

The contact with Rex energized me in ways I could not explain. Better days were coming; I could feel it, and I was at last not content to wait for opportunity to bang on the door. If I moved slowly, perhaps I could be forgiven, but the point is that I moved. In mid-November, I made a field trip to the English department at the university, which proved not merely fruitful but quite encouraging. I was pleased to discover—twelve years after graduating—that half a dozen of my former professors were still on the staff, and they remembered me fondly (and my grandfather too, of course).

When I asked about the master's degree program for literature, they were most insistent that I apply to begin my studies in January. A scholarship had recently been established in my grandfather's name in accordance with his will, and I was told I could quite possibly be eligible to receive the very first one, in spite of the family connection. I was assured that a teaching assistantship would be available as well, which included a stipend.

One of my old professors had moved into Granddad's former office, and I took a peek, with the new tenant's blessing. Minus the familiar books, the creaking wooden chair, framed photos and memorabilia, and the man himself, however, I couldn't get sentimental about it. I filled out the application online that evening and posted it before I went to bed.

Mom and Dad were proud of me for taking the step, and I knew just how Granddad would have felt, too—especially when I got the letter in the mailbox a month later informing me that I'd been accepted into the program. The envelope also included a contract for a teaching assistantship. I would start the new year as a student again for the first time in a dozen years, but also as an instructor for two sections of English 102, a course designed to teach freshmen how to write an effective research paper.

My parents were as pleased with the news as I was myself.

Scotty kept in touch, and I enjoyed his company but was grateful that he didn't press for anything more. I think we both knew we were still carrying our respective torches—his for my grandfather, mine for Ranger. Occasionally, Scotty and I shared a night at his place or mine, but even those trysts became less frequent. He finally admitted he'd found a man closer to his own age who was interested in commitment. We celebrated and bid each other a fond farewell. I had the usual propositions from one or another of the country club clientele, but I'd had my fill of married men and gently declined. A little celibacy wouldn't hurt. I let my boss know I'd be quitting for good at the end of the year.

I decked my grandfather's halls for Christmas as he used to in the years before he decided it was too much trouble: a wreath on the door, electric candles in the front windows, twinkling lights around the porch railing, a modest evergreen tree by the fireplace in the living room. The ornaments had been carefully stored in tissue paper in the attic, including several that were likely made by my dad as a child.

I persuaded my family to join me for the Christmas feast. It would be my first real dinner party and the first time I'd entertained on that ambitious level at any time. I wanted to prepare the same traditional holiday meal we'd always enjoyed together, and a week before Christmas, I stopped by to borrow my mom's recipes and pick her brain for cooking tips and advice.

I noticed that the old Buick had disappeared from the backyard. As my father had made no further mention of the restoration project, I was certain that Mom had insisted on his getting rid of the wreck. I didn't even ask my dad, not wanting to scratch open a sore spot. Nothing I knew about Ranger suggested that he would actually commit to the restoration venture that Dad suggested, and I could not imagine him tolerating Ranger's company and cheerful vulgarity for more than a single day before giving up in disgust. And what would have prompted Ranger to offer assistance for the project anyway? He'd have learned immediately that Dad didn't know the first thing about vehicle restoration, and the bulk of the work would be Ranger's full responsibility. I could not imagine his having the patience to teach the necessary skills to my father, starting from scratch.

But I put it out of my mind. I had work to do. I wanted Granddad's house to sparkle when my father and grandmother walked in. They hadn't seen its interior in more than half a century, and I wanted them to be impressed, though I had no delusion that they would actually feel at home. On Christmas Eve, I scoured and dusted and vacuumed and wrapped presents. Christmas morning found me out of bed before dawn, with a turkey to dress, cranberry sauce and green bean casserole to prepare, eggnog to blend, a pie to bake, and a table to set. Mid-afternoon, I lit a fire in the fireplace, plugged in the tree lights, and put some leisurely holiday jazz on the stereo. I fixed myself a cup of cocoa and took it to the porch to enjoy the last of the fading sun on a brittle but beautiful afternoon. Snow began falling, which seemed to be a good omen. I didn't think the day could be more perfect.

When my family arrived, we stood on the porch for a minute to exchange holiday greetings and hugs. I didn't want to rush anyone; my mother had never been inside and would be more curious than anything, but I suspected the experience would be more emotional for Dad and Grandma.

"Ready?" I said.

My dad took a deep breath and nodded, and I ushered them in. I was glad I'd taken the time to decorate and light the fire. The front room positively glowed with warmth and sparkling light. I served eggnog all around, and we exchanged our gifts. I was pleased to unwrap a briefcase, the first I'd ever had, and an appointment planner for the new year, which would come in handy once school started.

My dad was surprised to notice the handmade tree ornaments, which indeed had been his handiwork—school art projects, he said. He hadn't expected that Granddad would have kept them all those years.

I encouraged Dad to accompany me on a tour of the house. It had been, after all, his home too, in the distant past—and because it was mine now, I wanted him to feel welcome. Mom wanted to see the place too, of course, and even Grandma allowed herself to be persuaded to follow along. She limited her comments to the fact that the furniture had held up well and that I kept a clean house.

Dad kept his composure until we looked into his old bedroom, which had been left exactly as it was when he was a boy, with some of his old books and toys still on the shelves and the same spread on the bed. (I'd seen no reason to change anything.) He asked if he could sit in the room for a minute, and I told him he could stay as long as he wanted.

I excused myself to make the gravy and put the biscuits into the oven. Mom and Grandma came with me, offering their assistance to put dinner on the table. When Dad joined us later, I could tell that he'd been crying. I offered a hug, and he was grateful.

The whole meal worked out splendidly, from the golden turkey and fragrant dressing right down to the mince pie and coffee. My parents were lavish with praise, and I was more than pleased with the results.

Later, after they left, Rex called to wish me the merriest. When he asked about Ranger, I realized I'd been so wrapped up in the preparations for the dinner and for the holiday in general that I'd completely forgotten: Christmas Day also marked Ranger and Marlene's first wedding anniversary.

How, I wondered, had they celebrated this day?

I settled into my dual teacher-and-student role at the university in January with surprising ease. Because I started halfway through the academic calendar year, I missed the usual first-teaching experience of

English 101, the freshman composition class required of all university students, no matter what their choice of major. Instead, I tumbled headlong into the research-writing course. It proved to be a good fit. New teaching assistants like me had a week of orientation before the semester started, seminars and discussions about teaching methods and appropriate practices about grading, academic integrity and fairness, the challenges and rewards of using the internet as a tool, and an introduction to the required textbook. I would be expected to put in at least four hours of office time in addition to my two days of teaching per week. I was assigned a cramped cubicle in the basement of the department headquarters building with a dozen other graduate students, all younger than I.

I loved it.

Quitting the bartending job had been a good choice. I didn't need the money, but I did need the entire week to read and study for my own classes, as well as prepare lesson plans and grade papers for my students. I fell into a routine and found it immensely satisfying. All the pieces fit.

I had very little time to dwell on the fact that I was by myself.

I gave my English 102 students a relatively straightforward assignment: a detailed research paper, at least fifteen pages in length, about the legacy of any nineteenth or twentieth-century American author of the student's choosing. Each would be required to find primary and secondary sources, including works by the author, collected letters, interviews, critical texts, and so on—and not just online. I'd make sure they could locate a book or periodical in the library stack, even if such skills wouldn't necessarily serve them in the future. I argued that tradition had a place in research.

With no prompting from me, I was pleased that two of my students chose Mark Twain for their subject of study. And I was thrilled when both of them included articles written by my grandfather in their bibliographical research, without even a hint from me.

However, I couldn't see spending more time in the classroom than necessary. After all, the class focused on research methods. Whenever possible, I convened my students at the library so they could use the time to their advantage, with me available as a resource where I could do the most good. I positioned myself at a central table near one of the reference desks and dispatched the students to their individual projects, requiring only that they check in at the end of our session to show me their progress.

The hours at the library passed quickly, and I never felt bored. A steady stream of questions kept me engaged—and alert. On more than one occasion, I was stumped, and the best I could tell my student was "Let's find out." Off we would go on some literary treasure hunt. The kids grew more accustomed to seeing a "back in ten minutes" sign in my chair than finding me sitting in it. When I returned after one such search, I found two students waiting, and while I assisted the first with his questions about proper bibliography format, another guy joined the queue. Only he wasn't a student; it was Ranger, with a wicked grin on his face as he eavesdropped avidly.

A young woman slid into the chair next to me. "Mr. Graham, I can't find much information about my author at all. There's nothing in the library catalog except the four novels she wrote, and I can't get much from the blurbs on the book jackets."

"Have you checked out the periodical index online? I bet you'll find some up-to-date sources, and most of them are probably available. If we don't have the journals you need in the current periodicals collection or online, you can request materials through inter-library loan. You can access the index from any of the library computer terminals, or from your tablet, if you brought it with you. Also, check for videos. Maybe she was interviewed on a talk show or podcast, and you could get some direct quotations."

"Okay, I'll see what I can find. Thanks, Mr. Graham!"

Ranger slid into her vacated seat. "Hey there, Mr. Graham."

"Well. It's been a long time, Ranger."

"I had a hell of a time finding ya. Good thing I took a half-day off." He rattled off the details of his adventure, how he'd called me but gotten no answer (I turned my phone off when I was teaching), how he'd gone to the bar at the country club and discovered that I'd quit and returned to school. The university operator had found my name listed in the campus directory and let him know the location of my office in the English department. Ranger had looked for me in the office and my classroom and finally tracked me down here.

"I been chasing ya 'round this goddamn school for the last two hours, and I finally got ya cornered." He was clearly pleased with himself for his resourceful detective work and its successful conclusion.

"What do you want? I'm flattered that you went to the trouble, but why, exactly?"

"I wanted to see ya."

"So here I am."

"Ya look good, Neil."

So did he. Damn. But I would resist. "How is everything these days?"

"All right, I guess. Same old same old. Working for Buick. Still not drinking. Over seventeen months now. Well. Discounting that one time."

I remembered. "Congratulations. How's Marlene?"

"Okay, I guess. We don't talk so much. How ya doing?"

"Well, I'm a student again, and an instructor, as you know, thanks to your brilliant sleuthing. The semester started three weeks ago. I'm teaching two classes and taking four, and keeping office hours. I've got lessons to prepare, papers to grade, and a mountain of reading to do. It keeps me busy. When I finish the program—which I might be able to do in about eighteen months, if I apply myself—I'll look for a teaching position. I hope to find something around here, but I won't know until I start looking."

"Do anything ya want. Ya know I don't care, long as it's something ya like. But I'm glad ya got out of bartending. Always said ya could do better."

Marlene, he said, was finally making a move in the direction of the door. She promised she would be filing divorce papers this month—it took her long enough since the weekend at the camper, didn't it?—and he wasn't sure how he'd find the money to pay for another divorce, but he'd scrape it up somehow, wouldn't he? He could get some overtime hours at Buick, and that would help. Not drinking kept his expenses down like I wouldn't believe, he said. And he was making an effort to cut down on the smoking, which would save him a couple of hundred dollars a month, too.

His chatter contained no mention of a car restoration project, and I didn't ask, but after a couple minutes, I began to lose patience.

"What do you want exactly?"

That deflated him a little, and I was immediately sorry I'd been so blunt.

"Ya ...miss me?" His voice was small.

Did I? Hmm. I confess I got a charge out of seeing him at the library. Reminded me of the old days. But I was surprised that the answer was "not really." Slowly, I shook my head. "A long time ago, I met a guy driving drunk, stark naked in his pickup truck. He invited me into the cab to swap blowjobs. It's the best sex I ever had in my life. I miss that guy. He was kind of fun after he'd had a few beers."

He scowled. "So if I want ya back, I gotta start drinking again? I get it."

"Horseshit!" I used lexicon he could understand, though I did lower my voice. "You don't get anything. Whether you drink or not has nothing to do with it. I never know where I stand with you! And how could I, when you won't even admit that you're gay? I was good enough to be your bedmate when you were drunk. And you enjoyed it. But when you sobered up, you didn't want anything to do with me. In case you never noticed, I was always the same man whether you were drunk or sober. I wanted to be with you all the time, but if that mattered at all to you, you never showed it."

"I will now. With Marlene out of the picture, ain't nothing to stand in the way."

"Stand in the way of *what*? Us? How can I be sure you won't get tired of me too after a while and start looking for something else? Look at your track record. Have you ever made a commitment that you kept?"

He looked ashamed. "I been sober all these months."

He had a point. "Yes. I'm proud of you. I mean that. But does it keep you warm at night?"

"It don't. That's why I'm here, Neil."

"Just because we both like dick doesn't mean we'll ever really have anything in common. You call me a faggot because I'm willing to live my life as a fully-out gay man, but you won't come out at all because you're a coward."

"I ain't, neither! What I do inside my own house ain't nobody's business but my own. I ain't selling tickets."

"I've known too many men like you who are too scared to admit they're gay, but they're hot to meet you after dark to swap blowjobs. But I can't be one of them. Not anymore. I need a man who wants to get naked with me on the roof of the house in broad daylight for all of heaven and earth to see. A man who'll kiss me in public no matter who else is watching. You're not the man, Ranger."

"I could be. How d'ya know, if ya won't give me a chance to?"

One student and then a second and a third had lined up a polite distance away from the table where Ranger and I were deep in conversation. One poked at her phone, bored. The other two carried on a whispered conversation of their own, patiently waiting their turns.

"I'm sorry. I have students waiting, and this is their class time. They've got a right to my undivided attention during this hour."

"And I ain't." Defeated, he pushed back his chair and stood up. "Sorry I wasted yer valuable time, Neil."

I sighed. "It's not like that. It's just that—well, between the classes I take and the classes I teach, I just don't have time for anything extra right now."

"Yeah. Well, maybe I'll just wait around, at the edges, if ya don't mind too much. See if ya can find a little room for me one of these days."

He pushed back his chair, stood up, walked away, his head down. I'd told him almost exactly the same thing long ago, but I couldn't think about that right now. I beckoned the next student in line.

"Susan, how can I help you?" She took a seat and explained a problem she had with the interpretation of a critical text. As we examined it together, abruptly, and to my complete surprise, our consultation was interrupted by a man in a cowboy hat who came up from behind me, wrapped an arm around my neck, leaned around, and kissed me full on the mouth, tangling his mustache in mine long enough for me to taste his hunger, and long enough to know that it matched my own.

"There, ya son-of-a-bitch," he said into my ear. "It ain't the same as fucking yer ass on the roof, but it's the best I can do in a goddamn library." Without another word, he separated himself from me and marched off. I could not see his face, but he walked tall and proudly.

My students—three others in line now, in addition to Susan—burst into polite, hushed applause.

"Is he your boyfriend, Mr. Graham?" Susan asked.

I sighed. "No, but he surely wants to be."

"Why don't you let him? He's hot."

The rest of the hour at the library was taken up with questions and consultations, and if I could lose myself in the finer points of bibliographical form and the merits of one academic source over another, I still could not shake the nagging feeling at the back of my brain that maybe Susan was right.

Because Marlene was on my mind, I wondered about the coincidence when she called me not long after Ranger appeared at the library.

"You want to get together for a cup of coffee or something, Neil? I haven't seen you in a while, and it would be nice to have a talk, just the two of us."

I did want to see her. We made a date for the following week. We met mid-morning, between classes at a little diner in town, after the breakfast rush, and before lunch, so we had the place mostly to ourselves. She gave me a spontaneous hug without the least self-consciousness, and I returned the embrace. Since I'd last seen her, she had gotten an entirely new hairstyle, a straight bob instead of the girlish ringlets, and it made all the difference.

"I love your new 'do, Marlene."

"Really?"

"Absolutely. It's gorgeous. And extremely flattering. I mean that sincerely."

"Thank you. It was time. I had my hair cut the same way since high school, and I was tired of it. So I went to the salon and asked the stylist to give me something new. Ranger didn't notice for more than a week."

We both ordered coffee; instead of a pastry, I ordered a plate of fresh fruit that Marlene could share. She appreciated the gesture.

"Thanks for not ordering sticky buns or doughnuts."

"I don't eat that junk very often myself." I offered her the sugar substitute in the blue packet, and she smiled.

"You remembered."

"Of course."

"Any girl would be lucky to have you for a boyfriend. Someone considerate."

"Thanks, but—"

She giggled. "I know. I should've said any guy would be lucky."

We sipped our coffee.

"So, how have you been?"

She sighed. "Not real great, to tell you the truth."

"I'm sorry."

She shrugged. "Thanks. Everything in my life turned upside down when my first marriage ended, and here I am with a second one ruined too. I just didn't expect it. I feel like a failure, somehow."

If I expected sorrow or tears, there were none. I heard more resignation than anything else.

"You shouldn't. And I hope you know how sorry I am that I played any part in the whole mess."

"It's not your fault. How could I have known what went on between you two before I met him? Ranger might have at least been honest with me upfront. You could have told me yourself—but I can see why you didn't."

"By the time you started dating, we weren't even involved anymore, not since he quit drinking, and I never figured we'd get back together. For all I knew, Ranger really *did* want to be with a woman. I should have left him be after he married you."

"I wish it could have been me Ranger really wanted. I really hoped things would work out for us. He was so easy to fall in love with. A little rough around the edges. But that's part of his charm, darn it. Makes a girl want to move right in and take care of him, like you would a little boy or a puppy." She blew across her coffee to cool it. "But I needed someone to take care of me, too. And all the romantic stuff, going for walks or out to dinner or the movies. Maybe go dancing. That kind of stuff."

"Do you like to dance?"

"I love it. And I'm pretty good. How about you?"

"Hopeless, actually, but I like to try. Ranger is an amazing dancer."

"He is?"

"He can two-step better than anyone I've ever seen. Didn't you know?"

She shook her head. So it was one more thing they had in common, along with their shared triumph over an addiction. Something they might have enjoyed as a couple. I wonder if there were other interests that could have drawn them together instead of driving the wedge deeper between them.

"Huh. He never said anything about it. We could have had some fun."

"Did you tell him you liked to dance?"

She shook her head again. "Never thought about it. Guess I figured it was just something else he would make fun of." She sipped her coffee and nibbled a strawberry. "Early on, I hoped we might even have a child. I didn't find out until later that he had himself fixed. Naturally, he didn't think to tell me before we were married."

"He mentioned it to me, too. Actually, I can't imagine Ranger being a dad."

"Me, either. Now. That's the way it goes, I guess. It's all water over the dam."

"So what are your plans?"

She sighed again, resigned but not defeated. "Everything works out for the best. I was real mad for a long time, but I got over it. What's the point? The way I see it, the marriage was broken from the start, only I didn't know it. The sooner I found out about it, the sooner I could do what I had to do to fix it."

At least, she said, there had been no hurry. She'd been promoted to manager at the restaurant, which meant more hours, a pay raise, and benefits too. She'd found a small but comfortable house to rent, affordable and close to town. She'd asked Ranger to hire a couple of guys to help her move, and he'd agreed.

"I offered to leave some of the extra furniture for Ranger, since I don't have room—the dining room table and chairs and the pink bedroom set that was mine when I was a little girl. He could've painted it. But he won't take it—doesn't want any reminders of me around, I guess."

"I don't think it's like that."

"I do. Anyway. He's been awful darn polite lately, even if he hasn't been around much. I don't know where he goes after work, but he doesn't get home most nights until late, after I'm asleep, and he's usually gone before I get up. Doesn't even eat breakfast at home. I hardly see him on the weekends, either. I wonder what he's up to. Not that I care a whole lot now. I kind of assumed he was spending time with you."

I shook my head. "He offered, but I'm not really interested. It took me a long time to realize how selfish he is. I don't like how he manipulates people. You never knew the old Ranger, but he changed a lot after he quit drinking. They say there is truth in wine, and maybe that's so. Ranger seemed to be so honest in the old days, more so than he is now. He seems to have developed a mean streak along with the self-righteousness that recovering alcoholics have sometimes. It doesn't make him a very nice guy."

Marlene nodded, sympathetic. "So you and him won't be getting together?"

"It doesn't look that way."

"That's too bad. You might be good for him."

"Maybe. But I don't think he'd be good for me."

"You're probably right."

The waiter brought us more coffee.

"So what are you up to these days? Still working at the bar?"

"No, I quit. I don't have time. I'm enrolled in graduate school for my master's degree in literature. I want to be a teacher and follow the path that my grandfather blazed—and maybe I'll find a way to strike out on my own and accomplish something new. Classes just started in January, and it's crazy already. I'm up to my neck in it. I haven't been a student for twelve years, and it's so different these days. I've had to learn how to study all over again. I'm used to library books and professors lecturing to an auditorium full of students, and now we do so much online. It's a strange new world, but it feels right for me."

"Well, congratulations! So you're the big man on campus now."

"Hardly. I'm definitely the *old* man on campus, and next to my professors, I'm the oldest guy in all my classes. But at least I finally got off my lazy backside and enrolled in the program. That's a huge step for me, even if it doesn't sound like much. To tell you the truth, though, I'm having a blast."

"Good luck to you, then."

"Thanks. I could finish up in eighteen months, unless I decide to get a doctorate too. I'll see how it goes."

We finished our coffee and the fruit plate, and there didn't seem to be anything left to say. We stood to say goodbye.

"Maybe I'll see you around town, Marlene."

"I'll be here." We shared another wholehearted hug. "Good luck, Neil. Thanks for everything. And I mean that."

After everything we'd been through together, all the rough patches, the heartache and heartbreak, the surprises and revelations, the hate and accusation and recrimination, the spite and the rueful understanding and reconciliation that sometimes (fortuitously) comes as a result, I wished her nothing but the best. She deserved a good man, a good life, someone who could and would love her and share the things she believed to be important. I only hoped Ranger would allow her to exit with some dignity and grace.

23

Four Sundays later, mid-morning, the sun shone fiercely for the first time in a couple of weeks, and spring was gunning down the last of winter. The snow had melted, and even the puddles of water had mostly dried from the ground. The thermometer—by sheer force of will, I think—had pushed itself to fifty degrees. I sat at the dining room table, the drapes wide open to let in the warmth and light. They spilled across the table and me and the newspaper spread out before me as I enjoyed a second cup of coffee. A classic Dave Brubeck Quartet record on the stereo soundtracked a perfect day.

I was startled from my reverie by the sound of a car horn from the driveway. Not a single honk; it repeated, loud and insistent, calling for me, and it kept up until I set down my cup and came out on the front porch to see what could possibly be so urgent. I stepped outside—and sitting in my driveway was a 1941 Buick 46S Sport Coupe, sleek and elegant and gleaming like a black mirror, like a decadently sinful, wonderful life, its chrome so shiny it could blind a man. My father was at the wheel, and next to him in the front seat sat Ranger, both of them grinning like madmen.

I couldn't even move. My dad tapped the horn another couple of times to punctuate a job done exceptionally well. When they stepped out of the car, both of them lit up, glowing like neon from inside, like gangsters who'd just pulled off a career-capping heist and gotten away, scot-free.

"Surprised, Neil?" my dad said.

I couldn't even nod.

"Have you ever in your life seen such a beautiful machine?"

I shook my head.

"Come down and have a look!" I made my way from the porch to the driveway, and my father put his arm around me and gave me a tour of the vehicle, inside and out, back to front, top to bottom. He couldn't hold in his excitement; it kept spilling over his sides.

"And this guy," he said, clapping a hand on Ranger's shoulder. "This guy! He's a genius! So smart. So talented! And what a taskmaster. I've never known a more dedicated man. He was over at the house nearly every day after work, and every weekend, too. And he stayed until all hours, even after I went to bed. Five solid months of work! I thought your mother was going to kick me out of the house! Of course, Ranger did most of it. I didn't know the first thing about how to restore a vehicle, but this guy—this guy! Not only does he have the skills and tools, but the dedication, experience, and love to make sure it's done right."

Ranger protested. "Good grief, Clem. How ya do go on. You had as much to do with this durn thing as I did."

Good grief?

Durn?

Could this be the same Ranger? I listened for a hint of mockery, but there was none. My dad continued, extravagant about his indebtedness toward Ranger, how they'd gotten off to a bit of a rocky start together (I could just imagine), and how they'd overcome their initial differences.

Taking turns, they outlined the whole process for me in exacting specificity, but I confess I hardly even heard. I couldn't get over the wonder of it, as the pair of them happily chattered about the steps required to turn a rusty pile of old Buick into a textbook example of a classic automobile, more detail than I could ever process, and with an animated enthusiasm I don't think I'd ever seen in either of them. Dad went on about the difficulty of finding parts, how they'd driven across three states to find the proper struts and plugs and tires, of salvaging the seats that had nearly been destroyed, about the dozen coats of paint required to create the shiny lacquer-hard finish, of rebuilding an engine that hadn't run in more than half a century. Ranger lifted the hood to show me the gleaming motor, clean enough for a museum piece.

And also from Ranger, who shared as much information as my dad, not a single "fuck" or "goddamn" or even "Jesus Christ" in his entire narrative, though he resorted a couple of times to "Judas Priest" and "dang it all." I'd never known him to talk at such length without a colorful adjective or two flavoring the discussion. He never seemed at a loss for words, either.

Proudly, they went over every inch of the car, and I couldn't "ooh" and "ahh" enough for their satisfaction. It truly was an incredible piece of work—but I was just as amazed at the other piece of work, the fact that my father and Ranger seemed to have forged a deep bond over their late nights in a cold garage, working side-by-side.

Finally, exhausted, the saga of the restoration complete, they stopped talking long enough to catch their breaths. I went inside to get Granddad's camera, and Ranger and my father posed on every side of the Buick for photos, the sun as brilliant as their pride in the accomplishment. Finally, as we stood around, spent, a little bashful with nothing left to say, Ranger proposed to take his leave.

"Clem, I got to be going."

"You can't walk home from here," I said.

"My truck's over at your dad's. I can walk. Ain't but a mile."

"Let me drive you back," my dad said.

"Nope. Thanks, Clem, but I think y'all need to take a long drive in this car right now."

He was right. My dad opened the passenger door for me. He slid behind the driver's seat, checked the rearview mirror, and carefully backed out of the driveway. As we passed Ranger, hiking down the block, we waved and honked. He waved back, a beautiful stupid grin on his face.

"Pull up for a second, Dad. Please?"

He came to a stop by Ranger, and I rolled the window down. He stepped over and leaned in.

"We need to talk," I said.

He nodded. "It's about time. Give me a call. Or come by. Ya know where I live."

"Okay. See you later."

My dad stepped on the gas. We drove around the block and headed downtown. He particularly enjoyed the admiring glances, the thumbs-up responses, and envious finger-pointing as we made our way, and I reveled in his pleasure, too. I doubted that he would ever tire of it, and I predicted that there would be many excuses to bring the Sport Coupe out of the garage to transform even a trip to the grocery store into a special occasion.

I was thrilled to be with him.

"You've hardly said a word, Neil."

"I'm practically speechless, Dad. I've never seen anything like this. I didn't think it was possible. I can't tell you how proud I am of you."

"I can't believe it myself. This old heap sat in your grandfather's garage for more than fifty years, and it probably would have sat in our backyard for another fifty if it wasn't for Ranger. He made me swear I wouldn't tell you we were working together on this project until it was done."

"Ranger is an interesting guy. I'm seeing sides to him I didn't know he had."

"Is that good?"

"Yes. What did he tell you about himself?"

My dad laughed. "Pretty darn near everything. I was a little surprised, I admit, but I guess when you work so closely with someone, all those late hours, there's not much else to do besides talk. He told me right off that he's a recovering alcoholic, sober going on two years."

Had it been that long already? I guess it had.

"I admire him for that," my dad said. "I don't think it's been easy for him. He told me how much he appreciated this project. He said it gave him something to look forward to every day, and it helped keep his mind off the craving. I can't imagine how difficult that must be. Or why he'd let it get that bad in the first place. Who knows?"

For all my father's intelligence, he had never come face-to-face with any kind of addiction, though I suspect he fed many of them, directly or indirectly, in his position as a pharmacist. But I let it go. As a bartender, I'm sure I did the same, an unaware enabler of behavior I would not otherwise condone. I did so with Ranger early on, so desperate was I for his attention.

"He told me how he learned to fix cars by going to the vocational-technical center while he was still in high school, and how he had the knack for it right off. He did such a terrific job restoring that old red pick-up truck of his. As soon as I saw that, I knew he was the right man for the job."

The previous October, Dad had spent half a day cleaning the weeds from around the car, washing off the dirt, and taking a good, hard look at it for the first time, he said. Having it sit out in the rain and heat all summer hadn't helped its condition, but Ranger was optimistic when he came over to look at it. They agreed on a rate of twenty-five dollars an hour for the work.

That sounded a little more like the Ranger I knew.

"I wrote him a check every week, but after the first month, he stopped cashing them. I asked him why, and he said he just forgot. He still has them. He certainly earned every dollar."

I let Dad tell the story; he needed to, needed a rapt audience, and I was pleased that he turned to me.

The first task had been to get the car under cover and make a detailed checklist and plan for the restoration, then compile a list of necessary parts and supplies. Ranger had most of the tools. Finding the parts proved considerably more difficult, as the car was over eighty years old. There were trips to auto-supply stores, junk yards, and swap meets, sorting through websites, bidding against other collectors at online auctions, and haggling with dealers face-to-face.

"I tell you, Neil. I learned a whole new language," my dad said sincerely.

I bit my tongue. It would not do for me to laugh. "Would you ever tackle a project like this again?"

"Not by myself. But Ranger said he'd ask me to help if he ever does any more restoration work. I promised I would. He said we made a good team." I'm sure that made my dad proud. We drove in silence for a while.

"Ranger knew your grandfather too."

"Yes. When I told him about Ranger, Granddad insisted on meeting him. They got together for dinner one time."

"I...um...got the impression that perhaps you and Ranger have something in common."

"You're right. Several things, probably."

"He told me how you met, when you were walking home from work and he just happened to come by in his truck and offer you a ride home. He said you became friends right off the bat."

I doubt if Ranger had told my dad about being naked and the radio blasting and the consensual oral sex and whatnot. But never mind. He'd told my dad that we met and we liked each other, and I appreciated that.

"He was still drinking when we met. Did he tell you *exactly* how good a friend he was at first?"

"I'm not sure what you mean."

"Well, I don't want to spoil your opinion of him, but in those early days, Ranger and I found ourselves doing all sorts of things you would— most likely not approve of." That was about as delicately as I could put it.

"He didn't exactly go into detail, but I sort of figured it out." I waited for some kind of judgmental comment to follow, but it didn't.

"Not anymore, though, and not for a long time. Since he quit drinking, he also made the decision to get married again. To a woman."

"He seems to do that on a regular basis."

"He's a fool."

"I'm inclined to agree with you in that respect. If there's anyone who can speak firsthand about the dangers of a man getting married to a woman when he's—"

"Gay," I prompted.

"Yes. Anyway, we did talk about it, and I think Ranger is sorry that he dragged that innocent woman into it."

I was certain that Ranger felt sorry.

"Have you met her?" Dad asked.

"Yes. Marlene is her name. I spent some time with them together, and I met her alone for coffee not too long ago. She's a good-hearted person, but it took me a long while to see it. She just got caught up in something she had no business being caught up in, because Ranger wasn't honest with her at the start."

It occurred to me suddenly that my grandparents had weathered the same storm, compounded by the fact that my father was in the picture.

I had told Ranger at the library that I didn't think people could change. What you *want* can change, and how you choose to go after it can change *you*. There are no lifetime warranties in the box when you enter into a relationship. You have to accept who you are and accept your partner for who he is. I could hope for happily ever after, but I couldn't guarantee it. But even if we weren't destined to spend the rest of our lives together, whatever time we shared could be an adventure—fun, at least, and definitely interesting.

Minus the alcohol, Ranger was a different man. Was he a better man, or a diminished one? He'd lost the serrated edge, the reckless unpredictability he had when he was drunk. Is that what attracted me to him in the first place? As I'd told Ranger, I couldn't forget the skinny, furry, naked guy in his pickup truck at one in the morning, singing along to Hank Williams. Could Ranger be that man again? I didn't know. But I knew I wanted him next to me as he became the man he would be. Could Ranger surrender to himself and enjoy our mutual attraction? I couldn't risk not knowing. Since Ranger hated being alone, maybe I could be all the companionship he needed.

Why *not* me? Wouldn't it be worth the risk?

"Neil, I want you to know I really like Ranger. He's conscientious and hard-working, and I suspect he'll stick by you, right or wrong."

"What does Mom think?"

"I don't get it, but I think your mom actually has kind of a crush on him. She seems to think he's a diamond in the rough. She wanted me to be sure and tell you that she finds him quite—sexy, I think, is the word she used. So consider yourself told."

"Thanks, Dad. I'm inclined to agree with her in that respect."

My dad sighed. "It's your business, son. Anyway, your mom has welcomed Ranger into our home, and I think she will be very disappointed if she doesn't see him anymore."

"Thanks for letting me know. I should warn you that it's possible."

"That doesn't surprise me. I rather think you would make Ranger a very happy man." Something in me ached to hear my dad say that it would be okay with him too if I showed up at home with Ranger in tow. How could I explain to my father? If he could accept Ranger and me, then maybe he might—almost, maybe, at the very least—be able to make peace with his own dad?

"I won't tell you to be careful because you know that already. I won't tell you to do the right thing, because I'm confident that you will. And your mom and I will support you any way we can. We've all got weaknesses, and the best we can do is try not to let them defeat us. Ranger probably knows that better than most. But we do like him. We like him a lot. He certainly has a good heart under his shirt."

"Thanks, Dad." That was close enough for me.

"I love you, Neil. I haven't told you often enough. Pop never stopped telling me, but after our family exploded, I didn't see how it could possibly be true. Now I do, even if it's too late for him and me. I will always regret that I was too stupid to see, too certain I was right and he was wrong. I loved my father too, even if he was convinced I didn't, but I could never bring myself to show him. More than anything, I yearned for him to be happy, but I don't think he ever was. I want you to be happy too, and content, with the right partner—whether that's Ranger or anyone else. Or by yourself, if that's what you decide."

"In his own way, I think Granddad was content. He lived his life as he saw fit, even though he recognized that a lot of people wouldn't understand—and would judge him for it. I know how hard it was for him in the years after the divorce. But he certainly would be pleased to hear you say that."

"You really think so?"

"I know it."

We drove in silence for a mile or two.

"Dad, what's the story behind this car? Where did Granddad get it, and why did he hang onto it for so many years when he never did anything with it? I asked him about it a couple of times, but he only said it belonged in the past, and it would have to stay there."

My father was silent for a minute, and I thought at first he didn't know—or, if he did, he wasn't going to reveal any secrets. But he did, starting with a little history about the 1941 Buick 46S, nicknamed the Sedanet—presumably because it was something of a junior sedan. Over eighty-seven thousand were manufactured during the only year it was made, and it was very popular. But the bombing of Pearl Harbor that December put a stop to it as the automobile factories turned their efforts to wartime production. Granddad acquired the car in the early 1970s when my dad was four years old. He didn't recall the circumstances, but he could vividly recall when the car was towed to the house, and his father and a couple of other guys pushed it into the garage. The Buick hadn't been in running condition then, either.

"I was absolutely crazy about this car when I was a kid. I used to play in it for hours at a time, all by myself, pretending I was racing in the Indy 500 or maybe that I'd just robbed a bank and was making my getaway." He grinned, a little sheepish.

"Sounds like a lot of fun."

"It was my favorite toy ever. Pop told me he bought the car in the first place because it was the same age as him. The guy who owned it was going to sell it for scrap, but Pop couldn't bear to see it destroyed because he remembered what a fine car it was in its day. I bet a week didn't go by that Pop didn't promise me that when I turned twelve years old, we'd start restoring this old Buick together. We'd fix it up and get it running. It would be our special project, just us alone. It never occurred to me that Pop didn't know the first thing about bodywork or engine work, either. Maybe that's why he wanted to wait until I was older, so he'd have some time to learn how. And then—well, you know what happened."

How could I forget? Just as Dad never could himself.

"I'm sorry you never got to work on the car together."

He sighed. "On my twelfth birthday, Pop phoned and asked if I was ready to get started on the Buick. I told him no. I wasn't ready, even if your grandma would have permitted it. Every birthday for four or five years after that, he called me and asked again, and I always put him off. And then, he just stopped asking. I'm sure every time I said no, it was like a knife in his heart. So much for honoring thy father. I hated him so much for what he did to our family because I looked up to him—and loved him so much. Over time, it was easier to keep the pilot light burning under the hate. How could I let that happen?"

My father started to cry. He eased the car to the side of the road and slowed to a stop. As best as I could in the front seat, I embraced him until his sobbing let up.

"You did the best you could, Dad. And just look at what you've accomplished. Your project is done, and it turned out beautifully. Even if Granddad didn't work on it with you, I know he was in the garage with you in spirit, every step of the way. And he'd be thrilled that you finished it because it meant so much to both of you."

"You really think so?"

"No doubt in my mind. You did it for him as much as for yourself, and that's a good thing. This accomplishment belongs to both of you. Maybe this whole project was a kind of penance."

If there's one thing my dad could understand in context, it was penance. The whole Catholic Church is built on the concept of guilt, of confessing sins and atoning for them—and being forgiven, released to go forth and sin no more. Or sin quite a lot, with the reassurance and the relief that the whole redemption process could be repeated indefinitely as long as one lived.

"You committed the sin, if that's how you want to look at it, and sticking with the restoration project gets to be your punishment. I hereby absolve you of this transgression. And every other sin you forgot to mention." I raised my hand and drew an elaborate sign of the cross in the air.

That drew a wan smile from him. He started the car again and eased us out into the light Sunday traffic. "Where shall we go?"

I recalled something I'd learned during our disastrous lunch date months earlier. "Let's go to Dairy Queen for chocolate-dipped vanilla cones. Not a word to Mom, though—or Grandma, either."

I couldn't have come up with a better idea. "Brilliant," my father said. "Absolutely perfect." He steered in the direction of the Dairy Queen, and, well, we spent the rest of the day together, riding in the Buick until the sun started its descent, going everywhere and no place in particular, aimless and purposeful all at once. I'm sure my grandfather was in the back seat somehow with us. It was the best day I'd ever had with my father.

When Dad dropped me at the house again, I invited him in. After a moment of hesitation, he agreed. I knew he still felt a bit awkward coming inside, but I wanted him to feel at home again, to feel welcome. I persuaded him to stay long enough for a cup of coffee and extracted a promise from him that he would do so again.

24

A restless week passed. I didn't hear from Ranger, but it was my turn, as he'd already made his case at the library. At that time, I'd been unwilling to accept the revised version of him. Possibly, I could not believe that he had truly changed. But I never thought to figure a 1941 Buick 46S Sport Coupe into the equation.

Finally, after a sleepless Thursday night, I realized that enough time had gone by—and it really was up to me to initiate contact. Mid-morning Friday, I decided to invite him to lunch, and we'd see what developed after that. I drove to the car dealership to surprise him, but I found out from the receptionist that he'd gone to the Alcoholics Anonymous meeting at the Methodist church.

"Does he go very often?"

"A couple times a week," she said. "He's doing real good, though."

I thanked her for the information and checked my watch. So much for my plan to hijack him for a lunch date. The meeting would start any minute, and by the time it ended, he'd be due back at Buick.

I checked my appointment book, and the next afternoon I had available would be a week later. I decided I was too impatient to wait. I jumped in the car and headed for the church.

My experience with Ranger and Alcoholics Anonymous suggested that AA was a tolerant group. People who let their lives bottom out in a pool of booze and thrash their way through the wet and dark to make their way into the dry and light are pretty hard to shock. Maybe because they've seen so much, seen what people can do to themselves and to each other. Maybe listening to so many stories—dozens, hundreds, thousands, millions—that all start the same way has taught them to be compassionate and broad-minded, to withhold judgment until the facts became clear and sometimes even then. When you've heard and seen so much, it's easy to be forgiving. There but for the grace of whatever god you choose to kneel before ....

In the church hall, a dozen men sat in the circle. Most ate their lunch from fast-food bags and slurped beverages from paper cups. As I came in, every head turned—curiosity, mostly, but each offered a welcoming smile. The leader beckoned me to join the group, and I pulled up a chair directly opposite Ranger. He eyed me warily, uncertain if not downright suspicious; in the past, I'd always remained in the background when I accompanied him.

What could I possibly be up to? I offered a salute in his direction, and he furrowed his brow.

"Welcome, sir," said the moderator. I remembered him as the same man I'd seen over a year earlier when I'd brought Ranger to the meeting after his one binge.

"Thank you."

I looked around the circle at each man, ranging in age from perhaps his early twenties to an elegant old gentleman who could have been my grandfather's age. They were attired variously: three-piece suits, jeans and flannel, khakis and sport shirts. One sported Army fatigues, another the uniform of a local pizzeria. Ranger wore his loose-fitting dark-blue coveralls from the garage (unzipped far enough in front to suggest that he wore nothing underneath, as usual) with his name in red script over the pocket. And, damn, he looked sexier than ever.

I listened as several of the men shared their stories, the young man struggling through his first week of sobriety, and the leader, who reminded me that his name was Frank and that he had now accumulated more than eleven years and nine years of sobriety, and several others. Ranger merely introduced himself and announced that he was eight months and fourteen days sober (since his single transgression at the one-year point). He shot dark looks at me each time we made eye contact.

After everyone had spoken, Frank said, "We have a newcomer. Would you like to introduce yourself?"

"Sure. My name is Neil, but I have to confess that I'm not actually an alcoholic."

"That's okay, Neil," Frank said. "We've all got to come to terms with our problems—claim ownership and accept them. Call yourself anything you want. The labels aren't important."

Ranger interrupted. "Neil's right. He ain't no alcoholic. He got no business here."

"Now, just hold on a minute. Everybody's welcome. And remember, no crosstalk and no interrupting when someone is sharing."

"He ain't no alcoholic," Ranger insisted. "Hardly ever even takes a drink."

Others in the group shushed him. He crossed his arms and scowled.

"All you need is the desire to stop drinking, Neil," Frank said. "You have to realize that you are powerless over your addiction and that your life has become unmanageable as a result."

"I'm ready to admit that I'm powerless over my addiction and that my life has become unmanageable."

The group applauded.

"Very good. Thank you for sharing that." Frank picked up an aluminum token from the table and a copy of the "Big Book" and offered them to me. "How long since you had a drink?"

I had to think about that; the last one I could remember was a glass of champagne to celebrate the arrival of the new year with Scotty. I hadn't specifically avoided it since then; I just hadn't had the inclination. "Probably about four-and-a-half months ago."

Frank was mystified. "I don't think I follow you."

"I don't mean to mislead anyone. My life has become unmanageable, but not because of alcohol."

"That's all right. But there might be another group that would be more suitable for you—I can give you some phone numbers. Maybe Narcotics Anonymous or Al-Anon?"

"They can't help me. It's here or nowhere."

Frank tried to be patient. "Then what can we do for you?" Several of the men in the circle glanced at their watches. It was considered bad form, even disrespectful to leave the group while anyone was sharing, and I was holding them up if I had nothing relevant to offer.

"What happens at the meeting stays at the meeting, right?"

"Of course. That's one of our cardinal rules."

"Okay, then. My name is Neil, and I'm a—cocksucker, I guess you would call it. In the literal sense, I mean." My grandfather was right; there is tremendous satisfaction to be gained from the proper use of the term at the proper time and place. And this was decidedly the proper time and place.

Frank's confusion was understandable. "Umm...I don't think you need a twelve-step program for that."

A couple of the men chuckled. Ranger muttered "Jesus fuck" and sighed, deep. I was not deterred.

"I'm proud to call myself a cocksucker, though I'm a little ashamed to admit how long it's been. I had an offer back in January from a guy, and it was very tempting, but I turned him down. I can see now that maybe I was a little too hasty, and that's why I'm here."

The dozen men attending the meeting—including Ranger—perked up considerably. I suspect many years had gone by since an AA gathering had shaped up to be as interesting as this one promised to be, and no one wanted to miss a word. I made up my mind: why not give them a show? So I dived in, head first, and the water was fine. I suspected that more than one of the attendees would be talking about this one back at the workplace and later on, over dinner.

"You see, I wasn't sure I could trust this man. I'm still not positive, but I want to give him a shot."

A man spoke up. "What's holding you back?" I looked at him, a courtly older gentleman in a smart sport coat and conservative tie, shyly handsome behind his brown spaniel eyes.

I offered my hand and he shook it. "Neil."

"Bruce."

We shook hands. "I'm not an alcoholic. I hope you don't mind."

"Not in the least. I've been sober for five years and change myself. And as a matter of fact, I—ahem—like dick myself." He looked around; the crowd was mesmerized.

"I'm pleased to make your acquaintance. It's always a pleasure to meet a handsome man." I whispered the last part to him: "Especially one who likes dick."

He grinned. "So what exactly is preventing you from getting together with this other fellow?"

"Nothing much. I just want him to admit to the world that he likes—the same thing. More specifically, that he likes me. I could commit to a guy like that."

"That doesn't sound like too much to ask," said Bruce.

"I agree. If you're in love with someone, you want to be able to share it in the light of day. Announce it for all the world to see."

"Not everybody wants to watch two guys making out," Ranger contributed.

"Hush up, Ranger," I said. "Nobody asked you."

"Like hell."

"No crosstalk!" Frank warned.

The man in the Army uniform spoke up. He was long and lean and much in shape. "Ranger, you seem particularly interested in Neil's situation. What's up with that?" He extended his hand to me. "I'm Dean, by the way. I'm a cocksucker myself, as you so eloquently put it, and proud of it. You won't find many lieutenant colonels willing to come out and say it, even if it's permitted now."

"*Another* handsome gent," I said. Dean appreciated the flattery as much as Bruce did. Don't we all? "Maybe I should start hanging around outside AA meetings."

Good-natured laughter followed. I had a rapt audience.

"What makes you think this guy is unwilling to make such a commitment?" Dean said.

"When we met for the first time, he was still drinking. Rather heavily, I might add."

"Ah," said Bruce. "And after he had a few, he was more willing to be amorous, eh?"

"Exactly. We used to have a great time together, and I suspect he used to have a great time with—let's say at least several guys before me—while under the influence."

"So what happened?" said Bruce.

"I hate to say it, but he quit drinking. And the truth of the matter is, after that, he didn't want to be with me anymore. He wasn't exactly unfriendly, but —"

"No more dick?" Dean said.

"Bingo." I appreciated his bluntness.

"He sounds like one sorry son-of-a-bitch," Dean said.

"Hey!" Ranger sounded like a wounded animal.

"Not drinking can certainly change a man," said Bruce. "Usually, though, it's an improvement."

"I'm certainly in favor of sobriety. In no way do I want to suggest that he should start drinking again just so he can enjoy being with me or any other man."

"Good," Frank said. "That's sacrilege, and you don't want to go there—especially inside a church."

General laughter.

"After he quit drinking, he got married again," I said.

Bruce was startled. "To a woman?"

I nodded. "For the fifth time." Everybody (but one) laughed. I hoped I wasn't giving away too many details; I didn't want to expose Ranger—though I would be in favor if he chose to expose himself.

"Five times. Sounds like another addiction," said Bruce. "Are they happy?"

"I'm afraid not. The marriage is just about over, in fact. It barely lasted a year."

"I feel sorry for the lady," Dean said.

"I do, too. She's a nice person."

To my surprise, Ranger spoke up. "Didn't ya say he came looking for ya in January? Went to a lot of trouble to find ya and finally tracked ya down and wanted ya back—and he was stone-cold sober too—and ya told him hell, no." He was triumphant.

"I wasn't convinced."

"And what would it take, I'd like to know?" Ranger demanded,

"Maybe if he could bring himself to say he loves me in front of witnesses, I'd believe him. And I think he could save himself."

Ranger mulled over my offer. I could see he was at war inside.

"I'm no detective, Neil, but I can only think of one reason why you shared your story with us," said Bruce. He lowered his voice conspiratorially. "One of us must be the culprit."

"Exactly. But I don't want to 'out' anybody. I'm pretty sure he'd rather keep it a secret."

Much head-shaking followed.

"So," Dean said. "We have a closeted cocksucker among us. I'm intrigued." Several of the men in the circle snickered.

Ranger worked himself into a lather until he could hold his tongue no longer. "Just a goddamn minute!"

"What's the problem?" Dean said.

"Jesus *fuck!*" he said, a world of anguish packed into possibly his single favorite word; perhaps he hadn't used it much lately and had quite a few in reserve. "It ain't fair."

"What's not fair?" I said.

"Coming here to ambush me—I mean, him. The guy. It ain't fair. Ya can't just come in here and call me—*him*, whoever he is—ya can't just call him a cocksucker in front of every son-of-a-bitch at this meeting."

"The culprit may very well have exposed himself," Dean said.

"No, I ain't," Ranger said. "What makes ya think it's me? Ya can't just call a guy out in front of everybody."

"He didn't," Dean said. "But I reckon you just did."

General laughter.

"Sweet Jesus fuck," Ranger muttered again.

"No sense wasting your time running after a man who's too stupid to let you catch him, Neil," Dean said. "If Ranger—excuse me—if Mister X isn't interested, why not chase someone else who might be? I'll throw my hat in the ring."

"Likewise," said Bruce. "And any other article of clothing you'd like me to remove—in private."

"Thank you both. Your offers are not only flattering but arousing."

More laughter.

Ranger looked as if he might erupt in fury—or perhaps tears.

"I'm off duty at four-thirty," Dean said.

"And I'll be finished before then," said Bruce.

"I've got the whole day free myself," I said.

Ranger, apparently, had enough. "Stop it! Just *stop.*"

"What's the problem?" I said.

"You! *You're* the problem, goddamn it. Ya can't just throw yourself at every cocksucker in the place —" and here he took a deep breath— "without giving me a chance to stake my claim to yer ass first."

I was stunned. "I don't get it. You're not gay. You told me so yourself. You were most insistent about it."

More general laughter.

"*All right!*" His thunder quieted everyone. "All right. I'm...I'm..." It was a big step, maybe the biggest he'd ever taken.

Frank eased in. "—an alcoholic? Good for you, Ranger, for owning it."

Ranger glared. "No interrupting!" Frank hid a secret smile in a cough.

"Damn it, Neil. Fine! I'm a fucking faggot! What difference does it make what I call myself? Ain't I already told ya I want what ya got for sale? Ya said in January ya didn't want me, and now ya go on like ya do. Make up yer goddamned mind, for Christ's sake."

"Ranger, explain to me why you're so eager to tell everyone you meet that you're an alcoholic, as if that's something to be proud of, but you're scared to death to admit that you're gay? When are you going to start being true to yourself? Who even *cares* if you like dick? Do you care if Ranger likes dick?" I addressed my question to Frank.

"Can't say as I do, actually," he said. "It's not my cup of tea, but it's a free country, and it takes all kinds." He was thoughtful for a moment. "We do stress honesty in AA."

"Like it says on the coin: to thine own self be true," Dean said.

"I'm all for that," I said. "Does anyone else here mind if Ranger prefers guys?"

Much vigorous head-shaking followed.

Ranger offered me an injured look and his extended middle finger. "Fuck you, Neil. Fuck you for putting me through this bullshit. It's nobody's business if I want to suck yer dick. Okay? But I do. And I want ya to suck mine. Whenever ya want, every goddamn day. Twice a day, if ya want. And I'll fuck yer skinny ass nine ways to Sunday, too. What does that make me?"

I thought about it for a mere second. "Mine, if you'll have me?"

That stopped him cold.

"Look, Ranger. If you want to call yourself a straight man who happens to prefer sex with other men, I won't argue with you. But if you want to be my partner, you better be willing to announce it from the rooftop."

He glowered. "Fucking hell. Okay. Maybe." He caught me smiling. "*Maybe*, I said. Wipe that damn grin off your face."

"And take me dancing."

"What?"

"Two-stepping. You have to promise that you'll teach me, and we'll go dancing at the Whiskey River." I told the group, "Ranger is a terrific two-stepper."

"Then, by all means, I would include two-stepping in the deal," Dean said.

Others contributed "Hear, hear!"

"Ranger?"

"Jesus fuck," he muttered. "Dancing. I mean Jesus *fuck*. All right. *All right*. But that's enough. What about me? Do I get to put in my two cents?"

"Of course. What are your conditions?"

He thought about it and took a deep breath. "I only got one. Don't be in such a goddamned all-fired hurry. That's all. This is new to me. It'll take me a little while to get in the habit. Like not drinking. I get used to doing things one way for so long, and it gets hard to quit. Ya gotta gimme a little time and be a little patient. And gimme room to fuck up, so I'm not afraid you'll dump me when it happens. Because I'll fuck up sometimes. I know it, even if it's by accident." He sighed.

"Of course, Ranger. Absolutely."

"Ya know I can't promise much. I gotta do everything I can to stay sober. It takes all my concentration sometimes, and it has to come first, because if I take a drink again, I don't know as I'd ever quit. I can't take that chance. I could do it alone, maybe, but I don't wanna."

"You don't have to. You can count on me."

"If I ever feel like I got to take a drink just so's I can put up with all this—*cocksucker* bullshit, then we're done. I'm out the door. Ya got that?"

"I've got it. Agreed."

The group broke into long and sustained applause. When Ranger's brain finally caught up with the things his mouth had said, he looked a little embarrassed. He dropped into a chair and buried his head in his hands, muttering "shit, shit, shit" under his breath. My father's good influence would only go so far, and these were stressful times.

"Ranger." He looked up. "Thank you for speaking your mind."

"Weren't my mind that was speaking," he said. "My mouth goes places without me sometimes."

"You want to take any of it back?"

"*No!*"

"Good. Because I've got eleven witnesses here to back me up." Maybe what happened at the meetings stayed there, but I had a suspicion that some of those assembled would take an active interest in our relationship, and they'd be anxious for regular progress reports. Ranger would certainly run into many of these men at other meetings around town. He'd known some of them for nearly two years already.

"Fine." His scowl suggested that everyone in the room (myself included) had turned against him. He probably suspected that every other AA group in the county would be abuzz with a blow-by-blow account of this meeting within a day or two. "Y'all are a bunch of Judases!"

No one believed him for a second.

"Maybe this wasn't the best forum for bringing all this to the table, and I apologize to everyone here for taking up their time," I said.

"No need to apologize," said Bruce. The others agreed.

"Meetings are all about being honest," Frank said. "All about facing yourself and admitting your weaknesses."

"Cocksucking is a pleasure. I wouldn't call it a weakness," Dean said.

"Me, neither," I said.

Bruce: "Nor I. Ranger?"

"Wouldn't even fuckin' dream of it," he muttered.

"Thank you," I said. "And thank you for being honest with me, Ranger. I know where you stand, finally—and I know where I stand. I've got some ground rules too, but here's the main one. If you ever try to deny me, then *I'm* out the door. And I'll never come back in. Ever. Okay?"

Ranger said nothing.

"Come on, Ranger," Bruce prompted. "You got that?"

He sighed. "I got it. Jesus fuck." Then, improbably, his face lit up with a grin that would brighten all dark corners.

"Well?" I said.

"Well, what?"

"What are you grinning about?"

"You. Standing there with your mouth going. Suppose you shut up, and let's go somewhere I can put my hands on you without all these critics around."

"I'm all for that."

The next thing I knew, he was next to me, and his arm went around my neck as he pulled my mouth against his and held on. I surrendered; I forgot all about the audience until the men in attendance gave us another round of applause.

"I reckon this meeting is one for the books," Frank said. "But we've gotten a little off track here, boys."

"Sorry," I said. "That wasn't my intent."

"No harm done, I guess," Frank said. "You're welcome to continue the discussion after the meeting, if you want to. No one is using the hall this afternoon. Anyone have anything else to contribute before we adjourn?"

No one did. After a quick, cursory thanks to a generic Higher Power, the meeting concluded. With the exception of Dean, Bruce, myself, and Ranger, the hall emptied.

Dean turned to me. "So what's Ranger got in his pants, anyway? Anything worth bragging about?"

"I guess it meets the satisfactory average."

"That's all?" Dean said, turning to Ranger.

"He's lying," Ranger said. "Don't pay no attention to him."

"Prove it," Dean said. "Put your money where your mouth is."

Bruce chuckled. "I think he really would prefer you put your *cock* where his mouth is."

"Maybe so," Dean said, grinning. "Whip it out."

"Only one gets near that piece of me is Neil," Ranger said.

"What about you, Dean?" I said. "Hung like a horse?"

"I never had any complaints. Want proof?"

"A big dick don't mean nothing," Ranger said.

"You're right," I said, "if the guy attached to it doesn't have any idea what to do with it. Sex is for the mutual pleasure of all concerned parties, and if your only goal is to get your rocks off as fast as you can, and then turn over and go to sleep, you're being pretty selfish."

"I never had any complaints," Ranger said.

"Maybe you were too wasted to hear them," Dean said.

"What the fuck would you know about it?"

"I've been there, Ranger," Dean said. "I remember how it was when I was drinking. Sex is a hell of a lot more fun now that I've sobered up. It's a lot more interesting, too. What do you say, Neil? Are you positive you want to go with this guy?"

"He's coming with me," Ranger said. "By himself."

"Can't blame a guy for trying," Dean said. He didn't seem too disappointed, though. He and Bruce walked out together, sharing some earnest conversation and loading each other's contact information into their cell phones. We followed them outside and they waved to us as they backed their vehicles out of the parking lot. I hope they spent the afternoon together.

Outside, in the blinking sun, Ranger seemed a bit shy. He—we—had made a monumental decision, and there seemed to be nothing left to do but commemorate, consummate, and celebrate, but he seemed unaware as to how to proceed.

"Ain't none of those guys ever gonna forget *that* meeting."

"I'm sorry about that, Ranger. Kind of."

"Horseshit. Don't ya go tellin' yer dad I just said 'fuck' about nine hundred times."

"He wouldn't mind one bit, under the circumstances." I knew it was true.

Ranger grinned. "What now? I reckon ya got school this afternoon, or ya gotta get back to the library, right?"

"I don't, actually. This is my day off—I only teach on Tuesday and Thursday, and my classes don't meet on Friday. So I'm actually free until Monday morning. But aren't you on your lunch break?"

He pulled his cell phone from his pocket, punched in a number, and barked into it: "Boss, I need to take the afternoon off. I got some business I need to take care of, and it's going to take the rest of the day and then some. Okay? Yeah, yeah. I'll come in tomorrow and work a half day instead. Right." He disconnected the line and put the phone back in his pocket. "Prick."

"Your place or mine?"

"Ain't nothing in mine."

The first time I spent a whole night with Ranger, his place was empty, too. A good omen, perhaps.

"I vote for your place," I said. I'll meet you there."

He nodded, got in his truck, and peeled out of the church parking lot. I followed. I'm sure we set some kind of land-speed record getting to his house. But in spite of the m.p.h., I had time to think. In our old days, Ranger had always been in a hurry. He cared nothing about the pleasure of the leisurely buildup that made climax so, well, climactic. He wanted to fuck or get sucked off, and he offered (mostly) similar services, presumably because that was the price I demanded.

I'd waited nearly two years for anything more than a kiss from Ranger, and this afternoon needed to be much more. Our future depended on it.

25

Ranger arrived home a minute before me. I parked the car and barely stepped out of the driver's seat into the driveway when he started yanking at the buttons on my jeans.

I told him to stop.

"No way." He laughed, sure I was kidding.

"I mean it, Ranger. Stop just for a second."

"Why?" He almost howled. "*Jesus H. fuck.* Ain't we waited long enough? What now?"

"Hold your horses, Ranger. I want the same thing you do, and we'll get there, but what's your hurry?"

He was confused.

"We can go from Point A, arousal, to Point B, orgasm, in about five minutes, I think. Maybe less."

"If you mean how long it will take me to come, you're right." He took my hand and pressed it against his crotch.

"Okay, two or three minutes. If that's all you want."

He was mystified. "What else is there?"

"Suppose I show you. Are you in a hurry?"

"I ain't. But my dick might be."

"I'll take care of that. Trust me. But think about it. This is the first time we've done this. The first time, because you're stone-cold sober and you've made the conscious choice to be here with me. You can't blame the beer. I've been hot for you since the first night in your pickup truck, but this is the first time you feel the same for me and you're sober at the same time. This is brand-new for us. As if we're starting from scratch here."

"Never thought about it like that."

"I don't want you to feel as if you've been talked into something you don't really want. You sure this is where you want to be, and what you want to be doing?"

"Fucking hell, Neil. Who invited who to this party? Not Dean. Not Bruce." He spat into the dirt. "Damn traitors!"

"They seem like very nice guys. I'll bet you didn't even know they were gay."

"Never thought about it one way or another. Ya sure ya wouldn't rather be with one of them right now?"

"Positive. I don't want to be in any man's driveway but yours, Ranger. I'm a sucker for skinny, hairy-chested old guys."

"Now ya think I'm an old man. Along with how ya think my dick ain't nothing to brag about, like you told them guys after the meeting. Thanks a lot, by the way."

"You've got more than enough for me, and I'm not bragging because I don't want to share with anyone."

"I'll give you that. Now, what's this about being old? And how's your dad, by the way?"

"Fine. We had a wonderful afternoon together in the old Buick. Thank you for working on the project with him. It meant more than you'll ever know. I don't know if Dad explained to you why he needed to restore that car. I didn't know myself until we took that ride together."

"He told me too, while we were working. We had plenty of time to talk. He said he was supposed to do the project with your granddad."

"That was the original intent. But Dad could never have done it without you."

"Anyone can restore a car. It ain't that hard."

"Maybe. But not everyone would have had the patience to work with him so closely. Teach him, and see the project through to completion. It's impossibly beautiful, and Dad will be grateful to you for the rest of his life."

"Nah," Modest he was, but nonetheless pleased.

"There were a lot of unresolved issues between my dad and my grandfather. Restoring the car helped Dad make his peace with Granddad. I'm sure of it. Thank you."

Embarrassed now, Ranger changed the subject. "Did ya know your dad is named for that writer guy your grandfather was so crazy about?"

"Yes."

"It's a cool name."

"I don't think my dad liked it very much. You will note that my name is not Samuel Langhorne Clemens Graham, Junior. But I think his dislike has a lot to do with what happened when he was a kid. How their family came apart."

"Your dad told me. It's a sad story. I'm glad I got no kids. Can you imagine me trying to be a dad?"

"Don't you remember telling me you got yourself fixed, that night we met your drinking buddies at the Whiskey River?"

He thought about it and shook his head. "Guess I don't. I knew damn sure I didn't want kids, and I didn't want any accidents. Doctor thought I was crazy, but I talked him into it. Of course, most of the ones I fucked wouldn't have got knocked up anyhow."

"Oh? Why is that?"

That rattled him, as if he'd suddenly realized he said too much and couldn't find a way to backtrack. It dawned on me. They weren't women. I laughed. "I knew I wasn't the first. Or even the second, after that story I got from your ex, Laura. How many were there, anyway?"

"None of yer goddamned business. Be content that you'll be the last, and shut the fuck up about it. Besides, ya notice I ain't asking *you* such questions."

Content, I let the subject rest. But I had one more. "Dad said you stopped cashing the checks he gave you. Why?"

"He was way too generous. After a while, I felt funny about it, so I quit. It wasn't work to me. I liked spending time with your dad. He's a good guy. And besides, I needed something to do nights and weekends. Something to keep my mind off the beer. If I had to go home to Marlene every night, I'd'a gone back to drinking sooner or later."

"I know she and I didn't really start off on the right foot, but that's partly your fault, you know," I said.

"Yeah. But it wasn't her so much as what she stood for."

"And what was that?"

"Everything under the sun that wasn't you," he said at last. "When yer dad came into the shop hunting for someone to help restore a car, as soon as I heard his name, I wondered if he was kin to ya. I could see the resemblance. First time I went over to his house after work, he told me the car was his dad's, and how they were supposed to fix it together but they never got around to it, and he didn't know where to start."

"But what was in it for you?"

"I knew I could make that '41 Buick Sport Coupe look like new and run even better. I was itching to get my hands on it. So we both got something good out of it."

"I'm surprised that you and my dad hit it off."

"Me, too." He grinned. "And so was he, I reckon. I never met a guy who liked to exercise as much as he does. He even got me interested. I got this contraption in the basement that's supposed to give ya muscles like Superman or something, but I didn't know what to do with it. He came over and showed me how to use it. Put together a plan, building up a little at a time. He said, if I stuck with it, he'd guarantee results by the time we finished restoring the coupe."

Proud as a schoolboy, he unzipped his coveralls all the way and opened them wide to me. Among other things, I'd missed putting my hands against his furry chest, and my fingers instantly reached out and raked through it. He didn't object; as I stroked, he murmured softly and closed his eyes.

"Trading one six-pack for another, huh? Very impressive, Ranger."

"Kind of hoped ya'd approve." I continued massaging his belly firmly, exploring its newly defined contours.

"You remember how much I used to like doing this?"

"Remind me." Happily, I obliged.

"So my dad helped you get in shape. Seems as if you'd want a little more compensation than that. I still think there's something you're not telling me."

"Well, I guess I hoped ya'd see that I wasn't just doing it for yer dad."

I'd figured it out. With his generous offer of time and talent, Ranger managed to accomplish something neither me nor my father nor grandfather had managed to do on our own: knit my family back together. Chance, luck, skill, time, love, Ranger, my dad, Granddad—all had conspired, and I could not have been more satisfied or grateful for the result.

"Ya think ya might reconsider me?" he said.

"I already have."

He sighed, content. "Been a long time since ya had your hands on me. Too goddamn long." He muttered something under his breath, and then he asked me to be honest with him. "Ya think I cuss too much, don't ya?"

"It's your native tongue."

"But ya think it's—kinda common, don't ya?"

"Common as fuck!"

"I'm serious, Neil. Yer dad asked me how come I cussed all the time.

"What did you tell him? You probably discovered that Dad isn't one to tolerate much in the way of swearing."

"You're telling me. I figured that out in about ten minutes. He was polite, but I could tell he didn't like it. When he asked me why I talk like that, I couldn't tell him. I didn't get it from my own dad. Maybe I was always scared, and I didn't want anyone to know it, so I talked big and loud."

"Why were you scared?"

He hung his head. "I think maybe because I liked dick."

"Ranger, you're in luck. So do I. As I have announced on a regular basis. And my opinion of you has only rocketed sky-high in the last half-hour. You can speak any way you like around me."

"Even so. Yer dad never asked me *not* to cuss, but after a while I decided myself that I didn't need to so much. I made the decision—me. My own self. It took a little concentration, but it got easier. I won't say it won't slip out sometimes. When I get pissed off, I might let loose with a couple."

Recalling the AA meeting, I knew he was right, but that had definitely been stressful for him. The unspoken half of his observation was that the surest, quickest way to get Ranger to do anything was to ask him for the opposite. Marlene wanted him to quit swearing, among other things, but had made no progress, in part because she kept insisting, and kept getting angry about it, which made the continuation of the habit only more satisfying for Ranger—a useful lesson for me, if he and I were to make any progress together. The challenge would be to convince Ranger that the change was desirable for him, not for anyone else, and then let him make up his own mind to adjust as necessary. Aren't we all like that, to some extent? Marlene had lost weight because she saw the necessity. No one and nothing else could have persuaded her to do it.

"Hey, Neil? If I recollect rightly, I was bragging at the meeting about how much I wanted to suck yer cock."

"You were."

"Ya want me to?"

"Very much."

"I got a lot to learn. I ain't got beer anymore to relax me beforehand. I'm not so reckless as I was back then."

"I'm willing to work with you. I'll be your mentor. You've got potential. We can practice anytime you want."

"Starting now?"

I nodded.

He put his mouth against mine and reminded me that his hunger matched my own. We stopped long enough to catch a breath, and then he kissed me again. When we separated, he grinned. For the first time, I became aware of the warmth of the sun on us and decided it was perfect.

"I love you, Ranger Melusky."

"I love ya too, Neil Graham." He laughed. "Never said that to a man before."

"Thank you for saying it to me."

"I been saving it up."

"Good. I'll take all you've got."

He grinned. "Now we got that settled, ya wanna come inside? We could do it right here in the driveway if you want. Or on the roof, even if it's a little cold out." He squinted at the sun. "I know ya won't be satisfied until we fuck on the roof."

"You're right. Come the summer, we can do that."

"Meantime, maybe we can just go inside and use the bedroom."

"I'm game."

We climbed the stairs to the porch.

"Marlene left a couple of days back. We spent three days packing up her stuff. I rented a big U-haul and hired a couple of guys hanging out at the Home Depot to load the boxes and move all the furniture. They went along with her to unload everything at the other end. She asked me to wish ya luck. Says you'll need it."

"I think she's right. It's nice of her to think of me, though. She's a better person than you ever gave her credit for."

"I know. And I should never have married her in the first place."

"I'm glad she's gone—for her sake as well as yours. Do you think you'll get married again?"

"If I meet the right girl."

I smacked his ass. "Like hell. After five times at bat, haven't you struck out enough?"

He grinned. "The sixth time, I bet I hit a home run."

"If you've got the bat, Ranger, I've got the balls."

I followed him inside the house. It was nearly as empty as it had been the first time I'd been in it, but he gave me the tour anyway—perhaps to prove to me that Marlene was nowhere to be found. Gone were the overstuffed furniture and the wall decorations. The giant kitchen table and chairs, the knick-knack shelf and its ducks, the coordinated cookware and matching china. The living room was empty except for a couple of framed photos on the wall—Ranger and my dad standing by the Buick Sport Coupe. (I'd mailed him the photos and had no idea what he'd done with them.) There wasn't so much as a frilly curtain hanging in a single window.

The master bedroom had likewise been cleared except for some hangers in the closet. Ranger's room, down the hall, was still a wreck, but even it looked as if it had been turned over and dumped out. Gone were the pink bed, dresser, nightstand, and chair that had been Marlene's as a girl. Only Ranger's clothes and belongings remained strewn across the floor, bedsheets and pillow in a pile, and the lamp with a dented shade in the corner.

He sighed and looked around. "Good thing I hung onto that old furniture and dishes ya gave me. It's in the garage."

"Yes. The last time I was here, I saw it out there. I also saved some of the furniture and extra stuff from my old apartment, so you'll have a solid kitchen table and chairs and a decent couch and so on. Everything is stored in the basement at Granddad's. We'll get you fixed up before you know it."

He nodded. "Just not today. We got better things to do this afternoon."

We stood facing each other.

"Remind you of anything?" I said.

"Like what?"

"The first time I visited your house, it was empty just like this."

"I do remember, come to think of it."

"One thing was different. We didn't have so many clothes on."

"That's easy to fix." In seconds, he shed his coveralls. "One other thing's real different. I ain't drunk."

"That's good. Congratulations."

"It still ain't easy. I got to work at it every day. Some days are harder than others."

"I know. I'll help any way I can."

He sighed. "Just one thing I want to know."

"What's that?"

"Why the hell would a smart guy like you want to hook up with a dumbass like me?"

I could not believe my ears.

"You say something like that again and I'll kick you out of my bed and never let you back in. You insult yourself and you insult me when you say that. You're smart. You're talented. You don't need a college degree to prove it to anyone. I'll never be able to fix a car, but I don't expect you to be an English professor, either. Everyone's got a talent, and if you're lucky, you find it, and the reward is the satisfaction of doing well in your chosen field. If you like your job, it doesn't seem like work. I know you don't get along great with your boss at Buick, but do you like fixing cars?"

"More than anything else I can think of."

"Then don't you think you're lucky to have such a great job?"

"Maybe so. I'm lucky to have you, ya son- of-a-bitch." He grinned and pulled my mouth to his, wrapping himself around me, nearly crushing the breath out of me. "Ya sure?" he whispered.

I nodded.

"Take yer shirt off." I obliged. He traced his index finger down my belly.

There was no furniture in the bedroom, but Ranger is a man of habit. For the remainder of the day and into the evening, we set off firecrackers with as much noise and sparks and smoke as any two men could generate. I stayed with him overnight, wrapped around each other on the floor, inside the same old blanket I'd retrieved from the trunk of my car. Just as we'd done nearly two years before.

One thing more was different: it would not be the last time I stayed with him until morning.

Acknowledgments

Sincere thanks to friends who read and commented on this manuscript in draft form: Jay Disney, Sam Wells, Ron Conard, Rand Morrison, and Curt Engeland.

About the Author

Richard Compson Sater retired from the U.S. Air Force after 24 years of service, attaining the rank of lieutenant colonel. He spent most of his career as a photojournalist, a veteran of both Operation Enduring Freedom (Afghanistan) and Operation Iraqi Freedom; and spent his entire career in the closet. *Thirst* is his second novel. His first, *Rank* (2016), is a romance between two male Air Force officers.

Sater earned a bachelor's degree in creative writing from the University of Pittsburgh, a master's in creative writing from Purdue University, and a Ph.D. in fine arts from Ohio University. He has at various times been a college professor, radio announcer, bookkeeper, bricklayer, bartender, clerk, voice actor, and window-shade salesman. A Seattle resident since 2007, he has expanded his creative efforts into screenplays and songwriting as well as fiction.